SHEILA ROBERTS

CHRISTMAS
on Candy Cane Lane

MIRA

MIRA

ISBN-13: 978-0-7783-1835-4

Recycling programs for this product may not exist in your area.

Christmas on Candy Cane Lane

FOR ADRIANA
WELCOME TO THE FAMILY

Dear Reader,

I'm so glad you've taken time to join me for a holiday trip to Icicle Falls. Christmas is my favorite time of year, and there's no place I'd rather spend it than in my favorite small town. This year we're going to be visiting the neighborhood of Candy Cane Lane, where folks take "decking the halls" very seriously. This may be something Tilda Morrison, supercop, is not quite ready for. She fell in love with the fixer-upper she bought. But will she fall in love with her over-the-top neighbors? Well, I did.

I had great fun writing this book and I hope you'll have as much fun reading it. And when you're done, who knows? Maybe you'll be in the mood to deck the halls, too.

By the way, I love hearing from you. You can find me on Facebook or reach me at my website, sheilasplace.com.

Merry Christmas! I hope Santa brings you everything you ask for, and may the Grinch steal all the calories from your Christmas cookies.

Sheila

CHRISTMAS
on Candy Cane Lane

Chapter One

"Here's an accident waiting to happen," Tilda Morrison said grimly. Just what nobody wanted on the day before Thanksgiving.

"Not if we get to her in time," said her partner, Jamal Lincoln.

"Why us?" Tilda grumbled to Cherie, the dispatcher. "This is a job for animal control."

"Chief said you'd say that," Cherie told her. "He also said to tell you that today it's a job for you and to bring a rope and get to work before somebody ends up hurt."

"I don't believe this," Tilda muttered as Jamal turned on the look-out-here-come-the-cops lights and shot their patrol car out of town toward the highway.

"We're in Icicle Falls. Believe it," Jamal said. "You still got that rope in the trunk?"

"Yes. It's there from the last time." Tilda frowned. "You know, this really isn't the job of the Icicle Falls

Police Force. I don't care if Stumpy Hodgkins is best buds with the chief."

"You gonna tell that to the chief?"

"Yeah, I am. As soon as we get back to the station."

Jamal grinned. "That's what I love about you, partner. You're fearless. You should've been a man. I swear you've got more balls than most guys."

"Thanks. I think."

Tilda knew she was a tough cookie, and she liked being tough. She liked being a modern woman, able to stand up for herself and hold her own against any man. But she also had a feminine side and, secretly, she fantasized about some man tougher than her, pushing her up against a wall and having at it.

She'd thought she'd found that man, but it hadn't worked out. He'd never bothered to look beneath her tough exterior and check out her sweet, soft side. Instead, he'd fallen for the kind of woman Tilda thought of as a cream puff. Maybe that was what all men really wanted, someone as sweet as honey and as elastic and bendable as warm taffy. Tilda wasn't a bending kind of woman. Sadly, there were very few men who appreciated that.

Jamal did, but he was her partner. Then there was Devon Black, town bad boy, the king of speeding tickets and barroom brawls, who thought he was God's gift to women. In fact, he thought he was God's gift to *her*. Christmas might have been just a month away, but she had no intention of unwrapping Devon Black.

She frowned, thinking of their last encounter. "What the hell?" he'd said angrily when she'd pulled him over a week ago for a broken taillight. "I wasn't speeding."

"No, you have a taillight out."

Instead of showing some respect and thanking her

for letting him know, he'd flashed her a cocky grin and said, "You're looking for excuses to see me." As if she had nothing better to do than chase after wolves dressed in blue jeans.

"If I wanted to see you, I could just wait till the next bar fight," she retorted. It was how she'd met him when he moved to town. Trouble followed Devon around like a lost puppy. "Now, do you want me to let you off with a warning or do you want to keep flapping that big mouth of yours and up the ante?"

That had shut him up—until she gave him his warning and turned to leave. "I'm working the bar at the Man Cave. Come on by after you get off work and I'll give you a beer on the house." As if he owned the place. It was his brother's. He just filled in on weekends.

"In your dreams," she'd called back over her shoulder.

"And yours, too, I'll bet. I can show you some new uses for those handcuffs."

"Oh, there's an original line," she'd muttered. *Fifty Shades of Devon Black.* No way, even if he *was* ridiculously gorgeous. So was a hot-fudge sundae, but look what it did to your butt.

"There's Stumpy," Jamal said, bringing her back to the present.

Sure enough, the short, old guy was hobbling as fast as he could down the side of the snowbanked road in his jeans and cowboy boots and leather bomber jacket, his hunting cap mashed down over his ears, a lasso dangling from his right hand and Daisy's halter from his left. And there, half a mile farther up the road, trotted his horse, the escape artist. Loose again. Not a good thing, considering the fact that the old paint was deaf.

"You can turn off the lights now," Tilda said, and Jamal obliged.

They pulled up beside Stumpy and Tilda lowered the window. "Stumpy, this is the third time this month she's gotten loose."

"I know, and I'm sorry. Daisy!" he hollered at the horse. "Dang it all, come back."

Sometimes Tilda wondered how deaf Daisy really was. Either she was faking it or she was psychic because the darned beast tossed her head as though she was saying, "No way." Then she started across the road. Oh, great.

An SUV came over the rise and Tilda sucked in her breath. The car skidded to a halt and waited while Daisy stood in the middle of the road, trying to decide what to do. The driver soon tired of waiting and honked. The noise didn't faze Daisy. She stood there, watching Tilda, Jamal and Stumpy as if wondering what they were doing out here on a cold winter afternoon. Then she strolled back to her own side of the road and continued her journey, probably looking for some other horses to spend Thanksgiving with.

"Give me the rope and get in," Tilda commanded. With Stumpy safe inside and the rope in hand, they set off in hot pursuit. Well, semihot, not wanting to end up hitting the animal.

"I'd'a gotten her," Stumpy insisted from the backseat. "I don't know why Mildred keeps calling you guys."

"Because she's seen the way you drive," Tilda said. They were lucky that Stumpy hadn't taken the horse trailer. The week before, he'd attempted to rope Daisy from behind the wheel, skidding into Dan Masters's truck and effectively blocking traffic for a good forty minutes while they sorted things out. Daisy, naturally, had gotten away and wound up at the llama farm.

They'd almost reached the horse. "Stop here," Tilda told Jamal. "We don't want to spook her."

"Everything spooks her," Stumpy grumbled.

The natural retort would be, "Then why do you keep the dumb critter?" But Tilda didn't say it. She knew why. Daisy had been their granddaughter Willow's horse. Willow had died two years earlier from a brain tumor. Stumpy could no more get rid of the horse than he could throw out the pictures of their only granddaughter that filled their living room.

Tilda got out of the car and shut the door as Daisy moved down the road a few paces.

"Go get 'er, cowgirl," Jamal teased.

"Ha, ha," Tilda muttered. Jamal was the size of Texas and could take down three men single-handed, but he was a city boy and no use whatsoever in capturing a deaf horse.

Tilda moved away from the patrol car. Daisy, sensing pursuit, trotted a few more feet, then stopped and looked around. *Neener, neener, neener. You can't catch me.*

Oh, yes, I can. You may be big, but you've got a brain the size of an onion. Tilda squatted next to the freshly piled snow on the side of the road and waited. She'd done her share of ropin' and ridin'. Gone to horse camp at the nearby guest ranch all through high school. She was not going to be outsmarted by a horse.

Daisy tossed her mane and then, to show that she wasn't even remotely worried about Tilda and her rope, decided to enjoy a little roadside snack, pulling up a mouthful of snow-tipped grass.

Tilda slowly stood and sneaked forward a few feet.

Daisy raised her head and Tilda froze. This was like playing Red Light, Green Light when she was a kid. Daisy went back for seconds. Okay, green light. Tilda moved forward again.

Daisy lifted her head and checked to see where Tilda was.

Frozen in place, of course.

The next time the horse went for some grass, Tilda moved in, and this time when Daisy lifted her head, Tilda swung the rope and…missed.

Daisy shied away and trotted off down the road, and Tilda swore.

"You rope about as good as you shoot," Jamal called from the patrol car.

Tilda gave him the finger and started the whole process again. Horses were such foodies. Tilda could have lured over any other equine simply by shaking a can of oats. Was there such a thing as horse hearing aids? If so, it would sure make catching Daisy a lot easier.

It took two more tries before she got the rope around Daisy's neck, although the third try wasn't exactly the charm. Daisy neighed and pulled away, and even though Tilda had planted her feet, the horse still managed to yank her over into the snow. "Oh, no, you don't," Tilda growled, struggling back to her feet. "Bring the halter," she yelled.

Stumpy climbed out, holding it. "We got her now," he said gleefully.

We. Yeah, right.

Finally Daisy was haltered and rewarded for cooperating with the police with a pat on the neck. "You'd better stop this escape-artist stuff or we're gonna ship you off to become dog food," Tilda threatened.

Daisy just tossed her head yet again. She knew Tilda was all talk and no action.

Tilda was equally stern with Stumpy. "You make sure your fence is well mended and you keep that barn door shut," she told him as she handed over the escapee. "We can't keep coming out to help you catch her." She felt bad about being mean to the old guy. He was in his seventies and had arthritis in both hips, and maintaining the house and barn on their five-acre spread was getting to be too much for him. His wife was ready to downsize. Maybe being in trouble with the cops would motivate Stumpy to find a home for Daisy and move someplace smaller.

Stumpy hung his head. "I know, Tilda. You guys have better things to do."

"In Icicle Falls?" Jamal cracked as they drove off, leaving Stumpy and Daisy to make their own way home. "Right."

"Hey, you want action? Go to New York or LA," Tilda said, and turned up the heat. They'd have to swing by her place so she could get some dry pants.

"No, thanks," he said with a grin. "No horses to chase in LA. Anyway, I'd probably get stuck riding with some clown who farts all the time. Besides, where am I gonna find a lady cop as cool as you?"

That made her smile. "If you're trying to flatter me..."

He snorted. "Like that would get me anywhere." He shook his head. "It sucks when the best woman in town also happens to be your partner."

"Okay, now it's getting really thick in here." She had a pretty good face and her body was in mint condition but, sadly, there were too many good-looking women and not enough men in this town. She glanced out the window at the snowy firs and pines. "Sometimes I think

I should've moved to Seattle." Except that Icicle Falls was her home and her roots ran too deep. Hmm. Maybe she was root-bound.

Jamal grunted. "You should've thought of that before you bought a house. Hey, we still on for Saturday?"

"Yep. When are you coming back from your mom's?"

"Friday morning."

"Good. You can help me finish packing."

"You know, some of us have to fill in for you and work that day. Who takes vacation on Thanksgiving weekend, anyway?"

Somebody who had a lot of vacation days piled up and more seniority than half the guys on the force. Tilda grinned at him and played the world's smallest violin on her fingers.

"All I gotta say is you better feed me."

"'Cause you're a growing boy?"

"Order something from the deli. I don't wanna get poisoned," he joked. "Where'd you not learn to cook?"

"From my mom."

"Come on, your mom owns Pancake Haus. She can't be that bad a cook."

"She hires people to do stuff in the kitchen, you dope." Tilda sighed. "The turkey will probably be dry and we'll have stuffing out of a box. But I like stuffing out of a box. And Mom's great with pickles and olives. And at least Aunt Joyce and the cousins will be bringing the candied yams and casseroles."

"What are you bringing?"

"Pumpkin pie."

"From?"

"What do you mean 'from'?"

"I know you ain't bakin' it."

Busted. Tilda shrugged. "Gingerbread Haus."

"Yep, you're gonna make some lucky guy a great husband someday."

"Oh, ha, ha."

He shook his head. "Somehow, I just can't picture you in a house."

"What should I be living in, a yurt?"

"More like an army barracks."

"I do have a feminine side, you know."

"Sure you do."

She did, and she could hardly wait to get everything all squared away in her new house on Candy Cane Lane. She'd have dried flowers on the dining table and she was going to give that quilted wall hanging her cousin Georgie had made for her a place of honor on the living room wall. The house had three bedrooms, two baths, a big living room with a fireplace and a den, which she was going to turn into a kick-ass party room where her pals from the force could come over and play Call of Duty and World of Warcraft. The kitchen was bigger than the one she'd had in her condo. Once she put in new flooring, it would be great. Lots of room to…heat frozen dinners. Or make cookies. She made a mean chocolate chip cookie. Maybe, with her fancy new kitchen, she'd graduate to cake or pie or something.

Expanding her cooking skills would have to wait, though. The house needed some serious work. It had been a bank repo and the previous owners had done a fair amount of damage. Walls would have to be repainted, gutters replaced and, of course, the kitchen set to rights. And she'd have to replace the carpeting, which was badly stained and a little on the smelly side. Well, okay, a lot.

She hoped she could afford to give herself new carpeting for Christmas, at least in the living room and den.

"I don't know, Tillie girl," her mom had said when they'd first gone to see the place. "Sure looks like a lot of work. You really want to mess with that?"

"Yes," Tilda had replied. "It's in a great neighborhood. It'll be a good investment."

"It'll be a pain in the patootie," Mom had corrected her.

Yeah, but it would be *her* pain in the patootie and she was ready for it. For the past five years she'd been envisioning herself in a house with a great guy and a couple of kids and a big, friendly dog. The guy thing hadn't happened and she'd decided there was no point in waiting around. She was going to get her house and the dog, too. Heck, maybe even a kid. These days you didn't need a man to have kids. These days, it seemed you didn't need a man for much of anything.

Tilda wanted one, anyway. There were still some things nobody did better than men, and she was darned tired of being the only one who ever saw the lacy bras and matching thongs she wore under her uniform.

A man with a handsome, swarthy face and an admirable set of pecs suddenly appeared at the back of her mind. Oh, no. Devon Black was not in the running for that cozy life with the house, the kids and the dog. Devon Black did *not* deserve to see her in her bra and panties. Or out of them.

Someday she'd find the right man. New people moved to Icicle Falls all the time. Maybe Santa would bring her the perfect man for Christmas next year. This year it was a house. And that was enough to ask for. After all, there was only so much the jolly old guy in red could fit in his sack.

Tilda brushed at her wet uniform trousers. "We need to swing by my condo. I need some dry pants."

"Aw, you'll dry out. What we need is a good bar fight to distract you."

"I'll give *you* a good fight if you don't go by my place," she threatened, which made him chuckle.

Dusk was falling and they'd hit the edge of the main drag through town when they saw a car coming from the direction of Currier's Tree Farm. Well, maybe it was a car. It looked more like a holiday float—a giant tree with wheels under it. The windshield was barely visible under all that green fir. How could the driver even see? Okay, so much for going to get dry pants.

"There's another accident waiting to happen," Jamal said as he flipped on the whirling lights that always made drivers so happy. "Is that a Mini-Cooper under there?"

"That's got to be Ivy Bohn," Tilda said in disgust. Who else would buy the biggest tree on the planet but Miss Christmas of Icicle Falls?

The tree pulled over and they stopped behind it.

"Wanna do the honors?" Jamal asked. "Have some girlfriend time?"

"Yeah, right," Tilda said, but she got out of the cruiser.

Having both grown up in this small town, she and Ivy knew each other. Sort of. But they'd never be buds. Ivy was a spoiled. entitled brat. She was always running late and seemed to think that speed limits were simply suggestions. The few encounters they'd had as adults hadn't been good ones. Usually, Ivy claimed she hadn't been speeding, and when Tilda ignored that and gave her a ticket, she demanded Tilda's badge number (as if she couldn't just call the station and use Tilda's name). Her family had been in Icicle Falls for three generations and she now ran Christmas Haus, one of the most popular shops in town. They had plenty of money and if you asked Tilda, Ivy had always been spoiled and conceited. Tilda hadn't been even slightly surprised when her husband had finally had enough and left her.

Tilda approached the tree car and heard the whir of the window being lowered. There was Ivy in all her perfect makeup and blond highlighted glory, peeping out between the boughs like a pissed-off Christmas angel.

"I wasn't speeding," she greeted Tilda.

"We're not stopping you for speeding."

"Then what?"

Ivy suddenly looked on the verge of tears, and for a moment Tilda felt sorry for her. It had to suck, being left by your man.

Tilda sighed. "Ivy, you're a menace. You can't see where you're going under that tree."

"Yes, I can," Ivy insisted, pointing to a two-inch gap between boughs.

"Why didn't you get Kirk to deliver it?"

"Because he's out of town and couldn't do it until next week and I wanted the tree today so I could put it up this Saturday. Besides, Jinx told me it would fit on the roof of the car just fine."

Of a Mini-Cooper? Really? Tilda was going to have a talk with Kirk's son. And his uncle Al, who ran Santa's tree lot. Al would happily pull the same kind of stunt if it meant a sale.

"Well, you can't drive with that on your roof," she said. "You'll run someone over."

"Okay, fine," Ivy snapped. "I'll take it off."

And dump it by the side of the road? Leaving someone else to clean up her mess... Tilda scowled. "Stay where you are."

"Oh, come on. Don't give me a ticket. For heaven's sake, it's Thanksgiving. Have a heart."

"Don't get your panties in a twist," Tilda said, barely holding on to her patience. "I'm not going to." She marched back to the patrol car. Who the heck bought a Christmas tree the day before Thanksgiving? Oh, yeah. Someone who was probably going to be very busy selling Christmas ornaments for the next month.

"So what are we doing?" Jamal asked when she got back to the car.

"We're taking the stupid tree over to Ivy's place."

Ivy's place...which turned out to be right next door to Tilda's new house. Why was she shocked? She'd run Ivy's information often enough. She knew the address. It just hadn't sunk in. The Mini-Cooper hadn't been in sight when she'd come to look at the house and neither had Ivy. Out of sight, out of mind. In any case, she'd been in the throes of house lust, so excited about her great find she hadn't stopped to think about who her neighbors were. Oh, well, just because she lived next door didn't mean they had to be best friends.

"Thank you so much," Ivy gushed once the tree was unloaded and safely stowed alongside her pretty, perfectly painted blue house, and Tilda and Jamal were covered in pitch.

"We're here to serve and protect," he said cheerily, making Tilda want to gag.

"No problem," Tilda added, then muttered, "That tree is ridiculous," as they made their way back to the patrol car.

"Hey, it's big. I'd think you'd like that."

"It's too over-the-top." Like Miss Christmas there, who was about to become her next-door neighbor. And like all the houses on her street. She was moving to the epicenter of Christmas craziness. "Some people take their decorating too far." She wouldn't be one of them, though. There was such a thing as overkill.

"Yeah? We'll see what you do once Candy Cane fever hits," Jamal teased.

"I'm never going crazy like these people," Tilda said with a snort. "They need to get a life."

Sometimes, when it was just her and a plate of food from the Safeway deli, she told herself the same thing—*get a life*—but she sure wasn't confessing that to Jamal. Or anyone else.

The next day was Thanksgiving, and talk around Dot Morrison's table quickly turned to the subject of Tilda's new house. "It sounds great," said her cousin Georgie, who was there with her new husband, Jay. Georgie was a super-girlie-girl with perfectly highlighted hair and nails that never had chipped polish, but Tilda loved her, anyway. When they were kids, Georgie was the queen of Monopoly. Now she and her husband had invested in a duplex in one of the newer neighborhoods in town, and it looked like she was going to score in real life the way she always had in the game.

"It's pretty cool," Tilda said, always the master of understatement. It was definitely an upgrade from a one-bedroom condo, or at least it would be once she'd fixed it up.

"Cool? It's freakin' adorable," said her other cousin Caitlin. With her Julianne Moore hair and stylish clothes, Caitlin was almost as much of a girlie-girl as Georgie.

Unless she was on a baseball diamond with Tilda's team, playing first base, then look out.

"Yeah, well, remember that the pictures you saw online didn't show the stains on the carpets and the bunged-up kitchen floor and the nonworking stove. I'm going to have to redo the cabinets, too. But it's all good. For the price I paid I'm willing to put in some labor."

Some labor? There was another understatement. One of the bedrooms had a fist-size hole in the wall. The other walls were grimy and in need of paint. The gutters needed replacing, and the yard had been let go, too. But that was all cosmetic stuff. The house itself was sound. It just needed some TLC.

"I'm handy with a hammer," Uncle Horace offered.

Actually, she'd seen some of her uncle's handiwork. Good thing he'd gone into insurance. She thanked him, anyway.

"The place'll be great once you get it fixed up," Caitlin said. Caitlin did love a project. Usually, though, her projects were of the human variety. She went through a lot of men who had what she called potential. Tilda could suggest another name for them—losers.

"You got a steal of a deal, but you couldn't *pay* me to live on Candy Cane Lane," Georgie said.

"I think it's charming," Aunt Joyce put in. "Remember how we always used to drive over from Wenatchee to see it at Christmas when you kids were little?" she asked her daughters.

"And here I thought you were coming over to see me," Mom cracked.

"Well, that, too," Aunt Joyce said with a smile.

"It's really cute, but they go overboard at Christmas," said Caitlin, who had seven pairs of Christmas-themed earrings, wore enough green in December to put a leprechaun to shame and played Christmas songs 24/7 all month long. "I wouldn't want all that pressure of trying to keep up with the neighbors."

"No pressure," Tilda said. "I can handle sticking some lights on the fir tree in the front yard."

Georgie cocked an eyebrow. "Yeah? If you think you can get away with just throwing up a string of lights, you've got another think coming. I've heard those guys are like the decorating police."

"Well, as far as I know, they don't have any covenants requiring you to go all Griswold Family Christmas, so I'm not stressing," Tilda said.

"You should be," Georgie told her.

"Why don't we get you a big blow-up Santa for your front yard?" Caitlin suggested.

"Good idea," Aunt Joyce agreed.

Tilda pointed a warning finger at her cousin. "Don't even think about it. I hate those inflatable decorations."

"I thought you'd appreciate getting a blow-up man for Christmas," Caitlin teased.

"Is everyone in this family a smart mouth?" Tilda lamented, and they all chorused, "Yes."

"So what time do we start moving you on Saturday?" Jay asked her.

"Around ten."

"Is Jamal helping you move?" Mom asked, trying to sound casual.

"Yeah, but don't get excited. He's not moving in or anything. We're partners."

Mom frowned. "Dumb if you ask me. What woman in her right mind would pass up a good-looking man who comes with his own handcuffs?"

The women all guffawed and Jay blushed. Uncle Horace just shook his head.

Conversation drifted to other topics and then, after dessert, the family settled in front of the TV to get in the Christmas spirit by watching *National Lampoon's Christmas Vacation*. "There's Tilda's house," Caitlin said as Clark Griswold set the night ablaze with his over-the-top outdoor decorations.

"That'll be the day."

"You'll catch Candy Cane Lane fever," Caitlin predicted.

Tilda frowned. "I don't have time for that."

"Yeah, well, we'll see." The movie ended, and that wrapped up another family Thanksgiving.

"Do you guys want to come our way for Christmas?" asked Aunt Joyce.

That worked for Tilda. Aunt Joyce was a good cook and she always sent Tilda home with leftovers.

She was just opening her mouth to say, "Great idea," when Georgie said, "I know what, let's do Christmas Eve at Tilda's new place."

"My place?" For Christmas dinner? What did she look like, freakin' Martha Stewart?

"Oh, good idea," said Aunt Joyce. "We can celebrate Christmas and have a housewarming."

"You can come over and spend the night with me on Christmas Eve," Mom offered to Aunt Joyce and Uncle Horace.

"This'll be fun," Caitlin said.

Getting her place pulled together by Christmas and putting on a Christmas dinner? *Fun?* Really? "Uh, guys. I don't cook. Remember?"

"Well, it's about time you learned," Aunt Joyce said,

showing no mercy. "Anyway, you can't do any worse than your mother."

"Thanks a lot," Mom said.

Tilda echoed that thought. But, oh, well. There were only seven of them. How hard could it be to stick a turkey in the oven? Even she could make dressing from a box and manage that green-bean casserole. Everyone else would bring rolls and dessert. They'd be fine. And maybe it *would* be fun to have the whole family over to celebrate the holidays at her new place.

"Okay," she said, "but don't expect everything to be perfect."

"If we wanted perfect, we'd never come to your mother's," Aunt Joyce pointed out, and went off to fetch her coat.

"We'll see you on Saturday," Caitlin said. "I'll bring the inflatable Santa. Maybe I'll bring two. We can double-date."

Fortunately, Caitlin didn't make good on her threat. It had snowed again Friday night but that didn't stop the family moving crew from showing up at Tilda's condo promptly at eight, along with Jamal and Enrico Abano, another of Icicle Falls's finest. Within an hour her furniture and the boxes containing her household items had all been loaded into Jamal's truck and the trunk of her and Georgie's cars, and the caravan was on its way to Candy Cane Lane.

The neighborhood was a mix of old and new houses, all well-maintained and beautifully landscaped. Her place, toward the end of the street, stood out with its dirty white exterior and hanging gutters like an unloved ugly duckling. But an ugly duckling with potential, she reminded herself—unlike Caitlin's loser boyfriends. A few repairs and touch-ups, a little TLC from Hank's Landscaping, and it would be good as new.

As they drove down the street she noticed that practically every resident was outside, bundled up in parkas, hats and gloves, hanging from ladders stringing lights or setting up prancing reindeer and nativity sets on their snow-covered lawns. And, of course, candy canes were everywhere.

"I'm thinkin' you'd better let me get you one of those inflatable Santas, after all," Caitlin said as they parked in the driveway. "Otherwise, they're gonna have you arrested for the house version of indecent exposure. This place looks bare naked compared to what's going on everywhere else."

"Not everyone overdoes it," Tilda said. The other Victorian beside hers didn't have more than a wreath on the door and a couple of candy canes on the front porch steps.

Even Ivy didn't have her outside lights up yet, but inside Tilda could see the tree that had taken over the world standing by the picture window. And there was Ivy herself, busy stringing it with a silver tinsel garland. She shouldn't be putting the thing up so early, even if it was freshly cut. It would dry out and turn into a fire hazard. If Ivy's house caught fire and it jumped to Tilda's place, Tilda was going to throw her in jail for the next million years.

Of all the people in all of Icicle Falls, I have to end up living next to you. Well, she'd mind her own business and Ivy could mind hers, and they'd get along just fine. As long as Ivy didn't burn down the neighborhood.

Georgie and Jay parked at the curb, and Jamal and

Enrico pulled up behind them in Jamal's truck, which was loaded with furniture and covered with blue tarp.

Georgie took several plastic grocery bags with food from the backseat and followed Tilda and Caitlin to the front door. "This place has so much potential. I can hardly wait to see the inside," she said to Tilda.

"Remember, it needs some work," Tilda cautioned as she balanced a box of video games on her hip and opened the door. They were greeted by a blast of eau de litter box.

Georgie wrinkled her nose. "Gross."

"It won't smell so bad once I replace the carpets," Tilda said as much to herself as her cousin.

Georgie made a face as they stepped into the living room with its stained carpet. "Tell me you're going to do that before Christmas."

"Hey, I'm not the one who volunteered me to have everybody over."

"Maybe it'll be better once it's aired out," Caitlin said, walking to a window. She unlocked it and tried to open it. "It's stuck."

"You are such a weenie," Tilda said in disgust. She marched over to the window and quickly discovered it was, indeed, stuck shut.

"Well, every house has its problems," Georgie said. She gestured to the counters. "I think we need to clean these before we put out any food. In fact, I'm afraid to even set the grocery bags down."

"The counter's probably safer than anywhere else," Caitlin said, eyeing the scuzzy vinyl. "Wow, were these guys trying to get into the *Guinness Book of World Records* for the most cigarette burns on a floor?"

Jamal was at the front door now, along with Enrico

and Jay. "What do you want to bring in first?" he asked. "The boxes or the furniture?" He pulled a face. "What's that stink?"

"The place has been closed up for a long time," Tilda said as she opened the kitchen door. At least that wasn't stuck shut.

"What's been closed up in it?" Jamal retorted. "A dead body?"

Tilda shot him a look that would've made lesser men quake in their boots. "Bring in the boxes."

"Start with the one with the cleaning stuff," added Georgie.

"Forget the cleaning stuff. We need a hazmat team," Caitlin said.

Tilda studied the gross living room carpet. "On second thought, don't bring in anything yet. We're going to yank up this carpet and get it gone."

"You'll be down to plywood," Jay protested.

"I'd rather have that than peed-on carpet," Tilda said.

Jamal conceded with a shrug. "Come on, guys. We need to hit the hardware store and buy some tools."

"Bring the cleaner and disinfectant first," Georgie called after him.

"There isn't enough in all of Icicle Falls to de-stink this place," he called back over his shoulder.

"Hey, while you're there, get her an inflatable Santa," Caitlin said with a smirk.

"Do it and you'll get dog shit for Christmas," Tilda hollered.

"I have something better than an inflatable Santa," Georgie said. "Be right back."

"What could be better than an inflatable Santa?" Caitlin joked as her sister dashed out to her car.

Maybe it was a quilt for her bed, Tilda thought hopefully. But when Georgie returned carrying a red gift bag with red-and-white-striped tissue sticking out of it, Tilda knew it wasn't a quilt. Too small. Her cousin was also toting her pink plastic toolbox, which meant this was something to hang. It would no doubt feature some corny saying like Home Is Where the Heart Is, but that was okay. Tilda rather liked those homey sayings—in small doses.

"I figured this would be perfect for Christmas," Georgie said.

So. a holiday decoration. Tilda took the bag and dug out her treasure. Yes, indeed, it was a sign. But wait a minute. "What the heck?"

"You're supposed to hang mistletoe at Christmas," Georgie said.

It was pretty, Tilda would give her that. Faux mistletoe berries were attached to a wooden plaque decorated with red ribbon; Kiss Me was painted on it in red script. "Thanks. It's cute." But what good did it do to hang mistletoe when she didn't have anyone to kiss?

Georgie took it out of her hand. "We can put it right here." She pointed to the archway between the hall and the living room.

"Now you have to find someone to stand under it," Caitlin said as Georgie got out her hammer with the pink handle.

There was the challenge.

They'd just hung the mistletoe when someone knocked timidly on the open door.

"Looks like they've already sent out spies," Caitlin said to Tilda.

Sure enough. There in the doorway stood a woman

clad in a pink parka trimmed with faux fur, snug jeans and black boots with little pom-poms on them. A jaunty pink wool beret sat on her head, half covering chin-length blond hair. She had brown eyes, flawlessly made-up, and wore pink lip gloss. Between the outfit and the bottle of wine she was carrying, she looked like she might be applying for some reality show about housewives.

"Hi," she said. Tilda could tell the minute her visitor caught a whiff of the stinky carpet. Her eyebrows pinched and her lips pulled down at the corners. But she gamely recovered and put the smile back on her face. "I'm Maddy Donaldson. I saw the truck outside and thought I'd stop by and welcome you to the neighborhood."

"Thanks," Tilda said, taking the proffered bottle. "I'm Tilda Morrison."

"Good to meet you." Maddy cocked her head. "You look familiar. Have we met?"

"Only if you ran a red light or robbed a bank."

Maddy blinked.

"I'm with the Icicle Falls Police Force."

Maddy nodded, smiling now that she got the joke. "Ah. Well, a policeman, er, woman, er, person living on the street, er, in the neighborhood. That'll be reassuring. And we're all happy someone's finally moving into the house. It was sad to see it standing empty for so long. It sure wasn't doing anything for the rest of the street, either." She shook her head. "The people who were here before—bad news. They never bothered to keep the place up. Which kind of brought down everyone's property values, you know."

"Yeah, I guess it would," Tilda said, unsure how else to reply.

"They never quite fit in, never got in the spirit of what

Candy Cane Lane is all about." Now Maddy studied Tilda. "Your Realtor did explain to you about the covenants."

"Covenants?" What was this woman talking about? Tilda hadn't seen any paperwork involving covenants.

"Well, nothing in writing, really. Just an unspoken agreement. We do have a reputation. I'm sure you're aware of that."

"Uh, yeah."

"It's a great neighborhood," Maddy assured her. "And we do go all out this time of year. Everyone loves it. As you can see, this is the weekend we start decorating. People expect to see us all lit up for the holidays," she finished with a little booyah hand motion.

"Well, I'm just moving in." They couldn't expect her to leave her boxes and furniture, and run right outside and string lights. Could they?

"Oh, yes, of course. Don't worry. You don't need to do much this time around. It *is* your first year, after all. Some lights will be fine, so if you could manage that this week, we'd be thrilled... And candy canes, of course. My husband has them down at the hardware store. I'm sure he'd be happy to give you a discount, to welcome you to the neighborhood," Maddy added with a neighborly smile that made Tilda want to arrest her simply for being irritating. "And I know he'd be happy to string your lights for you." Tilda found herself frowning. Did she look like the kind of woman who couldn't string some Christmas lights?

Maddy's cheeks, which were pink from the cold, got pinker. "Anyway, I guess I should let you get back to work. If you need anything, we're three houses down across the street," she said, pointing to a mint-green two-story Craftsman already dripping with lights.

"Thanks." Tilda held up the bottle. "And thanks for the wine."

"You're welcome." Then with another cheery smile and a quick wave, Maddy vacated the front hall and went down the steps, the pom-poms on her boots swinging back and forth.

Tilda leaned against the doorjamb and watched her go. "What have I done?"

Behind her, Caitlin said, "You'd better stock up on a case of that wine. I have a feeling you're gonna need it."

Chapter Two

Holiday decorations put everyone in a festive mood.
      —Muriel Sterling, *Making the Holidays Bright:*
              How to Have a Perfect Christmas

Okay, Maddy thought as she left Tilda Morrison, *not the warm and fuzzy type.* But then cops were like that, weren't they? They couldn't afford to be warm and fuzzy when they dealt with criminals all day long. Did Icicle Falls even have any criminals? If so, Maddy was sure her new neighbor would scare them onto the straight and narrow. And it would be good to have that comforting police presence right here in the neighborhood.

Not that they needed it. Everyone got along fine. Almost everyone, she amended as she caught sight of Mr. Werner, who owned the house next to hers. His generous girth was bundled up in winter clothes and he wore a red, knitted scarf around his neck and a matching hat on his balding head. The clothes said, "Merry Christmas." The facial expression said, "I hope you choke on a sugar cookie." He was bearing down on Maddy, carrying three candy-cane yard ornaments, the kind that were supposed to light up. Oh, boy.

She donned a pleasant holiday smile and called, "Hello, Mr. Werner. How was your Thanksgiving?"

"Never mind about that," he snapped, and brandished one of the candy canes. "I just bought these at your husband's hardware store year before last and they're already defective."

As if it was Alan's fault. "I'm sorry, Mr. Werner. But you know, Alan only sells them. He doesn't make them."

Mr. Werner scowled at her "Well, he should have better-quality things in his store."

"I'm sure he'll be happy to let you exchange your candy canes for some that work."

"For this year. But what about next year when those crap out?" the old man demanded.

"Well, then, I guess he'll let you exchange those, too." Honestly, Mr. Werner had to be the crankiest man in all of Icicle Falls. What a contrast to his sweet wife, who always made *lebkuchen* for everyone.

He grunted. "You women and your silly ideas. Candy canes and lights and snowmen. You get us poor men out here in the cold all day putting up this junk and then wonder why we get pneumonia."

Maddy hadn't heard of anyone coming down with pneumonia after hanging Christmas lights and, as she looked around the neighborhood, she saw plenty of women outside decorating, along with their husbands and children. She decided not to point that out to Mr. Werner. He wasn't exactly in a receptive mood.

"Being out in this cold doesn't do my old joints any good."

Okay, so he was in pain and cranky. Maddy looped her arm through his and started strolling them back toward his house. "Mr. Werner, you know you enjoy how pretty our street looks when it's all lit up. Why don't you let Alan take care of your outdoor decorations after church on Sunday? Then you won't have to be out in the cold."

Of course, now Alan would have to be out in the cold, and he wasn't all that fond of outdoor decorating himself. In fact, he'd been known to do his share of grumbling when he used his day off to set up the Donaldson light show. *Really, Maddy, do we need to hang this many lights? Just one Christmas I'd love to go away... someplace warm like the Caribbean where I don't have to so much as look at a candy cane.*

Whenever he complained, she liked to remind him that he sold a lot of candy canes, Christmas lights, mechanical reindeer, and inflatable Santas and snowmen at the hardware store this time of year. "And besides, how can you live on a street called Candy Cane Lane and not decorate?"

Whenever she used that argument he was swift to remind her that their street had once been named Laurel Drive and people had been free to decorate or not.

Well, that had been years ago, and thanks to her, the street was now a special one, unlike any other in Icicle Falls. Changing the name from Laurel Drive to Candy Cane Lane had been her idea, and all the other women had happily come on board. She'd worked hard to get the change approved, but it had paid off. Turning their little corner of Icicle Falls into something extraspecial had definitely increased everyone's property values. Why, only the year before, the Schumans had sold their house for twenty thousand more than they'd paid for it ten years ago.

She'd never understood why the Schumans had moved.

Now they were on Mountain Drive, where they claimed to have a better view.

They had a slightly bigger house, she'd give them that. But if you asked Maddy, there wasn't a bad view in all of Icicle Falls. How could there be, when the town was surrounded by snowcapped mountains?

"I can string my own lights," Mr. Werner said grumpily, bringing Maddy back to the unpleasant moment at hand.

"If that's what you'd prefer."

"I'd prefer not to do it at all. But if I don't, I'll never hear the end of it from Berthe. Or the rest of you. And now I have to waste half an hour taking back these useless candy canes."

Maddy and Alan and Jordan had enjoyed a lovely Thanksgiving with her parents and sister in Yakima. And on Black Friday she'd done a brisk business at her shop, the Spice Rack, where she was headed in just a few minutes. Everything had been going well and everyone she'd encountered was cheerful…until now. She wasn't about to let Mr. Werner tarnish her holiday glow.

"I'm sure you'll get it all sorted out," she said, giving his arm a squeeze. "Call us if you change your mind and want Alan to help you with your lights." Then, before he could do any more grumbling, she trotted off to her own house, which was already dressed for the holidays, lit icicles hanging from the roof, the windows and porch, and all the shrubs trimmed with blue lights. A crèche decorated the lawn and, of course, candy canes lined the front walk. Theirs was always the first house to be decked for the holidays and she liked to think it inspired her neighbors to get their holiday game on.

She was barely in the door before her thirteen-year-old

daughter, Jordan, was after Maddy to take her downtown to meet her friends at the skating rink. After that, there were plans to go to Herman's Hamburgers.

"Don't you have homework to do?" Maddy asked.

Jordan rolled her big blue eyes. "It's Saturday! I'll do it tomorrow. Come on, Mom. You don't expect me to sit around here all day while you and Dad work, do you?"

"No, I expect you to clean your room, which you've been putting off for the past two weeks." Her daughter washed her long strawberry blond hair every day, redid her nails the second she discovered even the hint of a chip. And lived in a minidump.

"I did it while you were out visiting the new neighbor."

That meant she'd shoved everything under her bed.

"Come on, Mom," Jordan wheedled. "Everybody's going."

Well, who wanted to sit at home on Thanksgiving weekend?

"And there's nothing to do here."

Other than homework and room cleaning.

"And you're never here," Jordan added, playing the guilt card.

She was around more than a lot of working moms, always home by 5:15. "Hey, I close early every day just so I can be with you."

This produced another eye roll. "And make me set the table for dinner. And after dinner you're out checking on the neighbors' lights or giving people candy canes."

Only during December. Honestly, Jordan was the princess of exaggeration. Maddy decided this was a discussion they didn't need to have right before she went to work. "If I take you downtown, you'll have to wait until I close the shop or you'll be stuck walking home."

"Afton's mom will bring me back. She's going skating, too."

Unlike some moms, who never have time for their daughters anymore. Of course, Afton's mom, the perfect stay-at-home mother, would hang around and skate with the kids. She had nothing else to do but try and relive her childhood. What happened to the days when kids didn't want their parents hanging around, anyway? It seemed as though lately all Maddy heard about was how "cool" her new friend's mom was. Afton's mom had hosted a spa night for the girls, whipping up egg facials for everyone and teaching them yoga. Afton's mom had made milk shakes for everyone after school. Afton's mom was into beading and had taught the girls how to make earrings. Afton's mom needed to find someone her own age to play with, Maddy thought bitterly.

Okay, she was jealous. No point in denying it. Maddy herself had done that kind of thing, too, BS (before the shop). After she became a small-business owner she didn't have endless free time. But this shop brought in a good income, and once it was paid off, Maddy planned on using that income to put Jordan through college. The shop was an investment in her daughter's future.

Alas, thirteen-year-olds cared more about the present. And right now the present offered ice skating. What could a mother do but cave? "That's fine, then."

"Thank you, Mom!" Jordan threw her arms around Maddy as if she'd granted her a week at Disneyland. She had friends to hang out with and a cute new boy in the picture who was bound to be at the skating rink, too, so this was probably just as good.

Maddy gave her a kiss and said, "Get your skates. I'm leaving in a couple of minutes."

With a whoop, Jordan was off to fetch her skates.

All right, Maddy thought with a smile, *that had to earn me the daughter seal of approval.*

She was grabbing her purse when the phone rang. She looked at caller ID and felt dread wash over her warm holiday glow like a giant bucket of ice water. *Don't pick up*, she told herself. She didn't have time to talk. She had to get to the shop.

The ringing stopped, thank God.

A moment later, Jordan was in the room, holding out the cordless from the rec room. "It's Grandma."

Maddy would rather have talked to Cruella de Vil. She took the phone, wishing they'd got rid of their landline and, forcing pleasantness into her voice, said, "Hello, Corrine. How was your Thanksgiving?"

"Quiet but pleasant, thank you. My son's not answering his cell. Is he home?"

And how are you, Madeline? How was your Thanksgiving? "I'm afraid not. He's at the hardware store." *The same place he is every Saturday.*

There was a silence while Maddy's mother-in-law digested that information. "Oh. I assumed he'd take Thanksgiving weekend off."

He hadn't done that since they'd bought the hardware store and moved to Icicle Falls eleven years ago. "Uh, no. Thanksgiving weekend is a busy time for retail." Why did she have to constantly remind her mother-in-law of this? Sometimes it was as if Corrine came from another planet and had to have the customs here on Earth explained over and over again.

"Of course. But since it's not yet ten, I thought maybe he'd still be home."

"The store's open from eight to six until after Christmas." Corrine knew that.

"It's really you I wanted to talk to, anyway," she said.

That had to be a first. "Here I am," Maddy said sweetly.

"Thomas and I are coming up there for Christmas this year."

"Up...here?" Oh, no. She had to have misheard. *Please God, let me have misheard.* "You won't be going to Monica's?"

"Monica has to spend Christmas with her in-laws in Utah this year."

Monica had probably begged her in-laws to rescue her from her sourpuss, nitpicky mother. Oh, wait. She was only sour and nitpicky around Maddy.

Sadly, they'd gotten off on the wrong foot fifteen years ago. Maddy'd had the nerve to get engaged to Corrine's son before Corrine could have a chance to meet (translation: inspect) her. It hadn't helped matters that Maddy and Alan had spent their first Christmas with her parents rather than trekking down to California to hang out with the in-laws.

In spite of their bumpy beginning, Maddy had tried to get along, sending birthday presents and a Mother's Day card. And going to see his parents the following Christmas. But by then it was too late. Anytime Alan forgot to return his mother's calls, it was Maddy's fault, and when they were on the phone and he said he had to go, she always imagined Maddy was pulling him away. Corrine didn't like to share. She especially didn't like to share her son. And most of all, she didn't like to share him with Maddy. He often went down for a few days in

the summer just so Corrine could have him all to herself. Which was fine with Maddy. She had no desire to
go where she wasn't wanted.

Too bad Corrine didn't feel the same way. "Well, of
course, we'll be glad to have you," Maddy lied. "When
were you planning on coming?"

"We'll be there by the twenty-third."

"Oh." *Goody.* "And how long can you stay?" *Please
don't say you're staying through New Year's.*

"We're going home the twenty-sixth. Your father-in-
law has a doctor's appointment the next day."

Father-in-law, not Dad. Although Tom had asked her
to call him Dad the first time he met her. Corrine had
never asked Maddy to call her Mom. "All right, we'll
see you then."

"Alan can pick us up at the airport."

God forbid they should rent a car.

"I'll try him on his cell again and give him the de-
tails," Corrine went on.

"Okay," Maddy said. "I'll let you go, then."

"Yes, I'm sure you have things to do."

"I do have to get to my shop."

"You're working today, too. What's my poor granddaughter doing?"

At the moment the poor granddaughter was seated
at the kitchen table, playing a game on her cell phone.
"She's going skating with some friends."

"That's nice. Give her a hug from her grandma," Corrine said, her voice softening.

At least her dislike of Maddy hadn't extended to
Maddy's offspring. "I'll do that. We'll see you soon."
And wouldn't that be fun? Maddy set the phone on the
table. "Okay, let's go."

"Are Grandma and Grandpa coming to visit?" Jordan asked as they walked to the garage.

"Looks that way." Okay, she should've tried to sound more enthusiastic. Hard to be enthusiastic when you were going to be entertaining Scrooge in drag.

"How come you and Grandma don't like each other?"

"We like each other fine."

"No, you don't. Grandma's always nice to me. Why is she mean to you?"

"I guess you'll have to ask her that," Maddy replied as they got into the SUV. It would be interesting to see what Corrine would answer.

Maddy backed out of the garage, then they set off down the street. The houses were all starting to look festive. By evening they'd be sparkling with colored lights, and reindeer would be prancing on lawns and rooftops. Come tomorrow night, the Christmas show would be ready for the holiday early birds, arriving with their cars packed with children to enjoy the sights. Thanks to all the women taking turns, a Mrs. Santa Claus would be somewhere on the street every evening from now through Christmas Eve, handing out candy canes.

Several neighbors smiled and waved as they drove past, and Maddy waved back. Seeing Candy Cane Lane come to life usually made her heart soar. But now, even though almost everyone seemed to be in a festive mood, she just wasn't feeling it anymore.

There was only one person to blame for that. Maddy didn't want to see the Grinch steal Christmas, but she wouldn't mind if he made off with her mother-in-law.

Chapter Three

With Thanksgiving weekend comes the promise of a season of holiday delights.
—Muriel Sterling, *Making the Holidays Bright: How to Have a Perfect Christmas*

Ivy Bohn had seen her new neighbor and crew pull in next door. She stopped stringing her silver garland on the tree to watch Tilda the cop climb out of her black Jeep, managing to look both sexy and kick-ass in jeans, black boots and black leather jacket accessorized by spiky dark hair. She'd worn her usual frown. Tilda Morrison always looked like she wanted to arrest the entire world. What kind of neighbor would she make? Probably not a friendly one. Ugh.

It seemed Ivy was doomed to have neighbors she didn't want. Before Tilda it had been the Schmerzes, who thought yard work was optional and house repairs were for other people. They'd run the house into the ground. Before them it had been Mr. and Mrs. Gordon, whose son was a sneaky little drug dealer. There'd been muscle cars screaming up and down the street, loud parties and juvenile delinquents coming and going. Mrs. Gordon had been oblivious to what her son was doing to devalue the neighborhood, but when it came to Ivy's dog, the woman had the radar of a bat. If Gizmo even came near her flower beds, Mrs. G. squirted him with her hose, sending the poor little guy somersaulting across the lawn. At least the Schmerzes hadn't cared when Gizmo escaped under the fence and got into the flower beds. Tilda probably would. She'd probably arrest Gizmo for trespassing.

Ivy sighed. Maybe Tilda would make a better neighbor than she did a friendly neighborhood cop. Ivy knew from experience how heartless she could be when she was in Dirty Harry mode. But the other day had been an exception, she reminded herself. Perhaps, under that icy exterior, there beat a warm heart. And maybe, when she was out of uniform, Tilda Morrison changed into a human.

She should at least give Tilda the benefit of the doubt. She'd made pumpkin bread to take to her parents' on Thanksgiving. She had half a loaf left. She could slice some of that, put it on a red plastic plate and bring it over.

"Mommy, Robbie's getting into the ornaments," tattled four-year old Hannah from the couch where she was watching cartoons on TV.

A solid thump pulled Ivy out of her reverie and she turned to see that Robbie Junior had tired of playing with his stacking blocks and acquired a new skill, escaping from the playpen. Oh, no. First the crib, now the playpen. There'd be no stopping him. He was already at the great room's dining table, a pudgy little hand reaching for the box of glass ornaments sitting on the table.

"Robbie, no!" Ivy dropped the garland and hurried toward him.

Too late. He had his fingers on the edge of the box.

He wasn't quite able to get a grip on it and the box tipped off the table and landed on the hardwood floor with a delicate crunch. Ivy wished she'd gone ahead and put in carpet the year before last, even though she and Rob had decided they couldn't afford it.

"Oh, Robbie," she groaned. He tried to pick up one of the broken ornaments and she grabbed his hand. "No! You'll cut yourself."

Unhappy at being thwarted, Robbie let out a wail.

"Mommy told you no." Ivy picked him up and plopped him back in the playpen, then gave him his favorite stuffed bear. "Here. Play with Teddy-boo."

He looked at the beloved toy in disgust and threw it on the floor. "No." He held out his hands. "Uppy."

"No, I'm not picking you up."

Okay, fine. Then I'll just climb out. He lifted one little jammy-clad foot in an effort to get out again.

She put his foot back on the playpen floor where it belonged. "No, you don't, buster. You're staying put until we get done with the tree."

This inspired a fresh wail of outrage.

There was no good time to cope with the terrible twos, but Christmas was the worst. It would've been helpful if her son had waited until he actually turned two to begin this behavior. Two was still six months away but Robbie had made an early start.

"When can we dec'rate the tree?" Hannah asked from the couch. Gizmo had joined her now and she sat with the corgi snuggled up next to her. Such an angelic picture.

Except Gizmo wasn't allowed on the couch, and with his stubby legs he couldn't get up without assistance. Rather than argue with another child, Ivy ignored

Gizmo's trespassing. "You can help as soon as I have the garland on. Just another minute."

Hannah got tired of waiting just another minute, and scrambled off the couch, Gizmo hopping down after her. She handed her brother his discarded bear and that shut him up. Ah, a peaceful moment.

A moment was about all Ivy got before she heard the scrape of a chair on the kitchen floor. This, she knew from experience, meant her darling daughter was up to no good. Sure enough, when she got to the kitchen, Hannah was climbing onto the counter, right in front of the cupboard where Ivy kept the bag of marshmallows they used to make Rice Krispies treats.

"Hannah Joy!"

Hannah gave a start and made an effort to climb back onto the chair. In her haste she missed her footing and tumbled to the floor. Robbie, unhappy about being abandoned, was once more crying for all he was worth in the living room and now Hannah was crying, too.

Ivy picked her up and sat on the chair, soothing her while checking for damage. "There now, it's okay. But you know better than to get into things without asking."

"I want to dec'rate the tree," Hannah sobbed, changing the subject.

Oh, this was fun. Nothing like trying to decorate for the holidays with two little ones.

She'd had two little ones the year before, but Rob had been around then. Although he'd been disconnected emotionally, he'd still been there to ride herd on the kids. Now it was just her, and she hated it.

Women do this all the time, she reminded herself. *You're not the only woman to wind up as a single mom.* And at least she had her parents. They'd retired, leaving the running of Christmas Haus to their daughters, and Mom, affectionately nicknamed Mutti, had been more than happy to help Ivy out with child care. But even with her mom's help, there always came that time when Ivy had to take her kids and go home to no one but the dog. When she had to bathe the kids and put them to bed and then find a way to fill the silence. Thank God for HGTV, Netflix and her new hobby of knitting. So far, she'd made scarves for everyone in the family for Christmas, as well as half a dozen hats.

"I know you're tired of waiting," Ivy said. "But can you be good for Mommy for a few more minutes?"

"I just want to dec'rate the tree," Hannah sobbed, not making any promises.

"Well, the sooner you start behaving, the sooner we can do that." There was no reasoning with a four-year-old. Why was she trying?

Her cell phone rang and, still holding her daughter, Ivy snagged it.

"Hey, Ivy," said her cousin Pete, "do you know if Deirdre's coming in today?"

"What do you mean?" Ivy shouted, trying to make herself heard above her crying children. "She's on the schedule." Her younger sister always worked on Saturdays. (Well, almost always, unless she got an offer to go to Seattle for the weekend with her girlfriends.) She got Sundays, Mondays and Tuesdays off. Very European of Deirdre to make sure she had a four-day workweek.

"Well, she's not here."

"Did you call her cell?"

"Voice mail."

If she'd gone skiing, Ivy was going to whack her with

a snow globe. *Now, what kind of thing is that to think?* she scolded herself. *That would just damage the inventory.*

"Nicole and I can't handle all the customers on our own. You know what this place is like Thanksgiving weekend."

Boy, did she ever. Thanksgiving kicked off the holiday tourist season in Icicle Falls. People came up in droves to enjoy fancy holiday dinners at the various B and Bs and restaurants, shop and, when there was snow, get in some skiing. There'd been snow and there would be skiers and shoppers aplenty this Saturday.

Normally, in the good old days before the divorce, when Ivy thought she was happily married for life, she would've been able to drop everything and rush right in. Rob worked in the warehouse at Sweet Dreams Chocolates and had Saturdays off. He would've held down the fort for the day, feeding their daughter junk food and watching cartoons with her. Not cleaning up a thing, of course. But he'd have been home, a watchful presence, someone to return to, someone who had her back. Now nobody had her back.

Darn it all, her sister had said she'd be happy to go in so Ivy could spend the day at home, decorating for Christmas. Ivy had already worked until seven on Black Friday. She'd had enough.

But this was the family business, and the holiday buck stopped with her. "Let me see if I can get someone to stay with the kids."

"What if you can't?" Pete asked, his voice filled with panic.

"Don't worry. I'll figure something out."

Hannah's crying had subsided to sobs and to reward her (or reinforce bad behavior), Ivy took down the bag of marshmallows and gave her one. "Do not put the whole thing in your mouth," she said, setting Hannah on her feet. "And eat it at the kitchen table."

Hannah complied and Gizmo accompanied her to the table, where he sat at Hannah's feet looking pitiful. No need to tell her not to feed the dog. Marshmallows were her favorite, and she wouldn't be inclined to share.

Robbie had finally given up crying and Ivy took advantage of the moment of silence to put in a call to her mother.

"Hello, darling," said Mutti. "How's the decorating going?"

"Lousy. Robbie's learned how to escape the playpen. He managed to get out and knock my Italian glass ornaments off the dining room table and break them."

"I told you not to bring those out this year."

"I know. Have you talked to Deirdre?"

"Since Thanksgiving? No. Why?"

"She hasn't come into the store yet."

A long moment of silence ensued, followed by, "Your sister needs to stop this irresponsible behavior."

Ivy's sentiments exactly, yet she found herself defending Deirdre. "Well, she did just lose a fiancé."

"He didn't die," Mutti said firmly. "He dumped her, the beast. She should be glad to be rid of such a man."

Same here, Ivy thought. Rob had ended things the day after Christmas last year, and by New Year's Eve he'd moved into the Mountain View Apartments at the edge of town. "I just don't know what I want," he'd said, as if wanting had anything to do with commitment and responsibility. She'd been so hurt and mad. And she'd missed him terribly.

To prove it she'd thrown a grapefruit at him when she

encountered him in the Safeway produce aisle after the divorce was final.

"Breakups can make you crazy," she said to her mom. But why, oh, why did her sister have to go crazy right now, when Christmas Haus was entering its busiest season? "Anyway, can you take the kids?"

"Oh, dear. Your father and I on our way out the door to visit Grandma."

And her grandmother, who lived in Issaquah, was not fond of little ones. Ivy still remembered trips to Grandma's house when they were young. They called it No-No House because everything in the place was off-limits. *No, no. Don't touch that. Look with your eyes, not your hands. Don't put your feet on the sofa. Those dolls are for decoration, not to play with.* Oh, yes, her grandmother would love to see her two kids, she thought as she went into the living room to make sure her son was where she'd left him.

She arrived in time to see him topple over the edge of the playpen. "Oh, no," she groaned. "He's really mastered this escape-artist stuff." And, of course, he was headed straight for the tree. She made a Supermom dash across the room, catching him just before he could pull on the branches and yank it over on himself. "No, Robbie," she said, scooping him up, which of course produced fresh wails. Ivy felt like crying herself.

She could barely hear her mom asking, "Is everything all right over there?"

"Oh, yeah. We're great."

"Oh, dear," said her mother. "We'd better take the kids with us."

That would not be fun for her poor parents. "Never mind. I'll see if I can get a sitter."

"Are you sure?"

"Yes, no worries." She dumped the kids on her parents enough as it was. She didn't need to do it on Thanksgiving weekend.

A weekend that was supposed to have been Rob's. She'd been both irritated and pleased when he'd called asking her to switch weekends with him. Pleased at getting the extra time on Saturday, but irritated that while she was in Icicle Falls, catering to hordes of shoppers, he'd be in Seattle with his new girlfriend, whooping it up. Oh, he hadn't told her he was taking the other woman to Seattle, but Icicle Falls was a small town. Things had a way of getting out. This was the second woman he'd been with since they split, but who was counting? Not her.

"Well, call me back if you get stuck," Mutti said.

"I will," Ivy said, and ended the call. Still holding Robbie, who was straining to get free, she thumbed the number for Cass Wilkes's daughter Amber, who helped her out a lot.

"Hi, Mrs. Bohn," Amber answered.

"Oh, Amber, I'm glad I got hold of you. I'm in desperate need of a babysitter," she said as Robbie cried, "Noooo," and started kicking his feet.

"I'm sorry. I'm at the bakery today, helping Mom."

Of course. With the many visitors in town, it was all hands on deck for local business owners.

"No problem," Ivy said. "I hope you guys do a ton of business."

"We already are," Amber said. "I'd better go. I have to ring up this customer."

"Oh, sure. Thanks, anyway." Ivy mentally crossed two other babysitters whose families owned shops in town off her list.

Who else could she try? Jordan Donaldson had taken a babysitting class through the Red Cross and was just starting to babysit. Maybe she'd like to earn some money.

Ivy called the Donaldson home, hoping Maddy hadn't brought her daughter to work. All she got was Maddy's cheery voice mail. "Happy Thanksgiving. You've reached the Donaldsons. Leave a message and we'll get back to you."

I can't find a babysitter and you were my last hope was probably not appropriate. Ivy didn't leave a message.

Her cell rang again. This time it was Nicole. "Please tell me you're on your way."

"I'm working on it," Ivy said. "I'll be there as soon as I can."

Next she tried her sister's phone. Of course that went to voice mail. "Where are you? They're swamped at the shop and I can't get a sitter."

Okay, she was going to have to bug her parents, after all, and her poor kids would have to go to No-No House. She called home again. No answer, which meant they'd already left. She tried Mutti's cell phone and it, too, went to voice mail.

Meanwhile, Robbie was kicking his feet and howling, a true poster child for the terrible twos.

Great. "I can't find anybody to watch the kids. Help!"

Robbie was still carrying on and Ivy finally snapped. "Stop it right now!"

He stopped and regarded her in affronted shock.

She continued her message. "Mom, if you're anywhere within range, can you call me back? Please?"

This was not how her day was supposed to go. She'd planned on a nice day with her children, a chance to recover from being on her feet for ten hours the day before, a chance to decorate the tree and drink cocoa and pretend her life was great. Instead, here she was in a mess. Deirdre was most likely off skiing, while Rob was in Seattle enjoying a different kind of sport. Everyone was having a blissful day but her. She looked at her barely decorated tree and wanted to shove the thing over. Instead, still holding her son, she fell on the couch and burst into tears.

Her crying shocked Robbie into silence. He studied her, as if trying to figure out this very un-mommy-like behavior. Then he put a little hand on each side of her face and kissed her.

"Oh, sweet baby." She hugged him to her and indulged in shedding some more tears.

A moment later her daughter was next to her on the couch. "Don't cry, Mommy," she said, patting Ivy's leg. "It will be okay."

"Yes, sweetie, it will," she agreed, and pulled Hannah close.

"Are we gonna dec'rate our tree now?" Hannah asked.

The doorbell rang, and that was enough to distract Hannah from the subject of tree decorating. She scooted off the couch and ran for the door. "I'll get it!"

"No, you don't open the door. Mommy does that," Ivy said, setting Robbie down and hurrying after her.

Hannah was already looking out the window panel. "It's Oma and Opa!" she cried, and, forgetting her mother's instructions, unlocked the door, turned the handle with both hands and swung it open. "Oma!"

"Hello, my darling girl," Mutti said, scooping her up as Dad picked up Robbie. "We thought we'd better make sure you found a babysitter," Mutti said to Ivy as she joined them in the hallway.

Ivy shook her head. "No luck. I was just trying to call you."

"You know she never turns that stupid phone on," Dad said.

"Oma, we're gonna dec'rate our tree," Hannah announced.

"Tonight," Ivy told her. "First, how would you like to go for a drive with Oma and Opa and get some ice cream?" A drive, no matter what the destination, always included ice cream.

Hannah bounced up and down in her grandmother's arms. "Yes!"

Robbie mirrored the action. "Oma!"

"Thanks," Ivy said to her parents. "You're lifesavers."

"No problem. What's retirement for?" her father said. "Anyway, I'd rather play with your kids than be in the shop today."

Actually, Ivy would have, too. She got the kids' things together and sent them off with her parents. Then she abandoned the unfinished tree, donned her dirndl (official work uniform of all Christmas Haus female staff members) and drove to work. The tree should've been decorated by now and she should've been putting out her flicker candles, her nativity set and the little ceramic angels that spelled *Noel.* Rob used to rearrange them to spell *Leon* when she wasn't looking.

He used to sneak into the snowball cookies and the fudge she made, too. "I can't help it, babe," he'd say whenever she caught him. "Your Christmas cookies are too good to resist."

But not good enough to keep him from getting restless. Maybe there was something to that seven-year-itch theory. After seven years of marriage, Rob had decided he was through.

Of course, they'd been together a lot longer than seven years. They'd been together since high school, for crying out loud. Could that be the problem? They'd gotten together too young? He'd missed his youth. After two babies she didn't look like she did in high school anymore.

But heck, she was only thirty-five. Her life wasn't over. She could find another man…to break her heart again. Maybe not.

Driving through town was like driving through a holiday movie set—trees festooned with twinkle lights, shoppers stopping in the street to visit with one another, people skating on the little skating rink. Ivy looked at the skaters and sighed. She'd love to have been out there, whisking around the rink, the wintry breeze caressing her cheeks. (These days that was the only caressing she got.) In the town center gazebo, Santa and Mrs. Claus were seated on festive thrones and families were lining up to get their pictures taken with them. Bah, humbug.

"Happy holidays," she muttered, and then indulged in one of her favorite mind games, making up new lyrics to old songs. "Happy holidays," she crooned. "I'm a rat in a maze. This was s'posed to be a good day but it's stinking through and through. Those merry bells are ringing but my life has turned to poo."

Well, that was inspiring. She frowned at her reflection in the car's rearview mirror. "Can you please not be so cranky? There are people starving in the world. People who don't have parents around to help them with their kids. People who are on diets and can't eat red velvet cake. People who've never seen *It's a Wonderful Life*." Okay, things could be worse.

What was Rob doing right now with that mysterious girlfriend?

Oh, who cares?

She pulled into one of the parking spots behind the store reserved for the Christmas Haus crew and went inside. A CD of Christmas instrumentals was playing "Angels We Have Heard on High" and she couldn't resist making up yet another lyric. *We have the best shop in town, always full of Christmas cheer. There's no place I'd rather work. I am always happy here.*

It was true. She loved her family business. The family had changed the name from Kringle Mart to Christmas Haus, which they decided was a better fit with the town's Bavarian theme. The outside of the building had a winter woodland fresco and the requisite flower boxes at the windows. Inside was pure magic.

She'd been working in this place since she was fifteen and she still felt a holiday high coming in, seeing the kaleidoscope of colors and hearing the happy sounds of Christmas. The shop was huge, taking up two floors. The bottom level held Christmas trees decked out in various color themes—blue, red, white, gold, pink. Ornaments of every shape and style, all arranged by color, of course, hung from the walls. A front corner of the shop was dedicated to snow globes. A back corner held Advent calendars, ranging from inexpensive paper versions to elaborate wooden works of art. Upstairs, customers could find more ornaments, as well as every imaginable kind of tree lights, night-light, tree topper, stocking hanger, flicker candle, scented candle, CD and music box. Christmas Haus was a holiday delight for the senses, and walking into the store always lifted Ivy's mood.

Today it didn't lift quite as high. She'd get there,

though. And soon she'd be too busy to think about her subpar morning.

At quarter to eleven, the place was packed with shoppers and poor Pete and Nicole, the shop's dynamic duo, were working like crazy to help customers and ring up sales. Pete had been working in the shop almost as long as Ivy. When he wasn't at Christmas Haus, he was over at Bavarian Brews, which he co-owned with his sisters, doing the books and ordering coffee and syrups. Come the New Year Pete was going to be moving on. He and his sisters were expanding their business empire, opening another coffee shop in nearby Cashmere. She was going to be sorry to lose him. He was the ideal employee, good with customers and totally dependable.

Unlike *some* people. Ivy had her hands full managing the store and dealing with the kids. The last thing she needed was having to deal with younger-sister-induced headaches, as well. Why couldn't Deirdre be more like Cousin Pete?

Because she didn't love the shop the way Ivy did. Obviously, since she couldn't even be counted on to show up and work the floor on one of the busiest days of the year.

Nicole was off helping a customer and three women stood in line, waiting to have snow globes and tree ornaments rung up. But no one was complaining. Pete could take credit for that. He was not only gorgeous, he was also the world's biggest flirt. Women loved him.

"My gosh," he said as Customer Number One stepped up with her purchases, "you aren't...? Do people know you're in town?"

She looked at him, confused. "Excuse me?"

He glanced sideways as if checking for eavesdroppers, then lowered his voice. "You *are* Julia Roberts, right?"

Yeah, if Julia had gained forty pounds and aged ten years overnight.

The woman's cheeks turned pink. She shook her head and smiled. "No."

"No? Really?"

"Really."

"I bet you get that a lot, don't you?"

Ivy was willing to bet she didn't.

"Well," the woman hedged.

Pete shook his head. "Darn, I could have sworn we had a celeb in here."

Pete himself looked like a celebrity with his dark hair and eyes and that big, toothy smile. He also had a drool-worthy body, and the customers were having no problem entertaining themselves while they waited, enjoying the sight of Pete in lederhosen.

"I didn't need to come in," she whispered to him as the satisfied customer handed over her charge card. "Everyone's happy to stand around and gawk at you."

Pete frowned at her. "Yeah, right."

"I can help the next customer," Ivy said, moving to the second computer.

Customer Number Two seemed almost disappointed as she stepped over to have her purchases totaled. Oh, yes, Ivy was going to miss Pete when he left.

The next hour rushed by as she rang up sales and assisted customers in finding their way around the store. At eleven-thirty someone new arrived, a pretty thirty-year-old with the same blond hair and hazel eyes as Ivy. She wore a dirndl and an apologetic expression.

Ivy wrapped a pink teapot tree ornament in tissue paper, placed it in a red Christmas Haus bag and handed it to the customer along with her receipt. "Merry Christmas," she said with a smile.

"Same to you," the woman responded.

Ivy turned to her sister, who'd slipped in next to her, and lost the smile. "You were supposed to be here at nine."

"I know, I'm sorry. I couldn't sleep last night. I finally took a sleeping pill at three. I just woke up."

"Just woke up" might've been a slight exaggeration considering the fact that Deirdre's makeup was on and her hair ironed flat. But Ivy let it slide. Now that her sister had arrived, her anger had dissipated and she could sympathize with Deirdre's unhappiness.

"At least you're here," she said.

"And you can go home and hang with the kids. Are they at Mutti's?"

"They're with Mutti, but they're on the way to Issaquah to see Grandma."

"Oh, poor them."

"So I might as well stay." Ivy took a new customer's snow globe to ring up.

"There must be something you can do." Deirdre took the snow globe from her and wrapped it in tissue.

She could go skating. She could go home and take a long bubble bath. She could play her piano and sing all her favorite Carrie Underwood songs. She could make fudge. She could finish the hat she'd started knitting.

Her sense of responsibility won out. "I'll stick around. We're pretty busy."

"Go already," Deirdre insisted. "If you don't, I'll feel guilty."

Making her sister feel guilty, that would be fun.

Pete had gone to help a customer and was back now,

carrying several boxes of tree lights shaped like peppermint candies. "Well, guess who showed up? Where were you, anyway, off giving Santa a lap dance?"

Deirdre frowned at him. "You are so disgusting."

"Thank you," he said, then got busy ringing up the sale and flirting with the customer, a middle-aged woman with a naked ring finger who was looking at him like a hungry woman eyeing a big chocolate Santa.

"Now that she's here you can scram," Pete said to Ivy. "We can handle this."

Ivy did need a break. "Okay, you talked me into it."

"Good." Deirdre nodded. "See you tonight."

Oh, yes. They were going to have a movie marathon night after the kids went to bed and consume a ton of popcorn and eggnog.

Meanwhile, all that free time was a present waiting to be unwrapped. She left work and went home via Gingerbread Haus, where she visited with Cass Wilkes and picked up some gingerbread boys and cream puff swans for her movie night. What the heck, why not? *'Tis the season to get fatter. Fa-la-la-la-la la-la-la-la.*

Okay, if she was going on an eating binge she should get some exercise first. The skating rink was calling. She'd throw on some warm clothes and enjoy a few turns on the ice.

As she drove down the street she saw most of her neighbors now had their lawns and houses ready for the holidays. Okay, forget the skating rink. She'd better put out her candy canes and hang the outside lights. There'd probably be people cruising down the street tonight, and if she didn't have something up, she'd hear about it from Maddy Donaldson. Except hanging the lights had always been Rob's job. The idea of doing it by herself was daunting.

"You can do it," she told herself. "You don't need Rob for anything."

Yes, she did. She needed him for a lot of things.

No, she didn't. She had her parents to help with the kids. She knew how to pay bills. And any fool could put up Christmas lights.

She pulled into her driveway and saw the truck and cars next door, and remembered that she'd planned to take some pumpkin bread to her new neighbor. She wondered if Maddy had been over to visit Tilda yet and offer a discount on the requisite candy canes. Tilda didn't strike Ivy as the candy-cane type. But she could be wrong. Rob hadn't struck her as the leave-your-wife type.

You never knew about people. After all, Tilda had surprised Ivy and helped her get her tree home. And hadn't given her a ticket. She put away her Gingerbread Haus treats, then changed into ski pants and a sweater. Okay, ready to hang lights. Ugh. She hated that job. Ivy sighed and started for the garage.

Oh, wait. The pumpkin bread first.

No, first let Gizmo out. He was ready for a potty break. Although he had a doggy door, he seemed to think that convenience was for lesser animals and preferred to wait for someone to let him out. At least, with the ground frozen, she wouldn't have to worry about him digging out under the backyard fence and going next door to make a nuisance of himself. She opened the back door, and he happily ran out and down the porch steps.

She sawed off several thick slices of bread (sampling a couple as she went), then arranged them on a plate, which she covered with foil. She dug out a bow from her wrapping supplies in the bedroom closet and stuck it on her goody package. There. She hoped Tilda liked pumpkin bread. And maybe Ivy's welcome-to-the-neighborhood visit would be the beginning of a new friendship.

She put on her parka and outdoor boots and made her way across the front lawns to Tilda's place. As she went up the steps to the front porch, she could hear banging and commotion and laughter. It took her back to when she and Rob had moved into their house. He and his buddies Eric Wallace and Bubba Swank had about killed themselves moving her heavy player piano. Bubba had dropped a box of pots and pans on Rob's toes. Rob and Eric had gotten the bed stuck in the bedroom doorway and had to remove the door. She'd nicknamed them Three Stooges Moving, which they had, perversely, taken as a compliment. Later, they'd hooked up speakers to Rob's iPod and had music blasting, and she'd ordered pizza from Italian Alps.

Those had been good times. Ivy sighed yet again and rang the doorbell.

A moment later the door opened, and there stood Tilda, a slight frown on her face. Behind her, two men and a couple of women were busy pulling up the carpet. The smell of cat urine wafted out to greet Ivy.

"Hi. I saw the truck." Wow, sparkling conversation starter.

Tilda nodded.

"I, uh, thought you guys could use something to eat."

Tilda took the offering and smiled just enough to be polite, but not enough to encourage friendly neighborhood relations. "Thanks."

"I wanted to welcome you to the neighborhood," Ivy

persisted. Did pumpkin bread count as bribing an officer?

"That was nice of you." Now Tilda looked past Ivy. Her eyebrows dipped, and so did the corners of her mouth. "Do you know whose dog that is?"

Ivy turned around to see Gizmo happily marking his territory—on Tilda Morrison's rhododendrons.

Chapter Four

Hanging those outdoor lights not only makes your house festive, it also puts your whole family in a festive mood.

—Muriel Sterling, *Making the Holidays Bright: How to Have a Perfect Christmas*

Ivy gasped.

So, she and the mutt, who was in the process of marking Tilda's lawn, had a working relationship. Figured.

"Gizmo, no!" Ivy hollered.

Gizmo. Great name for the four-legged shrub destroyer who was now in the process of taking a dump right in the middle of Tilda's lawn. "There's a leash law, you know." What a surprise that Ivy thought she was above it.

Ivy looked at her as if she'd said the meanest thing in the world. "I know. I left him in the backyard."

"Maybe you should rename him Houdini."

"Thanks for the suggestion," Ivy said irritably as she hurried to pick up the offender. Ah, yes, the true Ivy was surfacing once again. Pumpkin Bread Ivy had only been a facade. "Don't worry," she called over her shoulder. "I'll clean this up."

"You bet you will," Tilda said under her breath.

"Come look at this floor," Georgie called to her.

Tilda walked over to where the guys had torn up a big section of rug. "Wow, hardwood." It needed some refinishing, but it was still gorgeous.

"Total score, cuz." Caitlin pointed to the plate in Tilda's hand. "More gifts from the neighbors?"

"My next-door neighbor, having a human moment."

"Sounds like you already know her," Caitlin observed, taking the plate from Tilda.

Tilda snorted. "I should. I've given her enough speeding tickets."

"Oooh, a rule breaker. Not fit to breathe the same air as Supercop," teased Caitlin, helping herself to a slice of pumpkin bread.

"She's a princess," Tilda said.

"Princess or not, she sure makes good pumpkin bread."

"Then you'd better share," Jamal said, coming over to grab a piece, too."

"Hey, how about the rest of us?" Enrico demanded, and Jamal took the plate from Caitlin and brought it over to the other two men.

"It was nice of her to do that," Georgie said between bites.

"Everyone in this neighborhood is nice," Tilda said.

Caitlin elbowed her. "Enough to make your fillings hurt, isn't it?"

"Ha, ha."

The doorbell rang. "If it's someone else bringing food, be friendly," Caitlin told her.

This time it was a wizened old lady with wrinkles crisscrossing her face. She was holding a small poinsettia in one hand and leaning on a cane with the other. She wore an ancient wool coat over some bright pink slacks, probably the kind with an elastic waistband, and her silver curls had been sprayed until they'd turned to stone.

"Hello, my dear. I'm Elinore Walters, your other next-door neighbor. Welcome to the neighborhood," she chirped, and handed over the plant.

"Thanks," Tilda said politely. When it came to houseplants, she had a black thumb, but it had been kind of the old lady to think of her, so she'd make an effort to keep this one alive. Anyway, it only needed to last through Christmas. She should be able to manage that.

"Your mother told me you'd be moving in today."

"You know my mom?" Well, duh. Everyone in Icicle Falls knew her mom.

"Oh, yes. My sister and I go to Pancake Haus for breakfast on Saturdays and have the senior special. Your sweet mother always stops by to visit with us. And she sent me such a beautiful card when my Emmit passed on."

Her mom was a lot of things—funny, smart, hardworking—but sweet? Somehow Tilda had never thought of Mom as sweet. She wasn't even sure what to say to that. "That's, uh, good to hear."

Mrs. Walters was looking unsteady in spite of that cane and Tilda found herself asking, "Would you like to come in?" *And where's she gonna sit, on the floor?* Well, she could bring in a chair from the truck. But could Mrs. Walters stand long enough to wait for it?

"Oh, no. I can see you're busy," the little woman said with a wave of her free hand. That seemed to upset her equilibrium and she swayed.

Tilda caught her by the arm. "How about I walk you back home?"

"Now, that's very kind of you, but not necessary."

Tilda thought it was. "I don't mind."

"All right, then. I'd appreciate that. I don't do stairs so well."

And she was living in a two-story house? Oh, boy.

They made it down the stairs, Mrs. Walters's cane wobbling with each step. If they'd been racing a slug, the slug would have won.

"I can't tell you what a comfort it is to have a policewoman next door to me," she said. "I think someone tried to break into my house last night. I heard a noise."

A burglar on Candy Cane Lane? Yeah, and Santa smoked pot. "Did you call 9-1-1?"

"I did," Mrs. Walters said with a nod. "Two nice officers came out and looked around. I'm afraid by the time they got here, though, it was too late. The burglar was nowhere to be seen." She smiled up at Tilda. "I'll feel so much safer with you next door."

"Mrs. Walters, if you see anyone, you need to call 9-1-1."

"But you can get here so much faster. What number should I call?"

"Nine-one-one," Tilda said, making the old woman frown. "You know, Mrs. Walters, I often have to work nights. I'm not always home."

Mrs. Walters looked as if she might cry. "Oh."

Tilda felt like a big police meanie. "But when I'm here, I'll be happy to keep an eye on your place." Had she really said that?

Mrs. Walters beamed on her. "That's very kind of you, dear. You're as sweet as your mother." Not only did the word *sweet* not come to mind when Tilda thought of her mom, it didn't come to mind when she thought of herself, either. She hadn't exactly been sweet to Ivy Bohn, who had reappeared with a plastic quart bag and was now scooping dog poop off Tilda's lawn.

"Hi, Mrs. Walters," Ivy said. "How was your Thanksgiving?"

"It was lovely, dear," Mrs. Walters said, feeling the need to stop and watch the poop scooping. "Have you met our new neighbor? This is Dottie's girl. What was your name again, dear?"

"Tilda," said both Tilda and Ivy, whose cheeks were especially rosy and probably not just from the cold.

"Yes, I have," Ivy said, the picture of sweetness and light.

"You don't have your lights up yet," Mrs. Walters informed her.

"They will be soon," Ivy said. "And how about you, Mrs. Walters? Is your nephew coming over?"

"He can't. He's in Cancún. But I have a young man who's done work for me before coming to do it. And he's not even charging me, imagine that. He'll be here this week. He's not married," Mrs. Walters added.

Ivy's cheeks went even pinker, and Tilda's face was suddenly feeling warm. "We'd better get you inside," she said to Mrs. Walters. "It's cold out here."

"Oh, yes," Mrs. Walters agreed, glancing around as if she'd just realized it was late November in the mountains.

They made their painfully slow progress up the front walk and then up the steps. "Oh, my, that is a workout," panted Mrs. Walters once they'd reached her porch. "I wish I could manage stairs. I miss sleeping in my old bedroom."

So she wasn't trying to climb up to the second story; that was a relief. How she managed *anything* was a mystery to Tilda. "Are you okay living here on your own, Mrs. Walters?"

"Oh, yes, I'm fine," Mrs. Walters said with another wave of the hand that left her teetering and had Tilda putting an arm around her shoulders. "The Meals on Wheels people bring me lunch and dinner. A gal on the corner cleans for me once a week and hardly charges me anything. Ivy fetches my mail from the mailbox. Madeline down the street runs errands for me." She smiled at Tilda. "This really is a wonderful neighborhood."

So it would seem. The other people on the street had set the good-neighbor bar pretty high. Tilda hoped she'd be able to keep up.

It didn't take long to find Gizmo's latest escape route. A board in the back fence had come loose, making it easy for him to wriggle his way to freedom. A few well-placed nails—who needed a man?—and the yard was once more secure. Gizmo was in a time-out in his doggy bed in the family room. He whined as Ivy came into the kitchen to wash her hands.

"Yes, you're in trouble," she told him. "And no, you're not going out front with me while I hang the lights. Just stay in here and think about what a naughty dog you've been."

Gizmo let out another whine and put his head on his paws, a sure sign of penitence.

"Yeah, you should feel bad," she said, showing no mercy. "Tilda already hates me, you know."

And a few slices of pumpkin bread probably wouldn't change that. But at least she'd been trying. Oh, well. All the other neighbors liked her fine, so what did she care about one snotty cop?

A cop who helped you get your tree home, she reminded herself. Maybe, down the road, they could find their way to neighborly. If Gizmo would stay in his own yard. Sheesh. Every male in her life was a pain in the patootie.

The candy canes were a little hard to get in as the ground was frozen, and that required some serious chipping with a shovel. By the time Ivy was done she'd worked up a sweat. Good. With luck, she'd burned off enough calories that she could enjoy her cream-puff swan guilt-free when her sister came over later. Now, on to the lights.

It was encouraging to see that they weren't tangled. Rob had always been careful putting them in their plastic bin. "Too much of a hassle to untangle them," he used to say. He also used to complain about what a pain it was to put them up, but every year he'd buy more, and he'd taken great pride in dressing up the outside of the house while she decorated indoors. One year they'd won the prize (a bottle of Icicle Creek wine) for the best-dressed holiday home.

Ivy didn't plan on winning any prizes this year. She simply wanted to get this chore done as quickly as possible, before she turned into a Popsicle. She'd cooled down considerably standing around checking the lights and her nose felt like an ice cube.

She dragged the big metal ladder from its spot against the garage wall, then laid it down on the front lawn and extended it to its full length. Whew, that was a lot of ladder. She didn't like climbing ladders.

"You can do this," she told herself, then proceeded to pull it up and lean it against the house. The thing felt

twice as heavy once it went vertical and seemed to have
a mind of its own, waving in all directions like a giant
out-of-control wand. She finally got the ladder to make
contact with the roof, but at the last minute the stupid
thing fell off to the side, landing on the azaleas in the
flower bed. That was fun. At least it hadn't gone through
an upstairs window. She hauled it off the azaleas and
tried again. This time it fell in the opposite direction.
Okay, third time's the charm.

And, indeed, it was. She stood for a moment, panting
and admiring her accomplishment. She so didn't need a
man. Well, not the one who'd defected, anyway.

She stood for a moment, eyeing the ladder. It was not
an inviting sight. She didn't want to be out here, risking life and limb for the Candy Cane Lane cause. People fell off ladders all the time and broke arms and legs.
Necks even.

"Oh, stop it," she scolded herself. "You're not going
to fall." She picked up the string of multicolored lights
and began her ascent, singing as she went, changing the
lyrics to another Christmas classic. *It's so nice to fix your
home for the holidays.* And wouldn't the kids be excited
when they returned and saw all the pretty lights? Up another rung. Just a few more to go. Easy peasy.

Crap, it was high up here. *Don't look down.* She'd
heard that somewhere, probably not in connection with
hanging lights, but it seemed like good advice. She went
up another rung. Okay, time to stop and hug the ladder.
I don't want to be here for the holidays. She hugged her
new metal friend tighter and whimpered. Maybe she
didn't need to put up lights this year.

But she lived on Candy Cane Lane. She had to. "Just
another step," she told herself. "You can do this."

Fifteen minutes—five minutes per rung—later and she was within reach of the roof. And there were the little plastic hangers to hook the lights on. She could do this, no problem. She hung the cord on one. "You did it!" she cheered. The ladder wobbled and she grabbed it and closed her eyes. *This will all be worth it when you're done. This will all be worth it when you're done.* Oh, man. Why hadn't she hired someone? She took a deep breath and reached up and another piece of cord fell onto its hook. *There, now, was that so hard?* She'd have this done in no time. She leaned out to hang another section.

And then, suddenly, she was losing her balance, hovering over the azaleas like some kind of bat hanging around for the holidays. The ladder didn't want to hang around with her and started leaning to the right. *Noooo.* What to grab—the lights, the gutter? Or her hair and pull it out and shriek? Oh, yeah. She was already shrieking and her hair was under her hat. The ladder was now headed for the ground.

Like Tarzan grabbing for a vine, Ivy reached out desperately and caught the string of lights. *Aaaah!*

There was no swinging to safety. The lights pulled away from their moorings and down she went like some pathetic cartoon character.

She landed on top of the shrubs with the treacherous ladder crashing down just to her left. Oh, my. That could have knocked her out. As it was, she was seeing stars in spite of the fact that they hadn't come out yet. She lay there for a moment while her heart did a wild lap around her chest, and wondered if anything was broken. Her back? It sure hurt. Oh, no! If she'd broken her back she'd be stuck here like a living yard ornament. She wiggled her toes inside her boots. Okay, good. Her back wasn't

broken. But a branch was poking through her coat, trying to stab her to death. She vowed never to laugh again
when someone fell off a ladder in the movies.

"Ivy, what are you doing?" called a familiar male voice.

She didn't have to turn her head to know who it belonged to. Great. What was her ex doing here and with
such impeccably evil timing? Maybe she was halluci-
nating. She blinked hard, hoping he'd disappear. Nope.
Still there. How humiliating.

"I'm hanging the lights," she said through gritted
teeth.

"I can see how well *that's* going." He came over to
where she was sprawled and helped her down from her
prickly perch.

Solid ground. Thank you, Lord. "Thanks," she said
with a groan. And then, remembering what a rat he was,
demanded, "What are you doing here?"

"I got back to town early and thought I'd come by and
see if you needed help with the kids."

"I don't. They're with Mom and Dad in Issaquah,
visiting Grandma."

"Lucky them. So why aren't you at work?"

"Deirdre's there. They don't need me."

He gave a cynical grunt. "They always need you."

This had been a constant bone of contention when
they were together. Even though Rob had pitched in,
he'd also complained about how often the shop took her
away. He used to say they were like hamsters running
on a wheel.

"The shop owns you," he used to complain. "I might
as well be single for all I see you."

"It's mostly during the holidays," she'd remind him.

"Yeah, when people actually want to do things together."

He didn't like her working so much, but he certainly never complained about the double income.

But he did complain about what it cost them to earn it. "We don't need that much to live on," he'd been known to say. "Look, I'm not asking you to desert the family business. I just want you to take some time off. I want us to enjoy life a little."

Well, he was enjoying life now, the skunk turd.

"Let me finish this for you," he offered.

"You don't live here anymore," she snapped. "I can do it."

"Ive, don't get all stubborn on me, okay?"

"I'm not getting stubborn," she insisted, jerking away. "I don't need any help."

"You're afraid of heights. You need help. And what if you'd broken your neck? What if the kids were inside?"

"I'd have called 9-1-1."

"Got your cell phone on you?"

Actually, no. She'd left it in the house.

She was trying to decide how to answer when he said, "Yeah, that's what I thought."

He picked up the ladder and swung it effortlessly back in place, then retrieved the string of lights and started climbing. He had the best butt in Icicle Falls. Maybe even in the whole state of Washington.

She turned away with a scowl. *Never mind his butt!* "Fine," she said. "I'm going inside."

"Good idea," he agreed.

She went inside and made herself an eggnog latte, then sat down at the kitchen table to fume. She wasn't sure which hurt more, her back or her pride.

An hour later, he was done and knocking on the door that led to the garage. It still seemed weird, Rob knocking on doors rather than just coming into the house.

"Need anything else done?" he asked, poking his head around the door.

Looking at him still made her treacherous heart flip over. He was tall and lean, with deep-set brown eyes and brown hair. He wasn't movie-star handsome but he was cute and fun-loving and he was hers. Correction: he *had* been hers, once upon a time. Before Peter Pan syndrome had struck.

"No," she said, and realized she sounded surly. "Thanks," she added. And then, to be fair, told him, "You probably did save me from breaking something."

He smiled at that. "Yeah, because you would've climbed right back up that ladder again."

He said it kindly, and the way he was looking at her reminded her of the good old days when they were happy. She found herself smiling back, just a little.

"I don't mind helping you with stuff. Just because we're not together doesn't mean..." Here he stumbled to a stop.

"Mean what?"

He shrugged. "That I can't come over when you need me."

"Need you for what?" Changing lightbulbs, fixing a leaky sink? Sex? *No, no. Don't go there.* "I don't even know how to take a statement like that," she said, frowning. They were divorced. There was no more honey-do list for him. It was all hers now—twice the work needing to be done in the same amount of time. Not his problem. He'd skipped off to never-never land.

"Take it however you want it."

"With a grain of salt," she said.

Now he was frowning. "Fine. I'm out of here."

"Oh, wow, echoes of Christmas Past. You said the same thing last year."

No reply. Hunched into his coat, he slouched out the door and through the garage.

At the back of her mind Elvis started singing one of her parents' favorite songs, "Blue Christmas." Only Elvis had new lyrics. *I'll have a fine Christmas without you. I won't even be thinking about you. I'll be doin' all right on Christmas night. Yes, I'll have a very fine Christmas.* "So there!" she added as the closing garage door echoed with a metal clang.

She sat down at the kitchen table and stared at her half-finished latte. She'd meant to offer Rob one. Good thing she hadn't. He didn't deserve one. He didn't deserve anything but a lump of coal up his butt. His cute butt.

"Stop already," she scolded herself, and went off to soak in a tub full of Epsom salts.

Why *had* he come back early? *Oh, who cares?*

"You got the lights up," Mutti said when she and Dad and two sugar-buzzed kids returned to the house.

"You did that all by yourself, kitten?" her dad asked, a worried expression on his face. "I told you I'd come do it for you."

"I know. But I didn't want you to have to." The last thing she needed was her father falling off that darned ladder. If someone was going to break his neck, let it be Rob.

"It looks wonderful," Mutti said.

Ivy merely thanked her, deciding it was best not to share that Rob had been over. It would only raise her mother's hopes that they might get back together. Mutti had always liked Rob.

"Just because he flatters your cooking," Ivy had said bitterly after he split.

"And because he fit so well with our family," Mutti had added.

"Yeah, he fit so well he left."

"I think he's a little lost. He'll find his way back," Mutti had predicted.

"As if I'd take him back? The chances of that happening are about as good as Santa going on strike."

Rob had hurt her too badly. Once he walked out the door, that was it, and she'd told him as much. She'd told herself the same thing when they'd met with the lawyers and he seemed almost regretful. She'd said it again the day they stood before the judge, him the guilty love criminal, her wishing him a lifetime in solitary with no sex. Nope, that tree had left the Christmas tree lot. They were done, and she was going to have a perfectly good Christmas without him.

She repeated it to her sister that night after the kids were in bed.

"Hey, people make mistakes," Deirdre said, and Ivy knew she was thinking about the creep who'd dumped her.

"True, but I'm not going to make the mistake of taking him back. Anyway, he's not interested."

"Yeah, right. That's why he came over and hung your Christmas lights," Deirdre said, diving into the popcorn bowl.

"Don't you go telling Mom."

Deirdre shook her head. "And she believed you when you said you'd hung 'em?"

"Why not?"

"You've never hung Christmas lights in your life. And you're afraid of heights."

"Well, there's a first time for everything. Are we going to watch this movie or what?"

Deirdre made a face, but she started the movie and they watched as Orphan Annie sang about the sun coming out tomorrow.

Maybe it would, maybe it wouldn't. Either way, life would go on. And later, after her sister had left, Ivy found herself picking up the copy of Muriel Sterling's latest book, which she'd had kicking around, and taking it to bed. She propped it on her knees and read the title. *Making the Holidays Bright: How to Have a Perfect Christmas.*

"That's what I'm going to do," she vowed.

We expect so much of the holidays, wrote Muriel.

Everything needs to be perfect: the decorations, the cookies, the big meal and our interactions with the people in our lives. Sometimes, though, things don't go as planned. Decorations get broken, cookies get burned, people disappoint us.

"You can say that again," Ivy muttered.

But perfect isn't about how things turn out. It's more about our attitude. What makes the holidays perfect is what we bring to them. Bring an attitude of joy and appreciation to the season, do things with those you love, and I'm sure you'll have a wonderful holiday.

Okay, good attitude. She could do that. She checked out some of the recipes and tips for activities with family and friends. If she did all this, she'd be guaranteed a great Christmas. No husband required.

With that pleasant thought, she set aside the book and snuggled under the covers. Bring on the dancing sugarplums. Ivy Bohn was going to make the holidays fabulous.

Chapter Five

Our relationships are especially important this time of year.
> —Muriel Sterling, *Making the Holidays Bright: How to Have a Perfect Christmas*

After church the Donaldson family stopped by Safeway and picked up some essential items—the ingredients for fudge and the latest Pixar movie. Inspired (or maybe threatened) by Afton's mom, Maddy had declared that this would be family day. After lunch she and Jordan would make fudge while Alan was outside decorating, and that evening they'd all watch the movie. And eat popcorn, she decided, swinging by the snack aisle.

"Let's get caramel corn," Jordan said, picking up a box.

"Okay." If her baby wanted caramel corn, then that was what she'd have. This day was going to be perfect.

Back home, Maddy made her daughter's favorite lunch—grilled cheese sandwiches and tomato soup.

"Can I have another sandwich?" Jordan asked.

"Sure. How about you, hon?" she asked Alan.

He pushed away from the table. "I think this'll do me.

Anyway, I want to get the Werners' lights hung before the temperature drops any more."

Maddy tried not to feel guilty for having volunteered him to do Mr. Werner's house. By the time the crotchety old man had gotten to the hardware store, he'd decided to take her up on her offer. Better to have the seller of faulty candy canes out there freezing his ass off than him, he'd kindly informed Alan.

Alan had come home from work in a grumpy mood, so Maddy refrained from pointing out how many candy canes and other holiday decorations they sold this time of year. And she certainly wasn't going to do so today, either. Maybe in January…or February. Or March, long after the decorations had all been taken down.

Alan went out, and she got busy at the stove. She and Jordan would have a lovely day, followed by some important family together time this evening. Meanwhile, Candy Cane Lane would come to life. By tonight the lights would be up on all the houses, and the first carloads of families would start driving through to experience the magic. As good as anything Disney could produce, if you asked Maddy.

She put the grilled cheese sandwich on her daughter's plate. Jordan was busy texting, but she managed to say, "Thanks." Learning to multitask at a young age.

"Who are you texting?" Maddy asked, more to make conversation and show interest in her daughter's life than because she needed to know.

"Afton. She and her mom are baking cookies today."

Of course. Afton's mom probably needed the carbs after all her exercise on the skating rink.

"I told her we're making fudge."

Maddy smiled. The bragging tone in her daughter's

voice said it all. Fudge trumped cookies. Yes, fudge had been a good idea. "We'll start as soon as you're done with your sandwich." The kitchen phone rang and she picked it up.

"Maddy," croaked Shirley Shank. "I've come down with the worst cold."

"Oh, no," Maddy said. "Were you able to do Thanksgiving?"

"Yes, it didn't hit until yesterday. But I feel awful today. My throat's sore and I'm sure I've got a fever. I just can't do candy cane patrol tonight."

Shirley was scheduled to pass out candy canes that night. "Oh," Maddy said as reality sank in.

"You've got to find someone else."

"No problem. I'm sure we can find a Mrs. Santa somewhere."

"Thanks, Maddy. I'm really sorry about this. I'll leave the costume by the front door for Harold to give to whoever takes over. Tell her I'll take her turn later in the month."

"Will do."

"What's wrong?" Jordan asked, her fingers still flying over her cell phone.

"Oh, nothing. Mrs. Shank is sick and we need another Mrs. Santa Claus to hand out candy canes."

"Not you, though. Right? I mean, we're watching a movie and having popcorn tonight."

"Of course not me. I'll find someone to take her place," Maddy said, and went to her list of Mrs. Clauses.

No one answered at Geraldine Chan's. They'd gone to Seattle for the weekend and probably weren't back yet. Maddy left a message in case she returned home in time and was in the mood for some fresh air.

Next she tried Gabriella Moreno. Thank heaven, Gabby answered. "Gabby, I'm glad I caught you at home."

"Only for a minute," Gabby said. "I'm almost out the door."

Crud. Strike two. "Oh?"

"My sister's in labor. I'm on my way over to watch the kids."

Well, babies were more important than candy canes. "Was there something you needed?"

"No, no, nothing urgent. Give your sister my love."

"I'll do that," Gabby said, and was gone.

"Mom, I'm done with my sandwich. Can we make fudge now?" Jordan asked as Maddy went on to the next name on the list.

The phone at the Williamses' was already ringing. Maddy held up a finger. "Just a minute. Hi, Diane. How was your Thanksgiving?"

Jordan sighed dramatically.

"Plate in the dishwasher," Maddy mouthed.

The plate went in the dishwasher and Jordan plopped down at the kitchen table, frowning and texting, probably complaining to Afton about the fudge production delay.

"Very nice," Diane said. "But I can't tell you how exhausted I am. We had all the kids here plus the five grandkids. I'm in my jammies, and I'm not moving."

This didn't bode well. "I guess I can't convince you to sub for Shirley, then? She was on for candy cane patrol tonight."

"What's wrong with Shirley?"

"She's sick."

"Oh, poor thing. I'll take her some turkey soup tomorrow."

Never mind Shirley, Maddy thought. *What about the candy canes?*

"Maddy, you know I'd do it in a heartbeat. I love passing out candy canes."

"And you make such a good Mrs. Santa," Maddy said, hoping to flatter her out of her jammies and into the Mrs. Santa wig.

"But not tonight."

Maddy accepted defeat. "I understand."

"Mom," whined Jordan.

"In a minute," Maddy said as she punched in another number.

Jordan shoved away her chair and flounced out of the kitchen.

"I'll just be another minute," Maddy called after her.

"I wish I could," said Louise Willis when Maddy asked her, "but we're having some friends over tonight. Trying to finish off those leftovers."

"Maybe your friends would like to help pass out candy canes," Maddy said. It was rude to push, but she was beginning to feel the teensiest bit desperate.

"Would you make your friends stand out in the cold and pass out candy canes?"

Yes. If someone was in desperate need.

"If there's no Mrs. Santa Claus for one night, it won't be the end of the world," Louise said.

But people had come to expect it. All those children would be disappointed. "I'll find someone," Maddy said. "Have fun."

"Thanks. And sorry I can't do it."

Sorry? Maddy highly doubted that. Louise hated wearing the Mrs. Santa Claus wig and specs and padding herself out. Getting her to take even one night was a challenge.

Twenty minutes later, Maddy was out of options. There was no help for it; she'd have to play Mrs. Claus tonight. Fortunately, she had candy canes left from last year, as well as her very own cute outfit—a red wool jacket that went over a red skirt and a striped red apron. She had an old-fashioned cap, and the wig and specs, of course. She made a pretty cute Mrs. Claus, if she did say so herself. Still, she wished she didn't have to play that role tonight, not when she'd planned to spend the evening with her family.

Ah, well. There was fudge to make. "Jordan," she called, "it's fudge time." No answer. She walked into the living room and found it empty, which meant her daughter was in her room, probably sulking. She went upstairs and knocked on the door. Loudly, since Jordan had her music blasting.

"What?"

Maddy opened the door. "We're ready to make fudge," she said cheerfully.

"Never mind. I don't want to now."

"Come on, now, sweetie, don't be like that."

"You spend all your time on the phone," Jordan complained.

Maddy noticed the cell phone on the bed in front of her daughter but decided now was not the time to talk about pots calling kettles black. "Let's go make fudge."

Jordan made a face and hurled herself from the bed as if she'd just been ordered to clean toilets. But once they were in the kitchen, assembling ingredients, she forgot about punishing her mother. Soon the kitchen was filled with the aroma of melting chocolate.

Jordan actually absorbed some sweetness after licking the spoon. "This is fun," she said, smiling at Maddy.

"Yes, it is." And this was the sweet daughter she knew and loved.

Alan came in later, his face red from the mountain air, and found Maddy in the kitchen putting together a meat loaf. "It's freezing out there," he announced.

"You look frozen to the bone. Let me make you a latte."

"Sounds good," he said, rubbing his hands. He peered into the mixing bowl filled with hamburger, eggs, onion and bread crumbs. "Whatcha making?"

She smiled at him over her shoulder. "Meat loaf." Meat loaf and mashed baked potatoes accompanied by green-bean casserole and pumpkin pie—all his favorites. Her daughter loved meat loaf, too, and Maddy had figured it would be a nice change from turkey leftovers. The meal had been meant to cap their day of family togetherness. Now it felt more like a bribe.

"All right! Is the fudge ready?"

"Yep. Help yourself."

He did, cutting himself a gargantuan piece. Maddy had hoped to take some to Mrs. Walters, but she had a feeling that by the time her husband and daughter were done, there'd be no fudge left. Well, she'd have to make more. She needed to get started on Christmas cookies, too. That was another thing she could do with Jordan. Maybe they could bake gumdrop cookies tomorrow night, follow up on the good fudge feelings. Muriel Sterling had a recipe in her new book that looked yummy. They should make some spritz Christmas trees, too. Then Jordan could bring a little plate to Mrs. Walters. The poor dear couldn't stand for very long anymore and Maddy knew she missed being able to bake.

"So when's dinner?" Alan asked.

"Five. I'll set everything out for you," she said, and braced herself.

"What do you mean?"

"Well, I'm afraid I've pulled candy cane patrol tonight." She didn't look at him. Instead, she watched the milk swirl around in her frothing machine.

"You had somebody else lined up for tonight."

"She's sick."

"Oh, for Pete's sake, Maddy. This is supposed to be a family day, remember?"

"It has been. Maddy and I made fudge."

"And we got a movie for tonight. We were all going to watch it together."

"You and Maddy can have some father-daughter time this way," Maddy said, putting a positive spin on the situation. "Or you can wait until I come back in. I won't be away that long."

"I've seen how that plays out," Alan grumbled.

The milk was done. She poured it into a mug, adding peppermint syrup and a shot of espresso, and handed over her creation.

He was frowning when he took it and still frowning after the first sip.

"How is it?" she asked, hoping to change the subject.

"Fine," he said, his tone of voice still grumpy.

She went to him and slipped her arms around him. "Come on, Alan. Cut me a little slack here."

He heaved a long-suffering sigh. "I know this whole Candy Cane Lane business means a lot to you."

"It's made such a difference in our neighborhood—raised our property values, brought us together."

"Yeah, it sure brought old man Werner and me together."

"It's only once a year."

"And it's a time of year we should be doing things together as a family."

"We do lots of things together," Maddy protested.

He shook his head. "We get fractured at Christmas. We're already busy enough with our stores."

She pulled back and frowned at him. "Don't tell me you wish I hadn't bought the Spice Rack."

"I'm not saying that. I'm just saying with both of us working full-time, you might need to cut back on some of the extra things you do. There are plenty of other people on the street who could hand out candy canes."

"I tried everyone," she said miserably. "They all had an excuse."

"That should tell you something."

"What?"

"That they all have higher priorities than passing out candy canes on a weekend that's usually reserved for family."

"We were stuffed to the gills with family only three days ago." She'd had her sister's brood over for Thanksgiving dinner, along with her widowed aunt and cousin (the weird cousin nobody could stand). And she and Jordan had just made fudge, for crying out loud.

"Let the candy canes go for tonight. Nobody will miss them."

It was a tradition. People expected to see Mrs. Santa Claus and get candy canes when they came to look at the lights. "Like I said, I won't be out long."

"Suit yourself, but don't blame me when Jordan pitches a fit."

Maddy didn't tell him their daughter had already done that.

The second fit got pitched when Jordan followed her nose downstairs in search of dinner and saw her mother in her Mrs. Claus outfit. "Where are you going?" she demanded.

"I have to go outside for a little while and pass out candy canes."

Jordan's eyes narrowed. "We were gonna watch a movie."

"You and Daddy can watch it together. Or we can all watch it when I'm done."

"You'll be out there forever," Jordan complained.

"No, I won't."

"Why can't somebody else pass out candy canes?"

"Because everyone else is either sick or has commitments."

"Yeah, well, *you* had a commitment."

"Honey, I told you, I won't be out for long."

"Fine," Jordan said in her newly acquired snotty-girl voice.

Okay, the old patience was wearing pretty thin. "Jordan," Maddy said firmly.

Jordan crossed her arms and glared at her. "I hate Candy Cane Lane!"

"No, you don't. You've always enjoyed seeing everyone's lights and decorations."

"It's dumb."

"What we do here brings a lot of joy to a lot of people."

"Well, I don't enjoy it," Jordan said, her face a study in sullenness.

"Of course you do," Maddy told her. "Remember how you used to like helping me pass out candy canes?"

"I was a kid then!"

"It's still fun." She paused. "I know. Why don't you come out and help me tonight?"

There was that clean-the-toilets look again. "It's cold out there. And handing out candy canes is boring."

"Never mind," Maddy said stiffly. "You don't have to. I just thought it might be fun to do together."

"We were supposed to watch the movie together," Jordan said.

Maddy sighed. "Like I told you…"

"Never mind. I don't want to watch it now, anyway." With that, Jordan ran back up the stairs to her room, probably to text Afton about her mother's perfidy.

"Jordan, come back down," Maddy called. "Dinner's almost ready."

"I'm not hungry," Jordan called back.

When had parenthood gotten so hard? Alan came out from the den. "What's going on?"

"Jordan's not hungry."

"Pissed at you, huh?"

Maddy sighed. "I'd take it personally if I hadn't been the same way with my mother when I was her age. Hopefully, she'll outgrow it before she turns every hair on my head gray." Not that it mattered, thanks to regular visits to Sleeping Lady Salon.

"You'd look cute with gray hair. You look darned cute in that wig," Alan said, and kissed her.

"Alan Donaldson, you are a truly wonderful man," she said, smiling up at him. "I think I'm going to have to keep you."

"I think you are, too," he said, smiling back. "Who

else will you get to put up your over-the-top Christmas lights? Speaking of lights, you'd better get out there. Your public awaits."

She stuck her tongue out at him and left her warm, cozy house for the cold, dark night. Well, semidark. Thanks to the thousands of lights coming at her from all directions, it was hardly dark. But it *was* cold. Oh, the sacrifices she made for Candy Cane Lane.

Still, it was worth it, she thought, looking around her. Every house on the street (except for the newcomer's) twinkled with lights of all colors and dripped with icicle lights. Shrubs and trees were adorned with red, green and blue. Santas waved from lawns and rooftops. Mechanical deer grazed on snowy grass (preferable to real deer, who loved to nibble the tops off her tulips every spring). Several lawns, including hers, had nativity scenes commemorating the Reason for the Season, and one of the newer neighbors had set up an elaborate lit Christmas train on the roof. The Whitakers, as usual, had their outdoor speakers rigged with Christmas songs to greet visitors to the neighborhood and their gigantic inflatable snow globe was producing a regular blizzard. Ah, yes, it was a lovely sight, positively soul satisfying.

A compact car came slowly down the street, crunching through the light dusting of snow. Obviously visitors taking in the sights. Maddy waved and the car pulled to a stop next to her. The driver's window slid down to reveal a man somewhere in his thirties. In the seat next to him sat his wife.

"Welcome to Candy Cane Lane," Maddy said. "Would anyone like a candy cane?"

"I would," chorused two little voices from the back, and Maddy handed them the treat.

"We love coming here," gushed the woman. "It gets better every year."

"Thank you," Maddy said. "We all enjoy doing this." Well, most of them did. Mr. Werner was the exception. The more popular Candy Cane Lane became, the crankier he got.

"We've been coming ever since we moved here," the man told her. "The kids love it."

Her daughter used to love it, too. It was so easy to take a good thing for granted. "I'm glad you all enjoy it. Merry Christmas," she said, and stepped away so they could continue their tour.

"Same to you," called the woman.

"Don't ever stop doing this," the man added.

"We won't," Maddy assured him. *Even if our daughters don't appreciate our efforts.*

The happy family had barely continued their tour when a black SUV turned onto the street, cranked-up music and a thumping bass announcing its presence. Teenagers out joyriding, probably some of the same oversize marauders who crashed through the neighborhood on Halloween, harassing the younger kids and demanding candy from the grown-ups. Honestly, where were their parents?

The vehicle drew close to her and the windows slid down. Teen boy laughter and catcalls spilled out.

"Hey, tell Santa to bring me some condoms for Christmas," shouted one as they cruised past. He looked all of fourteen, with shaggy blond hair, and was obviously applying for membership in Future Creeps of America.

Maddy frowned. This was a family neighborhood.

The other occupants of the vehicle thought their friend was hilarious and yukked it up even as the driver gunned

the motor, screeching out past the car with the young
family and driving over a parking strip, nearly taking
out an inflated snowman. Then they whipped a U-turn
and roared off down the street, too fast for Maddy to get
the number of the license plate.

If she had she would've reported them. With that
crazy driving, they could have hurt someone.

They'd had their fun. Most likely, they wouldn't be
back. At least she hoped not. But she'd send an email
about this to all the neighbors so they could be on the
lookout. Meanwhile, here came another car with another
family, eager to take in the holiday finery of Candy Cane
Lane. No requests for condoms from this bunch. Candy
canes would do just fine.

Maddy passed out the treats and gave them a final
wave as they moved on, her heart warmed by the com-
pliments she'd received.

The whole neighborhood was ablaze with lights, and
visitors were already on the street checking it out. *It's
Griswold Town*, thought Tilda, standing at her living
room window with her spiked eggnog, taking it all in.
But hey, people in Icicle Falls enjoyed getting into the
holiday mood. The downtown merchants went all out
and, of course, the big tree at the center of town was a
thing of wonder. That was how it should be. That was
how it had always been, ever since Tilda was a kid. And
it was great for the tourists. She supposed Candy Cane
Lane was, too. A lot of people cruised this street in December, enjoying the lights. It was a pretty impressive
sight.

Until you got to her house. She heaved a sigh. She'd
planned to go to the hardware store on her way home

from work later in the week and get some candy canes, figuring she'd put them out the next weekend. Now she was thinking she should've left some of the inside stuff until later and gotten the outside of her house dressed up for the holidays, like everyone else. This was the Christmas equivalent of being the one party-pooper house at Halloween that kept its porch light turned off and its candy under lock and key.

But a woman couldn't do everything in one weekend, and since she was spending more time indoors than out, she'd focused on the inside of her new home. She'd set up her computer and TV and sound system, and her latest version of PlayStation. She'd hung Georgie's quilted wall hanging in the living room, and the poinsettia she'd received from Mrs. Walters stood in the middle of her oak dining table. The mistletoe was hanging over the living room entryway, waiting for a stray male to wander by. Not that she'd be kissing any of her gaming pals, but it did add a festive touch. The floors were freshly mopped, and although the wax cleaner Georgie had used on the living room hardwood floor didn't make a huge difference, it did show its potential. The bathrooms and kitchen had been cleaned and the food stowed away. Yeah, the inside was coming along.

She glanced over at Mrs. Walters's place. Even that was now dripping with red and green lights. When had *that* happened? Elves had obviously sneaked over while she was taking a break, eating her leftover deli sandwiches and enjoying the episode of *Justified* she'd recorded. She caught a glimpse of a man in a parka and knit cap going into the garage with a ladder. Oh, yeah. The guy Mrs. W. had hired to fix up her place.

Hmm. How much did he charge? She pulled her coat

out of the closet and put on her boots, then hurried outside to catch him before he drove away.

She was halfway down her front walk when she noticed the truck parked in front of Mrs. W.'s. *Oh. Never mind.* She did an about-face and started for the porch as fast as she could without looking like she was in a hurry to escape. Which she was. *Idiot,* she scolded herself. She should've seen the gas-hog, big-wheel truck, and it should've registered. Where were her powers of observation lately?

"Well, hey, there," called Devon Black. "You out on foot patrol?"

Great. Frickin' lovely. If there was a man on the planet Tilda would less rather stand out in the cold with, she couldn't think of him. "Nope," she said over her shoulder, and kept moving.

"Hey, wait up."

No way. Here was the porch now. Here was the door.

And here was Devon Black, looking like the devil's best friend with that five-o'clock shadow on his perfect, square chin, his eyes dark, his mouth… *Oh, good grief, stop it!* "What do you want?"

"You."

"Very funny," she snapped.

"So, you live here?"

"I do."

"It's kind of…naked."

Her thoughts exactly. Only when she'd used that word, it hadn't produced the same holiday glow it did when Devon said it. "I just moved in," she said defensively.

"Yeah?" He was eyeing the place now. "It needs some work." He pointed to her droopy gutters.

"I'll get to them."

"I could fix 'em for you."

"That's okay."

"What, you gonna do it yourself?"

"I might. Well, it's been nice talking to you. I'm sure you've got a tavern brawl waiting over at the Man Cave."

"Ha, ha," he said sourly. "One little misunderstanding and I'm branded for life. Is that it?"

"I understand who you are," she said, aiming a finger at him.

"A few speeding tickets."

"You have no regard for the law."

He scowled. "I do, too. When was the last time you caught me robbing a bank? Shooting someone?"

"Doing drugs," Tilda added sweetly.

"I kicked that four years ago. Anyway, I only did weed, which as you know is totally legal in Washington."

"It wasn't four years ago."

"I wasn't here four years ago."

"Yeah, well, you were here when you were drunk and disorderly. Seems to me that's how we met."

"Aww, you remembered."

"I can remember more than one occasion."

"Hey, that last time I didn't start it."

"I guess not, if you don't count hitting on another guy's woman."

"How was I supposed to know they were together? Come on, she was flirting with me."

Yep, God's gift to women.

He crossed his arms, leaned against the house and grinned at her. "Sometimes I think you're prejudiced, Officer."

"What?"

"You heard me. You're prejudiced against normal people."

"That's ridiculous," she said with a snort.

"Yeah? Then how come you don't like me?"

Because you're immature, obnoxious and conceited. "You really need to ask?"

"Hey, you keep confusing the old me with the new me. Anyway, I'm not so bad. Ask my brother. Ask Dan Masters."

"And how many women should I ask?"

He smiled. Oh, yeah. She could smell sulfur. Where was he hiding the pitchfork? "Can I help it if the ladies like me?"

"Look, I'd like to stand out here all night listening to your line of bull, but it's cold," she said, opening the door.

"Yeah, it is. Let's go inside." The smile got bigger, showing off his even, white teeth and making her suddenly think of the big bad wolf. *The better to give you a love bite, little girl.*

He started to follow her in, but she stopped him with a hand to his chest. "I don't think so."

"Come on, Tilda. Show me your new place."

And your black thong. Whoa, where had that come from? As if she couldn't guess. Devon Black had a gift for waking up her sleeping hormones. "I've got stuff to do."

"I'll help you do it."

Do it. Yes! Okay, no more spiked eggnog. Time to cut herself off before her sex drive ran her off the road. "That's okay. I can manage alone." Thirty-two and still managing alone. That sucked.

But it would suck worse to hook up with a bad boy

like Devon Black. She was on the side of law and order
and self-control. He was…trouble. Beautiful, gorgeous,
tempting trouble.

And, of course, that was why she couldn't stand
him. He'd want to talk her into doing all kinds of bad
things. Skinny-dipping (indecent exposure). Wild party-
style drinking (which would lead to indecent exposure).
Speeding. Oh, not in a car, but into a relationship that
would drive her completely crazy. Tilda had her act together. She was strong and disciplined and straight as
an arrow. Some people confused that with having a stick
up her butt, but they were idiots. And she'd be an idiot
to encourage Devon Black.

"Being alone sucks," Devon said as if reading her
mind.

"So does being with the wrong person," she said, and
shut the door on him.

His muffled voice came through the door. "You don't
know I'm the wrong person."

"Oh, yes, I do," she said. There was someone out there
for her, but it sure wasn't Devon Black.

Chapter Six

Who doesn't love secrets and surprises at Christmas?
— Muriel Sterling, *Making the Holidays Bright:*
How to Have a Perfect Christmas

The first Saturday in December had been marked off on Ivy's calendar for months. Her friend Missy Monroe was getting married and Ivy was one of her bridesmaids. Ivy used to love weddings. Not so much now.

Not that she wasn't happy for her friend, of course. Missy was the Miss Congeniality of Icicle Falls. Everyone loved her. A single mom for years, she'd had some rough bumps along the way, but she'd finally met her Prince Charming when she and her kids came to Icicle Falls for Christmas a couple of years back. She'd since moved to town and was working at Sleeping Lady Salon, making the women of Icicle Falls beautiful.

This Saturday she was making her bridesmaids beautiful. The wedding was at seven, but photos were scheduled for six, and Ivy and Maria Gomez were going to the salon at four so Missy could do their hair.

"Are you sure you want to do that?" Ivy had asked

her. "I mean, you'll have enough to do getting yourself ready."

"Courtney's helping me with our hair," Missy had said. "And I'm just wearing mine down. That's how John likes it. We'll be done in plenty of time to get into our dresses."

So at 3:50 p.m. (after putting in half a day at work because, as usual, Christmas Haus was swamped), Ivy made her way over to the salon. It was packed with women getting haircuts and highlights for their various holiday parties. Sleeping Lady Salon was charming and kitschy, with vintage chairs from the fifties in the waiting area. A wall clock shaped like a black cat hung on the wall, its tail and its eyes swinging back and forth. Instead of pictures of beautiful men and women showing off various hairstyles, the walls were decorated with black-and-white photos of stars from Hollywood's golden era and of women in salons of bygone years getting beautified. A Kewpie doll sat on the reception desk, right next to the business cards. Hair dryers whirred and customers chatted and laughed. The aroma of coffee mixed with the usual hair salon smells. To most of the women in town, these were the sights, sounds and smells of their home away from home.

Sarah Gabriel, who'd owned the salon since the dawn of perms, was at the reception desk. "Ivy, it's lovely to see you. How's everything at the shop?"

"Busy," Ivy replied as she hung her coat on the coat tree.

"I can imagine," Sarah said with a smile that deepened the crinkles at her eyes.

No one knew exactly how old Sarah was and she never said, but most surmised she had to be in her sev-

enties. If that was the case she was certainly well pre-
served. Other than those laugh lines, she didn't have a
lot of wrinkles on her face—Sarah was a big believer
in chemical peels—but her hands had the crepey skin
and raised veins that accompanied age. Her hair was as
white as Santa's beard and she wore it in a short bob.
Her clothes were always stylish, and today was no exception. She wore the latest jeans, along with a black
sweater and a blue fringed scarf. "The rest of the bridal
party's already here," she told Ivy.

Missy's corner station looked like a miniparty. Missy
was working on Maria Gomez while Courtney, who was
Missy's maid of honor, stood by, eating a cookie and
watching. Missy's daughter, Lala, excited to be a flower
girl, was dancing in place and serenading her captive au-
dience with an off-key rendition of "Jingle Bells."

"Would you like a latte or some tea?" Sarah asked.
One of the many perks of coming to Sleeping Lady.
"Tea would be great," Ivy said. She'd seen the lavender-
colored Tea Time box and knew it was bound to have
lavender cookies from Bailey Sterling Black's tea shop.
Lavender cookies and tea. Nothing like it to sweeten
up the day.

"A little honey?"

"Why not?" Ivy said with a smile, and started across
the salon to join her friends.

On the way she stopped to say hi to some of her favorite customers at Christmas Haus.

Justine Wright, who'd been the driving force behind
the Icicle Falls information booth forty years ago and
still haunted the place once a week, was getting her hair
permed. Like Sarah, she didn't believe in cooperating

with Mother Nature, and she kept her hair the same shade of brown it had probably been when she was young.

"Ivy, you look pretty as a picture," she greeted Ivy, catching her hand and giving it a squeeze.

"You're looking good yourself," Ivy told her. Considering Justine's age, it was no lie.

"The older you get, the harder it is to maintain," Justine said with a wink. "Oh, to be your age again. Those years go so quickly." She patted Ivy's hand. "Use them wisely, dear."

"I will," Ivy promised, and moved on. She was sure going to be more heart smart in the future.

Muriel Sterling, who bought Christmas ornaments at the shop for her daughters every year, was doing maintenance on her chestnut curls and visiting with Maddy Donaldson (one of Ivy's best customers). Maddy was also getting a color job. A girl never referred to the fact that someone was covering gray hairs—that was the unwritten beauty-salon code—so Ivy said hello to Maddy and then asked Muriel how her latest book was going.

"Slowly," Muriel admitted. "But it's not due until April, so for now I'm simply enjoying the season. And isn't it wonderful to be able to kick it off with a wedding?"

In her present frame of mind, Ivy could think of better ways, but she kept that to herself and said a polite yes.

"I love a Christmas wedding," put in Maddy. "Of course, I love all things Christmas, and I'm really enjoying your book, Muriel. Have you read it?" she asked Ivy.

"I'm reading it right now, and I'm determined to make my family's Christmas perfect this year."

"I'm confident it will be, Ivy," Muriel said. "How could it not, with those two adorable little ones?"

How indeed? It was a good reminder of how much she still had to be thankful for, she thought as she moved on to Missy's station.

Lala had finished her performance and, at the sight of Ivy, gave an excited squeal and came running to greet her. "Hi, Ivy! How are you? Mama did my hair special. It sparkles." She shook her cornrows to demonstrate.

"It's very pretty," Ivy said.

"My grandma's coming to the wedding and so is Grandpa Claussen," Lala continued, grabbing Ivy's hand and towing her to Missy's workstation. "And Carlos and I get to stay up late."

"*¡Hola!*" called Maria.

"Good. Hair to work on," Courtney said with a grin. "I was getting bored standing around."

Missy glanced up from the creation she was forming with Maria's curls and beamed at Ivy. She'd swapped the glasses she wore when she first came to town for contacts but she still had her own unique look. Her hair was longer and had lost its former blue tint. Instead, she'd turned it dark red. The red now had sparkly threads woven through that gave it a Cinderella twinkle. She was still in her leggings and sweater but she already had that special glow all brides wore on their big day. Ivy remembered the glow, the thrill of coming down the aisle and seeing Rob waiting there, gazing at her as though she was the most beautiful girl in the world. He'd obviously developed blindness since then.

What did the new girlfriend look like?

Who cared about her! A song began dancing around Ivy's head. *He's makin' a list, he's checkin' it twice. Santa knows that you weren't very nice. You'll get what is coming to you.*

Okay, now, speaking of nice, that wasn't. With her bad attitude, Santa would be flying right over her house.

She hugged Missy. "You're going to be a gorgeous bride."

"Aw, thanks," Missy said. "It seems like I've been waiting for this day forever. I can't believe it's finally here. I'm marrying John!"

Her fiancé had been a regular visitor to Icicle Falls for the past year and had recently landed a job at Cascade Mutual. He'd be moving into the cottage on Juniper Ridge that Missy and the kids rented from Garrett Armstrong, one of Icicle Falls's firefighters. John was a good guy, and Ivy was sure he'd be the kind of father you saw in those old TV sitcoms. Missy's life might have started out crummy, but now it was going well. Ivy thought that was better than everything starting out great and then winding up like hamburger that had gone bad.

"You deserve to be happy," she said to her friend.

"So do you," said Missy. "And hey, who knows? Maybe you and one of John's friends will hit it off."

Ivy had met one of John's friends a couple of months ago. Barry Woofort was the stuff dreams were made of—if you were in the cast of *The Big Bang Theory*. He was short, scrawny and had no idea how to wear glasses as a fashion statement. He was so shy that talking was as painful for him as it was for the unlucky woman he was talking to. Unless he got to pontificating on the Fibonacci sequence or how to hack into Microsoft. He'd done plenty of pontificating when he and Ivy and Missy and John had gone out to dinner on one of John's previous visits to town. (A subtle attempt on Missy and John's part to give them both a life.)

Groomsman Number Two was nice but had weight issues. He would surely lead Ivy into carb temptation.

Ah, but then there was Groomsman Number Three, Clint Clayton, recently divorced and lonely. Missy was convinced he and Ivy would be a perfect match. After meeting him the night before at the rehearsal dinner, so was Ivy. At least he'd be perfect at helping her forget Rob. Clint Clayton. It was the kind of name that belonged to a Civil War general or a fifties TV cowboy. In fact, with his broad shoulders and dark hair, that cleft in his chin, he looked like a modern version of an old TV star. Put him in boots, jeans and a cowboy hat (forget the shirt) and he'd be yummy. He'd been fun to talk to, avoiding the subject of exes—thank God!—and instead comparing favorite holiday movies with Ivy. (How could you not like a man who appreciated *The Family Man*?)

"Here's your tea, dear," Sarah said, handing over a china mug. "It'll go well with those lavender cookies Missy brought in."

"Have another," Missy said, motioning to the box.

"Don't mind if I do," Sarah said. She took one from the box, then held the box out to Ivy, who also took one.

"Me, too?" asked Lala, her little fingers hovering over the box.

"No, you've had enough," Missy replied, and Lala's lower lip jutted out.

"You gotta save room for cake, kid," Courtney said, and that diminished the pout.

"Just gorgeous," Sarah said, watching Missy deftly work the same shiny threads into Maria's dark locks that she and Lala and Courtney were sporting. "You girls are going to look so beautiful. But, of course, you're all beautiful to begin with so we're only gilding the lily."

"I have no idea what that means," Missy said. "You mean the store?"

Sarah patted her arm. "Never mind. It's an old saying. I'm dating myself."

"Is that possible?" Missy teased. "You're always stylin', Mrs. G."

"Well, style is what we do here, and thank God I have you young girls around to keep us current. You all have fun," Sarah added, and returned to the reception desk to check in a new arrival.

"I hope I look that good at her age," Maria said.

"Me, too," Ivy chimed in.

"You'll both end up looking just as good," Missy predicted. She sighed. "Me, I'll probably be fat and dumpy by the time I'm forty."

"I don't think John will care," Ivy told her. "That man is crazy for you."

Missy smiled at that. "And I'm crazy for him. He's the best thing that ever happened to me. Well, and all you guys and Icicle Falls. I'm so excited!"

"You guys are gonna be real happy together," Maria said. "Hey, and maybe it'll prompt Eduardo to finally commit."

"I think he's committed to you," Missy said.

"Sure, as long as he can come and go as he pleases. Men," she said disgustedly. "They're like dogs, always looking for the next fire hydrant."

Yes, that was Rob. He should change his name to Rover.

Seeing the frown on Ivy's face, Maria blushed. "Oh, Ivy, I didn't mean your... I'm sorry."

"Don't be," Ivy said. "It's true. You're right about

men. Except for John," she added, dutiful friend that she was. "He's the exception to the rule."

"Don't worry," Missy told her. "You're gonna find a good man, too. I just know it."

"Well, then, let's get her lookin' hot," Courtney said, and commanded Ivy to sit down so she could get to work, which she did with Lala serenading them.

Once her hair was done (complete with sparkly threads) and she was in her red satin bridesmaid's dress with its matching red bolero and her I-want-sex red heels, she was feeling pretty darned hot. Maybe that heat would attract someone.

Although she wasn't sure she *wanted* to attract anyone.

Rob. She wanted to attract Rob. Not because she wanted him back, but because she wanted him to see what he'd lost. No, not lost. Cavalierly tossed away. Too bad he wasn't going to be at the wedding.

There were plenty of other men at the wedding, though. Most of them with dates.

Except for Clint Clayton, urban cowboy, Missy's choice to escort Ivy down the aisle at the conclusion of the ceremony. A cowboy in a tux. Yum. Rob had the kids for the weekend. She could stay out all night. *Save a horse and ride a cowboy.* He smiled at Ivy as she made her way down the aisle of the Lutheran church past pews trimmed with silver ribbons and white roses. What a smile. *Yee-haw. Git along, little dogie.*

Ivy reached her spot, then lassoed her wandering thoughts and turned to watch her friend come down the aisle. "Look how pretty my mama is," Lala whispered.

Missy was, indeed, beautiful in her white wedding gown, its bolero jacket trimmed with white faux fur.

John had bought her a necklace, a gold heart trimmed with diamond chips, and she proudly wore it around her neck. Instead of a veil she had on a white faux-fur pillbox hat trimmed with tiny poinsettias. James Claussen, her unofficial father, walked her down the aisle, resplendent in his black tux with a white rosebud in the lapel.

Ivy had always wanted a Christmas wedding, but Christmases were too crazy at the shop, so she and Rob had gotten married on New Year's Eve. Every year they'd start out celebrating their anniversary. It had all sounded so idyllic. It *had* been idyllic.

Until it wasn't.

Oh, never mind him.

The pastor made a few remarks on the sanctity of marriage (too bad Rob wasn't there to hear), then guided the couple through their vows. A friend of John's sang the popular Rascal Flatts song, "Bless the Broken Road," while John and Missy lit a red unity candle surrounded by Christmas greens. They exchanged rings and then were given the blessing for their first kiss as husband and wife, which they did to much cheering and applause. Then off down the aisle they went.

And here was Clint Clayton smiling at her and offering her his arm. She was walking down the aisle on the arm of a handsome man, about to go to a big party at Festival Hall. Life was good, darn it all, and it was going to get better.

To prove it, once she got there, Ivy snarfed down half a dozen crab-stuffed appetizers and an equal number of mushroom sliders and miniquiches before they even started on the dinner buffet, which was catered by Bailey Sterling Black. Dinner was delicious—garlic prawns, jasmine rice, chicken and an Asian salad, all favorites of the bride and groom. Cass Wilkes, who owned Gingerbread Haus, had provided the wedding cake, a spice cake with buttercream icing and loaded with red frosting roses and silver bells. Ivy devoured her slice. *What the heck? Calories don't count at a wedding.*

They especially didn't count when you were divorced. Ivy sneaked another piece of cake when no one was looking.

"Good cake, isn't it?" said a voice at her shoulder.

She gave a start. Busted by Clint Clayton, Mr. Cowboy in a Tux.

Mouth full, she nodded and set down her plate. *I'm really not a pig. I'm just eating this to be polite.*

He picked it up again. "Go ahead. I won't tell."

More Brownie points for Clint Clayton. "Thanks," she said.

People were beginning to move around, catching up with friends, changing tables. He scanned the room. "I bet you know everyone here."

"I do. I've lived here all my life."

"What's that like, living in a small town?"

"I love it," she said, waving at Bailey, who was busy circulating among the guests with more champagne to toast the bride and groom.

"You have so many people watching out for you."

Hildy Johnson stopped by the cake table with her husband, Nils, in tow. "I see you're on your second piece, Ivy. The cake must be very good."

Watching out, was that what you called it? "It is," Ivy said, and moved away, Clint with her.

"Of course, I guess the downside is that everyone knows your business," he said.

"You can say that again." Suddenly she wasn't in such

a festive mood. When Rob left, it had been the talk of the town. People had come into the drugstore more to sweep around the dirt with Hildy than to buy skin cream or fill a prescription. She'd walk into Bavarian Brews and see everyone's eyes swiveling her way. Their thoughts came at her as loudly as the whir of the espresso machines. *She couldn't keep him, you know. He was miserable for a long time. She always seems nice when you go into the store but I bet she's a nag at home.*

Bailey came by with her tray of champagne glasses. Ivy took one and chugalugged.

Clint was looking across the sea of linen-clad tables with their poinsettias and candles to where Kevin and Heinrich, the owners of Lupine Floral, stood yukking it up with James and Olivia Claussen. "Not always fun when that happens, but some things are bound to get out eventually, no matter how hard you try to hide them. And maybe that's for the best. People should know who you really are."

Ivy frowned at her empty glass. She needed more champagne. "Sometimes people *think* they know who you are," she said, picturing the way Tilda Morrison always looked at her, as though she was a spoiled prom queen, "but they're wrong."

"Good point. I think I see someone I know. Excuse me," Clint said, and moved away.

What? Was it something she said? Ivy frowned as she watched him walk across the floor, joining Heinrich and Kevin and the Claussens, watched him introduce himself and shake hands all around. She didn't feel so hot in her hot, red dress anymore.

She found Bailey and snagged another glass of champagne, then drifted over to take shelter from the cold with Maddy Donaldson and her family. "Isn't this a lovely reception?" Maddy asked.

In Ivy's present frame of mind, no.

Fortunately, Maddy didn't wait for an answer. "And Missy's a beautiful bride. She and John are such a cute couple. I know they're renting that cottage on Juniper Ridge, but I heard that the Schwarzkopfs down the street are thinking of moving to Arizona. Their house would be perfect for Missy and John, and I'm sure they'd love living on Candy Cane Lane."

At this, Maddy's daughter rolled her eyes. Obviously, not everyone loved living on Candy Cane Lane.

Maddy did, though. Ivy had seen her out the night before, when she was on her way to the wedding rehearsal. Maddy had been wearing her Mrs. Santa Claus outfit and handing out candy canes.

"All right, everyone," the DJ said, "it's time to toast the bride and groom."

As Missy's maid of honor, Courtney went first. "You guys are meant to be together."

Someone had said that about Ivy and Rob once.

"And I'm so happy you found each other. Missy, I know you had to kiss a lot of frogs, but you finally found your prince."

That was the problem. Ivy hadn't kissed enough frogs. Only the one she'd married, who'd come disguised as a prince.

"So here's to happy-ever-after," Courtney finished, raising her glass.

"To happy-ever-after," everyone echoed, and drank.

"To frogs," Ivy muttered, and guzzled half her new glass of champagne.

Barry's toast was a little shorter. "Live long and prosper," he said, and did that weird *Star Trek* thing with his fingers.

"And have beautiful babies," Olivia called out, making everyone chuckle.

After the toast, the bride and groom took the floor for their wedding dance, gazing up at each other like they were Adam and Eve on a first date in the garden. At the end of the dance, he dipped her. Sigh.

And then the DJ started playing Bruno Mars's "I Want to Marry You" and practically everyone hit the floor. Except Jordan and a friend of hers, who sat together and began texting each other. Ivy searched the hall for someone to talk to and spotted Dot Morrison with Muriel Sterling. She was halfway there when a heavyset older guy escorted Muriel onto the dance floor.

That left Dot all alone. Ivy and Dot didn't exactly hang out, but she knew Dot from the Chamber of Commerce. Unlike her daughter, Dot had a sense of humor. Maybe she'd like some company.

"Hey, kiddo," Dot said when Ivy got to her table. "How come you're not out there dancing?"

"I don't know. I'm…" Busy drinking. How much champagne had she had? She needed to cut herself off or she wouldn't be able to drive. Hmm. She'd probably reached the no-driving stage already. She'd have to get a ride home. Better that than trying to drive. If Tilda caught her, she'd wind up in jail.

"You never struck me as bashful," Dot said. She nodded to where Clint Clayton stood, talking with Heinrich and Kevin. "I saw you and that hotsy-totsy groomsman flirting a few minutes ago. Go ask him to dance."

Ivy never asked guys to dance. She'd never had to. Guys always asked her. And then she'd had Rob. But she didn't have Rob now and almost everyone was paired up tonight. If she wanted to dance…heck, if she wanted a new life, a new man, she'd have to get out there and go for it. Clint was probably ready to hit the dance floor and not sure how to politely extricate himself from the conversation. That was it. He'd appreciate her offering him an excuse to escape.

She weaved her way over to him. "Do you want to marry me?" she asked playfully. "Or at least dance with me?"

Clint looked a bit embarrassed. She'd only been joking! But he smiled gamely and said, "Okay. To the dancing, I mean."

He was a great dancer, and she told him so after the song ended. Now the music had morphed into slow and sexy. Aerosmith's "I Don't Want to Miss a Thing." Positively inspiring. "I bet you're good at a lot of things." *Mr. Cowboy Tux.*

He rubbed his forehead. "Uh, yeah. How much champagne have you had, Ivy?"

"Just a little." She slipped her arms around his neck, ready to start another dance.

"How about we sit this one out?" he suggested, gently loosening her grip.

"Okay." Sitting, lying, whatever. *Easy, cowgirl. You just met this man.*

He led her to a table in a dark corner occupied only by a couple of empty champagne glasses. The ideal spot to share a kiss.

Once they were seated, he took her hand. "Ivy, you're a lovely woman."

"So I've been told. And you're a lovely man." Was she

looking at him all goofy? Probably. But it didn't matter. *'Tis the season to be goofy. Fa-la-la-la-la la-la-la-la.*

"And I know Missy and John were kind of hoping we'd get together."

That could be arranged. "Well," she said, deciding it was time to act coy.

"But there's something they don't know about me."

"What, you're an ax murderer?" Ivy teased, leaning in close.

"No. I'm gay."

She sat back and blinked. "You're what?"

"I didn't choose to be, even though I know these days it's accepted, even understood, by most people. But I was raised…" He stopped and bit his lip. That gorgeous lip. The lip that had no interest in locking with hers. That gorgeous, lying lip.

"So you married your wife even though you preferred men?"

"It wasn't that I didn't love her. I tried to make it work. I couldn't."

It's just not working. Might as well have been Rob sitting there talking to her. "You rat. You big, chicken-livered rat. You used that poor woman as cover."

"I did love her," he protested. "Just…"

"No, you didn't. If you did, you never would've married her, never have put her through all that hurt." She stood abruptly, vaguely aware of her chair tipping over. "You're a frog. You're all frogs!"

And it was time for Cinderella, or whatever fool woman went around kissing amphibians, to leave the ball. Ivy tottered back to her table, grabbed her cell phone and called the only man who had his act together. "Daddy, I need a ride home. Please come get me."

"You okay, kitten?"

"Yes, I'm fine, but I've had enough." Enough of weddings, enough of men, definitely enough champagne. And she'd had more than enough of herself. Clint Clayton might not have been any Prince Charming but she sure hadn't behaved like a princess.

"Okay, I'll be right there."

"Thanks. You're the best." The best man in the whole world. The only decent man in the world.

She'd hardly ended the call when she got a text from her sister. How's the guy?

No go, Ivy texted back.

It was all for the best, she told herself. This simply confirmed what she'd already known. There was no man in her future.

Which meant she could drink all the eggnog and eat all the Christmas cookies she wanted. Who cared if she turned into a tree trunk? If she grew the biggest butt this side of Seattle? If she wound up being able to use her tummy for a TV tray? She didn't have anyone to impress. This Christmas she was going to follow the advice she'd read in Muriel Sterling's book. She was going to make her Christmas perfect even though it wouldn't be. So there.

"That was a fantastic wedding," Maddy raved as she and her family drove back home. "A wonderful way to start the holidays."

"Good food," Alan said.

"And wasn't it cute that they passed out candy canes to everyone?"

"Yeah, like we don't have a ton of those already," Jordan said from the backseat.

"You can never have enough candy canes," Maddy said lightly, refusing to be brought down by her daughter, the baby Grinch.

"Yeah, you can."

"Well, then, you can give me yours and I'll pass it on to some deserving child tomorrow."

"You're doing that again?" Jordan asked in disgust.

"Probably, for a little while."

"You were just out there."

"I know, but people are getting sick."

"Let it go tomorrow, hon," Alan suggested. "Let's have a cozy night in and play some Farkle."

"We can play games in the afternoon," Maddy said. It was Sunday. They had all day for family bonding.

"She'd rather be outside, talking to people she doesn't know," Jordan muttered.

"Oh, honestly."

"Anyway, Afton invited me over for dinner tomorrow. Can I go?"

"Sure," Alan said just as Maddy said, "No."

"We always have Sunday dinner together," Maddy told her. Then, to sweeten the pot, she added, "I'm making lasagna."

"Everyone's going to Afton's tomorrow. Her mom's making pizza."

"I guess pizza tops lasagna," Alan joked.

Maddy wasn't laughing. "Well, this time the gang will have to eat pizza without you."

"Thanks, Mom. You get to have a life and I don't?"

Who was this alien in the backseat? "You are my life."

"Yeah, right." They'd pulled into the garage now and Jordan got out of the car and slammed the door, then stalked into the house.

"I'm not sure what's happening here," Alan said as he and Maddy made their more sedate exit from the car. "She seems to be pissed off all the time. What is it, hormones or something?"

"Or something."

"Maybe you should let her go to Afton's."

"After that little snit fit? I don't think so."

"She'll make us pay," Alan predicted.

His prediction came true. Jordan was a sphinx on the way to church the next day. On the way home, Maddy tried to engage her in conversation, asking how the youth service was, and got a terse teenage, "Fine."

Jordan set the table for Sunday dinner, then disappeared into her room. She came out to eat, but when Alan suggested playing a game, all he got was a snotty, "No thanks," and then she was gone again, her bedroom door banging shut behind her.

"Well," he said to Maddy, "what do you want to do?"

"Besides throttle our daughter?"

"Uh, yeah."

"Why don't you and I play some Farkle? I feel lucky."

She *was* lucky, she reminded herself. She had a charming house, a sweet husband and a good kid who'd been temporarily kidnapped by aliens. The aliens would put her back in her body eventually. Maybe when she was around twenty.

They were at the kitchen table, halfway through their dice game, when Jordan came down in search of further sustenance in the form of potato chips. "You want to join us?" Alan offered.

Jordan shook her head, took her Pringles and vanished.

Maddy watched her retreating backside, covered in

very expensive jeans, and frowned. "She's trying to guilt me into changing my mind."

"That would end the battle," Alan said.

"But not the war. If she doesn't want to have fun with us today, she can just not have fun. Period."

"I suspect she is having fun. She's probably up there texting half the kids in Icicle Falls."

"Let her," Maddy said with a shrug. Let her tell Afton what a rotten mother she had. Maddy and the aliens knew the truth.

The cold war continued clear up until bedtime, but Maddy decided that her daughter wasn't going to sleep without her usual good-night kiss. She knocked on the door and got no answer; she opened it, anyway. Jordan was in her pj's sitting on the bed listening to music on her iPod. She pretended not to see Maddy.

Nice try. Maddy came in and sat on the bed beside her.

"All my friends think you're mean," Jordan informed her.

"All your friends should check their source. It might not be accurate," Maddy responded calmly.

Jordan rolled her eyes. Too bad there wasn't an eye-rolling gymnastics event. Jordan would've brought home the gold.

"I'm sorry you didn't want to spend time with us today."

"You don't want to spend time with me," Jordan shot back. "You made me stay home just to be mean."

"No, I made you stay home because we were going to do something as a family. You chose not to."

Jordan looked away, feigning interest in the top of her bedroom window.

"I'm sorry you had such a miserable day, but pouting isn't the way to get what you want."

"You don't care what I want!"

Okay, they weren't going to ride the night train to Hysterics Land. "That's enough now," Maddy said firmly. She kissed the top of her daughter's head. "I'll send Daddy up to say good-night."

"Fine," Jordan snapped. "I'd rather see him."

Ouch. The claws were out tonight and they were scratching deep. And it hurt. Maddy left the room before her daughter could see the tears in her eyes. *This is what teenage girls do. They get angry and they lash out.*

All it would take to melt Jordan's anger would be one after-school shopping spree at Gilded Lily's. They could go later in the week, after they had some distance from the day's attempt at manipulation. No way did Maddy want Jordan thinking her mother was trying to buy her off. Even if she was.

With that resolved, she was able to go to bed later that night feeling pleased with herself, pleased with the whole world. She turned off the outside lights (she was always the last one on the street to turn hers off) and followed Alan upstairs to bed. The neighborhood was quiet now, all the visitors back in their own homes, their children enjoying the candy canes Mrs. Santa Claus had given them earlier. Okay, so she'd pulled candy cane duty a lot this first week of the season. But after tomorrow, she was done for a whole week and a half. That should make everyone happy.

By the time she was done brushing her teeth and applying her Retin-A wrinkle cream, Alan was already sawing logs. She climbed into bed and snuggled up next to him and soon she was drifting off, too.

At one point she thought she heard something. She sat in bed, straining to detect whatever noise had punctuated her husband's snores, but there was nothing. Maybe some neighbors letting their dog out? Who knew? And then she was asleep again.

And then it was morning and her alarm was going off, and Alan was pulling his pillow over his head. "Come on, time to get up," she said, wrestling it away from him.

Next she went to make sure Jordan was stirring. She knocked on the door. The room was dark and her daughter was a lump under the covers. She tiptoed in, drew the covers back and kissed her daughter's cheek. "Time to get uppy, guppy."

"Go away," Jordan groaned, trying to brush her off as if she was some giant gnat.

"I'll go away, but I'll just come back. Give up and get up."

Another groan.

"I'm making French toast."

Jordan groaned a third time, but she sat up. Oh, yes, French toast always did it.

Maddy put on her favorite Mannheim Steamroller Christmas CD and began humming along with the music as she worked. Ah, yes, nothing like a family breakfast.

Alan was the first one downstairs. "Here's your French toast," she said, sliding it onto a plate.

She waggled the plate in front of him and he eyed the treat. "Well, okay, I guess I've got time."

He'd wolfed it down with a cup of coffee and was out already in the car when Jordan came downstairs. Maddy heard the garage door open, heard the car leave and then heard her phone ring. It was Alan's cell. Why was he calling her from the driveway?

She picked up the phone as she set Jordan's plate on the table. "What did you forget?"

"Nothing, and I've got to get going, but you'd better come take a look at the yard."

"What on earth?" She hurried to the front door and opened it and got a horrible shock.

The candy canes along her front walk had all been knocked over. Not only knocked over but stomped on. They lay every which way, broken and sad. Ruined. The Gordons, her neighbors to the left, hadn't fared much better. Their Santa had been deflated and tied in a giant knot. She looked down the street and saw another yard with its candy canes no longer standing. Vandalism on Candy Cane Lane?

Now Jordan stood behind her. "Wow! What happened?"

That was what Maddy wanted to know. And she was going to find out.

And when she did…

Chapter Seven

*You'll enjoy the holiday so much more if you look
on each new day as a new adventure.*
—Muriel Sterling, *Making the Holidays Bright:
How to Have a Perfect Christmas*

Tilda and Jamal had been on the job almost an hour
and a half, and Jamal was lobbying for a stop at Bavarian Brews when the call came in. "Vandalism on Candy
Cane Lane. Looks like you moved into a high-crime
neighborhood," he teased.

"Oh, man, do we have to take this call?" Tilda groaned.

"What, you gonna send Big Jer out to investigate?"

"I wouldn't mind." In fact, she'd love to dump this
on their lone detective. Jerry didn't have that much on
his plate.

"Not his department unless it's a hate crime."

"It might be."

"Yeah, somebody hates candy canes."

By the time they pulled onto the street, several neighbors were gathered in front of the Donaldson residence.
Jamal had just parked the patrol car when Maddy Donaldson came storming up to them, the pom-poms on her

boots swinging wildly. She looked mad enough to bite the head off a tiger.

"I'm gonna let you take the lead on this," Jamal said as they got out of the car.

Tilda scowled at him. "Thanks."

"We have vandals!" Maddy pointed to the ruins of her candy canes. "They knocked over our candy canes and smashed them. They knocked over the Welkys', too, and they wrecked the Gordons' Santa. Who would do such a hateful thing?" she demanded as if Tilda were psychic.

"Kids, probably."

Maddy made a face. "Kids whose parents don't keep an eye on them. Juvenile delinquents. You know, just last week we had a carload of boys tearing through here."

"Did you report it?"

"Well, no. I didn't get the license number. But it was a black SUV."

That narrowed it down to half the vehicles in Icicle Falls. "You really should report these things when they happen."

"Well, I'm reporting it now," Maddy snapped.

Mrs. Team Spirit was now Mrs. PMS. "Okay," Tilda said in her most calming voice.

"I expect you to get to the bottom of this. We can't have all our holiday displays getting ruined. People will be disappointed."

"I understand," Tilda said.

The tightly wound spring that was Maddy Donaldson unwound. "Thank you. I know you'll give this your full attention." She began making introductions as if they were all at a holiday cocktail party. "This is Tilda Morrison," she told the others. "She bought the Schmerzes' house. Tilda, this is Carla Welky."

"I'm Geraldine Chan," said a petite, fortysomething woman. "We live three houses down," she added, pointing to a house that had almost every square inch covered in lights.

"Was anything damaged at your house?" Tilda asked.

"Oh, no," Geraldine said airily.

"I'm Gabriella Moreno," put in another woman. "Welcome to the neighborhood."

Tilda thanked her and turned her attention back to Carla Welky, a woman in her fifties with a parka thrown over her pajamas and a knitted cap pulled over black hair with not a hint of gray. "Did you see anyone loitering around your place?"

Carla Welky shook her head. "It's hard to imagine someone doing something like this." She gazed up at Tilda as though they were in a war-ravaged city and Tilda was their rescuer. "Thank God you're living here now. Once those vandals learn there's a police presence in the neighborhood, they won't dare to try anything."

"We can hope," Maddy said. She didn't sound very confident of Tilda's protective powers.

A pretty girl, perched on the edge of becoming a teenager, approached the group. Tilda was no fashion queen but she knew trendy, expensive clothes when she saw them. She was willing to bet this kid was Maddy Donaldson's daughter. Of course, the fact that she was the spitting image of her mother helped Tilda reach her brilliant conclusion. At this rate she'd make detective in no time.

"Mom, I'm gonna be late for school," the girl said.

"Just a minute," Maddy responded. "Get in the car." The daughter heaved a sigh and trudged back to their car and Maddy looked expectantly at Tilda, waiting for her to go into *Law and Order* mode.

"Did you see or hear anything suspicious last night?" Tilda asked Mrs. Welky.

"Like a black SUV?" Maddy asked, helping Tilda do her job.

"Mrs. Donaldson, please," Tilda said. "I'll ask the questions."

Maddy blinked in surprise. "Oh. Yes, of course. Did you, Carla?"

"No," the other woman said. "I took a melatonin."

"Maybe Earl saw something," Maddy persisted. "Her husband," she added, obviously for Tilda's benefit.

"Mrs. Donaldson, why don't you take your daughter to school?" Tilda suggested.

Maddy managed to look insulted, hurt and reproachful all at the same time, but she did start for her car. "Don't forget to talk to the Gordons," she said over her shoulder.

Oh, for heaven's sake. "Don't worry," Tilda called back, then returned her attention to Mrs. Welky. "How about your husband?"

"He'd sleep through an earthquake."

"Okay, well, if you think of anything else, don't hesitate to call the station."

"Or come over to your house?"

"Just call the station," Tilda said, and moved on to the next scene of the Christmas crime.

The woman who lived there was outside now, too, and Maddy had taken a detour to talk to her, as well as a hefty old man and a couple of older women. Big excitement on Candy Cane Lane. On seeing Tilda's approach, Maddy, who'd still been hovering, made a beeline for her car. The others stood and waited, talking among themselves, shaking heads and frowning. The old man scowled at Tilda as if this was somehow her fault.

She reached the little group just as Maddy drove off. Thank God she was at least rid of the Queen of Candy Cane Lane. "Which one of you is Mrs. Gordon?"

"Well, it's not me," the old man said.

Everyone's a comic. Oh, goody.

"I am," said the youngest woman in the group. She seemed to be somewhere in her midthirties. Tilda had seen her around town with a couple of school-age kids in tow.

"Did you see or hear anyone out in your yard?" Tilda asked.

The woman shook her head. "We were busy helping the kids with their homework until nine. Then we watched a movie and went to bed. I didn't hear anything outside. But I go to sleep listening to music on my iPod."

"Was anything else damaged besides your Santa?" Tilda asked as Jamal went over to examine the decoration, which was tied in a giant knot.

"I wish they'd damage *my* candy canes," muttered the old man. "Give me a good excuse not to put the stupid things out every year. They're cheaply made, too. Don't buy any."

Tilda ignored him and studied the Gordon woman.

She shook her head. "They left our candy canes alone. And, actually, I don't think the Santa's damaged. I think we can untie him and inflate him again, and he'll be fine."

Tilda nodded. "Did *anyone* see anything?"

The others all shook their heads.

Okay, she was done here. "Well, if you do…"

"We'll call you," said one of the women.

"Call 9-1-1," Tilda instructed her. "That's the best way to get a quick response."

"Unless you're home, right?" the same woman asked.

"Even if I am home." Why did people think that just because a cop lived nearby she'd be on call 24/7? Probably because if something did happen in the neighborhood she wouldn't ignore it. No cop would.

The grumpy old man gave her some parting advice. "You catch these little shits and teach 'em a lesson. Make 'em spend a night in jail, that's what I say."

Tilda acknowledged him with a curt nod. She suspected that if his property was damaged he'd be out for blood simply for the fun of it. But he had a point. Kids needed to learn to respect other people's property.

"That's the most excitement we've had all week," Jamal said as they drove away.

Tilda frowned. Something didn't add up. "Hard to picture any of our local JDs out at night in the cold stomping on a few candy canes."

"Well, whoever did it probably isn't gonna stop. Hey, that could make second watch interesting next time we're on it."

"I just hope they don't go near Maddy Donaldson's again," Tilda said. "She'll have a stroke."

"What is wrong with kids these days?" Maddy fumed as she chauffeured Jordan to school.

"How come you think it's kids?" Jordan asked.

"Well, who else would do something so immature and inconsiderate?"

Jordan shrugged. "I dunno."

"That's because there is no one. No sane adult would do such a thing. Where are these kids' parents?"

"Who cares, anyway? It's just a bunch of dumb candy canes."

"It certainly is not 'just a bunch of dumb candy canes,'" Maddy corrected her. "It's people's property. You can't go around wrecking things that belong to others. I'm going to write a letter to the editor."

"Whatever," Jordan said.

"Don't you *whatever* me, young lady," Maddy snapped. "Some things are important."

"Yeah, like doing stuff with your daughter."

"We did do stuff. We made fudge Thanksgiving weekend. And I would've watched the movie with you and Daddy if you'd waited for me."

"We got tired of waiting."

Okay, so she'd stayed out a little later than she intended that night, but the cars had kept coming and she hadn't wanted any child leaving the neighborhood disappointed. Anyway, they could've had some time together the day before if Jordan hadn't confined herself to her room.

There was no sense bringing that up, though. "We'll do something tonight," she promised. Thank God someone else would be on candy-cane patrol so she could earn back her good-mother merit badge.

"Like what?" Jordan asked suspiciously.

"Like making Christmas cookies."

Jordan perked up at that, and by the time Maddy dropped her off at school, pouting Alien Implant Jordan had been replaced by Sweet Jordan. Okay, the day could only get better.

Once she entered her shop, she definitely felt better.

All was well here, shelves lined with glass jars filled with every imaginable kind of spice, from smoked paprika to curry. Her shop also offered herbs, spice rubs, fancy barbecue sauces, vanilla beans and a variety of exotic extracts. Her customers ranged from tourists to epicures and foodies, and Maddy enjoyed helping them find that special something or that hard-to-come-by seasoning, and talking about recipes.

At lunchtime Ivy Bohn came in looking for rose water. "I'm going to make Christmas cookies with the kids tomorrow," she told Maddy. "I'm using my mom's recipe and she always flavors the icing with rose water."

"I'll have to try it. Jordan and I are making cookies tonight." Maybe she'd put rose water instead of almond extract in the spritz Christmas trees.

"You should. It's really good."

"Anything with butter and sugar is good," Maddy said with a smile.

"You're right about that."

"And making Christmas treats together, that's such a special tradition to start."

"I think so," Ivy agreed. "I've got tomorrow off and I'm going to stay home all day and play with the kids. I'm following Muriel Sterling's advice about creating memories together."

"Great idea," Maddy said. "They grow up so fast." *Too fast.*

"Promise? Sometimes I think we're stuck in limbo." Ivy sighed. "Or maybe it's just me."

"You're still rebuilding your life."

Ivy made a face. "Is that what you call it?"

"You're making progress," Maddy assured her. "Your

shop is doing well, you're keeping your household running. That's what counts."

"I guess," Ivy said dubiously. "Hey, what was going on this morning? What happened to your candy canes?"

Now it was Maddy's turn to make a face. "Vandals. Some rotten kids were out last night tearing down candy canes."

"That's awful!" Ivy said. "What's wrong with people, anyway?"

"I have no idea. I just hope the police catch the little monsters who did this and throw them in juvenile hall."

"Or make them put up everyone's decorations next year," said Ivy. "Fit the punishment to the crime, and spare me from having to put up my lights. Not that I don't like *having* them up," she hurried to add.

"I understand," Maddy told her. "It's work. But it's worth it. Our neighborhood looks amazing."

"Yes, it does." Ivy nodded. "Well, I'd better get going. Let me know if the cops find whoever did it."

"I will." But she wasn't going to wait for the police to do something. Maddy Donaldson was on the job. Tonight she was planning to stay up and keep watch. If those rotten little miscreants returned, she had a cell phone and she wasn't afraid to use it.

Even though the day started out miserably, it ended happily. Alan came home on his lunch hour and set up new candy canes in their yard and the Welkys'. She made turkey chimichangas for dinner, which were a big hit, and after dinner she and Jordan baked Christmas cookies.

The cookie-baking led to great mother-daughter bonding, with Jordan catching Maddy up on all the latest school gossip. One of her friends had cheated on her math test and was in big trouble. Another friend had just had her first period. This was shared rather wistfully.

"You don't want to be in a hurry for that," Maddy said. "I mean, yes, it's an important rite of passage, but it's kind of a nuisance, too."

"I guess," Jordan said dubiously. "But what if mine never comes?"

"It will. Trust me."

That seemed to be all the reassuring her daughter needed. She went back to cranking out trees onto the baking sheet with the cookie press.

"Why don't we take some of these over to Mrs. Walters when we're done?" Maddy said.

"By that you mean me."

Maddy smiled. "You run over with the cookies and I'll stay behind and do cleanup. How's that for a deal?"

Jordan was no fool. She took the deal.

The conversation moved into new territory. Boy Land. The new boy at school was named Logan and he was an older man: fourteen. He was reeeally cute and looked just like Riker Lynch. ("He was on *Dancing with the Stars*, Mom. Remember?") Riker the Second was into video games and skateboarding. And could Jordan have a skateboard?

Skateboards. When Maddy thought of skateboards, she thought of kids with droopy clothes and bad grades. That might have been true twenty years ago but it wasn't now, she reminded herself, and switched to visions of her daughter flying through the air and breaking her wrist.

"We'll see," she said. "So, tell me more about Logan."

"What else do you want to know?"

"Is he interested in any sports?"

"No."

"What's his favorite subject in school?"

"I don't know," Jordan said, her tone of voice saying what she thought of that dumb question.

"Does he like school?"

Jordan merely shrugged.

So, not into learning. Maddy was beginning to get a bad feeling about this kid. "Where does he live?"

"On Alder."

A few blocks over, an older, run-down section of town. *Don't be a snob*, Maddy told herself.

"It's just him and his mom. His dad left when he was ten."

"Oh, that's sad." And it was. Was his mother managing to keep tabs on him?

Jordan switched to more interesting factoids about her dream boy. "He wants to become a street skateboarding champion. There's this big competition in Seattle. You can win a whole bunch of money." On she went, detailing Logan's dreams of glory, all the funny things he did in English to disrupt the class. Oh, yes, Logan sounded like a real winner. But at least he had goals.

Anyway, there was no point in worrying about her daughter and Logan turning into Romeo and Juliet. At thirteen, Jordan had a crush on a new boy every other month.

The subject finally changed to clothes and Maddy proposed a shopping trip. "Ace your math test and maybe we can reward you with those new jeans you want."

"Sweet," Jordan said with a smile.

Maddy smiled, too. Moments like this made up for the times when mother-daughter relations were strained. There'd probably be a lot more strained relations over the next few years, but she hoped they'd always have Christmas cookies to bond over.

Jordan dutifully delivered goodies to Mrs. Walters when they were done, then retired to her room with a handful of gumdrop and spritz cookies to study for her math test and no doubt text all her friends. At least she'd have good things to text tonight.

Alan and Maddy watched a movie on demand and then called it a night. Or, rather, Alan did. "I'm going to stay up awhile," Maddy said.

"You are? Why?"

"I want to see if whoever destroyed our candy canes comes back."

"They won't. They've had their fun."

"Well, I'm going to make sure they don't have any more."

"Suit yourself," said Alan, "but if you ask me it's a waste of time."

"Not if I catch 'em."

"Knock yourself out," he said, and kissed her good-night.

Alan went upstairs and Maddy turned off the lights and adjusted the blinds so she could peek out onto the street. Then she settled down with her e-reader. By eleven on a weekday, almost all of Icicle Falls was asleep; certainly all the visitors to Candy Cane Lane were long gone. The neighborhood light show was over and quiet reigned. She'd hear if any cars came cruising down the street, if any foot crunched on leftover snow. So far not a creature was stirring, not even a juvenile delinquent.

Maybe Alan was right. Whatever kids had vandalized their candy canes had moved on. But Santa help them if they returned because Maddy Donaldson was on the lookout, ever vigilant, her cell phone on the coffee table. No one would get by her. She was…

She was tired. It had been a long day. She peered out between the slats in the blinds. All was calm, all was dark. Yawn.

No, no. It was too early to go to sleep. She had to stay awake. Had to keep watch. Had to…

"Maddy."

"Wha?" Maddy opened her eyes to see a figure bending over her in the dark and let out a shriek.

"Babe, it's just me."

"Oh. Alan. I must have fallen asleep."

"Come on. Come to bed. I don't think you're going to catch any vandals at two in the morning."

By now it was freezing out. If their local criminals wanted to kick over candy canes, good luck to them. They'd be rewarded with frostbite. She took one last look outside. *Still all quiet on the candy-cane front.* Okay, she could leave her post on the sofa with a clear conscience. She followed her husband upstairs to bed. The mischief was a one-time thing, and there was no sense in losing beauty sleep over a one-time thing.

As she snuggled under the blankets, she wondered if she'd just experienced some Christmas version of Murphy's Law. Stay up waiting for vandals to show up and, of course, they won't. Or perhaps the vandals somehow knew that people would be watching for them from now on and decided not to risk another raid on the candy canes. In any case, it looked like the problem was past and Candy Cane Lane was safe.

With a smile on her lips, she shut her eyes and drifted off to sleep.

She dreamed that her mother-in-law had arrived early for the holidays. This was her reward for trying to watch over the neighborhood? *Sheesh. Thanks a lot, Santa.*

---

Chapter Eight

*Time spent baking cookies together is always time
well spent.*
— Muriel Sterling, *Making the Holidays Bright:
How to Have a Perfect Christmas*

Tuesday was Ivy's day off and it had started well enough.
She made pancakes shaped like Christmas trees and they
were a big hit with her daughter. Robbie didn't care what
shape his pancakes came in. He simply liked them, and
enjoyed making a mess eating them.

Once he was scrubbed down, his sister kept him entertained with his favorite toys while Ivy loaded the
breakfast dishes in the dishwasher and washed the skil-
let. Then she bundled up the kids and took them outside
so they could enjoy the newest couple of inches of snow
that had fallen during the night. She took pictures of the
snowman they made to post on Facebook later. Ah, yes,
creating happy family memories, just like Muriel Sterling had said to do. When the season was over, they'd
have a million of them to replace last year's memories
of Mommy yelling at Daddy. Muriel Sterling herself
couldn't design a more idyllic December day.

Once back inside the house Ivy discovered that the

washing machine was stuck between its rinse and spin cycles. Well, there was a fun little day-off adventure. She called Arvid's Appliances and got Arvid himself.

"You're in luck," he told Ivy.

"Oh, good," she breathed.

"We can get someone out there first thing tomorrow."

"Tomorrow? But my clothes are sitting in the washer today. What am I supposed to do?"

"Well, here's what you do. Get a big plastic tub and put all the wet clothes in it. Then take 'em to the kitchen and wring 'em all out over the kitchen sink. Then put 'em in the dryer."

"Thanks. That was really helpful." Just what she wanted to do with two kids underfoot.

"And don't you worry. We'll get it fixed for you."

"Tomorrow."

"Yep."

"Arvid. You're a pal," Ivy said, and hung up. She'd planned to flop on the couch while the kids took their afternoon naps and watch a couple of episodes of *House Hunters International* she'd recorded earlier. Now she'd be dealing with a tub of wet laundry instead.

Rob could probably fix it, whispered a little voice at the back of her mind.

Yeah, well, Rob doesn't live here anymore, she told it. She'd rather sprain her fingers wringing out clothes and pay one of Arvid's appliance elves a king's ransom than call her ex. Unless it had to do with the kids, she didn't need him, didn't want to need him ever again. For anything.

She fed the kids lunch and then put them down for their naps. She'd barely shut the door on Robbie before she heard the thump that signaled he was out of his crib, his newest escape accomplishment. Well, let him goof around in there. There was nothing that could hurt him. Falling asleep on the floor might convince him to think twice before he tried another great escape.

After struggling with their waterlogged clothes, she was ready to fall asleep on the floor herself. Instead, she fell asleep on the couch, halfway through looking at houses in Nuremberg. Just before she drifted off she'd seen shots of the town's Christmas market, one of the oldest in Germany. Christmas Haus imported a lot of ornaments from Germany. What fun it would be to go over there and check out all the beautiful ornaments firsthand, maybe take one of those river cruises and visit the markets in Rothenburg and Bamberg and Cologne, as well. How nice it would be to have a life.

You have a life, she told herself. And it was a darned good one, even without Rob.

She woke up two hours later to see that the light was fading outside her living room window. Her daughter was calling, "Mommy, can we get up now?" and her son was not happy with his escape-proof doorknob cover and was shrieking at the top of his lungs. So much for dreams of Christmas markets. Back to the real world.

She turned Hannah loose, then rescued Robbie from his prison and changed his diaper. "Now," she said, "guess what we're going to do."

"Eat marshmallows!" Hannah cried, jumping up and down.

"Lows!" Robbie mimicked, also jumping.

"No, but we are going to do something fun. We're going to make Christmas cookies."

"Cookies! Cookies!" Hannah chanted.

"Ookies!" Robbie joined in.

"Let's fix you two a snack, then Mommy will get everything ready for baking. Okay?" She should've done that before she sat down. Oh, well. Being organized was overrated.

She went to the cupboard and the cupboard was bare, at least of one of the key cookie ingredients. Where the heck was the sugar? She could've sworn she had sugar. She'd made sure to get the rose water for the frosting, but without sugar there'd be no cookies to frost. Darn it all. This meant a trip to the store. Unless she could borrow a cup from a neighbor.

Hmm. Maddy would still be at work. Mrs. Walters was off visiting her sister. There was no sign of her new neighbor. Even if there was, Ivy would rather have her acrylic nails pulled off than go sugar begging at Tilda's place. *Oh, just suck it up and go to the store.*

"Okay, guys, let's get our coats on. We're going to the store to get what we need for making cookies." Or maybe they'd just buy the darned things.

No, no, no. That was no way to make happy family memories.

So, once more, she bundled up the kids and out they went to the grocery store. Safeway was ready for the holidays, with cute plates and mugs for sale, Christmas cards, wreaths and an entire aisle dedicated to Christmas candy. All the checkers wore Santa hats and Christmas music was playing over the speakers.

"Can we get a candy cane?" Hannah asked.

"We're going to have Christmas cookies in a little bit. Remember?"

"I want a candy cane," Hannah whined.

"If I get you a candy cane, we can't make cookies," Ivy said, and that was the end of the candy cane requests.

They were almost at the baking aisle when she saw him, just off work and heading their way with a shopping basket. Why was Rob off work already? And why did he have to be here?

Hannah had spotted him, too, and took off at a run, crying, "Daddy!"

Not wanting to be left behind, Robbie was now trying to climb out of his seat in the shopping cart and follow suit. "Dada!"

"Oh, no, you don't," Ivy told him, putting his leg back where it belonged. This, of course, produced a howl that had everyone in the store staring. "We're going to go see Daddy right now," she said to her frustrated son. *And won't that be fun?*

Hannah ran to her father, arms outstretched. He scooped her up and she hugged his neck. "Daddy!"

Boy, Ivy never got that kind of reception when she picked up the kids at her parents' house. Was it just her or was it sick and wrong that the defector got such love and adoration?

Be a grown-up, she lectured herself. Still, it was hard putting a polite smile on her face. Rob had walked away and was living free as a wild turkey, whooping it up with other women, while she was stuck with the daily grind of the kids and the house and work and…making Christmas perfect. Just as well they were nowhere near the produce section. She might've been tempted to hurl another grapefruit at him. Maybe she could accidentally ram him in the shins with her cart. That pleasant thought put a real smile on her face as she wheeled up to him.

He sidestepped the cart, put Hannah down and picked Robbie up all in one smooth move. "Hey, there," he said to Ivy.

"Hi," she said stiffly.

"We're gonna make cookies," Hannah told him.

"That sounds like fun," he said, smiling at her. Then he looked at Ivy with a disgustingly wistful expression. "I always loved your sugar cookies."

Not *her*, her sugar cookies. "Okay, guys, we need to get our sugar. Tell Daddy goodbye."

"Can Daddy make cookies, too?" Hannah asked.

Yeah, at the North Pole. In nothing but his tighty-whities. "Daddy has things to do."

"Actually, I don't," said Rob.

Ivy gave him a look that threatened castration. "Yeah, you do."

He looked right back, half smiling. "No, I don't."

"I want Daddy to come home with us," Hannah insisted, wrapping her arms around her father's legs.

"Honey, Daddy lives somewhere else. Remember?" *Daddy has a new life and a new girlfriend.*

Hannah burst into tears. "I want Daddy."

Robbie, too, decided to cry.

Ivy felt like joining them. Yep, they were sure making holiday memories. "Honey, you just saw Daddy last weekend," she reminded her daughter.

"I want my daddy," Hannah wailed.

Half of Icicle Falls was in the store, and it felt as if everyone was watching this charming family vignette. "Explain to her," Ivy said to Rob the Rotten through gritted teeth.

He ruffled Hannah's hair. "Mommy said no."

"Oh, thanks. That helped," Ivy said as the crying got louder. Now she was Mean Mommy while Rob was… the biggest rat on the planet.

"Come on, Ivy, let me come over. What will it hurt?"

Her heart, that was what. But her children were both carrying on as if she'd just caused the end of the world, and she was trying to be a grown-up. She could handle this. "Fine." Not fine, really.

"Okay, kids," he said, lifting Robbie back into the shopping cart. "We'll go get what Mommy needs, then we'll pick up a frozen pizza."

"Pizza!" Hannah crowed.

Yeah, let's bribe the kids, Ivy thought bitterly. "I hope you're happy," she said to Rob as he accompanied them down the baking aisle.

"I am," he said. "This'll be fun."

"For you. You won't be the one stuck with the fallout when you leave."

"Then I'll stay."

The words made her heart twist painfully.

"I'll help you put them to bed and everyone will be happy."

"Until they wake up and find you gone. This is so typical of you, Rob. You never think about the fallout."

He bit his lip. "Sorry. You're right. I don't have to come over."

"Oh, that'll make the kids happy. You're committed now. You'd better see it through." Just like he should've seen their marriage through. He hadn't been able to handle that, but when it came to fun and games he was all over it.

To be fair, he'd always taken the kids when he was supposed to, and he would've taken them more often if she hadn't fought him on it. He was prompt with his child support, too. She supposed she should be thankful that he was no deadbeat dad.

Only a deadbeat husband.

They picked up the needed sugar and the pizza. Chicken Alfredo, Ivy insisted. The pepperoni and sausage kind would make Robbie sick. At the checkout Hannah hit Rob up for a candy cane.

"Sure," he said, plucking one from the display even as Ivy said, "Mommy told you no."

Rob hesitated, candy cane in hand. "Did you already ask Mommy?"

Hannah studied her pink snow boots. "I want a candy cane."

"We're going to have cookies. That'll be enough sugar. Unless you want to stick around and deal with these two on a sugar high," she said to Rob.

He put the candy cane back and Hannah pouted all the way to the car.

"No pouting, now. You're getting to bake cookies with Daddy," Ivy said to her, and that made Ivy want to pout, too. Here she'd planned this time with the kids, an opportunity to make a nice Christmas memory and now Rob had invaded her memory-making moment and was ruining it. Back at the house he put the pizza in the oven and entertained the kids while she prepared the cookie dough. It was almost like a normal family Christmas.

Except for her, the new normal was going to involve no kids on Christmas Day. She'd have them on Christmas Eve for the big family dinner at her parents' house and the Christmas Eve service and then, come Christmas Day, Rob would take them off and keep them clear through New Year's.

What was he going to do with them when he worked? she'd objected back when they were hammering things out with the lawyers. "That's what vacation time is for,

Ive," he'd responded. Yes, it would be vacation time with Daddy. What was Ivy going to do?

"Don't worry," Deirdre had said to her. "I'll keep you company Christmas Day. God knows I don't have anybody to spend the day with." Realizing how that sounded, she'd said, "We can watch Christmas movies and you can teach me to knit. Or we can go over and bug Mom and Dad."

Two losers, spending the day together. It was a poor substitute for being with her children. And that was another thing that wasn't fair. Rob was the one who'd indulged in a premature midlife crisis and left. Why did *he* get the kids on Christmas Day? Ivy watched him giving them piggyback rides around the living room and frowned. *Jingle Bells, that sure smells. Tie Rob to a sleigh. Drag him through the tree farm. Ha! Jingle all the way.*

Of course, there'd been a time when she'd loved watching him play with the kids. A time when she'd loved him, period. Now she loved to hate him.

Sometimes she loved to hate herself, too. Like Santa, she made a list of her wifely shortcomings, checking it twice. Gained an extra fifteen pounds after Robbie was born and only took off four. Asked Rob to do too much around the house (totally bogus, considering how much she did and how hard she worked, but irrational guilt kept that one on the list). Was cranky when she was tired. Wasn't always interested in sex because she was tired. Was tired too often.

Darn it all, she was done checking that list. She had done nothing—nothing!—that deserved having him walk out. He'd messed up their lives and now here he was, messing up her happy-memory making. Well, she wasn't going to let him.

She got out the cookie dough and the rolling pin and cookie cutters. "Okay, we're ready," she called.

That brought Hannah running to the kitchen, with Robbie in hot pursuit and Rob following at a more leisurely pace.

"I'm gonna make trees and stars. What are you gonna make, Daddy?" Hannah asked as Ivy put the child-size apron on her that she'd made earlier in the year. It was pink and decorated with teacups and teapots. Hannah loved wearing it when she was playing house or helping Ivy in the kitchen.

"I'm going to make Santas," Rob said.

"I like Santa," Hannah informed him.

"I know you do."

"Where's your apron, Daddy?" she asked.

"Daddy doesn't need one," Ivy answered for him. "Daddy never goes in the kitchen."

"He does now. I make a mean lasagna."

"Why is it mean?" Hannah asked, and he chuckled.

This would be so heartwarming if they were still together. Ivy would be recording it all on her phone.

But she could get a picture of Hannah in her apron. She picked up her phone. "Hey, sweetie. Let's get a picture of you all ready to make cookies."

"Come on, Daddy," Hannah said, reaching over and grabbing Rob by the sleeve.

Photo bombed by her ex, just what she'd wanted.

"Will you send that to me?" he asked.

"Yes," she said reluctantly. Then to Hannah, "Now, let's get one of you all by yourself like a big girl." Hannah beamed and Ivy snapped the pic. Yes, now *there* was a happy Christmas moment.

They set to work, rolling out dough and cutting out cookies, Robbie corralled in his high chair with toys, and laughing when Rob dotted his nose with flour. Rob kept Hannah amused with silly suggestions for what Santa might bring her. "Green eggs and ham? No? How about some chicken bunions? No? Hey, maybe Santa will bring you some elf earrings."

"Yes, I want elf earrings!" Hannah crowed. "Bring Mommy some, too."

"Do you think Mommy would like elf earrings for Christmas? What about some other kind of earrings?" Rob asked, looking over their daughter's head at Ivy.

"Maybe Santa will bring Mommy a new boyfriend for Christmas," Ivy said sweetly. "One who gets her diamond earrings."

Rob's smile fell away. "Did you meet someone at that wedding?"

Was he just a little jealous? Oh, how she'd love to serve him a holiday helping of what he'd given her, even if it was only a small one. "Maybe." And maybe that someone was gay, but Rob didn't need to know that.

"Mommy doesn't have a boyfriend, Daddy. She has you," Hannah said. "Are you gonna stay with us tonight?"

"No," Ivy said, and it came out sounding snippy. "You know Daddy has someplace else to stay."

Hannah's mouth turned down at the corners. "I want him to stay with us. Why can't you stay here with us, Daddy?"

Rob was still looking at Ivy as if she could, somehow, provide the perfect answer. She had all kinds of answers, none of them perfect. And she sure wasn't going to help Rob with this question. She cocked an eyebrow at him.

"Well, honey, sometimes mommies and daddies don't end up staying together."

Because the daddies are immature jerks suffering from Peter Pan syndrome.

"Why?"

"Yes, do tell her why," Ivy said, and turned to take cookies out of the oven.

He sighed. "Sometimes daddies are dumb."

Ivy paused in the middle of placing her cookies on the cooling rack. Well, here was a first.

"Daddy, are you dumb?" Hannah asked, incredulous.

"Afraid so. Hey, there's our first batch of cookies. Think Mommy will let us sample one?" And that was the end of that conversation.

But not the end of the thoughts it had triggered. Did Rob regret leaving? No, probably not, not when he was moving on with a new woman. But then why say something like that? Did he want to get back together? Would she take him back if he did?

When the mountains all fell in and Icicle Falls became a desert.

After an hour the baking was done. Robbie had crumbs all over himself and frosting on his face and in his hair, and Hannah was covered in almost as much frosting as the cookies were. Rob stayed and helped Ivy bathe them and put them to bed. Watching him kneel by Hannah's bed, listening as she said her prayers, tugged at Ivy's heart and that made her want to whack him with her rolling pin. "God bless Mommy and Daddy and Opa and Oma and Aunt Deirdre and Grandma and Grandpa B. and Robbie and Gizmo and the elves and Santa and

Missy and Lala and Carlos, even though he called me a baby. And please let Daddy come home to stay. Amen."

"Amen," said Rob.

Ivy kept quiet.

He followed her downstairs and into the kitchen, where she got busy stacking mixing bowls in the sink. He began rinsing them and loading them in the dishwasher.

"You don't have to help with this," she said.

"I helped make the mess. I should help clean it up."

She sighed, thinking about the big mess he'd made of their family.

"Ive, did you meet someone at the wedding?"

"Is that any of your business?"

"No, it's not." He leaned on the counter and studied her as she wiped down the table.

She could feel her cheeks heating up. "Why are you asking?"

"No reason," he said, and went back to loading dishes. Then, "I broke up with Melody."

Ivy stopped her scrubbing, frozen in place. *Okay, so what?* She got busy again, pushing the sponge around the table hard enough to take off the finish. "When?"

"Thanksgiving weekend."

"Why, did you find out she can't make pumpkin pie?"

"I found out I made a mistake."

"Why are you telling me this?"

"I just thought you should know."

"I don't care one way or the other." *Liar, liar, Christmas stocking on fire.*

"Don't you? Not at all?"

"Why should I, Rob? You broke my heart."

He dropped his gaze. "I wish I hadn't. I just…"

"Oh, let's not go over that again," she said irritably.

"Sometimes I wonder..."

She stopped her scrubbing and frowned at him. "What?"

"Never mind."

"No, what were you going to say?"

"Okay, sometimes I wonder what I was thinking when I left."

"We know what you were thinking. You told me what you were thinking."

"I was thinking stupid, okay?" They stood there for a moment, having their own silent night.

Then she broke the silence. "I'd take you back if..."

He looked at her hopefully. "Yeah?"

"If I was brain-dead. But since I'm not, that isn't happening, so I hope you weren't counting on some miraculous Christmas reconciliation." She'd landed a nice blow to his pride, and she watched in satisfaction as the muscle in his jaw twitched while he fought off disappointment and humiliation.

"I don't blame you," he said. "I don't deserve another chance."

"You're right, you don't. You hurt me, Rob. You violated a sacred trust."

"I know. But I thought maybe, for the kids' sake..."

"Don't you dare bring the kids into this," she snarled. "Were you thinking of the kids when you walked out?"

"No," he said miserably. "I was only thinking of myself. I admit that. It was the stupidest thing I've ever done."

"And you're just now realizing this? Funny how that coincides with dumping the hot girlfriend."

"I broke up with her because I realized it was all wrong!"

Like what he'd done to her. "Well, too late. Too, too late. And speaking of late, isn't it time you went home?"

"Yeah, I guess it is," he said, his voice filled with anger. As if he had any right to be angry!

"Good." She returned to viciously scrubbing the table.

She kept scrubbing until the front door shut. Then she sat down at the table and cried. Oh, yeah, she'd sure made memories tonight.

Chapter Nine

It's especially important at this time of year to reach out to those in need of love.
—Muriel Sterling, *Making the Holidays Bright: How to Have a Perfect Christmas*

On Wednesday Tilda stopped at the hardware store on her way home from work to pick up some candy canes for her front walk. Somewhere between the candy canes and the checkout she caught a bad case of keeping up with the Joneses. (Or, in her case, the Donaldsons, the Welkys, the Gordons, Ivy Bohn and even Mrs. Walters. Not to mention all the other neighbors who were putting her to shame.)

Lights. She needed lights. She couldn't not have lights. Sitting in darkness amid all those happy, sparkly houses made her place resemble a haunted house. She liked the white icicle ones. Those would look good strung along her roofline. Hopefully the gutters wouldn't come crashing down once she'd strung them. Did you string lights on gutters? Nah. Under them? She had no idea. Well, she'd figure it out.

And hey, look at this—an animated T. rex wearing a Santa hat and holding a gold box wrapped with red ribbon. It was so tacky. And so funny. And no one on the street had a T. rex. Santas, crèches, reindeer, trains and angels, but no Christmas dinosaurs. This guy was one of a kind, the only one in the store and he was already marked down twenty percent.

"Nobody wants you, huh?" she said, picking him up. "Well, you can come home with me." He beat a blow-up Santa all to heck. Okay, icicles, candy canes and Mr. T. That should do it. Although she should put some colored lights around the windows or on the bushes.

Wait a minute. What was she thinking? Did she really want to be an Ivy Bohn or Maddy Donaldson? But there was probably no chance of that, considering what she'd just picked up for her yard. She decided to stop with what she had. "Buying candy canes?" the store owner greeted her. "You must be our new neighbor."

"I am," Tilda said. "And you must be..."

"Alan Donaldson. I think you've met my wife."

Oh, yes, the Queen of Christmas. "I have," Tilda said. "Thanks for the wine."

"The least we could do, since you're buying candy canes from us," he joked. "And boy, we've had a run on them today."

She'd noticed. There hadn't been many left. Woe to anyone else in Icicle Falls who wanted to decorate with giant candies.

"One of our local construction guys was in here buying up a bunch." Alan's expression was slightly puzzled. "I thought he lived in an apartment."

Construction guy? Nah, couldn't be. What would he want with candy canes?

"Anyway, looks like we'll have to try and order some more."

"I would imagine everyone's gotten their decorations by now," Tilda said. Except her, the newcomer.

"Pretty much. But it's always good to have extras on hand, in case some get broken."

"Or vandalized?"

He nodded. "That, too. I suspect that was a one-time deal, but you never know."

"You're probably right. We don't have a lot of vandalism this time of year. Too cold."

He smiled at that. "Almost too cold to be putting up outdoor decorations. I hope you'll have some help."

"I can handle it," she said.

"I'm sure you can," he agreed, and finished ringing her up.

Yikes. That much for a bunch of electricity-sucking... stuff? Oh, well, 'twas the season. She took out her credit card and swiped it through the gotcha machine. Okay, now she was committed. Or should be committed.

As she approached her driveway, she saw a familiar truck parked at the curb and her headlights shone on... whoa, what was this? The frozen ground along her front walk had been pickaxed to death and lighted candy canes had been planted, a dozen altogether, the same number as she'd just purchased. A ladder leaned against her house and on that ladder stood a man in jeans and a parka, hanging colored lights. Devon Black.

With a scowl she pulled into the driveway and got out, marching over to where Mr. Fix-It was hard at work. "What do you think you're doing?"

He smiled down at her. "Merry Christmas to you, too."

"You're trespassing."

"No, I'm surprising you."

"Well, it's not a good surprise." She pointed at her Jeep. "I just spent a small fortune on stuff for my house."

He went back to desecrating her roofline with multi-colored bulbs. "You can always return it."

"I don't want to return it. I don't want friggin' colored lights. I want icicles and that's what I bought."

He shrugged and started taking down the colored bulbs. "Okay, fine. We'll put up icicles."

"There's no *we* here," she informed him.

He stared down at her, his easy smile missing. "No. There's only a you, and not a very nice version if you wanna know the truth," he said, unhooking some more lights.

"I have no nice version," she snapped. Hmm. Did she really mean that? "Damn it all, Black, I don't need people coming around and hanging my lights for me. I can do it myself. I'm a big girl."

The smile was back. "In all the right places."

She pointed a finger at him. "Watch it."

"Come on, Tilda, lighten up and let somebody do something nice for you."

"I would if he didn't have ulterior motives."

"All men have ulterior motives. Look, if you want icicles, I'll put up your icicles."

Actually, the colored lights did look pretty. "Never mind," she said. "You've already started with those. You might as well finish."

He shook his head and went back to hanging lights. "Thanks for the appreciation. And don't say you didn't want the candy canes. You can't live here and not put 'em somewhere. Anyway, breaking up that ground was a son of a bitch. Did *you* want to do that?"

No, but she didn't want to be in Devon Black's debt, either. "I'm not helpless, you know."

He frowned at her. "What is it with you? Most women would be happy to have somebody lend a hand."

"I'm not most women."

"You got that right. Most women have a heart."

"Hey, I've got a heart."

"Where, buried under the house?"

"Oh, ha, ha," she said grumpily. "Just remember that no one asked you to come here and hang colored lights all over my place."

"Yeah, 'cause God forbid you'd ever ask anybody for anything. What's it like to be perfect?"

It took a lot to rattle Tilda and she could always give as good as she got, but there was something about Devon Black that made her want to stamp her feet. She resisted the temptation and marched over to the car, pulling out her candy canes. Then she dumped them in the back of Devon's truck. He could return them and get a refund. She'd pay him for the colored lights, and then they'd be even.

"What are you doing now?" he called from the ladder.

"I'm giving you the candy canes I just bought."

"So that's why you're mad."

Dumb as a box of toadstools. "No, that's not why. Anyway, you can return mine and get your money back. I'll pay you for the lights you're putting up."

"Fine," he said irritably, "if it'll make you feel better."

"It will," she said, and took out Mr. T.

"I didn't know you had a twin," Mr. Helpful said from his ladder top.

"He was looking for a Neanderthal and heard you were over here," she retorted.

Setting up her Christmas dino took exactly five minutes. After that there was nothing left to do but stand out in the cold and watch Devon freezing his hindquarters off or go inside and stay warm while he was freezing his hindquarters off.

Okay, there was one more option. She could play nice. She went into the house and dug out her box of packaged cocoa from the kitchen cupboard, then heated the water in the electric teapot her mom had given her. In a minute she had hot cocoa. There. She could be gracious.

She went outside to deliver it and found him coming down the ladder. In silence. He folded it up. In silence. And took it to the truck. In silence.

"Okay," she called after him. "I'm a bitch. So sue me."

"I might," he called back, not turning to look at her.

"But first have some cocoa."

That did get him to turn his head.

She held up the cup. "Peace offering."

He walked back to her, although he was careful not to smile. "You know, you and T. rex have a lot in common."

She handed over the mug. "I know. We're both cute."

"That wasn't what I was thinking."

So she'd almost taken his head off. He'd had it coming. Still… "It was kind of you to hang my lights."

"And put in your candy canes," he reminded her.

"Them, too. Although I could have done it myself."

"You don't need a man for anything, do you?"

"I never said that."

He grunted and took a sip of cocoa. "Where's the marshmallows?"

"I don't have any. Don't get picky."

He did smile at that. "Let me take a guess here—you don't do stuff in the kitchen."

"I can do stuff in the kitchen."

"Yeah? What?"

"I can make chocolate chip cookies." Her one claim to fame.

His smile grew. "Prove it."

"I'm out of chocolate chips."

"I'll go buy some."

"Drink your cocoa and go home."

"I knew you were lying."

"I am not. I can make cookies."

He handed her the cocoa. "I'll be back."

"Oh, come on. Just because you strung up some lights."

"And busted my back getting those candy canes in the ground," he added, walking to his truck.

"This is not the beginning of a beautiful friendship!"

He acknowledged her warning with a wave, then climbed in his truck and varoomed off down the street. He was probably going to speed.

With a frown she went back inside the house. Darn it all. She'd wanted to get her lights up, relax and play some video games, eat some canned chili and her leftovers from the Safeway deli. Now, instead, she had uninvited company coming and she was going to have to bake cookies.

Might be kind of fun, came the traitorous thought, obviously planted in her brain by her neglected hormones.

Oh, no, it wouldn't. Well, okay, maybe it would, but she didn't want to have fun with Devon Black. She didn't want to do anything with Devon Black. He was cocky and irresponsible and not at all what she was looking for. When he came back she'd tell him as much. Meanwhile, though, she'd get out of her lady-cop clothes.

And when she did, lo and behold, there was the black thong and matching lacy black bra, reminding her that she was a woman and she wanted a man in her life.

Not him!

She pulled on jeans and a black T-shirt. All right. Nothing in that outfit to say Welcome Back.

It'd been a long day, though, and she needed to freshen up. She spritzed on some perfume so she'd feel better about herself, not because she wanted to impress someone. Then she brushed her teeth. And put some gel in her hair, spiking it a little. It had nothing to do with Devon Black, though. No. This was all just a matter of self-esteem.

She went to the kitchen and took stock of what was in the fridge. He probably hadn't eaten yet. It would be rude to eat in front of him, so what could she make? There wasn't much to choose from, just the usual pickles, mustard and mayo, half a bag of salad mix, that chicken breast from the deli and some milk. And beer. Couldn't forget that. Well, okay, she had some cheddar and some butter. And bread. She could manage grilled cheese sandwiches.

Fast and easy. She'd stuff one down him, throw a beer at him, make half a dozen cookies and then send him on his way.

She had the bread out and the cheese sliced when he returned. Yep, he'd sped.

"You were speeding."

"I was not," he insisted, walking through the door. He was carrying a large grocery bag. "Got some beer," he said, and sauntered out to the kitchen.

Even though she'd intended to offer him one, she bristled at the fact that he'd assumed this was going to be some kind of party. "I hope you're not planning on staying all night," she said. "I've got things to do." She hoped he wouldn't ask her what.

"I just saved you a good hour. You've got that much time, right?"

She leaned against the kitchen counter and frowned at him. "Why do you keep thinking I want to hang out with you?"

"Why'd you put on perfume?"

Now her cheeks were sizzling. She turned her back on him and got busy laying cheese slices on Oatnut bread. "I always put on perfume when I get home."

"Liar." He moved to stand behind her, close enough to make the sizzle spread farther down. Way farther down. "Are you cooking for me? That's so cute."

"No, I'm not cooking for you. I'm cooking for me. You just happen to be here and I don't want to be rude."

"There's a first."

She ignored him, pulling out a frying pan and setting it on the stove burner.

"Kind of a small burner for that pan, isn't it?" he asked.

"It's the only one that works."

"Ah."

She turned the burner on and slapped some butter in the pan.

"You should butter the bread and then put it in the pan."

She frowned at him. "You want to do this?"

He held up a hand. "No, no. You're proving you can cook. I don't wanna mess with that."

He'd rather mess with her head. She turned up the heat and added the sandwiches.

"Did I ever tell you I'm a good cook?" he asked.

"Did I ever ask?"

He didn't reply to that. "Yep, I had this girlfriend," he went on, "who had a cooking show on one of the local channels when I was living down in sunny California. She was ten years older. She's the one who taught me."

"All part of your misspent youth?"

He was quiet for a moment. "A lot of it was misspent. A lot of things didn't go according to plan."

"Like what?" she asked, lifting the sandwich with a spatula to see if the bread was browned.

"Like a pro-ball career."

She flipped the sandwich. "Sucks to be you."

He grunted. "It did actually. One minute I thought I was on my way to the majors and the next I was on my way to the hospital."

That made her turn around. "Seriously?"

"Baseball is something I'm always serious about."

"What happened?"

"What didn't? First my shoulder benched me, then I trashed my knee and that was the end."

Way to go, Tilda. "I'm sorry. I had no idea."

He shrugged. "Shit happens. And hey, I've made my share of shit since then. I know that."

"But now you're a new man?"

"I'm workin' on it."

This she highly doubted. Devon Black would always be a rebel, a bad boy.

"Your sandwiches are burning."

She swore and pulled the pan off the burner.

"Yeah, you sure can cook," he teased.

"I like my grilled cheese sandwiches well done," she said as she slid them onto plates. She took a bite of hers. "Mmm."

He laughed. "You really are a liar."

"Shut up and eat your gourmet sandwich." She pulled a beer out of the fridge. "Here. I'm only giving you one. Make it last."

"I'm good at making things last," he said with a devilish grin.

She returned to the kitchen table and plunked down on a chair. "There are lots of women in Icicle Falls. Why do you keep bugging me?"

He joined her. "Bugging you—is that what I'm doing?" He took a bite of his sandwich and regarded her.

"Yeah. You've been trying to flirt with me ever since you came to town. You got some kind of fantasy about doing it with a cop?"

He took a swig of beer. "Nope. Only about doing it with you. What can I say? I like you. I know it's sick, but there you have it."

"I'm not your type."

"You don't know what my type is."

"Oh, yeah, I do. Someone like that cute little blonde I saw you hitting on in Safeway last week." They'd been checking out the oranges and each other.

"Pfft, I was just being friendly."

"Yeah, I've watched you being friendly."

"You were watching, huh?"

She rolled her eyes.

"I didn't even ask for her phone number."

"I guess you'll have to hope she runs out of oranges."

"Funny. I like a woman with a smart mouth."

"Well, I don't like a man with a smart mouth."

"Lying again."

She shook her head. "You are so not my type."

"Okay, what is your type? Oh, wait, let me guess,

someone who walks around wearing a gun and who'll use handcuffs on you."

"Cute," she said, and left the table. "I'm making cookies now, and after you've had your cookies and milk, you're going home."

"Okay, Mom," he said, and took another swig of beer. "I'd offer my help but you're such a whiz in the kitchen I know you don't need any."

"I don't." She set the oven to three hundred and fifty, then got busy melting butter.

"So, getting back to your type of man," he prompted.

Tilda measured brown sugar into a bowl. "Someone who's got some muscle."

"Check," Devon said, and raised the bottle to his mouth. "What else?"

This conversation was getting a little uncomfortable. She downed some beer, too. "Someone who's a responsible adult." She turned and pointed her mixing spoon at him. "And don't say 'Check.'"

"I've got a steady job and I pay my bills. And my speeding tickets. I do my own laundry and my own cooking and I clean my own place. I'd say that all counts as responsible."

"Okay, fine. Let's say you're responsible." She added granulated sugar and her melted butter to the bowl.

"Good idea. Let's say that. What else?"

She shrugged. What she'd wanted was someone fit, with a six-pack, but also someone kindhearted, someone who did something noble for a living, like fight crime. Or fires. *Uh-uh*, she told herself and put her straying thoughts under house arrest.

"Come on, spill," he said.

She mixed in the other ingredients. "We're ready for the chocolate chips."

That brought him over to the counter. He watched as she stirred them in, then dredged out a finger full of dough and stuck it in his mouth. "Not bad."

"They don't have my secret ingredient in them yet," she said.

"Yeah? What's that?"

"Nuts."

"That's original."

"I'm out of nuts."

"We'll have to make do," he said, and snitched some more dough.

She whacked his hand with the spoon. "Stop that. There won't be any left." It suddenly dawned on her that they were getting way too chummy here. How had that happened? Okay, she needed to get these cookies done and get him gone. What kind of cologne was he wearing?

Never mind that! She started dropping dough onto the cookie sheet in fast motion.

"So, back to your perfect man," he said as she slid the cookies into the oven.

Her cell phone rang. Saved by the bell. "Hey, Jamal," she answered.

"You busy?" Jamal asked.

"Busy? Nah."

"Yeah, you are," Devon told her. "You're baking cookies."

"I just picked up a pizza at Italian Alps. Wanna play some Call of Duty?"

"Sure. Come on over."

"Who's Jamal?" Devon demanded.

Tilda frowned at him. "Is that your business?"

"Who are you talking to?" Jamal asked.

"Just someone who's leaving soon."

"It's gotta be a cop," Devon deduced.

"Okay, then," Jamal said. "I'll pick up some beer."

"I've got beer."

Devon frowned. "Not mine you don't."

Tilda ignored him. "See ya soon."

"You and this cop seeing each other?" he asked as she ended the call.

Partners were off-limits and Jamal was too much like a brother, anyway, but she wouldn't mind a Jamal clone. Sadly, the other guys at the station were either married or had girlfriends. There wasn't much left to choose from at the fire department, either, especially now that Garrett Armstrong was taken. *Forget it*, she told herself. *You'll just feel…* She didn't even want to think about how it would make her feel remembering that she'd lost out on Garrett. "Hello, there. You having an out-of-body experience?" Devon's question yanked her back to the moment at hand.

"Yeah, and I thought maybe you'd be gone by the time I came back." Just her luck that the only guys who appreciated her were ones who were completely wrong for her.

"So what are you and Robocop gonna do?"

"Like I said before, none of your business."

Devon's easy smile was now long gone. "Is he your type?"

"Maybe."

He studied her, then gave a knowing nod. "I see how it is. You're into superheroes. Anyone else won't make the team."

"What?"

"You're looking for a cross between Rambo and Batman. If I ran into burning buildings or beat up crooks for a living, you'd be all over me."

"We don't beat up crooks."

Devon shook his head. "Jeez, Tilda. I knew you were a hard-ass, but I was okay with that. You weren't like the airheads I used to date who just wanted to spend my money and have a good time. You were interesting, different. And yeah, out of reach. But I kept thinking, *What the heck, give it a try.* Now I'm beginning to wonder if you're worth the effort."

"Oh, thanks a lot. Way to impress a girl."

"Hey, I'm done trying to impress you. I'm gonna find someone who's not stuck-up."

"I'm not stuck-up!" she protested.

"Oh, yeah, you are. You think you're better than everyone else because of what you do for a living. Building houses doesn't count for squat. You're prejudiced against plain, old, normal people. I was half kidding when I said it the other day, but I was right, wasn't I?"

"That's ridiculous!"

"Yeah, it is." He marched for the door. "Have fun with your superhero."

"Hey, I never asked you to chase after me!"

"Don't worry. I'm done with that." He yanked open the door just as the doorbell rang and there stood Jamal, all six feet four inches of him, looking like an escaped Seahawks fullback. Devon wasn't a small man, but Jamal dwarfed him. Jamal the superhero. "Have fun," Devon snapped at him and left.

Jamal strolled into the living room wearing a puzzled frown. "What was that loser doing here?"

Even though she had the same attitude—okay, so *was*

she stuck-up?—Tilda found herself jumping to Devon's defense. "He's not a loser. He's got a job."

"A flunky at a construction company? Tell me you're not interested in him, Til. You can do a hell of a lot better."

Yeah, that was why the men were lining up at her door. "He was here hanging Christmas lights."

"I coulda done that for you."

"I could have done it myself." Did everyone in Icicle Falls suddenly think she was helpless?

He sniffed. "Is something burning?"

"Crap! My cookies." She pulled on an oven mitt, opened the oven door and grabbed the cookie sheet. The cookies were definitely well done—just like the grilled cheese. "It's this oven," she said, looking for a scapegoat.

"Good thing I brought pizza." Jamal set the box on the kitchen counter. "By the way, I like your T. rex. Might have to get one of those to put up outside my place."

"Too late. I bought the last one."

"Figures." He opened the box and took a slice for himself. "If you have any more stuff to put up, let me know. I'll come over and help."

"Stop already. I don't need any help. Anyway, I'm not putting up any more. This is enough."

"Yeah, I bet that's what everyone said when they first moved here." He tried a couple of cupboards, looking for dishes.

"Plates are in the one to the right of the sink," she said.

He got one out and dropped his pizza on it, then got one for her, too. "Come on, eat your pizza and let's play."

So that was the end of the conversation about Devon Black. But he didn't leave. He stayed at the back of Tilda's mind, constantly poking at her with a guilt stick.

So what if she preferred men who had noble occupations? So what, so what, so what? There was nothing wrong with that, and it didn't make her prejudiced. It wasn't her fault that Devon Black wasn't her kind of man.

The whole baseball thing, though—she hadn't known about that. It must've been hard to lose such a big dream. Still, it was no excuse for barroom brawls and speeding and walking around like you were God's gift to women. And the only reason he wanted her was because she didn't want him.

No, she didn't. No, sirree. She could do better than Devon Black.

She said as much to him when he showed up in her dreams later that night. There she was, a member of the Seattle Mariners, the only woman on the team. (Very impressive, but then she always was in her dreams.) She was playing second base and here came Devon Black, playing for the other team. (Who in the American League wore pink uniforms?) He slid into the base, knocking her off balance and making her fall on top of him. He grinned up at her and, lo and behold, he had little red devil horns poking up through his batting helmet.

"You're a loser," she informed him.

"Yeah? Well, then, how come I already got to second base?" he murmured, slipping a hand under her baseball jersey. Before she could say anything else, he kissed her.

Oh, man, it was a great kiss. Long and luxurious, and who cared about those horns? She kissed him right back, and there they lay, going at it until the umpire, who just happened to be Jamal Lincoln, showed up and said, "You're both benched. Get a room."

The next thing she knew, they had a room and she was standing in the middle of it, asking herself how she got

there. It was pink (ick!) and had a circular bed and mir-
rors on the ceiling. And in the middle of the bed stood
Devon Black, wearing a Halloween devil costume and
holding a baseball. He wound up and threw it at Tilda. It
caught fire and sailed directly at her. She wanted to duck,
but she couldn't. She just stood there, unable to move, as
the flaming baseball rocketed toward her head. *Eeeeek!*

She woke up with a strangled screech and the strong
wish that Devon Black had never moved to Icicle Falls.
And right along with that was the niggling question—
did he kiss as well in real life as he did in her dream?

Chapter Ten

The holidays have a way of bringing out the best in people.
— Muriel Sterling, *Making the Holidays Bright: How to Have a Perfect Christmas*

Ivy had been on her feet and going nonstop since nine that morning. Now it was six-thirty and she was just getting home. Thank God Mutti had fed the kids, but nobody had fed Ivy since Pete fetched lattes from Bavarian Brews at ten. She was hungry and tired and cranky, and the kids were bouncing around the house like twin Slinkies on speed, Gizmo chasing them and barking at the top of his little doggy lungs.

I'm dreaming of a calm Christmas. And that would happen only in her dreams. Older women like Muriel Sterling and Janice Lind loved to remind her how fast children grew up, and they cautioned her to enjoy these precious moments while she had them. Either she was the most ungrateful mother in all of Washington State or these women were forgetting that some moments weren't all that precious.

She captured Robbie and plunked him in the playpen (as if that was going to do any good), and put on a DVD of Christmas songs complete with cartoon characters so the kids could sing along while she put together a quick sandwich in the kitchen. She'd just spread tuna fish on some whole-wheat bread when the doorbell rang. Oh, good grief, now what?

"It's Mrs. Walters," Hannah yelled.

By this time of day, the temperature was dropping and the ground was getting slippery. Mrs. Walters should've been in her house rather than out risking a broken hip. She usually called if she needed anything, so the fact that she was at the door meant she was delivering something, probably candy for the kids. Mrs. Walters loved doling out sugar buzzes.

Ivy left the kitchen and started down the hall just in time to see Hannah opening the front door, Gizmo there beside her. "Hannah!"

"It's okay!" Hannah shouted back.

No, it was not okay. She didn't want Hannah in the habit of opening the door, partly for safety but also because of—oh, no, there he went! "Gizmo!"

Too late. Dog gone. He'd smelled freedom and bolted for it. Ivy raced down the hallway, hoping she could lure him back before he got too far away.

Mrs. Walters was holding two large, plastic candy canes filled with candy. "Oh, my, your little doggy just got out," she told Ivy.

What to do first? Scold Hannah, go looking for Gizmo or get Mrs. Walters in out of the cold. Mrs. Walters took top priority. "Come on in," Ivy said. Then, as the old lady tottered inside, Ivy turned to her daughter, "What has Mommy told you about opening the door?"

"But it was Mrs. Walters!"

And now, here was another escapee. "Uppy!" said Robbie, reaching his hands toward her.

Ivy picked him up and continued her lecture. "But what if it had been someone you didn't know?"

Her daughter refused to follow her logic. "I know Mrs. Walters."

"You also know you're not supposed to open the door. You leave that to Mommy. Now I'm going to have to go find Gizmo." Just what she wanted to do in the freezing cold, go out and search for her dog, the great escape artist. "Mrs. Walters, would you mind staying with the kids for a few minutes?"

"Not at all, dear," Mrs. Walters said.

So everyone paraded back into the living room and Ivy inserted Robbie into his playpen once more. Of course, he wasn't happy and sent up a howl. "You stay there," Ivy said firmly. "If you don't, Mommy's going to be very mad."

Robbie paid no attention. Instead, he continued to howl and put one foot up on the railing.

She put it back down. "No!"

"Waaaah!"

"Oh, don't cry, sweetie," cooed Mrs. Walters.

Robbie increased the volume level and Mrs. Walters turned down her hearing aid.

"I'll just be a few minutes," Ivy said, and hoped that was true. "If Robbie gets out of his playpen…" What then? She didn't want Mrs. Walters breaking her back trying to put him in again.

"Why don't you let him sit next to me on the couch," Mrs. Walters suggested. "We can read a nice story. Would you like that, Hannah?"

Hannah nodded eagerly.

"Well, then, you pick out a book and we'll read until Mommy gets back."

Ivy plucked Robbie out of his playpen and the howling magically stopped. Hannah had found her favorite *Little Bear* book and was already settling in next to Mrs. Walters. Ivy parked her son on the couch on the old woman's other side, and he promptly shut up and stuck his thumb in his mouth. Aah, blissful peace and quiet.

Too bad she couldn't stay inside and enjoy it. "I'll hurry," she promised.

"Take your time, dear. We'll be fine," Mrs. Walters said.

Until Robbie got tired of sitting still… Maybe they'd luck out and he'd fall asleep in the middle of the story. It was moving toward bedtime for him.

Ivy pulled her parka from the closet, stuffed her feet into boots and went out into the cold night. This was *not* what she wanted to be doing after a long day at the shop. Of course there was no sign of Gizmo. "Gizmo, here, boy!" She heard an answering bark from what sounded like a million miles away. And then another bark. Great. Which one was Gizmo? She couldn't tell. On she trudged.

Cars were cruising up and down the street, admiring her neighbors' light displays. *Oh, Gizmo, whatever yard you're marauding, stay there until I can find you.* She stopped and called him. No bark this time. Boy, this was it. He was never getting dog treats ever again. And this time she meant it.

Headlights shone from behind her, and she turned to see the now-familiar Jeep that belonged to her new neighbor. Tilda's window slid down and she called out, "Everything okay?"

Nothing was okay these days. "My dog got loose."

The Jeep pulled over to the curb and stopped. Super. She was going to get a lecture about the leash law and some sort of ticket. Could cops give you tickets when they were off duty?

Tilda got out. "I'll take the other side of the street."

What was this? Officer Meanie moonlighted as a good Samaritan? "You don't have to help me." That wasn't how their relationship, such as it was, worked.

"I know. What's his name again?"

"Gizmo."

Tilda nodded and moved off. And then there were two of them calling out Gizmo's name. It took fifteen more minutes before the runaway decided he'd had enough fun for the night. Tilda found him, and Ivy nearly burst into tears at the sight of her little dog happily riding along in the woman's arms. He saw Ivy and barked and wriggled to get down.

"Oh, no, you don't," Tilda said, and Gizmo whined. To Ivy she said, "I caught him peeing on the Donaldsons' candy canes."

"Oh, man, I'm glad Maddy didn't see him. She'd have strung him up by his tail."

"I figured as much," Tilda said. "How'd he get out this time?" Surprisingly, her tone wasn't judgmental.

"My daughter opened the door and let him out."

From the expression on Tilda's face, Ivy could tell that she'd changed her mind and put on her judge's robes. *Ivy Bohn, guilty of poor parenting.*

"She's not supposed to open the door," Ivy hurried to explain in case she got a lecture on child safety. "But she saw Mrs. Walters out the window and…" The sentence trailed off. Ivy had been on the verge of saying something about her daughter thinking it was okay to break the rules, but she could envision Tilda replying, "Like mother, like daughter." Okay, so she'd gotten stopped for speeding once in a while. So she'd slid through a stop sign or two. She wasn't a serious rule breaker. She was a responsible adult. Extraresponsible these days, since she was the only adult in the house.

"Who's with them now?"

"Mrs. Walters stayed to watch them."

"Uh, she can hardly walk."

Ivy realized she was gritting her teeth. "I left them on the couch with her reading them a story."

Tilda shrugged as if to say, "Not sure that would hold up in court."

What did she know about kids? Or single parenting?

Ivy reached over to take the dog and Tilda handed him to her. "It's colder than a penguin's butt out here. Come on. I'll give you a lift back."

It was only four blocks, but Tilda was right. It was freezing out and Ivy didn't want to walk around in the cold anymore. "Thanks," she said, both surprised and grateful, and followed her nemesis to the Jeep. It was a sporty thing, the kind of vehicle an adventurous woman would drive. Sometimes Ivy wished she owned a Jeep. But she wasn't all that adventurous. And she had kids. She had a minivan.

Once inside the Jeep, she found herself at a loss for conversation. Tilda wasn't helping. She sat there behind the wheel, exercising her right to remain silent. Finally Ivy asked, "So what would you have done if you were me?"

"Gotten an electric fence."

Of course. Solutions were easy when it wasn't your

life. Ivy decided to shut up. At least it was a short ride to her place.

Tilda stopped at the curb. Ivy thanked her and then—out of gratitude, perhaps, or temporary insanity?—said, "Listen, we've never had a chance to get to know each other. I'm about to put the kids to bed and make some hot buttered rum for me and Mrs. Walters. Why don't you join us?" *What are you thinking? You want to hang out with Tilda the Terror?*

Tilda hesitated. Of course she'd say no. She hated Ivy. Then she nodded. "Okay. Sure."

Ivy blinked in shock. "Really?"

Tilda nodded again, as if confirming to herself that yes, she'd just committed herself to something she didn't actually want to do. "Yeah. I don't have anything planned."

They had nothing in common. What a dumb idea. What Ivy had really wanted to do that evening was curl up in front of the TV and turn into a zombie. Instead, she was going to be stuck with Tilda, who was probably regretting her rash decision to accept Ivy's invitation.

Except Mrs. Walters would be there to act as a buffer. They'd all drink a hot buttered rum and then Tilda could give Mrs. Walters a police escort back to her house and they'd resume hostilities in the morning.

"Okay," Ivy said, trying to sound happy about the whole thing. "Come over in half an hour."

Tilda nodded, and Ivy and Gizmo got out of the Jeep.

"Look what you got us into," Ivy said to him as they went up the walk.

Gizmo whined and licked her face.

"It's a good thing you're so cute."

He barked to show his agreement.

Once inside the house the four-legged troublemaker trotted into the living room as if nothing had happened. "Gizmo!" Hannah cried, and jumped from the couch to hug him.

"I'm so happy you found him," Mrs. Walters said. Robbie was leaning against her, fast asleep.

"Thanks so much for staying with the kids." Everyone was still in one piece. CPS would not have to be called tonight.

"I was delighted to help," Mrs. Walters said. "It's a treat to spend time with little ones again."

A treat. Was that what you called it? "Okay," Ivy said to Hannah. "Go get your jammies on."

"I'm not sleepy," Hannah told her, and yawned.

"You will be when we get you tucked in. Say goodnight to Mrs. Walters."

Hannah said good-night, then started for the stairs, Gizmo trotting alongside, and Ivy picked up her sleeping son.

"Well, dear, I should get home," said Mrs. Walters.

"Stay a while," Ivy urged. "I'm going to make some hot buttered rum and I've invited our new neighbor to join us." *And I need you to be a buffer.*

"My, it's been years since I've had hot buttered rum."

"I made the mix myself."

"All right, thank you."

"Good," Ivy said, relieved. "I'll be back down in a few minutes."

By the time she had the kids in bed, the water heated for their drinks and cookies on a plate, Tilda was knocking at the door. She came bearing a bag of potato chips. "Thought we might want something to snack on." Then she entered the living room and saw the plate with the cookies Ivy had made with the kids. "I should've known you'd have that covered."

"Hey, I like potato chips."

"Me, too," Mrs. Walters said from her seat on the couch. "How are you, my dear?"

"Fine." Tilda smiled and sat next to her.

"I see that nice Devon Black got your lights up for you."

Tilda's cheeks suddenly looked a little on the pink side. What was going on there? "So you had help?" Ivy asked.

Tilda frowned. "Yeah, although I was going to do it myself."

Ivy shook her head. "I tried that. Fell off the ladder."

Both of Tilda's eyebrows went up.

"My ex came over and finished the job," Ivy said with a shrug. "He's still got his uses."

"Oh, men are very useful," Mrs. Walters said cheerfully.

"Mrs. Walters, you got a good one," Ivy told her.

"Most of them are good," Mrs. Walters insisted. "You just have to find the one who's right for you."

Tilda's eyes widened, as though Mrs. Walters had just told her she could easily fly to the moon. Ivy knew how she felt. She'd thought Rob was the right man for her and look how that turned out.

"I'll get our drinks," she said, and went into the kitchen, hoping that when she returned, Tilda would have escorted Mrs. Walters down a new conversational path.

Mrs. Walters must have refused to go because when Ivy came back with their drinks, she was still on the subject of men. "Of course, none of them are perfect."

Ivy frowned as she handed over a steaming mug. "You can say that again."

"But most of them try their best," Mrs. Walters continued, taking the mug.

"Mine didn't," Ivy said.

"It's a crapshoot," said Tilda. She tried her drink. "This is good."

"Yes, it is," agreed Mrs. Walters.

"Thanks," Ivy said.

"Where'd you buy it?" Tilda asked.

"I didn't buy it. I made it."

Tilda looked at her as if she'd confessed to inventing the formula for calorie-free cookies.

"It's not hard," Ivy said.

"If you're good at doing stuff in the kitchen."

"Even if you're not," Ivy assured her.

"Yeah?" Tilda sounded dubious.

"I used to love baking," Mrs. Walters said wistfully. "I don't do it anymore. I can't stand for long periods of time. Oh, to be young again," she concluded with a sigh.

"It's not all it's cracked up to be," Tilda said, and took another drink.

"Tilda, dear, you shouldn't talk like that. You have your whole life ahead of you. You'll find a nice man, fall in love."

"Get divorced," Ivy muttered. *Whoa, let's add some bitters to that hot buttered rum.* "Sorry, sometimes I have a very bad attitude."

"But you make good hot buttered rum," Tilda said, and downed the rest of hers.

"Want some more?"

"Yeah. Why not?"

"I'll have a little more, too, dear," said Mrs. Walters, holding out her empty mug. Wow, she'd polished that off fast.

Ivy freshened their drinks and Mrs. Walters waxed poetic on love and marriage, then apparently decided to pry. First she turned to Tilda. "Are you seeing that young man?"

"I'm not seeing anyone right now, Mrs. W.," Tilda replied.

"Oh, I thought you were when I saw him hanging your lights," Mrs. Walters said.

"I didn't ask him to come. He just showed up," Tilda said irritably.

"How sweet! He's obviously interested in you."

"Well, I'm not interested in him."

"Why on earth not? If I was younger…"

"Mrs. Walters, he's not my type," Tilda said.

"You young girls." Mrs. Walters shook her head. Now she turned her attention to Ivy. "I saw your husband over here the other day."

Mrs. Walters didn't miss a thing. "He's not my husband anymore," Ivy reminded her.

"You two are such a sweet couple."

Tilda shot Ivy a sympathetic look. Bonding over embarrassment. Who said she and Tilda didn't have anything in common?

"Some things weren't meant to be, Mrs. Walters," Ivy said.

"No, I suppose not. Still, it seems a shame." She glanced from Ivy to Tilda. "Two lovely young women all alone."

"It's getting late," Tilda said. "I should get going."

Ivy hadn't been excited about being left alone with Tilda, but now she wasn't feeling that enthusiastic about spending any more time with Mrs. Walters in her current matchmaking frame of mind. "Would you mind walking Mrs. Walters home?" she asked Tilda.

Tilda's expression said, "Thanks a lot," but she answered, "Not a problem. You ready to go, Mrs. W.?"

Mrs. Walters seemed surprised that the party was ending just when she had their party theme all picked out. "Oh? Yes, of course." She pushed off from the couch and, after a wobbly moment that had Ivy holding her breath and poised to catch her, managed to get to a standing position. "I sit too long and I stiffen up," she explained.

Ivy could practically hear Tilda thinking, *And this is who you left your kids with?* "Thanks for not giving me a ticket tonight," she said.

"Hey, I was off duty."

"Or a lecture."

As Mrs. Walters was fiddling with her coat, Tilda said in a low voice, "When I was around three, my mom and dad separated for a while. I remember my mom left me to go find our cat. She took a scarf and tied me to a front porch rail. I wouldn't want to be a single mom."

Maybe Tilda Morrison wasn't so bad, after all. "I'll give you that recipe for hot buttered rum if you want it."

"Yeah. Thanks. I might make some for Christmas presents."

"What a lovely idea," said Mrs. Walters, and hiccupped.

Ivy watched them go, Mrs. Walters weaving slightly, Tilda steadying her with a firm hand. Okay, Tilda Morrison definitely wasn't so bad.

It was three in the afternoon on Friday, and the Spice Rack was having a temporary lull. Maddy was taking advantage of it, filling glass jars with spices, when her daughter called.

"I got a B on my math test," Jordan announced.

This was definitely an improvement over the last test, which she'd barely passed. "Great job! I'm proud of you."

"So can we go shopping? Gilded Lily's is open till six tonight."

"Oh, honey, that wouldn't leave us much time. And I have to pick up some more candy canes to give out this weekend."

"You *promised*," Jordan reminded her.

"We'll go tomorrow. Gilded Lily's is open all day. I'll take a long lunch break and we can shop and get hamburgers at Herman's. How does that sound?"

"Okay," Jordan said reluctantly. "But for sure?"

"For sure."

"Can I spend the night at Afton's?"

"Why don't you see if Afton would like to come to our house instead?" Maddy suggested. "I'll pick up a pizza on my way home."

"I guess," Jordan said. Obviously a night at home couldn't measure up to an evening with Afton and Fab-o-Mom.

"I'll get makings for root beer floats, too," Maddy said.

"Okay." There wasn't much increase in enthusiasm. It was more a case of Jordan realizing this was the best deal she was going to get.

"I'll be home by six. Have her come over then."

Jordan gave her another resigned, "Okay," and ended the call.

All right, pizza and root beer floats. What else could she do to make her house the place to be? Maybe she'd rent the latest Pixar movie for the girls. Or get out a board game so they could all do something interactive.

WWAMD? What would Afton's mom do? Board game, of course. Fine, they'd play Clue.

She left the shop later than she'd intended. Hildy Johnson came in looking for lavender just as Maddy was ready to turn the sign on the door to Closed. "I'm going to make sachets for everyone for Christmas," she said, and then proceeded to go into great detail about what she was serving for dinner, who was coming, who couldn't and why. She continued talking long after the lavender buds had been measured out and payment made. And the wall clock kept ticking. Five minutes past closing time, ten minutes past closing time. Fifteen.

Finally Maddy started moving the conversation toward The End. "Hildy, it sounds like a lovely celebration…"

As if sensing a premature end, Hildy broke in. "Well, you know, last year was a disaster, because of that awful woman Kevin brought home. But they're not together anymore, thank God. This year is going to be perfect."

Was she reading Muriel's book, too? Maddy didn't dare ask. That would give Hildy even more to talk about.

"We're pulling out all the stops."

"I'd love to hear more, but I've really got to close. My daughter has a friend coming over tonight and I promised I'd bring home pizza."

"I hope you already called in your order. Otherwise, you're going to have quite the wait."

"Well, I'd hoped to beat the rush," Maddy said, and hurried to the back room to get her coat and purse. "I guess I'll have to call it in on my way."

"You'd better not let Dot's daughter catch you talking on your cell phone and driving," Hildy warned her. "That young woman is as tough as they come. She actually gave me a ticket the other day. No warning, no nothing. As if I haven't known her since she was in diapers."

Hildy continued talking even though Maddy was now out of range. Maddy could hear her droning on as she called Italian Alps and ordered a large pepperoni, Jordan and Alan's favorite. When she came out of the back room, Hildy was still talking. "But motherhood isn't easy, as I'm sure you're finding out."

How they'd gone from pizza and traffic tickets to motherhood, Maddy had no idea, but she nodded politely and started moving Hildy toward the door. Once outside she said, "It's been great catching up with you but I have to run. Good luck with your sachets."

"Oh, I know they'll be a hit," Hildy said confidently. "It's always nice to get something homemade."

"Yes, it is," Maddy said as she walked off. Hildy was still talking and she hated to be rude but she had candy canes and a pizza to pick up, and Afton would be arriving at the house any minute.

Safeway was packed as townspeople and tourists alike stocked up on eggnog, weekend snacks and dinner makings. Every checkout line stretched to the end of the world. At this rate she'd never get home.

She called Alan. "Can you close up early?"

"Babe, I've got some customers in here right now, so no, not really. What's wrong?"

"I'm stuck in line at the grocery store and I still have to pick up pizza for tonight. Jordan's friend Afton is coming over."

"Well, they'll be fine on their own for a few minutes," Alan said. "I'll be home a little after seven."

Yes, the girls would be fine. They didn't need her

there, hovering. Still, she called her daughter to let her know she was on her way.

"Have you got the pizza?"

"Not yet. I'm waiting to pay for the candy canes."

"Mom, we're hungry."

"I know. I'll be home soon."

"Right." Her daughter's voice was sullen.

"That's enough of that, young lady. You're not going to starve to death in the next half hour."

"You'll be longer than that. You still gotta drop off those stupid candy canes and you'll end up talking."

"No, I won't. Meanwhile, you girls go ahead and find something to snack on. But don't eat too much. You don't want to ruin your appetite."

"Okay."

"Bye. Love you," she added, but Jordan had already ended the call.

She finally got home to find the girls texting on their cell phones and giggling, having obviously survived pizza deprivation. Afton wasn't nearly as pretty as Jordan—she had a long nose and narrow eyes—but she was sweet and polite, a good friend and, hopefully, a good influence. Maybe she could influence Jordan to abandon her crush on the unsuitable Logan.

Or not. As it turned out, that was who both girls were texting with. Logan, it appeared, was spending the night with a friend only a couple of blocks away. "Can they come over?" Jordan asked.

The last thing Maddy wanted was little Mr. Unsuitable hanging around. "Let's keep it just girls tonight," she said lightly, which earned her a scowl from her daughter and a "Why?"

Because this boy sounds like a loser. "Another time,"

she said, not wanting to have this particular discussion in front of company.

Jordan's scowl worsened and Afton gave her a sympathetic look.

Maddy pretended not to notice. "So, who's ready for pizza and root beer floats?"

The pizza and root beer floats were a big hit. Playing a board game not so much. The girls vanished into Jordan's room, where they streamed a movie on her iPad and continued texting and giggling, leaving Maddy out of the equation.

"You've still got me," Alan said, giving her a hug once they'd settled in the family room.

Maddy shook her head. "I thought we could have some fun together."

"I think those days are gone, at least for a while. They don't want to hang out with grown-ups."

"They hang out with Afton's mom." Why was that? And what was Maddy doing wrong?

"Not as much as it sounds like, I'm betting."

"I don't know. She goes skating with them."

"Just because she's on the rink doesn't mean she's part of the tribe."

"She makes taffy with them."

"Probably supervises. Once it's made you can be sure they're up in Afton's room. Come on, you remember what it was like. You didn't want to hang out with your mom when you were that age."

"I guess you're right," she said.

"Forget about it. Let's watch a movie."

"Okay. But first, let me take some cookies up to them."

"What, they don't know where the kitchen is?" He shook his head. "Bribery never works."

"Sure, it does," she said with a grin.

She loaded a plate with some of the goodies she and Jordan had made earlier in the week and went upstairs. She knocked on her daughter's door, then opened it, poking her head inside.

Both girls gave a guilty start and Jordan's face turned as red as a Christmas stocking.

What had they been talking about? Her? If so, it hadn't been anything good.

"I thought you'd like some Christmas cookies," Maddy said, ignoring her daughter's guilty flush.

"Thanks, Mrs. Donaldson," said Afton, whose face was also a little red.

Maddy resisted the temptation to linger outside the door and eavesdrop. Ignorance wasn't bliss, but it beat overhearing whatever complaints were being shared inside the teen confessional.

She'd just come back into the family room when her cell phone rang. Alan groaned. "Don't answer it."

"It might be an emergency," she said, picking it up.

"What, someone's out of candy canes?"

"Very funny," she said, and answered.

It was Carla Welky, who was on candy-cane duty. "I think I just saw those kids."

Good. "Call the police."

"They're not doing anything. They're just cruising down the street with the music turned up."

"Well, get the license-plate number, anyway," Maddy said. She parted the drapes and peered out the window. She could see several cars, but not the black SUV she'd encountered the other night.

"Okay. Oh, wait. There they go. They're speeding!"

"Did you get the license-plate number?"

"No, just the *WA*."

That narrowed it down. "I'm gonna follow them," Maddy said decisively. "Come on, Alan, get your coat."

Alan looked at her as if she was nuts. "What?"

"Don't bother," Carla told her. "They already turned the corner. You'd never find them."

Maddy accepted defeat with a frown. "Call me if they come back."

"Will do."

"And who were we going to follow?" Alan asked as Maddy set down her phone and flopped on the couch.

"Those rotten kids were back."

"Did they wreck anything?"

"No," Maddy said irritably. "Not yet."

"Well, then, it wouldn't have accomplished anything to follow them," Alan said. "Anyway, you need to let the police handle it."

"They haven't been handling it, and those brats are back."

"They were probably just out joyriding."

"Or scoping out the neighborhood."

"Yeah, next thing you know they'll be stealing mechanical reindeer and selling them over in Wenatchee. Are we going to watch this movie or not?"

Maddy sighed. "Yes. I need a laugh."

"Come on." Alan kissed her on the cheek. "Life's not that bad."

Easy for him to say. Their daughter wasn't complaining about *him* behind his back.

Still, there was nothing she could do about the mystery juvenile delinquents. Jordan was going through a bratty phase but she'd come out of it. Everything would be fine.

The rest of the night went smoothly. The girls giggled and carried on until eleven-thirty and then settled down. Maddy let them have their fun, not wanting to provoke another display of brattiness from her daughter. But tomorrow, when she and Jordan went shopping, they'd have a little talk about her attitude.

Hmm. In the middle of mother-daughter bonding? Maybe not. A more opportune time was bound to present itself. With that resolved, she drifted off.

At one point something woke her up. She lay in bed, listening. Somewhere a dog barked. A car crunched down the street in the snow. And then all was quiet again and she fell back to sleep.

The next morning she woke to sunlight filtering in through the bedroom blinds. A sunny day—that was a good omen. She didn't have to be at the shop until ten, which meant she could make the girls breakfast before Afton's mom came to pick her up. At noon she'd take Jordan out for hamburgers and then to Gilded Lily's. She fired up the Keurig, then went to the living room and opened the drapes to the view of Candy Cane Lane.

And of broken candy canes lying every which way along her front walk.

Chapter Eleven

One of the best gifts you can give anyone is a second chance.

—Muriel Sterling, *Making the Holidays Bright:*
How to Have a Perfect Christmas

Tilda was still in bed when her doorbell began ringing. That was followed by knocking. Followed by more doorbell ringing. What the heck? Had Icicle Falls been invaded by aliens? There'd better have been at least an avalanche for somebody to be bugging her on her day off.

She stumbled out of bed and drew on some jeans and a T-shirt over her red Victoria's Secret baby-doll nightie and shoved her feet into her fuzzy zombie slippers. "Coming!"

The banging kept on with 9-1-1 urgency.

"I'm coming already," she snarled. She opened the door to find Maddy Donaldson on her porch looking like a one-woman lynch party.

"It's happened again!" Maddy pointed a shaking finger in the direction of her house. Tilda ran a hand through her hair. A sexy fireman had been carrying her from a burning building and telling her how much he liked her nightgown, and she'd been dragged away from that for this? "Did you call the station?"

If Maddy got any angrier, her head was going to spin off her neck and take off for parts unknown. "You're the officer of record. Do something!"

Tilda rubbed her face, wishing she could scrub away the vision of Maddy in all her pink glory, having a fit on her porch. "I'm not on duty today, Mrs. Donaldson. I think you should call the station."

"And I think you should *do something.* For heaven's sake, this is your neighborhood. Don't you care what happens? Do you want to see irresponsible little vandals get away with this?"

"Of course not, but you really need to…"

"Good. Now what are you planning to do about this?"

Nothing. But she wasn't going to tell Maddy that. "We can have a patrol car drive by tonight and keep an eye on things."

"Was anyone doing that last night?"

"I don't know. I wasn't on duty last night."

"Well, when *are* you on duty?"

"Not today," Tilda said. "But I'll be happy to put in a call and make sure someone swings by tonight. Did you see anything last night?"

"Yes. Well, no, not me. Carla Welky saw that black SUV again. I'm positive it was the same kids."

"Did she get the number of the license plate?"

Maddy frowned. "No."

"That would've been helpful."

"I know that," Maddy said through gritted teeth. "We obviously need professional help."

You could say that again.

"Are you going to interview the neighbors?" Maddy demanded.

"Not at this time."

"Well, then when?"

"When someone reports damage to their property," Tilda said. She needed coffee.

Maddy thumped her chest. "*I* just reported damage to my property."

"And I'm talking to you right now," Tilda said, using her most diplomatic voice, even though she wanted to throttle the woman. "But I'm afraid that since you didn't see anything and you don't have a license-plate number, there's not much I can do."

"You can check out the scene of the crime, which I might add is growing," she said, pointing to a lawn where two mechanical reindeer had been spray painted and were now on their sides, taking a nap in the snow.

Tilda sighed inwardly. "Let me get my coat." What she really wanted to get was some coffee, but she knew Maddy was in no mood to wait while she took care of her caffeine needs.

Boots and coat on, she walked down the street with her new neighbor, Maddy sputtering all the way. "I don't know what this world is coming to when people go around damaging Christmas decorations. It's…un-American."

"It is sad," Tilda agreed. Considering how much the darned things cost, she'd be pissed, too, if hers had been ruined. Especially Mr. T.

They got to the Donaldsons' house and Maddy pointed at her neighbors' home on the other side. Like Maddy's, their candy canes had been stomped to death.

"Look, they got the Werners this time. Maybe one of them saw something."

"I'll ask," Tilda said. "Meanwhile, why don't you go inside?"

Maddy's eyes narrowed. "Are you trying to get rid of me?"

Yes. "If you think of anything else, be sure to call the station," Tilda said.

Maddy got the hint and marched back inside her house.

Tilda stood for a moment, looking at the carnage along the Donaldsons' front walk. As before, each candy cane had not only been tipped over but crushed. Somebody sure hated candy canes. She walked next door to the Werners' place. Only two of theirs had been ruined. The vandals must've been interrupted or scared off halfway through their fun. Tilda shook her head. No concept of what property rights were all about. She hoped she did catch them. But Icicle Falls had a small police force and the odds of getting the sneaky little monsters were pretty slim.

Mr. Werner answered his door after several knocks. He scowled at Tilda. "Whatever you're collecting for, we already gave."

He started to shut the door and Tilda put up a hand. "I'm Tilda Morrison with the Icicle Falls Police Force. I was here earlier in the week with my partner."

"Oh. Well, we're not donating to the policemen's ball, either."

"Sir. I'm here about your candy canes."

"What about 'em?" he asked. Then he looked past Tilda and his eyes got as big as oversize Christmas balls. "What on earth?"

"There was more vandalism last night," Tilda explained.

"Well, why didn't you do something about it?" Did these people think she wore a red cape under her uniform?

"Did you or your wife see anyone wandering around the neighborhood who didn't seem to belong here?"

"This street is full of people who don't belong every night. Carloads of 'em."

"Maybe someone on foot? Some teenagers, perhaps?"

He frowned and scratched his head. "No, no. The missus and I are back in the TV room by seven, watching *Jeopardy!*"

This was a waste of time. Tilda nodded. "Okay, well, thank you."

He nodded in return. "You catch whoever did it. And tell Donaldson I'm not buying any more damn candy canes."

He shut the door and Tilda went down the steps thinking that if anyone ever did a remake of *It's a Wonderful Life*, old man Werner would make an excellent Mr. Potter. She walked back to the carnage in front of the Donaldsons' and squatted to inspect the footprints in the snow. There appeared to be three sets. One was larger than the other two. One big guy and two smaller ones? Even if she had dental stone, she doubted it would do much good in this stirred-up mess. She did pull her cell phone out of her coat pocket to take some pictures. That probably wasn't worth the effort, but if Maddy Donaldson was watching from her window—and no doubt she was—she'd at least feel the cops were doing something. The evidence wasn't any better at the house where the reindeer had been assaulted and, like the Werners, the residents there hadn't seen anything, either. The best Tilda could do was call Enrico, who was on second watch that night, and fill him in on the latest fun and excitement in her new neighborhood.

"I can swing through a couple of times tonight," he said. "Sure can't figure who'd want to be out freezing their butts off just to mess with some Christmas decorations."

It was a mystery, but one she wasn't going to worry about on her day off. She had other things to ponder—like buying a new stove, a project that required family assistance. Back home she showered and dressed in jeans and her favorite black T-shirt. Then she pulled on her parka and boots and drove to her mom's restaurant.

Her cousins Georgie and Caitlin had already scored a table at Pancake Haus. Along with her cashmere sweater, Georgie was wearing enough jewelry to start her own store. Caitlin wore her red hair down and it fell in a perfect sheet to her shoulders. She'd accented her white blouse with a red fringed scarf. They both looked like fashion models. If you asked Tilda, they were a little overdressed for stove shopping.

"You two going to a fashion show after we're done?" she asked, sliding into the booth next to Caitlin.

"Just trying to be a good example for you," Caitlin retorted.

Georgie eyed Tilda's naked fingernails. "We should all get manis and pedis today."

Tilda snorted. "Yeah, pink fingernails will really make people take me seriously."

Georgie obviously didn't buy that argument. "What have you got against being a girl, anyway?"

"Nothing." She was a girl. The red lace under her jeans proved it.

"We know you can dress hot when you want to," Caitlin said.

Georgie raised both carefully penciled eyebrows. "She can?"

"I've seen it. Back when you were after…"

"Enough." Tilda cut her off. She looked around. "Where's Mom?"

"Betts said she didn't come in today," Georgie replied. "She's sick."

"She is? This is the first I've heard about it."

"She's got a cold," Caitlin added.

Tilda shook her head. "I told her she needs to slow down."

"And we all know how well Aunt Dot takes that kind of advice," Caitlin said.

"She never listens to me," Tilda complained. "She makes me crazy."

"You were already crazy," Caitlin kindly pointed out. "Hurry up and order your pancakes. I'm ready to go shopping."

"It's not that exciting shopping for a stove," Tilda informed her. Although secretly she was kind of pumped about getting a shiny, new stove for her kitchen. Maybe she'd even learn to cook on it.

"Are you sure you want to go to Arvid's, though?" Georgie asked. "I checked and he doesn't have the best rating."

"Of course I do," Tilda said. "This is my town. I support my local businesses."

"Even Arvid can't screw up delivering a new stove," Caitlin said.

"Let's hope," Georgie muttered. "Betts," she called to their waitress. "We need pancakes for Tilda."

Georgie was so darned bossy. "What if I wanted eggs?"

"You always order pancakes."

"Well, this morning I want eggs."

Georgie shrugged. "Make that an egg-white omelet."

"Make that a regular omelet," Tilda amended. "And bacon. And pancakes," she added. Georgie was right; she did like pancakes.

"Why aren't you fat?" Caitlin said in disgust.

"Clean living."

"That means no life." Caitlin heaved a sigh. "That's me these days."

"I have a life," Tilda insisted.

"Being one of the boys doesn't count as a life," Georgie said. "You need a man."

You could say that again. "All the good ones are taken," Tilda grumbled.

Georgie flicked back a lock of perfectly highlighted blond hair. "I still think you and Jamal should get together."

"That can't happen when you're partners."

"Then ask for a new partner," Georgie said.

"Or, better yet, give him to me," Caitlin said.

Georgie took a sip of coffee. "You two need to get online. That's where everyone finds a match these days."

It was where Georgie had found hers. But… "I don't know. Finding someone that way just seems too efficient or something. Not very…" Okay, she was going to look like a total cream puff if she said that word. Maybe, deep down, she was.

"Romantic?" Georgie supplied as if reading her mind. "You think Jay and I don't have any romance?"

"I didn't say that." But meeting Mr. Perfect via laptop seemed pretty darned sterile. Lurking at the back of Tilda's mind was this image of someone big and strong flirting with her in line at Bavarian Brews, or hitting on her at Bruisers when she was doing her workout.

Or showing up at her house to hang Christmas lights. No, no, no—who invited Devon Black to sneak into her fantasies?

She was suddenly aware of Georgie snapping her fingers. "Hello, are you paying attention?"

"Of course I'm paying attention."

"What'd I just say?"

"You and Jay are romantic," she guessed.

"That's right. We're absolute soul mates. And we might never have found each other if we hadn't been deliberate about it. Going online you weed out all the losers. You guys should both try it," she said, and the look she sent her sister said, "Especially you."

"I know," said Caitlin. "I sure can't pick 'em."

"I hope you're better at picking stoves than you are men," Tilda said as Betts arrived with their breakfasts.

As it turned out, she was. Caitlin zeroed in on a stainless-steel model with a glass cooktop. "This one's nice."

"And self-cleaning," Tilda read.

"They all are these days," Georgie said.

"Not that you need that feature since you'll hardly ever use the thing," teased Caitlin.

"I'll be using it Christmas Eve."

"Yeah, that could be a mess. On so many levels," Caitlin said with a grin.

"It's got a warming drawer, too," Georgie said.

"I'll get it," Tilda decided.

"Don't you want to look at some of the other models?" Georgie asked.

In Tilda's opinion, when you'd seen one stove you'd seen them all, but she dutifully checked out a couple of other brands. "I think the first one is fine." And the price was right. The more bells and whistles, the higher the price. She wanted to be able to cook a turkey, not have a show on the Food Network.

"It's going to make that old, white fridge of yours look pathetic in comparison," Georgie said. "Why don't you replace that, too?"

"Uh, because I don't want to wipe out my savings."

Caitlin waved away her logical reasoning. "Savings, schmavings. That's what credit cards are for."

"Easy for you to say," Tilda responded.

"Yeah, it is," Georgie put in. "Hers are all maxed out."

Now Arvid himself was with them. The middle-aged shop owner was a tall, scrawny guy with straight hair and the kind of rodent-like face that would have qualified him as an extra in a Western movie, one of the bad guys who was always taking shots at the hero from the roof of the saloon.

"Hello there, ladies. See something you like?"

"This one," Tilda said, giving the stovetop a friendly pat.

"Very good choice." He nodded approvingly. "And it's got a one-year parts-and-labor warranty."

"Wow. One whole year," Tilda said.

Arvid either missed the sarcasm or chose to. "We can deliver it next week."

"That's good, because I need it by Christmas."

"No problem," he said. "Now, did you see this refrigerator?"

"Yes, I did. Let's just get the stove today."

"I'll give you a deal," Arvid persisted.

"On the stove? Great."

"On the fridge if you buy it now."

Arvid sure had great hearing when there was a potential sale involved. "Nice try," Tilda told him. "Let's stop with the stove."

He shrugged as if to say, "Oh, well, I tried," and ten minutes later Tilda was the proud owner of a new stove and Arvid was about to own a piece of garbage with only one working burner.

"Which he'll pretty up and sell to some poor sucker for a small fortune," Georgie predicted as they left the shop. "There's something oily about that guy."

"He's been here for years," Tilda said. "Mom bought her washer and dryer from him." Hmm. "It did take him a long time to get someone out to fix the dryer when it broke."

"Oh, well. You're not going to have problems with a new stove," Georgie said. "At least not before Christmas. Unless it's operator error," she added.

"You two sure are funny," Tilda said with a frown. "Remind me again why I hang out with you."

Caitlin gave her a friendly nudge. "'Cause no one else will put up with you. Well, other than guys who are stalled out at fifteen and want to play video games all night."

"There's nothing wrong with being a gamer," Tilda said.

"And there's nothing wrong with hanging out with men who want to play slightly more grown-up games, either," Georgie said.

She'd tried that. And lost. "Let's not talk about my love life again, okay?"

"Nothing to talk about," Caitlin teased. She threw an arm around Tilda. "We're sisters in celibacy."

"Like I told you," Georgie said, "you need to…"

"Go online," Tilda finished with her. "I'll think about it."

"Let's both start an online hunt," Caitlin suggested. "We can compare notes."

"After Christmas." She had enough stress over getting ready for Christmas dinner. She didn't need to be worrying about impressing a man.

"Okay, that's a deal," Caitlin said with a smile. "My New Year's resolution is going to be to find someone who's not a waste of my heart."

"A very good resolution," Georgie said. "You two both deserve the best."

"We sure do," Caitlin agreed. "So let's go to Gilded Lily's."

Where Tilda would get talked into parting with more of her hard-earned money. "I should visit Mom."

"You can see her when we're done," Caitlin said, and steered her toward the shop.

All of downtown was now teeming with visitors enjoying the holiday atmosphere. And Icicle Falls provided plenty of atmosphere. Little trees in front of all the shops wore twinkling white lights, and the streetlights sported fat, red bows. In the town-center gazebo, Mr. and Mrs. Santa Claus were taking toy requests while the Icicle Falls Glee Club, all dressed in red, sang Christmas songs. Come five o'clock, the famous tree-lighting ceremony would begin with a ho-ho-ho or two from Santa, a prayer by one of the local ministers and a community

Christmas-carol songfest. Then there'd be the big count-down and the giant tree in the town square would come alive with an uncountable number of colored lights. All the other Christmas lights would be set ablaze, and the entire downtown would glow like a giant open treasure chest nestled among the mountains.

Tilda had been going to that tree-lighting ceremony since she was a kid, and even though it was the same hokey thing every year, she never got tired of it. The event had become so successful that the town now staged one every Saturday in December, and it was the bait that drew visitors from all over the country to enjoy the holiday celebrations and check out all the cute shops.

Gilded Lily's was a favorite female destination for locals and visitors alike, and it was all decked out for the holidays with a wreath on the front door and the mannequins in the store window modeling holiday finery. They seemed to be whispering, "Think how good you'd look wearing this outfit."

Tilda knew she could look good when she tried, but sexy clothes only took you so far when a guy was determined to chase after a cream puff. She'd pretty much sworn off Gilded Lily's after things imploded with Garrett. Still, as she entered the shop, it wasn't hard to get in touch with her feminine side.

By the time she was done, she had black leggings, a midnight-blue jacket and a light blue chambray blouse that Caitlin insisted had to be left unbuttoned down to… "Whoa, what's this?" she asked, peering at Tilda's lacy bra. "You *are* a real girl, after all."

Tilda clutched the blouse to her chest. "Don't be cute."

"When did you start wearing Victoria's Secret?" Caitlin demanded. The minute the words were out of her mouth, her face turned red. It wasn't hard to figure out, and nobody wanted to remind Tilda of her romantic failure.

Georgie rushed in to smooth over the awkward moment. "Okay, now we really need to find you a man. You can't be wasting your inner sex goddess like this."

"I don't have an inner sex goddess," Tilda mumbled. If she did, she would've snagged Garrett.

"Of course you do," said Caitlin, trying to fix her misstep. "I suspected it all along. Otherwise, you'd never have bought that leather jacket and those red heels."

Way back. A million years ago. "Those didn't work out," Tilda said. Why she still had them in her closet she had no idea.

"You used them on the wrong man," Georgie said. Thankfully, that was *all* she said.

Both cousins had known about what she'd hoped was her blossoming relationship with the sexy fireman, a relationship that ended up going nowhere. And after a night of helping her forget with wild huckleberry martinis at Zelda's, neither of them had ever brought up the painful subject again.

"You just wait until the New Year. We're going to find you someone who really appreciates you," Georgie promised.

Maybe it was that easy. Go online, put in your order for a perfect match and bam. There he was. Part of her wished she already had that perfect man, someone to watch Christmas movies with, to kiss under the mistletoe Georgie had hung up, someone to bake cookies for.

You baked cookies for Devon Black.

Not him! Her hormones needed to get a grip.

"Hey, it's way past lunchtime," Georgie said. "Let's go over to Zelda's and get something."

"I'll pick up a salad for Mom while we're there," Tilda said.

They were just leaving as Maddy Donaldson and her daughter entered the shop. "Tilda, hello," Maddy greeted her. "Have you made any progress on our case?"

"Not yet, but we'll have a patrol car come by tonight."

"Good," Maddy said with a nod. "I hope you catch those rotten kids before they do any more damage."

"We'll try," Tilda said, careful not to make any promises.

"What's that all about?" Caitlin asked as they left.

"Someone's trashing candy canes," Tilda said.

"Did they steal your T. rex?" Georgie asked.

"No."

"Too bad."

"Hey, he's cute."

"Tacky," Georgie said, rolling her eyes.

"The picture didn't do him justice," Tilda said. "You have to see him in person."

"No, I don't."

"So, getting back to the candy canes," Caitlin said. "Is that all?"

"Pretty much. They've stomped on a few. Tied a blow-up Santa in knots."

"Weird," Caitlin said. "Who'd want to mess around with the stuff on Candy Cane Lane?"

"Who'd want to mess with Maddy Donaldson?" Tilda said. "When it comes to all that Christmas stuff she's... I don't know, Queen of the Street or something."

"Protecting her turf?" Caitlin guessed.

"That's about it," Tilda agreed.

"Her daughter looked a little embarrassed by the whole thing," said Georgie.

"She's about the right age to be embarrassed by her mom." Tilda remembered the time she'd commanded hers to drop her off a block away from school. Commands didn't work with Dot Morrison. "Too bad your mom's not Cybill Shepherd," Mom had said. "Deal with it." And then she'd dropped Tilda off right in front of the school. How humiliating.

Now Tilda was nothing but proud of the woman. Tilda's dad had died when she was in high school. Dot had picked up the pieces of their shattered lives and forged them into a family of two. She ran a successful business and made a habit of helping anyone and everyone who needed a job, a fresh start or simply an infusion of cash into their business. Yeah, she was one zany old broad, but there wasn't anyone in town who didn't love her. And that included her daughter.

They got sidetracked on the way to Zelda's when Georgie saw a holiday serving platter and insisted Tilda buy it. "This'll be perfect for your turkey," she said.

It would. Tilda picked it up.

And then set it down again.

"This thing is seventy bucks!"

"That's because it's fine china."

"Too fine for my bank account," Tilda said wistfully. "Come on, guys, let's go eat."

After Tilda drove to the old Craftsman-style house she'd grown up in to deliver Zelda's popular Christmas salad with spinach, blue cheese, dried cranberries and pecans. "Hey, sickie, where are you?" she called as she walked in.

As usual, the place smelled like an ashtray. She'd tried

any number of times over the years to get Mom to quit smoking, but the stubborn brat refused and no amount of pleading, bribery and scary information from cancer websites seemed to work. "We all have to die of something," Mom liked to say, to which Tilda usually responded, "How'd you like to go with me throttling you for being so stubborn?" That, of course, always made her laugh. Yeah, ha, ha. New Year's resolution—lock Mom in her room and make her quit cold turkey, whether she wanted to or not.

"Out here," came a croak.

Okay, that didn't sound good. Tilda walked into the family room to find her mom sacked out on the couch with a mystery novel, an afghan thrown over her skinny legs, her bed pillow behind her head. She was wearing her newest Christmas sweatshirt, sporting a yellow Minion in a Santa hat.

"You sound like crap," Tilda said.

Mom let out a hacking cough. "I feel like crap."

Tilda set the salad on the nearby coffee table and took a seat in the rocking chair her mother had had ever since Tilda could remember. "Have you gone to the doctor?"

"For a cold? Of course not."

"It seems to be in your chest now."

"I just gave myself a mustard plaster."

Oh, yeah. Tilda remembered those dreaded mustard plasters. They stung like the devil and they didn't work. "If you get bronchitis, you'll be down for the count."

"I won't," Mom assured her, and then quickly changed the subject. "So, did you get a stove?"

"I did. Arvid says he'll deliver it next week."

"Which really means in two weeks, but at least you'll have it by Christmas." Mom blew her nose on a fresh tissue, then deposited it in the wastebasket she'd set next to the couch.

The thing was practically full. Tilda picked it up and emptied it in the kitchen garbage can. "Are you going to be well by Christmas? I'm counting on you to help me pull off this Christmas Eve dinner."

"Of course I'll be well by Christmas," Mom said, and coughed.

At the rate she was going she wouldn't even be well by New Year's. "Have you been eating?"

"Food. Bleh."

Tilda returned and sat in the rocking chair. She picked up the container. "I brought your favorite salad."

Mom waved it away. "I'll have it later."

"Later when?"

"Later when I feel like eating," Mom said with a scowl. "Honestly, Tillie, you can turn into such a nag."

"Yeah, well, I wouldn't nag if you'd act like a grown-up when you got sick."

Mom pointed a warning finger at her, a reminder of where she got her own finger-pointing habit. "I brought you into this world. I can take you out."

"Yeah, I'm scared. I'm going to the Safeway deli to get you some chicken soup."

Mom sighed and leaned back against the pillow. "Okay."

Tilda bent and kissed her head. "I'll be right back. Don't move."

"I wasn't planning on it."

Chicken soup wasn't going to do it. What Mom needed was to go to the doctor. Why was she so darned stubborn, anyway?

Tilda skirted the busy downtown, taking the back roads to the store. Fresh snow was falling, which would make downtown and all its pretty shops look like the inside of a snow globe. It would also create slippery driving conditions for all the visitors who'd taken their chains off after coming through the pass. Especially the ones with all-wheel drive who considered themselves invincible. Before the day was over there'd be at least one accident.

The Safeway parking lot was a zoo, packed with cars easing in and out, people dashing into the store, dogs inside cars and trucks, barking at passersby.

Speaking of trucks, there was Devon Black's. If she hadn't promised her mom chicken soup, she would've turned around and left. Collaring punks, facing gunfire, breaking up fights—none of those situations fazed Tilda. She knew what to do and she did it well. Social situations, on the other hand, particularly situations where you ran into a guy you wanted nothing to do with, a guy who'd had the nerve to tell you off when you didn't deserve it—well, those were a challenge. She could already feel her heart rate picking up, as if she was about to walk into a dark, abandoned warehouse filled with criminals all lying in wait.

She sat in her Jeep, considering her options. As far as she could tell, she only had two. Keep sitting there until he left and hope he didn't notice her, or go in, get her soup and hope she didn't run into him.

And if she did, then what? She'd nod her head, acknowledge his presence and move on. That was how she'd always treated him. He'd strung some lights for her and hung around and made a pest of himself, but it didn't change anything. He was still a pain in the butt and she was still not interested. Not. Interested. Remember that.

With her plan in place, she entered the store. It took her no more than a couple of minutes to fill a container with soup. She'd be out of here in no time. And the sooner, the better. Not only did she want to avoid Devon, she was ready to get away from the woman behind her in line and her wound-up kid.

"No, James, you can't climb up there," she said after her son's second attempt to follow the chips and apples onto the checkout conveyor belt. "He's three," she said to Tilda as if that explained it.

Before Tilda could respond, James was busy again, this time helping himself to a candy bar from the impulse-buy rack.

"No, baby, give that to Mama."

"I want it," he protested as she took it away.

"Not today. We're getting corn chips instead."

"I want candy," he whined.

"Remember what we said. You had to be good at Grandma's."

Obviously, James hadn't been good at Grandma's.

Now he was on an invisible spring, jumping up and down, bouncing into the old woman behind him who let out a yelp when he jumped on her toes.

"Oh, dear," fretted his mother. "I'm so sorry. James, stand still."

James was either hyperactive or on a sugar high. He was also a good argument for birth control if you asked Tilda. She paid for her soup and got away from the pair.

She was almost at the door when Devon approached from a check stand farther down. He hesitated for a second, looking half hopeful, half embarrassed, then he prepared to march past her.

"I'm not stuck-up," she informed him when he got within hearing range. Was she responding to something he'd said when he was at her place or later when he'd invaded her dreams? She wasn't quite sure and now she felt like a fool.

He stopped right in front of her. He wore dark jeans, boots and a navy pea coat, and the beginning of a five-o'clock shadow was darkening his chin.

Like chocolate-dipped potato chips from Sweet Dreams Chocolates, Zelda's chocolate-kiss martinis and all such things that were bad for a girl, he looked ridiculously tempting.

"Yeah, you are," he said.

"I am not," she growled.

"Prove it."

Just then the kid who'd been in line went racing past. "James!" his mother shouted.

James was enjoying his temporary freedom far too much to heed his mother. The automatic door had opened and the whole world (or at least the parking lot) was before him, a snowy wonderland. Out he bolted.

"Crap!" Tilda dropped her soup and went in hot pursuit.

A car with two old ladies in the front seat had slid into the parking lot and was now sledding its way toward the child. Tilda registered it all as a few seconds stretched into slow motion. The one in the passenger seat was Mrs. Walters. The driver had to be her sister. Mrs. Walters held both hands to her cheeks and had an expression of terror on her face. Her sister looked just as terrified. She'd obviously slammed on the brakes and lost control of the car. A woman screamed. A baby cried. Someone swore. Oh, yeah. That was her.

As Tilda bolted for the boy, a bigger body shoved past her and scooped up the child, handing him off to Tilda like a two-legged football. The car sent the rescuer sprawling, then came to a stop, colliding with a display of Christmas wreaths, toppling them and spilling them in all directions.

The boy's mother took him from Tilda, tearful and grateful. "You and your friend saved my son's life."

The friend was covered in Christmas wreaths and struggling to get up. If it hadn't been such a serious rescue, it would have been comic.

Tilda ran to Devon's side. "Don't move. You might be hurt."

Of course, he ignored her. "I'm fine," he snapped, brushing fir needles from his coat. "Ow. Shit!"

"Yeah, I can tell. Sit down. You need someone to check you over."

"How about you check me over?"

"Sit down," she ordered. She helped him to a nearby stack of bundled kindling. He was limping and his head was bleeding. She took out her cell phone and called the 9-1-1 dispatcher.

"Seriously?" he said.

"Yeah, seriously. You're limping. Your hand's bleeding and so is your head. You could have a concussion."

He took quick advantage of that observation. "Someone should stay with me all night to make sure I'm okay."

"If that's the case, I'll call your brother."

He made a face. "Gee, thanks."

She could already hear sirens, which meant help was on the way. "Stay put," she said, and went to check on the two older women, who were struggling to get out past the car's air bags. Both were going to have some lovely bruises.

"Are you all right, Mrs. W.?" she asked Mrs. Walters.

Mrs. Walters looked around her as if trying to figure

out how she'd gotten into this predicament. "That little boy, is he…?"

"He's fine. Don't worry. How do you feel?"

"Well, dear, to tell the truth, I feel…a bit shaky."

"Come on, let's get you and your sister inside where it's warm."

"And that young man," Mrs. Walters continued. "Isn't that Devon?"

"Yes, it is."

"Well, he's a true hero."

It looked that way. But then, looks could be deceiving. Next time Tilda saw him, he'd probably be in a fight over at the Man Cave.

Still, he'd risked life and limb to save that kid. Maybe there was more to Devon Black than met the eye. Or *her* eye, anyway.

By the time she got Mrs. Walters and her sister calmed down, her fellow officers had arrived on the scene, as well as the aid car. She could leave now. She glanced over at Devon Black. Someone had brought him a roll of paper towels and he sat on that pile of kindling, stanching the flow of blood and looking like a wounded warrior.

Or a hero.

Chapter Twelve

Always make going to see Santa an outing for the whole family.
—Muriel Sterling, *Making the Holidays Bright: How to Have a Perfect Christmas*

Ivy had slipped away from the shop early, leaving the rest of the gang in charge. She didn't feel too guilty since she'd be back the next day right after church. In retail during the month of December, there was no such thing as a free Sunday. Her day off always had to come on Monday or Tuesday. And there was only one Saturday in December when she traditionally left a little early. That was Santa Saturday, the day she took the kids to visit Mr. and Mrs. Claus in the town center.

She liked to time her visit so she could stick around for the tree-lighting ceremony afterward. No one would miss her then, as Christmas Haus would be practically void of shoppers. The town square would be filled with visitors and locals alike, all singing Christmas carols and waiting to see the giant tree come to life. She drove to her house where Mutti was on kid patrol and also waiting for Arvid's repairman to come fix her washing machine.

Ivy had gotten most of the water out, but the appliance was still useless and the laundry was piling up.

Two familiar cars were parked out front. One belonged to Mutti. The other... She pulled into the driveway with her jaw tightly clenched. What was Rob doing here?

Her son was already in his white shirt and bow tie and black slacks, and Mutti was in the process of buttoning up his little red vest. She looked up at Ivy with a smile that was as guilty as it was welcoming.

"What's Rob doing here?" Ivy demanded.

"He stopped by to drop off treats for the kids."

"Mama!" cried Robbie, and ran to her, hands outstretched. "Uppy!"

She picked him up and kissed his cheek. "It's *my* weekend." Okay, did she sound snippy and selfish?

"I know, dear," her mother said calmly.

"Well, then, why's he here?"

"He stopped by to see if you were taking the kids to see Santa, and Hannah told him the washing machine is broken. He's in the laundry room fixing it."

"Him? Where's the repairman from Arvid's? He was supposed to come this afternoon."

"He had a family emergency."

"That's the second time they haven't shown up when they said they would."

"Rob offered to help." Mutti shrugged. "I figured since he was here, anyway... And you do have a civil relationship now, right?"

"Define civil."

"You haven't thrown anything at him recently."

"Ha, ha."

Her mother patted her on the shoulder. "Really, dear,

I'm sorry. But I assumed that in the long run you'd want to have your washing machine fixed."

"No, actually, I don't." Not if it meant having Rob here, trying to work off his bad behavior.

Mutti sighed. "I figured it was the least he could do after…"

Ivy bristled. "There is no *least* he could do. He left us, Mom. And coming back and fixing a washing machine doesn't make up for that."

Her mother put an arm around her. "I know he hurt you, sweetheart. And this past year hasn't been any fun."

Her mother had no idea. She'd never been left. She and Dad were devoted to each other. Why, oh, why couldn't Ivy have found someone like her father?

"But you have to forgive him."

"I may have to forgive him, but I don't have to take him back."

Her mother blinked. "Who said anything about taking him back?"

This was a can of Christmas worms Ivy didn't want to open. "Never mind," she said. "Here, hold Robbie a minute, will you?" She dumped her son in her mother's arms and marched double time to the laundry room. Rob and his wrenches could go find some other washing machine to play with.

Hannah was seated on the floor in her red velveteen Christmas dress, watching while her father put away his tools. "Daddy fixed our washer machine," she told Ivy. "He's gonna take us to see Santa!"

Daddy didn't look at Mommy. He was very intent on shutting his toolbox.

Ivy was now an exploding pressure cooker. "Go tell Mutti to get your coat," she said to her daughter, and

Hannah happily skipped off. The second she was out of the room, Ivy turned on him. "How dare you?"

"Hey, I'm sorry. Hannah wants me to take her to visit Santa. What was I supposed to say?"

"That Mommy's taking her," growled Ivy.

He nodded and stood slowly. "Look, they're my kids, too."

She couldn't argue with that. She moved to more solid ground. "And who asked you to fix my washing machine?"

"Our daughter. She told me it was broken. I thought maybe it was a simple fix and I could help."

"I didn't ask you to help!"

"I know you didn't, but I wanted to. I know I can't undo what I did…" he began.

"That's right. You can't." Fixing a washing machine couldn't fix a broken heart. There was nothing he could do to make up for the way he'd hurt her.

Hannah was back again, coat on and ready to roll. She took Rob's hand and started towing him out of the laundry room. "Come on, Daddy, let's go see Santa."

Darn it all, Ivy didn't want to share with her undeserving ex. "Baby, Mommy's going to take you."

Hannah frowned. "But I want *you* to come, Daddy. Mommy, make Daddy come."

"Daddy has to be somewhere else," Ivy said. Preferably somewhere far away, like the moon.

Hannah's lower lip began to wobble. "But I want Daddy."

Oh, great. Ivy glared at Rob. *Look what you've done.* "If you're going to cry we won't go," she warned.

"I don't want to go. I want my daddy," Hannah wailed, and flung her arms around Rob's legs, clinging to him.

He picked her up. "Hey, is this any way to act? Santa's not going to bring you anything if you're naughty."

"I'm not naughty," Hannah insisted through her tears.

"Good. Now Mommy's right. You need to go with her."

He looked so stoical, so noble. Disgusting.

"You go with Mommy, and on Christmas Day we'll do something fun. Okay?"

Bribery, a time-honored parental tool. But, somehow, in this instance it felt wrong. Since when did a dad have to bribe a child to go see Santa with her mother? Oh, yeah. When Mother was being mean. *You're a mean one, Mrs. Grinch.* Except she wasn't being mean. It was sneaky and wrong of Rob to come over and start manipulating the kids like this.

Hannah's wails were downgrading to sobs and she was nodding. Resigned to going to see Santa with Mean Mommy. And right now there was nothing Mean Mommy would rather do than beat Daddy the Jerk over the head with a Christmas tree.

"Why did you come over?" Ivy demanded.

"Didn't your mom tell you?"

"I mean really."

"I found some chocolate Santas at Sweet Dreams."

"Daddy brought us candy," put in Hannah, still sobbing.

"Well, that was very nice of Daddy, especially since he could've given them to you next weekend when you came to visit," she added, glaring at Rob.

"Daddy brought you candy, too," Hannah said.

"Employee discount on the Sweet Dreams Christmas box," he said.

The special Sweet Dreams Christmas box. An elegant

gold box wrapped with a red ribbon, containing all the Sweet Dreams specials—mint truffles, rum bonbons, little dark-chocolate Santas spiced with cinnamon and their signature white-chocolate-rose truffles. He'd gotten it for her two years ago and she'd savored every bite. Last Christmas there'd been no chocolate, and then no husband. This Christmas…okay, she'd keep the chocolate, but the man could go live in Whoville for all she cared. Did he really think he could bribe his way back into her heart with a box of chocolates?

"Chocolate, that makes everything all right again, huh?"

"I'm not sure what will make everything all right again," he said, "but I have to start somewhere."

She reached to take Hannah from his arms, and her stubborn daughter clung to him like a limpet. "I want Daddy."

Ivy gave up. "Okay, fine. Daddy will come with us."

The sobs stopped instantly now that victory had been achieved. Giving in to a child's tantrum, bad. Letting the child's father come with her to see Santa, good. So was this good parenting or bad? Who knew? Was it good for her heart? Definitely not. They'd take two cars. Rob could hang around for some ho-ho-hos and then he'd go his way and Ivy would go hers.

"Thanks, Ive," he said.

"I'm not doing this for you and you know it," she snapped.

"I know. Thanks, anyway, though," he said, and followed her out to the living room, where Mutti was bouncing Robbie on her knees.

"All ready?" she asked, her expression a mixture of concern and guilt.

"Yes," Ivy said.

"Daddy's taking us to see Santa," Hannah told her grandmother.

Now Mutti really looked guilty. "Oh. Well. That will be nice."

"For some of us," Ivy said. Rob and the kids were going to have a great time, but he'd managed to ruin the day for her. Ooh, she'd like to give him a lump of coal in his stocking and a lump on the head to go with it.

They went out the door and Mutti made a quick exit. Rob helped Ivy load the kids into the minivan, then started walking to his car.

"Daddy, come with us," called Hannah.

"Daddy will meet us there," Ivy said. She got in the car and locked the doors.

"But I want Daddy to come with us," Hannah whined.

"He is. He's coming in his own car." And as soon as they'd seen Santa, they were going to ditch him.

Downtown was a holiday beehive, teeming with people. She parked in the employee parking slots in back of Christmas Haus, and then made her way with the kids to the town center where Santa and the missus, played by James and Olivia Claussen, were enthroned, surrounded by plastic reindeer and pots of miniature Christmas trees festooned with colored lights. The line to see them stretched halfway down the block. Oh, good, a nice, long wait with her ex. Maybe he wouldn't find a place to park. One could always hope.

But no, here he came, as hard to get rid of as Thanksgiving leftovers.

He joined her, and they walked to the end of the line with Rob carrying the baby and Hannah skipping alongside. Samantha Preston and Cecily Goodman, members

of the Sterling family who owned Sweet Dreams Chocolates, were at the end of the line with their husbands and
children. Samantha's husband held their toddler, Rose,
who was dressed all in pink. Cecily was almost at the
end of her first pregnancy and showing off the expectant-
mom glow. Her stepdaughter, Serena, who was a couple
of years older than Hannah, wore a plaid wool coat with
a red scarf and matching knit tam. She was holding her
daddy's hand, jumping up and down with excitement.

Both sisters did a double-take, seeing Ivy with Rob in
tow, but recovered quickly enough, greeting them with
smiles and hellos.

"We're going to see Santa," Serena said to Hannah.

"I'm going to ask Santa to bring my daddy back
home," Hannah confided.

Blake smiled politely. Luke cleared his throat and then
said to Rob, "Hey, how about those Seahawks?" while
Cecily looked speculatively at Ivy.

I'm going to die of embarrassment. Ivy did her best
to gloss over the moment by asking the sisters how everything was going at Sweet Dreams.

"It's been our best year yet," Samantha said. "And I
assume things are great over at Christmas Haus."

"Our best year so far, too," Ivy said. At least something in her life was going right. She liked the Sterling
sisters a lot, but she couldn't help envying their perfect
lives. Beautiful children, husbands who were in it for the
long haul and who didn't resent their women's busy lives.

As the men chatted and the children kept one another
occupied, Cecily lowered her voice. "I know it's none of
my business, but are you and Rob...?"

Ivy shook her head vehemently. "No. We're just doing
the Santa thing together with the kids."

Cecily nodded, her expression thoughtful. Cecily had a reputation in town. Before returning to Icicle Falls to live, she'd worked as a professional matchmaker in LA. When it came to romance and who should be with whom, she had a sort of second sight.

"What are you thinking?" Ivy prompted.

"Me? Oh, nothing," Cecily said airily. "It's just nice to see you two together, is all."

"We're not together."

Cecily's cheeks, already pink from the frosty air, reddened. "No, of course not."

Did she know Rob had bought candy for Ivy? Did Samantha know? Did it matter? He could buy a sleigh load of chocolate, and it wouldn't change Ivy's mind about taking him back.

As the line moved forward, the conversation shifted to plans for the holidays. "We'll be with Blake's family Christmas Eve, then with ours on Christmas Day," Samantha said. "How about you?"

"The kids and I will be with my family on Christmas Eve," Ivy said. And the next morning, she'd drop them off at their father's. This would be the first year she didn't have her babies with her on Christmas Day. She could feel the tears rising in her eyes.

Cecily reached out and patted her arm. "Holiday adjustments can be hard."

Ivy nodded and wiped away a tear. She even managed a smile. Yes, those adjustments could be hard but she'd make them. She had to.

Finally it was their turn to see Santa, with only five minutes to spare before his next appearance in the gazebo to kick off the tree-lighting ceremony.

James Claussen was one of the town's newer residents.

He'd been a professional Santa for years and he had the girth and thick, white beard, as well as the jolly smile that made him perfect for the job.

"Well, look who we have here," he said, holding out a white-gloved hand to Hannah. "You're a very sweet little girl," he said as she perched on his leg. "I'll bet you want something special this year."

Hannah nodded eagerly and Ivy captured the moment with her cell phone camera. "I want my daddy to come back home to stay."

Ivy was aware of Rob standing next to her, holding Robbie. She could feel her cheeks heating with embarrassment and—what? Not guilt. She had nothing to feel guilty about. She wasn't the rat who'd broken vows and walked out.

"Daddy doesn't live at our house anymore," Hannah went on to explain.

"That's because Daddy wanted to live somewhere else," Ivy said with a fake smile for Rob.

He moved close to her and lowered his voice so only she could hear. "I'd give anything for a second chance."

"Well, don't hold your breath," she said sharply. Darn him, he was bringing out the absolute worst in her. She had to stop letting him do that. "Tell Santa what else you'd like," she prompted Hannah, infusing her voice with holiday cheer.

Hannah considered a moment, then shook her head. "That's all."

Ivy felt an ache pounding at her temples. Whose idea was it to come here, anyway? "Okay, sweetie, it's your brother's turn on Santa's lap," she said.

Hannah dutifully thanked Santa and hopped off his leg, and Rob moved in to replace her with Robbie. Their son took one look at the big guy in the red suit and burst into terrified tears.

"Robbie, ask Santa to bring Daddy home," Hannah coached.

This was like some sort of Christmas nightmare. Ivy took a quick shot of her son, then picked him up. The crying shuddered to a stop and he laid his head on her shoulder.

"Well, now, next year our young man will be ready to sit on Santa's lap," said James. He smiled sympathetically. "You have a good Christmas."

"Thanks," Ivy murmured, and thought, *Fat chance*.

Rob picked up Hannah, who beamed at him. "I know you'll come home now," she said. "Santa promised."

"No, sweetie, he didn't," Ivy corrected her as they moved away. "Santa only brings toys, not daddies."

Hannah seemed downright shocked by this and looked to her father to refute it.

"It's true, baby. But Santa will bring you something nice."

Hannah didn't say anything to that. And she didn't seem particularly happy with the outcome of her visit to the jolly old guy. Well, that made two of them, Ivy thought miserably.

They walked to a nearby bench that would give them a view of the goings-on at the gazebo, Ivy holding Robbie and Hannah perched on her father's lap. "I don't like Santa," Hannah muttered.

Thanks, Rob. "Oh, but he likes you," Ivy said.

"I just want you to come home, Daddy."

"Daddy likes where he lives now," Ivy told her. "And you like going to visit him."

Hannah considered this and then answered with a shrug.

Who could blame her? Having her parents living apart was a poor second to having them both with her every day.

But hey, people got divorced all the time. Kids were resilient; that was what everyone said. This first Christmas with the new arrangement would be hard, but after that the holidays would get easier. And at least Mommy and Daddy still lived in the same town. That was almost as good as sleeping in the same bed.

Bed. No, don't even think about it.

Too late. A flood of images assailed her. Rob wearing the boxers with red hearts she'd gotten him for Valentine's Day, standing in the middle of the bed, thumping his chest like Tarzan, then leaping off and gathering her in his arms. Rob kissing his way down her body. Rob spooning her when she was eight months pregnant with Hannah, kissing her neck and telling her she was the most beautiful woman in the world.

Those were old, out-of-date mental snapshots, she reminded herself. *Remember Rob coming to bed long after you did, getting under the covers and turning his back to you.* Or Rob sitting on the bed fully clothed with his head in his hands, saying, "I can't do this anymore. I want out."

Yeah, happy Christmas memories.

Santa was on the gazebo stage now, speaking into the microphone. "I know you've all been good."

Not all of us.

"And I'll be visiting your houses on Christmas Eve, so make sure you do what Mommy and Daddy say. Can you all do that?"

"Yes," chorused all the young children present.

"All right, then. Merry Christmas," Santa called, and waved.

Hannah, who only a few minutes ago had put Santa on her naughty list, waved eagerly. Then she hugged Rob.

He looked over her head at Ivy, his expression half pleading, half hopeful. "I really would do anything, Ive. Anything you asked."

"Good. Then why don't you go jump off Sleeping Lady Mountain?"

Now Pastor Jim was saying a prayer. "God, bless us all this Christmas season. Give us joy in our daily lives, forgiveness in our hearts and Your perfect peace."

Ugh. Ivy was currently lacking in all three of those.

"Peace on earth, goodwill toward men," Rob whispered.

"Men? How about immature, irresponsible little boys masquerading as men?" she retorted.

"Boys can grow up."

"Yeah? Well, it'll take a whole chorus of angels announcing it to convince me."

At that moment the carol sing began. "Angels we have heard on high," everyone around her began warbling, "sweetly singing o'er the plain."

"There you go," Rob said, trying for a light tone.

"Stop it," she said harshly. "Just stop it."

"Mommy, don't yell at Daddy," Hannah scolded.

"Mommy's not yelling," Rob said.

"Yes, she is. She's wearing her mad face."

Ivy forced herself to smile. She rubbed her daughter's arm. "It's okay, baby."

A text came in from her sister. How was Santa?

Bad. Rob came with.

Poor you. Want company tonite?

Yes! They could have a man-hating party.

K. See you at 7.

That worked. If Rob asked to stay she could tell him she was expecting company.

She tucked her phone back in her pocket and sat through "Deck the Halls" and "Santa Claus is Coming to Town." Then Mayor Stone began the countdown for the tree lighting.

Robbie's head came off Ivy's shoulder and he looked up to see what the ruckus was about. Hannah sat on Rob's lap, smiling as he counted down in her ear.

"Three, two, one... Merry Christmas!" called the mayor, and the giant tree came to glorious, sparkling life, along with the lights on the smaller trees in the town square and all the ones strung along Center Street.

Robbie gazed around in wonder and Hannah clapped her hands. Even Ivy, who'd been feeling pretty darned sour a minute ago, had to smile. Christmas in Icicle Falls was always magical.

The local glee club was on stage now, singing "We Wish You a Merry Christmas."

Could Ivy make her Christmas merry this year? She remembered what she read in the last chapter of Muriel Sterling's book.

Find joy in the smallest things and all those small joys will add up to a full heart.

Okay, here was one small thing she could find joy in—the lights were beautiful and her children were smiling. That made her smile, too.

Until she saw Rob smiling at her as if her happy moment had anything to do with him. That wiped the smile off her face. "Okay, gang. Time to go home and have dinner," she said, and stood up, settling Robbie on her hip.

Rob sighed and set Hannah down. She looked up at him and repeated, "Time to go home and have dinner, Daddy."

"No, Daddy can't come," Ivy said. "He has things to do."

Hannah's lower lip jutted out. "I want Daddy to come home with us."

"You'll get to go visit Daddy next week." Ivy took her daughter's hand and began to lead her away.

Hannah dug in her heels, trying not to move. "Noooo, I want Daddy."

"Well, I don't," Ivy said. "See you next week, Daddy," she called cheerily, and hauled off her crying daughter.

"Someone needs a nap," said an older woman as Ivy and her children passed by.

"I sure do," Ivy muttered.

Chapter Thirteen

One thing that blooms well at Christmas is love.
—Muriel Sterling, *Making the Holidays Bright:*
How to Have a Perfect Christmas

Tilda tossed aside the out-of-date issue of *People* magazine she'd been half reading. What was she doing here in the emergency waiting room? Oh, yeah. Waiting.

"You oughta get that hand checked out," Andy Mixon, one of the medics, had told Devon. "Might need a couple stitches on your head, too. Til, take him to the emergency room," he'd added. "If we give him a ride there for minor injuries, his insurance won't cover it."

"Yeah, Til, take me to the emergency room," Devon had echoed, grinning as though he'd made some sort of conquest. Did he really think she was that easy?

Maybe she was. Why else was she hanging around here? She could've told him to call his brother to come and get him.

Of course, it wasn't like she'd had big plans for the night. Except…crap. Mom's soup. She pulled out her cell and called her mother. "Hey, you doing okay?"

Mom answered with a phlegmy cough. "Sure. Where's my soup?"

"It's coming. I had to take a friend to the emergency room." Friend? That was stretching it.

"What happened? Did someone get shot?"

"I wish you wouldn't always sound so hopeful," Tilda complained.

"I have no life. I have to live through you."

"Yeah, right. And no, nobody got shot. A kid ran out into the parking lot and my friend—" there was that word again "—rescued him."

"What kind of friend, a man?"

"Don't get your hopes up. Just a friend."

"You know I want a grandkid before I die," Mom said, and coughed again.

"That would be funny if you weren't so darned sick. You know, stubborn old people who refuse to go to the doctor get pneumonia and die all the time."

"Who are you calling old?" Mom demanded, incensed.

"Not you. I'll be there as soon as I can with your soup. While you're waiting, eat your salad."

"Salad. Bleh. Pick me up some cookies."

Her mom, the nutrition queen.

Devon appeared then, two of his fingers splinted and his head bandaged. Even all banged up, he looked good. Better than good. Fireman-hot good. Tilda was glad she had an excuse to drop him off and leave him.

"Okay, gotta go," she said to her mom.

"If this is going to turn into something, take your time. Have sex. Get pregnant."

"Thanks for the motherly advice," Tilda said, and ended the call. "What's the verdict on your hand?" she asked Devon.

"A couple of broken fingers. Glad it's my left hand and not my right. Otherwise, I'd have to miss work."

"What about your head?"

"I could have a concussion. Someone needs to stay with me," he added, giving her the kind of smile that set her panties on fire.

"You can call your brother," she said, and told her panties to cool it.

"He's got a wife."

"He can bring her along. Come on, let's get you—" *to bed. No, no, don't say that! Don't think that, don't go anywhere near that* "—home."

She loaded him in the Jeep and drove him to the Mountain View Apartments at the edge of town. They were older, mostly inhabited by struggling single moms, divorced men and bachelors. She expected his apartment to be a mess, with clothes and magazines scattered around, dirty dishes in the sink and a mishmash of furniture. Surprisingly, it was clean and the furniture matched. He had a couch that looked like real leather and a matching chair. A couple of framed baseball posters hung on the walls.

"Where are the pictures of you in your baseball uniform?" she asked, glancing around.

He frowned. "In my mom's scrapbook."

Of course, he probably didn't want to be reminded of what he'd lost. She walked over to the coffee table, a smooth piece with simple lines carved out of maple. "Cool table."

"Thanks."

"Where'd you get it?" She could use one like that at her place. At the moment she was making do with a garage-sale special.

"I made it."

"You made it?"

"Don't sound so shocked. I have talents," he said, and fell onto the couch. "I need a beer."

"I bet the doc said no alcohol."

"What does he know?"

"More than you do. I'll get you some water."

"Whoopee."

She searched in the tiny kitchen cupboard and found the glasses. They weren't the cheapo kind she had. No, these were the kind her cousin Georgie bought from Crate and Barrel. She took one down and filled it with water.

"So why are you here?" she asked, handing it over.

"Why are any of us here?" He took a drink and laid his head back against the couch.

"Seriously. In this apartment, I mean. You've got all this fancy furniture and stuff."

"And I'm living in a dump. Well, what can I say? The furniture is left over from the glory days. The house got sold, though, and most of what I made went—never mind." He shrugged. "Bad choices equal starting over. I've got some money in savings. One of these days I'll get a fixer-upper. Or find someone with a fixer-upper," he said with another of those panty-burner smiles.

"You shouldn't have any trouble finding someone." Half the bimbos in Icicle Falls would fall all over themselves to be with him.

"I've gotten particular about the kind of someone I want," he said. "Can you get me an aspirin?"

"Didn't they give you anything?"

"A prescription. All I need is an aspirin. In my medicine cabinet in the bathroom. Down the hall."

The bathroom was dinky, with worn-out linoleum. It sure didn't match the furnishings. She opened the medicine cabinet and found it pretty understocked. Aspirin, some mouthwash and deodorant, toothpaste. Plenty of condoms. What a surprise. She took out the bottle and returned to the living room. "One or two?"

"Two," he said, and watched as she shook out two pills. "You know, you make a good nurse."

She held them out to him. "Not really. No bedside manner." Oh, no. Had she just said the *B* word? She had, because her cheeks suddenly felt as if she stood in front of a roaring fire.

Instead of taking the pills he caught her wrist. "Tell me more about your bedside manner."

Oh, this was ridiculous. That little bit of skin-to-skin contact had sent an electric current running up her arm. She needed to get out of there. "Are you going to take your aspirin or do I have to stuff it down your throat?"

He took the aspirin all right. Licked it off her palm. "Have you been watching *Fifty Shades of Grey*?" She snatched her hand back.

"I don't need all those extras. I'm good all by myself."

"You obviously got more brain damage than you realize," she said.

"You oughta give me a chance. I almost got killed today."

"You got knocked over."

"What does a guy have to do to impress you?"

She raised her eyebrows. "Is that why you pulled that little boy out of the way?"

His cocky expression disappeared and so did his playful tone of voice. "What do you think?"

"I think you're full of yourself."

He grunted and turned his head away, looking at something she couldn't see. "Not much to brag about these days." She was almost feeling sorry for him when the smile came back and he added, "Except *my* bedside manner."

But it was too late. He'd removed the facade he'd been wearing ever since he came to town and given her a glimpse of a different kind of man, one who'd been broken and had some trouble putting the pieces back together again. One who, maybe, wasn't such a bad guy, after all.

He still thinks he's God's gift to women, she told herself. He was a smooth-talking heartbreaker, probably out to rebuild his confidence with notches on his belt. Not what she was looking for.

"Sit down for a while. Keep me company."

Why did she have a feeling that sitting down could quickly lead to lying down...with a sexy male body on top of her? "I've gotta be somewhere."

He frowned. "Fine. I'll just sit here all by myself and hope I don't pass out."

"Call your brother," she said, not for the first time, and then left before she was tempted to join him on that big leather couch of his.

She went to the store and got more chicken soup and some cookies. "That was some rescue," Carol the checker said as she rang up Tilda's purchases. "I heard you took him to the emergency room. Is he okay?"

Ah, small towns. Everyone knew everything about everybody. "Yeah, he's fine."

"I tell you what, that Devon Black can rescue me anytime," Carol said.

Carol the cougar was twice his age and twice divorced. Probably just his style.

"Yeah, I know," she said, "call me Mrs. Robinson. But that boy is a delicious-looking hunk of beefcake."

"Yeah, he is," Tilda agreed, and swiped her charge card. "Just ask him."

Carol gave a snort. "Ah, Tilda. You know what your problem is?"

Tilda suspected she was about to hear.

Carol handed over the receipt. "You're too picky."

"Now you sound like my mom."

Carol grinned. "I'll take that as a compliment. I love your mom."

So did Tilda, but sometimes the woman drove her nuts. She was still on the couch, burrowed under her afghan, her face flushed with fever, when Tilda returned.

"You need to go to the doctor," Tilda said.

"I will if this gets worse," Mom promised.

"If it gets any worse, you can forget the doc and go straight to the morgue."

"Just give me my cookies."

"Soup first," Tilda said.

Mom struggled to sit up and Tilda plumped the pillows behind her and tried not to envision herself plumping up pillows behind Devon Black. What was wrong with her all of a sudden? The guy did one good deed, and now all of a sudden he was Superman? She needed to get a grip.

No, she needed to get a boyfriend. She should take Georgie's advice and get online, find someone pronto, maybe even before the New Year.

"So, tell me more about this man," Mom said as Tilda served her the container of soup.

"There's nothing to tell."

Mom gave her the all-knowing-mom look. "Oh?"

Tilda could feel a blush coming on. She hated it when she blushed. "He's not my type."

"You need to redefine your type," Mom said, and took a slurp of soup. "There aren't enough firemen in Icicle Falls to go around."

"I don't need a fireman."

"Or policemen. Unless, of course, you take up with Jamal. Now *there's* the man you should be locked up with for life."

"His mama wants him to marry a nice girl from her church."

"Well, you've got the 'nice' part down," Mom said, and spooned up some more soup. "You know what your problem is? You're too picky."

Where had she heard that before? "I'm not picky," Tilda insisted.

"Then quit looking around for Superman and go for Clark Kent. When he loses the glasses he's the same guy. And you know what? Deep down they're all really just Clarks, anyway."

Tilda had to smile at that. "Maybe you're right."

Maybe she was indeed. That gave Tilda plenty to think about as she drove back to Candy Cane Lane. Darkness had fallen, the big Saturday tree-lighting ceremony was long over and people had shifted from singing Christmas songs to going out to eat. Several cars were already starting to cruise Candy Cane Lane.

Tilda had almost reached her house when she saw a little girl in pink pajamas and slippered feet making her way down Ivy Bohn's front walk, a teddy bear clutched to her chest. First a dog and now a kid—what was with Ivy Bohn that some member of her family was always escaping?

Tilda parked the car and got out, greeting the little girl just as she reached the sidewalk. "Well, hi there. Remember me? I'm your neighbor."

"Hi," said the girl, and kept walking past her.

The kid's feet were going to be frozen. Tilda fell in beside her. "Where are you going?"

The little girl's expression turned mulish. "I'm going to my daddy."

Uh-huh. "Well, then, I'll tell you what. Let's get you a coat so you don't catch a cold on the way."

Now the expression morphed into sneaky. Yep, the kid definitely knew she was in trouble. "That's okay. I don't need a coat."

"Oh, I think you do," Tilda said, and picked her up.

Her cargo strained to get away. "Put me down!"

"I will as soon as we're inside. Your mom can get your coat."

No dummy, the kid knew she was being lied to. "I want my daddy," she cried, and tried even harder to break free as Tilda strode up the walk.

Tilda rang the doorbell. At least she hoped it had rung. It was hard to hear anything over the girl's crying.

The door opened and there stood Ivy Bohn, looking first puzzled, then horrified. "Hannah! What on earth?"

"I found her going down your front walk," Tilda explained.

"I want my daddy!" Hannah wailed as Tilda placed the kid in her arms.

"Hannah, what were you thinking?" Ivy demanded.

"Daddyyyyyy."

"Come in, please," Ivy said.

"I should get home." Tilda nodded to her dark house, where nothing was happening.

"Let me at least give you some wine as a thank-you."

Now another woman was there in the hallway. Tilda recognized her from when she'd been at Christmas Haus, shopping.

"She tried to run away," Ivy said.

"The door was locked," the woman protested as if a child couldn't figure out how to turn a lock.

"This is Tilda, my next-door neighbor. Deirdre's my sister. Dee, get her a glass of wine. I'll be right back," Ivy said, and started up the stairs with her crying daughter.

Deirdre watched them go. "Sometimes I wonder if I want to have kids."

"I guess everybody survives it. My mom did."

Deirdre smiled. "Come on out to the kitchen. We're just in the process of getting fat on wine and red velvet cupcakes."

Tilda really hadn't planned on staying. She and Ivy Bohn didn't have anything in common.

Except red velvet cupcakes. Okay, she'd stay for a few minutes.

Ivy's kitchen looked like something from HGTV, with granite countertops, a fancy island, elaborate bar stools. The walls were painted a sage green. It opened out onto a large family room, beautifully furnished, with only a toy box and a playpen to prove that kids lived there.

Deirdre must have caught her staring. "Yeah. That's my sis. The high achiever. The only thing she ever did wrong was marry Rob. Although nobody thought he was wrong when they first got together." Deirdre shook her head. "What is it with men that they can't settle down?" Tilda didn't get a chance to answer because Deirdre had already moved on. "So you're the cop?"

"Yeah," Tilda said cautiously.

"If we're nice to you does that mean you won't give us tickets?" Deirdre filled a wineglass with merlot and handed it to her.

Since she was smiling, Tilda assumed she was kidding. But considering who she was related to, you never knew. "Don't hold your breath."

"Guess I'd better spend the night, then, 'cause I plan on doing some serious drinking," Deirdre confided.

"You and me both," said Ivy, walking into the room. She picked up her wineglass and took a sip. "First she's opening the door when she's not supposed to and now she's running away. And she's only four. What's she going to be like when she's fourteen?"

"I don't think you want to know," Deirdre said.

"Thank God you came along," Ivy said to Tilda. "I owe you big-time."

"Nah. A cupcake will do," Tilda said, and helped herself to one. "I suppose you made these."

Ivy acted as though it was no big deal. "Cake mix."

"Really?" Tilda could handle a cake mix.

"Do you bake?" Deirdre asked Tilda.

"Not one of my skills."

"Anybody can make cupcakes," Ivy said.

Tilda took a bite. Heaven. "Not like these. And what's this frosting?" It was like eating whipped cream.

"Family secret involving a ton of butter."

"Oh, man," Tilda said, and took another bite.

"I know," Deirdre agreed. "Red velvet orgasm. About the only kind I'm gonna get these days."

"Her creep of a boyfriend dumped her," Ivy explained.

"Fiancé," Deirdre corrected, "which made it even worse. He got cold feet."

"And the hots for someone else," Ivy added in disgust.

"If he marries her, I'm gonna send them dead fish for a wedding present," Deirdre said, and drained half her glass.

"I know the feeling," Tilda said.

"You got dumped by a fiancé?" Ivy looked at her in surprise, whether surprised that Tilda got dumped or that she'd had someone in the first place, Tilda couldn't tell.

"Just a boyfriend." At least that was what she'd thought he was. She'd thought wrong. Stupid her for not putting two and two together when he kept playing the gentleman card and not trying to get her into bed. A heck of a lot different from... No, she wasn't going to think about Mr. Not Right.

"That sucks," Deirdre said.

Tilda shrugged. "Shit happens."

"Well, here's to shit." Deirdre raised her glass. "May it happen to someone else 'cause we've had enough of it. Can I get an amen?"

"You sure can," said Ivy.

"Make that a third," Tilda threw in, and they clinked glasses.

"Have another cupcake," Ivy said to Tilda.

"Don't mind if I do."

"And stick around," said Deirdre. "We're gonna watch *Gremlins*."

Tilda would never have thought of that as an Ivy Bohn Christmas movie pick. But then, there were a lot of things she'd never have thought about Ivy. Sometimes there was more to people than you realized.

"More wine?" Ivy asked as if assuming Tilda was staying.

"Don't mind if I do." She liked that movie. And she was beginning to like Ivy Bohn.

Chapter Fourteen

Sometimes things don't go according to plan, so stay flexible.
—Muriel Sterling, *Making the Holidays Bright: How to Have a Perfect Christmas*

Maddy was just dishing up Sunday breakfast when Alan's cell phone rang. "Yo, Mark," he said. "What's up?" His Sunday-morning smile fell away, which could mean only one thing. Alan had to go into work. "No, no worries. There's a lot of that going around."

A lot of not wanting to work, if you asked Maddy. Mark called in sick at least once a month, and always on a Sunday. "Don't tell me, let me guess," she said as Alan set aside his phone. "Mark has some mysterious ailment."

"Flu," Alan said, and ate some of her ham-and-cheese strata.

"More like allergies, if you ask me. I think he's allergic to work. Why you ever put him in charge on Sundays is a mystery to me."

Alan sighed. "It's hard to get good workers. Anyway, I can't leave Wink there all by himself."

"Couldn't Joe come in?"

"Would you have wanted me to go to work one week after our daughter was born?"

Good point.

Jordan found this interesting. "Did you take off work when I was born, Daddy?"

"Of course I did," Alan said, smiling at her. "I didn't want to miss a thing."

And he hadn't. Neither of them had, really. They'd been there for every school concert, every piano recital (until Jordan decided she didn't want to take piano anymore) and every Saturday soccer game (thank God she'd given up soccer). Granted, Maddy had been a little more MIA after buying the Spice Rack, but by then she'd figured Jordan's self-esteem was pretty well boosted.

"You're going to miss a few things today," Maddy said irritably.

Alan's brow furrowed. "What did we have planned?"

"Besides church and getting the tree? How about putting our candy canes back up?"

"We'll have to get the tree tomorrow night. As for the candy canes, I guess you and Jordan will have to deal with that."

Jordan made a face and Maddy could feel her own lips turning down at the corners.

"Or you can just not bother putting any more up."

"Alan Donaldson, what a thing to say!"

He shrugged. "It's your call. But if this batch gets ruined, you're out of luck. I've sold out at the store and I can't get any more in."

"Good. They're dumb, anyway," Jordan muttered.

"They're not dumb," Maddy corrected her—again.

"Someone sure thinks they are," Alan said. "I don't know, hon. This is all starting to feel a bit like Charlie

Brown, Lucy and the football. How many times are we going to keep getting suckered into putting up candy canes for someone to come along and trash?"

"Those candy canes are going up this afternoon," Maddy insisted.

"I thought we were going to see *The Christmas Card* this afternoon," Jordan said.

The latest holiday offering was now showing at Falls Cinema, and although it looked slapstick and silly, Maddy had promised they'd go. "We are. But first we're going to put our candy canes up."

Jordan rolled her eyes.

"And no eye rolling," Maddy told her. "You'll break your eye sockets."

Jordan performed another eyeball somersault. "Whatever."

Alan washed down one more bite of casserole with his coffee, then pushed away from the table. "I'd better get going," he said, and kissed Maddy and Jordan.

Maddy watched him go and sighed. So much for the nice family day she'd planned. Ah, well, the best-laid plans and all that.

So, it was only her and Jordan at church. Well, only her, since Jordan always sat with her friends.

Maddy consoled herself by visiting with as many people as possible before the service. A lot of families had come to church together. The Lindstroms, the Claussens, the Joneses. Muriel Sterling stood at the other end of the foyer with her clan all clustered around her. The Christiansens were making their way into the sanctuary, along with their daughters, Deirdre and Ivy, and the grandchildren. Poor Ivy. Being on her own had to be hard, even with her parents nearby to help her. Maddy found herself feeling smugly thankful that her husband was still loyal and in love with her.

She decided to slip into a seat next to Ivy, just to see how she was doing. Ivy hadn't volunteered to pass out candy canes this year, and Maddy hadn't pressed her, figuring she had her hands full adjusting to her first Christmas as a single mom.

Ivy greeted her with a polite smile and a hello.

"I keep meaning to tell you how nice your lights look," Maddy said, hoping to encourage her.

"Thanks," Ivy murmured.

"Did you put them up all by yourself?" Did she sound nosy? She didn't mean to be. She was simply making conversation.

"I had a little help. Have you found out who's been knocking over the candy canes?"

The mere mention of the vandalism was enough to make Maddy grind her teeth. "Not yet. I don't think the police are trying very hard, even though we have one living in our neighborhood now."

"Well, hopefully they'll catch whoever it is soon. Meanwhile, I'm just glad they haven't gotten down as far as our place. It's so much work getting all the decorations up. I'd hate to have to keep replacing things."

"It's not fun," Maddy said, thinking of her poor squashed candy canes.

The musicians had taken their places and the service was beginning, so that was the end of the chitchat. Maddy got swept up by the music and forgot about her irritations. Pastor Jim's sermon centered on the joy of Christmas and the importance of sharing that joy with others, advice she took as an endorsement of all the joy she and her neighbors were spreading with their festive light displays.

She said as much as she and Jordan headed home, hoping to instill a fresh appreciation for everything Candy Cane Lane represented.

"I thought he was talking about doing stuff together," Jordan said, which gave Maddy hope that her daughter actually listened to the sermons.

"Well, of course, that, too."

"So, we're still going to the movie, right?"

"Yes. But first I need to do a few things at home."

"Like what?"

"Like putting our candy canes back up. Remember? You can help if you want."

"No, thanks," said Jordan.

"Well, then, while I'm doing that, you can finish your homework."

That wasn't met with great enthusiasm, either. Big surprise.

After lunch Maddy bundled up and went out into the frosty air to set up her candy canes once more. Mr. Werner came out to supervise. "I don't know why you're bothering. The same little brats are just going to come by and wreck them."

"Now, Mr. Werner, you have to think positive," Maddy said. Really, Mr. Werner was the most unpleasant—no, make that second most unpleasant—person she knew. Her mother-in-law would always hold the first-place position.

"Waste of time," he said. "I hope they catch the brats, though. I'll be more than happy to press charges. Teach 'em a lesson."

"I couldn't agree with you more," Maddy said. That was one thing she and the old curmudgeon saw eye to eye on, anyway.

She was working up a good sweat by the time Carla

Welky and her husband, Earl, stopped by. "Here, let me help you," Earl offered.

"Oh, thank you, Earl. That would be great," Maddy said.

"It's the least I can do for our resident Mrs. Santa Claus," he said with a smile.

"Oh, and speaking of Mrs. Santa Claus. I was just over at Safeway to get some more candy canes for to-night and they're sold out," Carla told her.

"That can't be. I bought some there the other day."

"Well, they're out now. Won't have any more in until the middle of the week. I've only got half a dozen left. That won't last me very long tonight."

"Don't worry," Maddy said. "I'll find you some." Johnson's Drugs probably had them in stock.

Once her decorations were put to rights, she called the drugstore. "We're all out," Hildy said, "We've got some coming in next week. You girls up there on Candy Cane Lane tapped us out."

"But you ordered extra," Maddy protested.

"Yes, and you've used them. The place gets more popular all the time. Like I said, we'll have some for you next week."

Next week didn't help her now. "Okay, thanks. Can you think of anyplace else that might have them?"

"Safeway," Hildy said.

"They're out, too."

"Well, dear, you may have to drive over to Cashmere or Wenatchee."

Oh, no. That would take too long. She'd never make it back in time for the movie. She thanked Hildy, poured herself a cup of coffee and sat down to think. She'd have to call around and see if anyone else in the neigh-borhood had extra candy canes Carla could use. Half a dozen phone calls told her that the neighborhood supply was running on peppermint fumes. Great. What now?

Jordan wandered into the kitchen. "I'm done."

"What? Oh. Good. Good job."

"The movie starts in half an hour."

"Okay. We'll leave in twenty minutes," Maddy promised, and put in a call to Carla. "I can't find candy canes anywhere."

Jordan plunked down at the table, pulled out her cell phone and got busy texting.

"I'm going to be out in no time. You know Sundays are big nights for families."

"Well, there's not much we can do. Hand out the ones you have and call it quits," Maddy said.

"Next year we should just order a whole bunch online." *We*, of course, meaning Maddy.

"Good idea." Maddy wished Carla luck, then hung up, feeling frustrated.

"Who cares if you run out of candy canes, anyway?" Jordan said.

"You cared when you were little," Maddy retorted, annoyed by her daughter's callous attitude.

"Kids just want candy. They don't care if it's candy canes or not."

Maybe her daughter had a point. Maddy called Johnson's Drugs again. "Hildy, do you, by any chance, happen to have peppermint discs?"

"Yes, we've got a couple of bags hanging in the candy section. But you didn't say you wanted discs."

"They'll do in a pinch. I'll be right there to pick them up." Maddy gave Jordan a kiss on the forehead. "You're brilliant, my darling daughter."

"Huh?"

"I'll be right back," Maddy said, grabbing her purse.

"Mom, where are you going?"

"To get some candy."

"But the movie…"

"I'll be back in time."

"No, you won't!"

"Yes, I will. Don't worry."

And she would've been—if there hadn't been a Sunday rush at the drugstore, with people standing in line to buy everything from cough drops to skin cream. Good grief. She finally made it out of there with her treasures and barreled toward home. She'd dash out of the car, throw the candy at Carla, then dash into the house. Jordan would be ready and waiting. They'd be a little late getting to the theater, but they'd probably only miss the commercials and the previews of coming attractions.

She was so intent on getting the candy to Carla and getting Jordan to the movie on time that the flashing lights didn't even register. Until the car behind her— yikes, a patrol car!—gave a short blast of its siren.

Oh, no. She didn't have time for this. But how was she going to explain her situation to the officer? There were some things men didn't understand. Two men. Groan. Oh, wait. One wasn't a man. Thank heaven. The officer getting out of the car was her new neighbor. Good. They could have a quick woman-to-woman chat and Maddy would be on her way.

She lowered her window and donned her most diplomatic smile. "Hello there."

Tilda didn't smile back. "Mrs. Donaldson, do you know how fast you were going?"

"Well, no, not exactly. I don't suppose, being neighbors and all…"

"You were going forty-five in a thirty-mile-an-hour zone. Is there some emergency at home?"

"Sort of. You see, we're out of candy canes for our Mrs. Santa Claus to pass out, and I had to run to the store and…" Did this sound kind of lame? Judging from the expression on Tilda Morrison's face, yes. "I promised my daughter I'd take her to see *The Christmas Card* and I'm late getting home and…" Now she'd gone from lame to ridiculous. "Just give me the ticket."

"License and registration, please."

Maddy dug around in her purse and produced the necessary information. "I know this is going to sound a little strange, but could you hurry, please?"

Okay, that had not been a smart thing to say. Tilda's eyes narrowed and for a minute Maddy was afraid she'd be asked to step out of the car and take a sobriety test. Because surely only someone under the influence would be stupid enough to say something like that to a cop.

"Mrs. Donaldson, I'm not sure you understand the danger of going so far over the speed limit, especially at this time of year when the roads are hazardous."

Maddy sighed. "I do. I'm sorry. It's just that I promised my daughter and… Never mind. Take your time."

Which, of course, she did. What was she doing back there, playing Trivial Pursuit with her partner? *How many tickets are given out on Sundays to women who promised to take their daughters to a movie and tried to squeeze in a run to the drugstore for peppermint candies?*

Maddy called her daughter's cell.

"Mom, where are you?"

"I'm almost home. I got stopped."

"Are you talking to someone?"

You could say that. "I got pulled over by the police."

"Jeez, for what?"

"Speeding. We'll be a little late to the movie."

As it turned out, they were a lot late. Tilda Morrison had, indeed, taken her time giving Maddy her present from the Icicle Falls Police Force, then followed her home to make sure she drove like a good citizen. She left the candies on her front porch and called Carla as she and Jordan made their way (at twenty-five miles an hour) to the theater, telling her about plan B. They arrived at the theater after the commercials, after the previews of coming attractions and after the heroine's best friend had died and her boyfriend dumped her on Christmas Eve. Well, at least they got to see her find someone new and live happily ever after.

Too bad Jordan wasn't inclined to help her mother put a happy holiday spin on the situation. Jordan sat through the movie looking as if she'd been sucking on a lemon, and even popcorn and a Coke couldn't put a smile on her face.

The smile never surfaced on the drive home, either. "I *said* you wouldn't be back in time."

"I'm sorry, sweetie."

"And there isn't another showing. I didn't even get to see Angelica die," Jordan finished on a wail.

"I know, I know. I'm very sorry. But the rest of the movie was good, wasn't it?"

Jordan didn't answer. She was now in ignore mode, texting. Probably telling Afton all about her mother's latest failure. Angelica had died and Jordan hadn't been there to witness it.

What would Muriel Sterling have said about this? Maddy didn't want to know.

* * *

Tilda came home from work to find that Mrs. Santa Claus was on duty, passing out candy. Maddy Donaldson's big emergency had been taken care of. That woman needed a life.

So do you, came the unbidden thought as she hurried to her bedroom to change.

No, she had a life. She had guys coming over to play video games and eat chips and salsa, and tomorrow her new stove was being delivered. Plenty of life.

And that, of course, was why she avoided looking in the direction of the stupid mirror some previous owner had hung on her bedroom door. (With all the stuff that had gotten bunged up in this house, couldn't someone have made off with the mirror?) As long as she didn't look, she couldn't see the black lacy bra and matching thong. And if she didn't see the fancy lingerie, she didn't have to think about the fact that not one of the guys coming over to play would be staying for more adult games later on. And if she didn't think about that, she wouldn't ponder the suitability of a certain bad boy who seemed to have a hidden good side, a certain bad boy who wasn't what she was looking for, even if he did have one lucky moment when he'd actually behaved like a grown-up instead of a teenager stuck in a man's body.

And what a body it is, whispered her hormones.

Stop that!

She pulled on jeans and an old Washington State sweatshirt that proved her loyalty to her alma mater, and went into the kitchen to put together the evening's refreshments—chips and salsa and beer. Half an hour later, she and three guys (two cops and one EMT thrown in for good measure) were whooping it up, drinking beer and shooting one another on her TV screen. Three and a half hours after that, it was just her and her lacy undies, getting ready for bed. Alone. Oh, well. Life wasn't all bad. Her new stove was coming tomorrow. Finally.

But on Monday there was no stove. She finally called Arvid's Appliances at one in the afternoon.

"We ran into a scheduling problem," he explained. "We'll have it to you tomorrow, no problem."

"Okay, but you need to deliver it by three-thirty." She was on second shift now and she couldn't wait around all day.

"We'll have it to you by noon. No worries."

No worries, huh? Well, okay.

But by two in the afternoon, it still hadn't arrived.

All she got when she called the appliance store was a voice message. "This is Arvid. Glad you called! We're open from 10:00 a.m. to 7:00 p.m. six days a week, ten to five on Sundays. If we're not answering it's because we're busy helping another satisfied customer, so leave your name and number, and we'll call you back. Then you can be a satisfied customer, too. Remember, we sell it, we fix it and we make your life simple."

Oh, yeah? "Arvid, this is Tilda Morrison. You promised to deliver my stove by noon and it's two and I'm still waiting. I have to leave for work at quarter to four. Call me. Or better yet, get my stove over here."

Arvid was either helping a lot of customers or he was hiding from her. Well, you could run but you couldn't hide from an Icicle Falls cop. She decided to pay Arvid a little visit on her way to work.

When he saw her walk into the store all dressed in her police uniform, accessorized with her 45 mm Glock, he blanched like a crook caught with the goods. "Oh,

Officer Morrison. I'll bet you're anxious to have that great stove."

"You could say that." She leaned on the counter. "What happened to my stove, Arvid?"

"I do apologize. We hit a snag."

"A snag. You were supposed to deliver it last week. And then you were supposed to deliver it yesterday. And now it's Tuesday and I still don't have it. I'm cooking dinner for my family on Christmas Eve, and I'd like to be able to use it once before then. You know, get the hang of it." She gave him the look that made even honest citizens tremble.

"I guarantee you'll have it," he promised, sounding like a human oil slick. "You'll get it…"

"Tomorrow," she finished with him. "Have you noticed what I'm wearing?"

"Very flattering," he said with a toothy grin.

"Glad you like it." Okay, she'd burn in hell for this. "What kind of car do you drive, Arvid?"

The grin faltered and Arvid's forehead began to glisten as tiny beads of sweat formed. "Oh, just a nondescript little compact."

"And I'm sure you obey all the traffic rules."

He blinked. "Of course."

"Because you're just as good a citizen as you are a businessman."

He nodded eagerly. "Of course."

"And my stove will be delivered tomorrow."

"Of course."

And, of course, it wasn't. Arvid had better drive very carefully.

Chapter Fifteen

A little impromptu party with friends at a local gathering spot is a good way to relieve holiday stress.

—Muriel Sterling, *Making the Holidays Bright: How to Have a Perfect Christmas*

"Let's do something tonight," Deirdre said as she and Ivy stood at their twin cash registers, ringing up sales.

"I'm too pooped. All I want to do is go home and flop on the couch for about a million years."

"You sound like an old woman."

"And what's wrong with that?" demanded a gray-haired customer wearing a Santa hat. "We old women have a lot of life left in us."

"Oh, yes," Deirdre murmured, her whole face glowing red. She took a string of candy-cane lights from the woman and rang them up. Once the woman had muttered a disgusted, "Hmmph," and departed, Deirdre returned her attention to her sister. "It's Rob's weekend to have the kids, right?"

"Don't remind me." The weekend was already stretching out in front of Ivy like a long, lonely, rock-strewn path, and she wasn't looking forward to rattling around in the house with only the dog for company.

"Come on, it's Friday. You can't sit around the house moping."

"Sure I can," Ivy said, and dredged up a smile for another customer. "Hello, Merry Christmas." *Bah, humbug.*

Nicole had joined them now, having just helped someone find an ornament shaped like the infamous leg lamp from *A Christmas Story.* "Are you guys going out tonight? I wanna come."

"Deirdre's going out," said Ivy. "I'm staying home."

"Like a lump," Deirdre said, obviously hoping to shame her into wanting to party when she was in a no-parties-ever-again mood.

"Come to the Man Cave with me," Nicole said. "There's a darts tournament tonight. Winner gets a bottle of peppermint schnapps."

Deirdre made a face. "The guys who go there are all such losers."

"Not all of them," insisted Nicole. "And what about that cute bartender?"

"He's married."

"I'm not talking about Todd. I'm talking about his brother, Devon. He fills in on Fridays." Nicole fanned herself. "Oh, my gosh. He's just what I want for Christmas."

"It might be kind of fun," Deirdre said. "Anyway, it beats sitting at home," she added, and looked meaningfully at her sister.

"I'll pass." The last thing Ivy wanted to do was go trolling for men in a seedy dump like the Man Cave. Actually, she didn't want to go trolling for men anywhere. What was the point? You fell in love, had a family and wound up alone. Whoo boy, the pity party was starting early. *Rockin' around the Christmas tree, guess that won't be me.*

"If you change your mind..." Nicole said.

"She won't. Once she decides something, it's set in cement."

Deirdre said this as if it was a bad thing and Ivy frowned at her. "What's wrong with that?"

Deirdre shrugged. "Nothing, I guess. Except sometimes it's good to change your mind, go with the flow. Live a little."

"I'll remember that," Ivy said, and greeted another customer.

Live a little. Easy for her sister to say. She didn't have kids. Who had time to live when you had kids?

A woman who didn't have hers for the weekend. She *should* do something.

But once she'd picked Hannah and Robbie up from her parents' and gotten home, she didn't have the inclination to do anything other than tap into her inner Scrooge. She had them ready to go by the time Rob arrived, Hannah's clothes packed in her pink-and-lavender princess backpack with its quilted castle and her name on it, and Robbie's diaper bag full to overflowing, in addition to his Thomas the Tank Engine backpack.

"Daddy!" Hannah squealed, and jumped for Rob's arms when Ivy opened the front door.

Not to be outdone Robbie stretched up both hands. "Dada, uppy."

He kissed Hannah, set her down and lifted up Robbie. Then he smiled at Ivy, the polite, wary smile of a man walking on thin relationship ice. "You look good."

No, she didn't. She looked tired. She needed to get

her hair done. Maybe she'd do that tomorrow, stop by
the salon on her lunch break and see how Missy had enjoyed her honeymoon in Hawaii.

"You got plans for the weekend?"

None of his business. But she'd let him think she did.
Going to the salon counted as plans, didn't it? "For tomorrow. Tonight I'm too tired to do anything." And why
was she confessing this to her ex as if they were buddies or something?

He nodded. "Figured you would be."

"Let's go, Daddy," Hannah said, grabbing his hand,
tired of sharing her father's attention.

"Okay, time to go get pizza."

Friday night was always pizza night when they were
married, and Rob was keeping up the tradition with the
kids. Ivy hadn't had a pizza since the divorce was final.
"Don't give Robbie pepperoni or sausage," she reminded
him.

"I know already. Don't worry," Rob told her.

She couldn't help worrying. But it wasn't her weekend. She didn't get a say in what the kids ate when they
were with Daddy. She didn't get a say in anything. *You
need a break*, she lectured herself. *Be glad he wants
to stay involved in their lives.* He wanted to be part of
hers, too. Tough. People didn't always get what they
wanted in life.

Once she decides something, it's set in cement. Nothing wrong with that. Cement was sturdy. It protected you.

"Daddy," Hannah said imperiously.

"Right. Off we go."

Ivy watched as they went down the front walk, Robbie
looking at her from over his father's shoulder, Hannah
skipping alongside Rob, the tassel on the red hat Ivy had

knitted for her bouncing. Ivy sighed and shut the door. She turned on her TV, got out her knitting and wished she was going out for pizza with her family.

No, no. She was better off sitting here on the couch, encased in cement.

Half an hour later, she was still on the couch, just a girl, her yarn and the TV, when the doorbell rang. She opened the door to find a man in jeans and a parka, bearing a large insulated pizza carrier.

"I didn't order a pizza," she told him.

"Someone ordered it for you." He handed her the box and a folded sheet of paper. "Have a nice night," he said and hurried down the walk to his car with the lighted Italian Alps sign on the roof.

Ivy shut the door and read the note. *So you don't have to cook. Rob.* She frowned. Now he was trying to bribe his way back. Well, she couldn't be bribed.

But darn, that pizza smelled good. She opened the box. Barbecued chicken, her fave. She carried it into the living room and set it on the coffee table. Now it was just a girl, her yarn, the TV and her favorite pizza. Come to think of it, she was hungry. No sense letting this go to waste.

Oh, wow, that was good.

But she was eating alone. She was going to spend the whole darn night alone.

Rob had a life. She should have one, too.

She finished her slice of pizza and went upstairs to take a bath. And shave her legs. And put on her tightest jeans. She was going out.

Eight o'clock found her walking into the dark, seedy den that was the Man Cave. Billy Williams, one of the town characters, was playing pool with two other guys all decked out in worn jeans and baseball caps worn backward to cover their bald spots. A hefty man sporting a Santa hat and a beer belly was working the pinball machine, while several men, most of them older, hunched along the bar at the far end of the tavern, nursing beers or whiskies. The real action was taking place in one corner. There, a couple of cute guys in their early thirties were busy playing darts and flirting with Deirdre and Nicole. Then there was the man standing behind the bar, washing glasses and observing the action. Devon Black. Oh, he was enough to make a woman consider a second chance at love. Except she'd seen him hanging around Tilda's place. If they were an item, she didn't want to poach. She would never poach another woman's man.

Unlike the cheap blonde coming out of the restroom. Ashley Armstrong. There wasn't a man in town she hadn't gone after since Garrett Armstrong divorced her, and that included Rob. In fact, she'd gotten her talons into him practically the second he moved out. Someone had seen them having dinner at Zelda's on Valentine's Day, and it had gotten back to Ivy faster than Cupid's arrow. He hadn't stayed with Ashley for very long, but she was still the other woman. Oh, this was beyond awkward.

She spotted Ivy and narrowed her eyes and tossed her long blond, split-ended hair. Then she sashayed over to where the dart players were partying and took a seat at the bar, picking up a half-downed glass of what looked like cola. Probably rum and Coke. Was she playing darts? More to the point, were Deirdre and Nicole playing darts with her, the traitors?

Ivy hovered near the entrance, trying to decide if she should go back home to her pizza. Yes. Bad enough to have been humiliated, but then to hang around and have

Ashley looking down on her with an I-took-your-man smirk. Eew.

Just then Deirdre saw her. She waved and called Ivy's name, drawing everyone's attention to her. Okay, if she left now, it would be a case of letting the other woman win—again. She had no choice but to join them. She should've stayed home. Why had she bothered to shave her legs? There was no one here she wanted.

"Well, if it isn't the perfect Mrs. Bohn," Ashley sneered as she walked past. "Except it turned out you weren't so perfect, didn't it?"

"And it turned out you weren't so sexy, didn't it?" Ivy retorted, making Ashley's face redden.

"I dumped him, you know," Ashley said. "He was lousy in bed."

"Funny, that's what I've always heard about you."

"Hey, now, ladies. No fighting," Devon said pleasantly. "What can I get you?" he asked Ivy.

"Give her some Icicle Orchards cider," Deirdre told him.

"Is she playing darts with you?" she asked Deirdre, nodding in Ashley's direction.

Deirdre bit her lower lip. "It's a tournament. We couldn't tell her to take a hike."

"I knew I should've stayed home," Ivy muttered.

Ashley, who'd been pretending not to eavesdrop, inserted herself in the conversation. "Then why don't you go home? You can't play now, anyway. The tournament's already started."

Ivy picked up her glass. "I'm just here to watch." She turned her back on the tacky man stealer and went to stand by Nicole, who was watching as one of the guys threw his darts.

"Wow, two triples and a bull's-eye," Nicole gushed. "I wish I could do that."

"Just takes practice," said her competitor. He smiled at Ivy. "Hey, there."

Nicole introduced her. Then, as he walked over to the dartboard to retrieve his darts, she leaned over and whispered, "He's the new guy who works at Safeway. Isn't he cute?"

Yeah, but he didn't have as cute a butt as Rob did. Right now Rob would be putting Hannah to bed, listening to her bedtime prayers. Maybe he was reading her a story. After that, he'd probably watch some action flick.

She remembered when they used to cuddle on the couch and watch movies together and suddenly felt like crying. Instead, she downed some more cider. That stuff had a kick.

The other guy, introduced as Ben, took a turn and his three darts all embedded themselves in one of the red bars in the middle of the circle.

"Nice," said his pal. "But I'm still kicking your ass."

"I'm gonna kick all your asses," bragged Ashley from her bar stool. Ivy wished she'd fall off and break hers.

It was now Deirdre's turn with the darts. Since when did she play darts?

Since never. Two of her darts bounced off the board onto the old wooden floor and one stuck in the wall. "Oops," she said, and giggled.

"Ha! She can't even hit the dartboard." Ashley chortled.

"Isn't it time for you to go home with someone?" Ivy asked her sweetly.

Ashley turned her back. "Give me another rum and Coke."

Another drink. Good idea. Ivy finished the rest of her cider and ordered a refill.

The competition went on, with the men doing backward math and writing numbers on the scoreboard. And Ivy sipped away at her cider and visited.

This was kind of fun...as long as she ignored Ashley. Oh, who cared about...Ashleeeey? Ivy's tongue was feeling fuzzy. Just like her head.

Deirdre stepped up to the line again, her lower lip caught between her teeth, concentrating on her target. One dart stuck at the outside of the wheel. The other two wound up on the floor.

"Another loser, just like her sister," Ashley said under her breath.

Ivy whirled on her. *Whoa, let's not turn around so fast.* "Talk about losers." Had that just come out as *looshers*? "You haven't been able to keep one single man you've latched onto."

"I kept yours. Until I didn't want him anymore. And that's more than you can say, isn't it?"

Critical mass, boiling point, had enough! With a screech, Ivy lunged for Ashley. Ashley lunged right back and suddenly they were pulling at hair, trying to scratch out eyeballs, bouncing off tables and pretty much putting on a show while the other patrons of the Man Cave cheered them on.

Ashley landed a solid punch to Ivy's right eye. Oh, look, the stars had come out in the Man Cave. Maybe Ashley would like an indoor night-sky tour, too. Ivy took aim and missed, her ring cutting Ashley's lip in the process, making her squeal like a stuck pig.

Of course, now that blood had been drawn, the fighting really started, with the combatants ricocheting off the bar, sending glasses and beer bottles flying and tipping bar stools. "I've got a ten on Ash," somebody called as another bar stool crashed to the floor.

Ivy was vaguely aware of her sister crying, "Call the police!" as she landed in some guy's lap.

"Don't spoil the fun," he said right before Ashley knocked her onto the floor.

Oh, yeah, they were having fun now.

"What a surprise," Jamal said as he hit the siren, "a brawl at the Man Cave."

"It beats lurking on Icicle Road, giving out traffic tickets," Tilda said.

"How much you want to bet we find your buddy Black at the bottom of it?"

"He's not my buddy," Tilda said through gritted teeth. Which of them was she trying to convince?

"I hope you've got better taste than that, Til."

So did she, but ever since she'd witnessed Devon Black scooping that little boy out of harm's way in the Safeway parking lot, she'd had the sneaking suspicion that her taste was beginning to change. Of course, they probably *would* find him behind the trouble tonight, back to his old tricks, hitting on other men's women, picking fights, showing his true colors.

The atmosphere as they entered the tavern was like a Las Vegas fight night, with men cheering and hooting, money changing hands as bets were made. There, at the center of the mayhem, were two women intent on beating the crap out of each other. And one of them was...

"Oh, for crying out loud," Tilda growled, and pushed her way through the spectators.

Jamal was right behind her and each of them took hold

of a combatant. In the process Ashley tried to throw a punch at Ivy and caught Tilda on the side of the head.

"Whoa, that's enough of that," Jamal said, pulling her away while Tilda hung on to Ivy.

"She started it!" Ashley cried. "You bitch!"

Ivy?

"I did not!" Ivy yelled back.

Tilda frowned at her. "What the heck are you doing?"

"I'm…" Ivy waved a hand about wildly. "I'm…"

"You broke a nail," Tilda informed her, and Ivy burst into tears.

"Who started this?" Jamal was asking.

Ivy's sister and another woman Tilda didn't know both pointed at Ashley. "She did!"

Tilda doubted they were unbiased witnesses. She looked around the little crowd of men gathered there listening as intently as they would to a Seahawks game on the radio. "Did anyone see anything?"

Billy Williams, aka Bill Will, said, "Nah. We were playing pool. Next thing we know, it's World War Z in here."

"Thanks, Bill Will. That was really helpful," Tilda said, frowning at him.

She went over to where Devon Black stood behind the bar, dressed casually in jeans and a black T-shirt stretched over an enticing set of pecs. "Can you tell me who started this?"

"Bet you thought it was me when you took the call."

That was exactly what she'd thought.

Fortunately, he didn't wait for an answer because that might've been embarrassing. "I don't know. I was busy pulling beer. One thing I can tell you, Ash has been taking potshots at the other chick all night long."

"Why?"

Devon shrugged. "I get the impression Ash and her husband were seeing each other for a while."

That would do it.

In the state of Washington, whoever threw the first punch was the one who got hauled away, but since nobody *knew* who threw the first punch... Aw, heck, she ought to haul 'em both off. Except she'd grown to like Ivy and she felt a little bit sorry for her. Bad enough to run into someone her man had been seeing, but then to make a fool of herself in public. Oh, boy. She was not going to be a happy camper come morning.

Tilda returned to where Jamal stood, trying to talk to the two women. Ashley was standing with her hands on her hips, glaring at Ivy and informing her what a sub-par female she was. Ivy was... Oh, no. "Jamal, move out of the way!"

Too late. Ivy upchucked on him.

"Shit!" He jumped back and looked at his chest in revulsion.

Tilda took Ivy by the arm and hauled her aside. "What the hell are you doing?"

"I'm...having a life," Ivy said, and burst into fresh tears.

"This is not the kind of life you want to have," Tilda said sternly. "Devon, come here."

Devon obliged, all business.

"Since it's unclear who threw the first punch..." Tilda began.

"Let 'em both off," Devon suggested, handing Jamal a bar towel.

Tilda shook her head. "With no consequences? Uh-

uh. I'm thinking you ladies need to pay for damages. And you need to eighty-six them," she said to Devon.

"That's not fair!" Ashley protested.

"Or we can haul your ass to jail," Tilda went on.

Ashley clamped her split lips shut, then winced.

Devon shrugged. "How about we ban them for a month? I don't think this one will ever be back," he said, nodding at Ivy, who was crying and apologizing to Jamal. "But a month will just about kill poor Ash."

Apparently it was already killing her. "Why me? I didn't start this."

Ivy jabbed a finger at her. "You started it when you stole my husband!"

"He'd already dumped you, and I can see why."

Tilda held up a hand. "That's enough."

Ashley crossed her arms and scowled, and Ivy hung her head.

"Take her home," Tilda ordered Deirdre, then said to Ivy, "I don't want to see you in here again. Ever."

"I don't want to be in here again. Ever," Ivy said, all the fight drained out of her.

"You need to arrest her," Ashley demanded. "She attacked me."

"You have no witnesses," Tilda informed her. "It's your word against hers."

"I'm gonna sue!" Ashley roared.

"You're going to stop making an ass of yourself," Tilda said firmly. "Now, I can either throw you both in the drunk tank, or you can agree to behave yourselves and not to press charges. Which is it going to be?"

"I just want to forget this," Ivy said miserably.

Ashley was pouting now, but she nodded her agreement.

"And you'd better not let me catch you driving," Tilda added, pointing at her.

Ashley flopped on the one remaining upright bar stool and grabbed her drink, still pouting.

"I'll take her home," Bill Will offered, probably hoping to get lucky, but as far as Tilda was concerned, Ashley was no prize.

"I need to get cleaned up," Jamal said as they walked back to the patrol car.

"I tried to warn you."

He shook his head. "Gotta say, that's the first fight I've ever broken up between women." He grinned. "Kinda sexy."

"You are a cretin," Tilda said in disgust.

The rest of the night was relatively quiet. A few speeding tickets and a DUI—good, old Ashley, the man stealer. Tilda smiled as they put her in the back of the squad car. She loved her job.

Chapter Sixteen

Think of drop-in company as a holiday bonus rather than an inconvenience.
—Muriel Sterling, *Making the Holidays Bright: How to Have a Perfect Christmas*

Something horrible was assaulting Ivy's brain. It sounded like a jackhammer. She pulled her pillow over her head to make it stop. Ow. The pillow felt like it was made out of lead. And the jackhammer kept drilling. She fumbled for the alarm clock, found it and gave it a good slap and the jackhammer subsided. But that didn't stop her head from hurting. And now someone was spinning the bed. *All I want for Christmas is to make this stop, to make this stop, to make this...oooh, please God. I'll never drink again.*

She lay in bed, stared at the ceiling and willed herself to feel better. She didn't have time for this. She had to get to the shop. Where she would throttle her sister for talking her into drinking that killer stuff. What a mistake.

No, the mistake had been going out in the first place. She should've stayed home and eaten pizza. She might have weighed a pound more this morning, but at least she wouldn't have had a hangover.

She eventually managed to get up, stagger to the bathroom and down a glass of water and some aspirin. The physical fallout from her girls' night out could be dealt with easily enough. Not the emotional fallout, though. She was now the fool of Icicle Falls and the idea of having to see anyone today made her want to throw up. Except she'd already done that last night, all over a cop.

She looked at herself in the mirror. Smeared makeup, tangled hair, dark circles under her eyes. Ugh. *Would you buy a snow globe from this woman?* With a groan, she turned on the shower. The hot water streaming over her skin felt good. If only she could wash away her humiliation.

She dressed and put on makeup, made herself some toast and peppermint tea, and went out to face the world. The one bonus was that she wouldn't see any of the occupants of the Man Cave in her Christmas shop. If she went straight home from work, maybe she could avoid seeing anyone who'd witnessed her abysmal behavior the night before.

She got in late, but thankfully Deirdre had already opened the shop. Clad in her favorite blue dirndl, she was waiting on an early-bird shopper who'd stocked up on glass ornaments. The shop was aglow with lit trees and bright ornaments. Brightness everywhere. Ugh. Ivy was tempted to leave her sunglasses on. Walking carefully, so as not to disturb the little gremlins playing baseball with that aspirin inside her brain, she went to the back room and stowed away her purse and coat.

She was barely out when a woman with two noisy children assaulted her, wanting to know where the nutcrackers were. "Right up the stairs, at the far end of the room," Ivy said, and breathed a sigh of relief as they moved away.

"How are you doing?" Deirdre greeted her.

"Just great. The whole world knows about Rob and Ashley now." But the whole world had known all along.

"They already did," Deirdre said, voicing her thought.

And last night she'd provided the gossips of Icicle Falls with another juicy tidbit. Ivy rested her elbows on the display counter and let her heavy, hurting head drop into her hands. "My life is a joke."

"It could be worse. You could have gotten in a fight at Zelda's and everybody goes there."

"Except Ashley, who was at the Man Cave." Ivy shook her head. *Oh, don't do that.* "I should've stayed home last night."

Deirdre put an arm around her. "I'm sorry, sis. I had no idea that skank would be there."

"It's not your fault I'm a loser."

"You are not a loser," Deirdre said.

"Public brawling." Ivy groaned. "Who does that?"

Now Nicole had joined them and was ringing up a purchase. "Someone who's provoked beyond reason," she said. "Anyway, Ashley's the loser. I'm glad she's been banned from the Man Cave."

"She ought to be banned from Icicle Falls," said Deirdre.

Nicole finished the sale. The customer left with a smile, and no wonder. She'd not only gotten some beautiful hand-blown glass ornaments, she'd also gotten a nice little serving of gossip.

"I thought she was with Bill Will," said Nicole.

"He must have come to his senses," Deirdre said. "Just like Rob did."

"No, he didn't. If he had he would've gone to Ivy

and begged her to take him back," Nicole said, her tone wrathful.

Now here was another customer, listening eagerly. "Guys, can we talk about this later?" Ivy whispered. Or not at all. Ivy pulled herself together. "Did you find everything you were looking for?" she asked the woman.

"Oh, yes." And then some.

"We're better than the soaps," Ivy said as the customer walked out. "I need another aspirin."

Two more aspirin, a quart of water and another couple of hours had Ivy feeling almost normal again. Maybe she was going to live, after all. Tonight she'd have some more pizza. *Oh, no. Not that!* protested her stomach. Okay, make that cheese and crackers. So, tonight she'd have some cheese and crackers, bring out the yarn, turn on the TV and stay put. Not very exciting, but it sure beat getting drunk and getting her hair pulled.

Tilda's stove arrived. It was a regular holiday miracle.

"There you go," said Arvid's son, Mike. "All hooked up and ready to roll."

Oh, yeah. It was a thing of beauty, with gleaming stainless steel and a glass cooktop, and it was begging her to break it in. *You can learn to use me. Come on, give it a try. Walk on the wild side.*

Well, why not? She got Mike out the door, promising not to give his dad a ticket—unless he was speeding—then put on her coat and drove to Safeway. On her way she called her mom. "I'm going to the store. Do you need anything?"

"A new body," Mom croaked.

She sounded awful. "Are you getting any better?"

"I don't know," Mom said, sounding both phlegmy

and grumpy. "This thing's gonna be with me until the Fourth of July."

"Well, you don't have until the Fourth of July to get well. We want you well for Christmas."

"I will be," Mom promised. "I'm not missing out on Christmas Eve in your new house. Did the stove come yet?"

"Just got here. I'm about to break it in."

"Don't break it," Mom teased, and then started coughing up a lung or two.

"You need to go to the doctor."

"I do not. What's he going to do? They can't treat a virus."

"You've probably got bronchitis by now," said Dr. Tilda. "If you don't go in, you'll end up with pneumonia."

"You worry too much."

"Let's see. You smoke, you work too hard. You stay up till all hours watching those dumb TV cop shows. Why would I worry?"

"They aren't dumb. Gives me a good sense of what you're doing."

Oh, yeah. The cops on those shows always had interesting cases or were in the middle of shoot-outs. Tilda chased deaf horses and broke up catfights. "Look. I really think you should see the doctor. I'll come and get you right now." The stove could wait.

"You will not," Mom snapped. "Go play with your stove."

"How about if I get you some more soup?"

"And some Oreos. Oreos will make me feel better."

"And some Oreos," Tilda repeated. Did getting her mom Oreos when she was sick make them codependent?

"Or better yet, bake me some cookies in that new oven of yours," said Mom. "Hey, and you could make some soup while you're at it," she added, then fell into a barking cough.

It'd be easier to pick up Oreos. "You never taught me to make soup. Remember?"

"That's what the internet's for." More coughing.

This was ridiculous. "You've got until tomorrow to get better. If you're not, I'm taking you to the emergency room."

Mom turned testy. "I don't need people telling me what to do. I'm not in my dotage yet."

"Maybe not, but I think all that coughing has unhinged your brain."

"I don't know how I ended up with such a smart mouth for a daughter," Dot grumbled.

"Heredity. I mean it, Mom. You really need to get some help."

"I will," Mom promised with a sigh—and another cough.

Tilda reiterated her threat to haul the stubborn woman to the doctor and then said goodbye before she could protest any further.

Once at the store, the first thing she did was buy more soup. Homemade soup? What was Mom thinking, anyway?

Making soup was out of the question, but she could do cookies. She picked up some red and green M&M's, then moved on to the baking aisle and got brown sugar. Oh, man, look at all those cake mixes. And there was one for red velvet cake. She could make cupcakes for Christmas Eve.

She'd just picked up the box and was studying the directions when a voice behind her said, "Well, hey, if it isn't the cooking cop."

Devon Black. Why wasn't he home, sleeping or hammering or…something? Why was he here, smelling like woodsy aftershave and looking all solid and manly and tempting? "What are you doing here?"

He held up a shopping basket filled with lettuce and tomatoes, cheese and flour tortillas. And was that a can of black beans she saw? Her basket seemed woefully undernourished in comparison, with her store-made soup and her M&M's. *And brown sugar. Can't forget the brown sugar.*

"Gonna do some baking?" he asked.

"My mom's sick. She wants cookies."

"And red velvet cake." He motioned to the cake mix.

"That's for Christmas Eve. I'm making cupcakes." As if he needed to know that. As if she needed to even tell anyone she was making cupcakes. One new stove and she was turning into Miss Food Network.

He nodded and faked looking impressed. "You're a regular Barefoot Contessa."

"Who?"

"Never mind. You might want to do a trial run on those cupcakes."

"I think I can handle it."

"Uh-huh." Devon moved farther down the baking aisle and she dropped the cake mix into her shopping basket, then started for the checkout at a good clip, intent on ditching him.

Ditching was one thing. Settling down her stirred-up hormones quite another. *Cut it out*, she told them. *We're not interested.*

Oh, yes, we are! they chorused.

Devon followed her to the checkout like a lost puppy. Lost puppy? Yeah, right. More like a wolf.

"You're not very good at losing a tail, are you?" he taunted.

"It's a free country. You can stand in line anywhere you want."

"Good, 'cause I want to stand behind you. The view's great."

She frowned at him. "You're…"

"Charming?" he supplied.

"That wasn't the word I was thinking of. More like obnoxious."

He shrugged. "I've been called worse."

"I can imagine."

"But not by women," he added smugly.

"Oh, brother."

"You know, I'm a lot of fun when you get to know me."

Let's find out, suggested her hormones.

Let's not. "Yep, fun just follows you everywhere you go. And then we get called to clean up the mess."

"Oh, yeah, I forgot. You're prejudiced. I'll bet you were real disappointed to get to the Man Cave last night and find you couldn't arrest me."

She pulled out her snottiest smile for him. "It *was* a disappointment."

"What can I say? I'm a lover, not a fighter."

That sent the hormones into a frenzy, dancing around and singing, "You're So Cute I Want to Wear You Like a Suit."

Tilda told them and Devon to knock it off.

He lifted both hands, palms up. "What? I'm stating a fact. Just the facts, ma'am," he said, waggling his eyebrows.

Damn, but he was cute when he did that. Tilda turned her back on him. Enough already.

"Hi, Til," Carol the checker greeted her. "Looks like you're getting ready to do some Christmas baking."

"That should be interesting," Devon said under his breath.

She decided to ignore him.

"I'm going to get all my baking done this afternoon," Carol said. "Just in case. You heard we're supposed to get hit with a big storm tonight or tomorrow?"

"No." That would make life interesting. Downed power lines, people skidding off the road. It would be a busy work night.

"Power outage?" Devon said. "Candlelight, fire in the fireplace."

"You don't have a fireplace," Tilda reminded him.

"No, but you do," he said with a grin.

Let it snow, let it snow, let it snow, sang the hormones, and it was all Tilda could do not to yell, "Shut up!"

"No cooking, either, so you'd better make everything now while you can," Carol advised.

"Good idea," Tilda said, and swiped her charge card. It was also a good idea to get out of here and away from Devon Black. "Thanks, Carol."

"Merry Christmas," Carol said as Tilda skedaddled on out.

Devon didn't say anything.

Back home, Tilda unpacked her grocery bag. She opened the M&M's and snitched a few. Then she melted some butter in the microwave, set the oven to preheat and started putting together her cookie dough. Cookies first. Then she'd make the cupcakes and run everything over to Mom.

She'd just finished with the dough when her doorbell rang. She went to answer it, hoping it wasn't Maddy Donaldson with some new crisis.

It wasn't Maddy. She would've preferred Maddy. "What are you doing here?"

Devon grinned at her and held up a package of cupcake liners. "You need these if you're gonna make cupcakes," he said, sauntering in.

"How do you know stuff like that?" Oh, yeah. The girlfriend who taught him how to cook. Among other things.

"My mom makes cupcakes all the time."

There was something about a man mentioning his mom that was like a secret sauce. Pour it over him and suddenly he was completely irresistible.

But she'd manage to resist somehow. "You had a mom. Gosh, I thought you were hatched."

"Hey, chickens are moms, too. So, need help?"

"No."

"You sure? Don't forget, I've seen you in the kitchen."

He thought this was the way to her heart? She narrowed her eyes and prepared to lambaste him.

"Come on, let me do my good deed for the day and help you. And you can make up for being so shitty to me last time I was over."

"Uninvited," she reminded him.

"You know, sometimes relationships are like cookies. You burn a batch, you try again. It turns out not so bad, and you think, 'Hey, I'm glad I gave it a second chance.' Did it ever occur to you we might be like that?"

"No," she said irritably.

He took a step closer, and she was suddenly aware of how solid and well put together he was. "You're too late on the cookies. I'm almost done," she said, and turned back to the kitchen. To prove it, she shoved the baking sheet in the oven.

"Whoa, nice oven."

"It'll get the job done."

"Yeah? We'll see," he teased. "You might want to set the timer."

Oh. Yeah. Now, how to do that? She studied the stove.

He reached around her and pushed the set-timer button, then chose the minutes and pushed it again.

"I was going to do that," she said, but they both knew she was lying. "Okay, I was going to do it as soon as I figured it out."

He grinned, even more roguishly than before. "I like a woman who can admit when she's wrong." Then his voice softened. "Can you do that, Tilda? Can you admit when you've been wrong about someone?"

He was standing so close, their bodies were practically touching. Was it getting hot in here? "You're not my type," she reminded him. Or was it herself she was reminding?

"Maybe you need to rethink that," he said softly. His lips were almost on hers. *Whoopee!* howled her hormones.

No, no, no. She was not taking up with the likes of Devon Black. He'd said it himself. He was a lover. And she knew what that really meant—a lover and a leaver, as in love 'em and leave 'em. Well, she wasn't going to be one of the 'ems.

Even though her black thong was about to spontaneously combust, she stepped away, leaving him kissing air.

He frowned at her. "You're a tease."

"Yeah? Well, you're a heartbreaker, so we can call it even."

"So, that's it. You think I'm going to break your little policewoman's heart?"

She narrowed her eyes and pointed a warning finger at him. "Don't you mock me."

"Cops are supposed to be brave."

"I am brave," she snapped. "And I'm not stupid." She marched over to the counter where her bowl of cookie dough sat waiting, then dug the mixing spoon in, pulled out a dollop of dough and slammed it on the second cookie sheet.

"I don't know. I think you're kind of chicken."

She looked over her shoulder. There he stood, leaning against the stove, arms crossed, surveying her with a frown that mirrored her own. "Just because I don't want the playboy of Icicle Falls messing with my head."

"The only one messing with your head is you," he retorted. Then he smiled. "I was more interested in messing with other body parts."

"Ha! That proves it. You're not serious. A man like you doesn't understand the meaning of the word *serious*."

His smile fell away. "Yeah?"

She shook her head and went back to her cookie dough. "Yeah. And we both know it."

"You don't know squat. You haven't spent enough time with me to know much of anything."

"All you want is to get drunk and get laid, and as long as you make enough to party, life is good." Okay, that was a pretty shallow summary, and she immediately regretted the words. She bit her lip. Too late to contain the harsh words that had come out.

He flinched. "You've got a real mean streak, don't you?"

He was right. She did. When did she get so mean?

"Did you ever stop to wonder if maybe I'm tired of relationships that go nowhere? Tired of being by myself, having nothing to show for my life but a bunch of newspaper clippings?"

The timer on the stove went off. Saved by the bell. Tight-lipped, Tilda put on the new oven mitt Georgie had given her. Equally tight-lipped, Devon moved out of the way.

Then he spoke. "Your oven's not hot."

She opened the door. No blast of heat greeted her. She pulled out the cookie sheet and found uncooked mounds of dough with red and green candies peeking out. "What's wrong with it?"

"Did you turn it on?" he asked.

She sent him a scorching glare. "What do you think?"

He looked at the little window at the front of the stove that said 350. Then he looked inside. "Your heating element's out."

"What?" She looked inside, too. Sure enough. Instead of glowing red, the dumb thing was black as a lump of coal. "I just bought this," she said in disbelief.

"From Arvid?"

She straightened and said a cautious, "Yeah."

"My brother and sister-in-law bought a stove from him last year. It was a lemon."

Great. She'd bought a four-burner lemon and Christmas Eve was right around the corner. "This can't happen, not now."

"Family coming?" he guessed.

Tilda's cell phone rang and she snatched it from the

counter, wishing she was grabbing Arvid by the neck instead. "There must be something I can arrest him for," she muttered. Irritation turned to wariness when she saw the called ID. "Hi, Mom. I got your soup."

"Tillie." Her mom's voice was a cross between a croak and wheeze. "I…"

"Mom! Are you okay?"

"I think I better…go to the doc. Having. Trouble. Breathing."

Oh, God. "I'll be right there. I'm calling 9-1-1 now."

"What is it?" Devon demanded.

"My mom." Tilda's voice broke. "I've gotta get her to the hospital." She scooped up her keys and ran out the door.

In less than a minute she was on her way, pedal to the metal. At the far end of Candy Cane Lane, one of her neighbors was crossing the street. Tilda didn't let up on the gas. She laid on the horn and the neighbor ran for her life. Tilda roared past her and barely registered the angry, "Slow down!" the woman hurled after her. She made good use of her Bluetooth as she screeched around the corner.

"We're on it, Tilda," said the dispatcher. "Don't worry."

Don't worry. Yeah, sure. Darn the stubborn old bat. They should have gone to the doctor this morning like Tilda wanted to do. This was the last time she was listening to her mother. Ever!

She beat the ambulance to the house, raced inside and found her mom on the couch. She looked awful and her breathing was labored. "Guess you were right," she wheezed.

"Don't talk," Tilda commanded. "Hang on. The ambulance will be here any minute." Tilda wasn't much for praying, but that didn't stop her from hedging her bets. *Please, God, don't let her die.*

As if in answer to her amateur prayer, she heard the siren. It got closer and louder, and then James Jensen, Harv Correll and two other medics were on the scene. In they came with their jump kit and oxygen kit. Tilda had spent plenty of time around medics over the years and usually managed to stay calm and cool in the face of blood and pain. But this was different. This was Mom.

"You took long enough getting here," she told James.

He ignored her pissy greeting and instead focused on Mom. "Let's have you sit up, Mrs. Morrison," he said, and Harv took out a stethoscope and listened to Mom's breathing. With that done it was time for questions. What meds was she on? Did she have emphysema? Harv put a nasal cannula on her face while another medic took her blood pressure.

The team worked with precision and efficiency, and Tilda almost calmed down until it was decided that Mom would get to take a ride in the ambulance.

Tilda was ready to take a ride, too, but James said, "Why don't you follow us in your car? That way you'll have a ride home from the hospital."

"I want to go with her."

James laid a hand on her arm. "Til. She's going to be fine. Okay?"

Tilda wanted to cry like a big baby, but she bit her lip and nodded.

She easily kept pace with the ambulance. Once at the hospital she insisted on sticking by her mother's side. Only after the doctor had examined her and she'd been hooked up to an IV with fluids and antibiotics did Tilda's heart rate start to return to normal.

By the time her mom was settled in a room and Tilda had talked with the doctor, she felt as if she'd been mugged in a dark alley and left for dead. Mom was going to be okay. She'd have to stay in the hospital for a couple of days, but the doc had assured Tilda that she'd be able to come home for Christmas.

It was such good news, Tilda nearly burst into tears. "Thanks," she said in relief.

"Don't let her overdo it," he cautioned.

Tilda was going to make certain Mom never so much as got off the couch. Which meant she was on her own for cooking the turkey. Oh, well, she could figure it out. No need to bug Mom. She'd just look it up on the internet.

"She's had a real scare," the doctor said. "Now would be the time to convince her to quit smoking."

Tilda resolved to go over to the house and round up all the cigarettes. Mom would be too weak to go off to get more.

She took the elevator down to the lobby, leaning against a corner and taking a deep breath. Mom was going to be okay, thank God, the cigarettes were finally going bye-bye and Christmas Eve was going to be great. The elevator door slid open and she stepped out wearing a smile.

Until she saw Devon Black slouched in one of the chairs in the waiting area, watching for her. He uncurled himself and came over.

"What are you doing here?"

"Thought I'd hang around in case you needed anything."

There it was again, the hint that Devon Black wasn't such a loser. That he was, in fact, a nice guy. And prob-

ably a masochist, considering the fact that he was hanging around after what she'd said to him back at the house.

She almost didn't know what to say after having been
such a jerk. "Thanks," she mumbled.

"No problem."

"About what I said…"

"Forget it."

That sounded like a good idea to her. She nodded and
started for the door.

He fell in step with her. "How's your mom?"

"She's going to be okay. She'll be home by Christmas."

He nodded. "Good. By the way, I put your cookie
dough in the fridge. That seems to work."

Which was more than she could say for her stove. "I
have to cook a turkey," she blurted. Okay, where had that
come from? Word association? *Broken stove, Christmas
dinner, turkey.*

"You can order a precooked one from the Safeway
deli. Pick it up on Christmas Eve and you're good to go."

So he wasn't such a great cook, after all. "And you
know this how?"

"I saw the flyer for it in the store."

Now, there was the way to cook a turkey. "I think
I'll do that."

"I've got a stove that works. Why don't you bring over
your cookie dough and finish your cookies at my place?
I have some Hale's Pale Ale."

They were in the parking lot now, but Tilda knew she
was really standing at a crossroad. She didn't know what
was more tempting—cookies, beer or Devon Black. Part
of her wanted to go all domestic goddess, wander down
the road to stupid with a man who was *not* what she was

looking for but exactly what she wanted. If she went over to Devon's, it would be like going into a dangerous situation without backup. She was wrung out, vulnerable.

Not gonna happen. She shook her head.

"Bad timing on my part?" he guessed.

Bad idea. Period. "Look," she began.

He held up a hand to stop her. "Let's just leave it as bad timing. I hope your mom feels better soon." With that he saluted her and walked off to his car.

She got into her Jeep and drove back to her house, where she filched some of the cookie dough he'd put in the fridge. She wished he'd stop doing nice stuff like that. It didn't fit his image and it was confusing her.

Right about now, an M&M's cookie would really help her think.

Let's go to Devon's, chanted her hormones.

We are not going to Devon's, she informed them. But she could use some company. What was Ivy doing tonight?

Chapter Seventeen

Remember, it's not about what you do or where you go but who you're with.
— Muriel Sterling, *Making the Holidays Bright: How to Have a Perfect Christmas*

Missy had managed to fit Ivy in for an afternoon color touch-up. She'd hated to leave the shop when it was so busy, but she'd decided that taking care of her hair would put her in a better frame to take care of business.

Or not. Missy had gushed like a geyser about her fabulous honeymoon. "We stayed at the most gorgeous place in Hawaii. The food was the kind of stuff you have in superfancy restaurants. We even went to a luau. And the sunsets. Wow."

Oh, yes. There was something about watching a sunset with the man you loved. Ivy and Rob used to sit out on the back deck with a beer on the long summer evenings and watch the sun set behind the mountains, painting the sky gold and pink, and turning the mountains lavender.

"Never mind the sunsets. Tell her how good the sex was," teased Courtney, who'd been managing to keep up a conversation with her own customer, as well as Missy's from her neighboring station.

Missy had blushed. "That, too. I'm so happy."

"And I'm happy for you," Ivy had said. Which she was. If anyone deserved a good life, it was Missy Monroe. But Ivy realized she was also a little jealous. She didn't need to go to Hawaii, but she sure could use some love.

You have love, she'd reminded herself. *You've got your family, your friends and your kids.* She could have Rob's love again, too. At least that was what he claimed. But there was no guarantee that if she took him back he wouldn't get restless and dump her all over again. Who wanted to risk that kind of pain?

You have to move on, she'd told herself. *Be grateful for what's good in your life. Don't think about sunsets and sex.*

Once Missy had finished up with Ivy's hair, she'd handed her a mirror so she could check out the back.

"Thanks. It looks great." And, indeed, it did. There was something about getting her hair done that always lifted a woman's spirits, and Ivy had found herself wishing she had somewhere to go after work besides home.

Except, by the time she got home from work, she wouldn't want to go anywhere but to the couch. No wonder Rob had left, she'd thought as she went back to the shop. All she did was work. When had she turned into a boring stick in the mud?

She remembered the night before. That had been very unboring. But not in a good way. Ugh.

Now it was five o'clock, and she was ready to leave Nicole to handle the post-tree-lighting shoppers, and then close up at seven. She was barely out the door when her cell phone rang.

"Ivy, I'm sorry to bother you when you're at the shop," said Maddy Donaldson.

"That's okay," Ivy told her. "What can I do for you?" Now, why had she gone and said that? A person should never ask Maddy what she could do for her, because at Christmastime, Maddy always wanted *something*.

Sure enough. "Well, we seem to be short a Mrs. Santa Claus for tonight and I was hoping you could take a turn."

On a Saturday night after being on her feet at the store all day? What was Maddy smoking?

"If you could go out for an hour or so, say from seven to eight, it would be so helpful," Maddy hurried on. "I wouldn't ask, except this bug that's been going around has knocked out a lot of our volunteers. I'd do it myself but I've got a commitment later in the evening."

Ivy knew she'd be pooped when she got home. "I can't. Sorry, Maddy."

"I just thought that since your husband has the kids this weekend... I did see him coming for the kids yesterday, didn't I?"

There was nothing Maddy didn't see on Candy Cane Lane. "Yes, he did. But..."

"I can take five to seven if you could take that last part of the night," Maddy pleaded.

Ivy had been a Mrs. Santa Claus slacker this year. She really needed to take a turn. "All right. I can do from seven to eight." Maybe the cold air would revive her. And doing something to make other people happy would take her focus off herself and remind her to appreciate the joys of the season.

"Oh, thank you," Maddy gushed. "Drop by the house

on your way home. I'll leave some candy on the front porch for you."

Doing things for others is one of the most wonderful ways to make your holidays bright, Muriel Sterling had written in her book. Ivy had been focusing way too much on her own misery lately. It was time she thought about other people. As she ended the call she was smiling. The weekend wasn't going to be a total loss, after all.

Thank heaven she'd found someone to do candy-cane patrol. At least this way Maddy would only be outside until seven. She'd move their dinner reservation from six to seven-thirty and they could dine fashionably late. Everything would work out.

Not everyone in the family shared her opinion. "You know I hate eating that late," Alan had said when she called to tell him about the slight change in plans. "It doesn't do my hiatal hernia any good."

"Honey, I think if you take a Zantac you'll be fine. When the store's open late, you don't get home for dinner until seven, anyway."

"In case you've forgotten, I don't often eat dinner at home this time of year," he pointed out. "But never mind. Do what you want. You will, anyway."

That was unfair, and now she felt insulted and hurt. "If it's going to be a hardship, I'll keep it for six."

Sweet man that he was, she figured he'd change his mind and agree to the change in plans, but he said, "Good. It'll be fun to have a family dinner together out from under the shadow of the candy canes."

"Alan," she protested.

"Sorry, hon, but you go overboard with this. If you're not passing out candy, you're looking for someone else to do it. And if you're not doing that, you're at somebody's house telling them some of their Christmas lights are out. Or delivering candy canes. Or on the phone talking about candy canes. Give us all a break and give it a rest."

"Alan, I'm only trying to make our neighborhood nice."

"I know. But for just one night, can you let someone else do it?"

Who did he think that was going to be? She was as tired of this as he was, but someone had to keep things organized, and the best someone was the person who'd come up with the idea in the first place. Still, she could delegate. "I get the message," she said.

"Good. So, when I come home, somebody else will be wandering the street."

A lovely way to phrase being a goodwill ambassador. "I'll be at the house by the time you get there." Thank heaven she'd convinced Ivy to take a turn.

She hurried home to change into her Mrs. Santa Claus outfit and then went out to be a goodwill ambassador. For a very short while.

Mr. Werner and his wife pulled out of their driveway. He stopped his Marquis on the street opposite where she stood and let down his window. "Have they caught the brats who wrecked my candy canes?" he called.

What Mr. Werner had to squawk about was a mystery to Maddy. His candy canes were only knocked over, not damaged. And he didn't even like them. "Not yet."

"Well, I hope they do," he said. He slid his window back up and the car crept down the street at the same pace he'd keep up all the way to wherever he was going.

Maddy sighed. Talking with Mr. Werner was about as uplifting as getting strapped to a boat anchor.

Oh, well. Never mind him. She only had to look around to lift her spirits again. The neighborhood was all color and festivity, and cars were already showing up, driving slowly, taking in the sights. Every house and shrub was alight, and all the larger-than-life inflatables were on display. She looked down the street at the lit-up dinosaur their newest resident had put out on her lawn. Tacky. Maybe, if they were lucky, the vandals would strike again and make off with it. Ah, but everything else was a feast for the eyes. Oh, did the Shanks family know they had some nonworking icicle lights?

A car stopped next to her and Maddy greeted them. "Merry Christmas. Do we have some takers for candy canes?"

"You bet," said the mom. "The kids have been waiting for this all day."

Ha! Proof that she was doing something good, not just for their neighborhood but for the whole town. Too bad her own family didn't understand that.

More cars came by and she chatted with everyone. In fact, she got so busy she lost track of time. She only realized how late it was when she saw a familiar Toyota at the end of the street. Uh-oh. A holiday Cinderella, Maddy fled the party and ran up the steps into the house. It wouldn't take her more than a few minutes to change.

"Jordan, are you ready to go?" she asked.

"Yes," came the answer from behind Jordan's door.

She dashed into her own bedroom, shedding her wig as she went. Her hair was terrifying. No time to fix it now. She'd have to do that in the car. Off came the skirt.

"I'm home," Alan called up the stairs. "Everybody ready to go?"

"Almost," Maddy called back, and left the last of Mrs.

Claus on the bedroom floor. She could hear Jordan running down the stairs.

"Come on, babe. They won't hold the reservation," Alan said.

"Coming!" Oh, boy. She shouldn't have stayed out so long. Quick! Into her skirt, throw on the blouse. Grab a necklace to put on in the car. Shoes! Okay, she was ready.

But halfway to Schwangau, she remembered she'd forgotten to leave out the candy canes for Ivy.

"We're already running late," Alan said. "You know they don't hold reservations more than ten minutes."

"This'll just take one minute," she promised. "I'll call them and tell them not to give away our table."

"Schwangau," answered a soft female voice.

"This is Madeline Donaldson. We have a reservation for three people for six o'clock."

"Yes," said the voice.

"We're going to be a few minutes late, so please hold our table."

"As you may know, we have a strict policy regarding reservations. We only hold tables for ten minutes."

That gave them five minutes to do this one quick errand and then get to the restaurant.

"Are you on your way now?"

Pretty much. "Yes," Maddy lied.

"All right," said the voice. "We'll hold your table."

"Thank you," Maddy said. "There," she told Alan, "all taken care of."

"Good, because I'm starving, and I sure don't want to have to wait for a table." Jordan was busy in the backseat texting and didn't say anything.

Which was just as well, since these days most of her conversation consisted of complaints.

They parked in front of the house, and Maddy ran inside to fetch the new supply of candy canes from the closet in the guest room. There. Now she could go out and enjoy herself.

But when they got to Schwangau, she learned that her enjoyment was going to be considerably delayed. "I'm so sorry," said the hostess. "You're fifteen minutes late and we couldn't hold your table."

Maddy frowned.

"How long will we have to wait to get another one?" Alan asked.

Seeing all the people waiting to be seated, Maddy had the sinking feeling it could be a while.

The hostess consulted her seating chart. "An hour."

"An *hour*?" Alan repeated.

"I'm hungry," Jordan whined.

"Can't you get us in any sooner?" Maddy pleaded.

The hostess managed a sympathetic look but shook her head.

"Never mind," Alan said. "Let's go to Zelda's. They can probably fit us in."

On a Saturday night? Maddy doubted it.

"Maddy, I'm really sorry," Charley Masters said to her when they got there, "but we're packed."

She could see that. There wasn't an empty table in the popular restaurant, and here, too, people were waiting to be seated.

"How long is the wait?" Maddy asked.

"About twenty minutes," Charley said. "Do you want me to put you down?"

"Mom, I'm hungry," Jordan grumbled again.

"Well, that's it," Alan said. "Let's go to Herman's."

"Herman's?" That was going to be their big family holiday dinner out?

"We won't have to wait twenty minutes there," Alan said. "Come on, girls." Out the door he went, expecting Maddy and Jordan to follow.

There went Jordan, right behind him.

"I guess we'll come back another time," Maddy said, and left the restaurant, fuming.

"I can't believe Schwangau wouldn't wait just a few more minutes," she said, slamming the car door behind her. "After all the business we've given them."

"If they change their policy for one person, they have to do it for everyone," Alan said. "We knew what time we had to be there."

Maddy decided not to pursue this topic any further, since their tardiness could be laid directly at her door.

In her black skirt, heels and green satin blouse she was a little overdressed for a hamburger joint. Jordan was, too. Maddy had insisted she wear something other than jeans and under her coat she wore a dress. "I'm cold," she complained as they walked into the popular hamburger joint.

"I guess you won't want a chocolate peppermint shake, then," Maddy said.

Jordan ignored her, then turned to her dad. "I want a shake and a Herman Deluxe burger and garlic fries."

"What'll you have?" Alan asked her.

A nice glass of Gewürztraminer. That wasn't happening. Maddy sighed deeply. "A root beer and a cheeseburger." Oh, well. At least they were all together.

Sort of. They'd barely gotten seated when Alan's cell phone rang. He had a different ring tone for each of the women in his life. For Maddy it was Johnny Cash singing

"Ring of Fire." For Jordan it was "My Girl," and for his mother it was "Mission Impossible," which was playing now. Maddy's ring tone for her was "Ding Dong! The Witch Is Dead," which she never heard because Corrine never called her.

"I'd better take this," he said. "Hi, Mom... No, no. It's fine. We're just out getting a hamburger."

Having family time. Some family time. Now Jordan was busy with her phone. Maddy chomped down on a garlic fry. This was fun. She took out her cell. She could text, too. She sent one to Carla Welky. Family time. We're all on our phones. Yep, this was some good family bonding.

"You know, I'm not sure," Alan was saying. "Let me put Maddy on."

That really made the evening special. Maddy frowned at her husband and shook her head.

"She wants to know what a certain someone wants for Christmas."

"An iTunes gift card," Jordan said, not looking up.

Maddy took the phone and said, "Hello, Corrine," forcing politeness into her voice.

As usual, Corrine didn't waste time on pleasantries. "I need to know what my granddaughter wants for Christmas."

"It won't be long now before you're with us," Maddy said, maneuvering the old bat into polite conversation.

"Which is why I need to get my shopping finished tomorrow," Corrine said briskly. "What would she like?"

"She says she'd like an iTunes gift card."

"She's there?"

"We're all sitting here having dinner, Corrine."

"Now she'll know what we're giving her. I'll have to

think of something else. Honestly, I don't know why you eat so late at night. That poor child."

The poor child was busy slurping down a milk shake at the moment and didn't seem to be suffering in the least. Well, unless you counted being stuck with your parents.

"I hope you're not planning on such a late dinner time when we're there."

"We'll make sure you eat early," Maddy said as sweetly as she could. *Maybe then you'll go to bed early, too, and leave us in peace.*

"Good. Put my son on again, please."

Gladly. Maddy handed the cell back to Alan. She could tell he was getting a motherly lecture from the expression on his face. "No, Mom… Uh-huh." He got up and moved away from the table. Maddy could hear him say, "No, no. Maddy's looking forward to having you."

She was? News to her. Her phone dinged, announcing a text from Carla. Ha ha. Sounds like us. At least Maddy wasn't the only woman in Icicle Falls coming in second place after a cell phone.

"I've got to go, Mom. We'll see you soon," Alan said, and ended the call.

"Is she getting me a gift card?" Jordan asked.

"We'll have to wait and see," Maddy replied.

"She's not," Jordan said irritably, not even glancing up from her phone.

"I'm sure someone will give you a gift card." That someone would probably be her or her mother, since Corrine would now go her own stubborn way and get Jordan something she couldn't care less about like a stuffed bear or a child's yoga mat. Oh, wait, that was what she'd gotten Jordan last Christmas. Maddy had taken them to Goodwill.

"Anyway, Christmas isn't just about getting," Maddy reminded her. "It's about giving, too."

Alan reached over and squeezed her hand. "And being together."

Ah, yes, and here they were, together, but not really.

Jordan texted through half the meal until, exasperated, Alan told her to put away her phone. Then her friend Afton came in with her mom and a couple of other kids, and Jordan was off like a shot. Afton's mom was wearing leggings and a black sweater, along with a very cool scarf under her parka. Her boots looked expensive. Maddy knew her Coach purse was. The kids all ordered and she paid for everyone. Big deal. Maddy would have done the same. She needed to encourage Jordan to have her friends over more.

Except for that tall, gangly boy Jordan was flirting with. Maddy took in his gangsta-wannabe clothes and scraggy hair, the way he flipped it out of his eyes. And he had gauges in his ears. At such a young age? This had to be Logan. Blech.

"Who's that kid?" Alan asked, irritation in his voice.

"A boy Jordan has a crush on."

"Looks like a loser to me," Alan said in disgust.

"They all dress like that these days," Maddy said, and wondered why she was coming to the boy's defense when she'd thought pretty much the same thing. Probably because she hated to think of her daughter having such poor taste.

"I guess," he said dubiously. "Isn't she too young for boys?"

"At thirteen? No. The hormones are just starting to kick in."

Alan sat for a moment, watching the flirting and listening to the squeals. "Sometimes I wish she was still a little girl."

Maddy knew exactly how he felt. One blink ago, their daughter had been a toddler. Now high school was right around the corner.

"We don't have many years left with her," he said sadly.

As whiny as she'd become, maybe that wasn't a bad thing.

"What do you think about going to a movie?" Alan asked.

Hang on to her a little longer... "Good idea," Maddy said.

"At least she won't text through the movie."

Want to bet? "We can always hope." Maddy continued to study the boy. Why did he seem familiar? Suddenly she flashed on the image of a kid leaning out the window of a car filled with other teenage boys, taunting her. *Hey, tell Santa to bring me some condoms for Christmas.* It was the same kid. Double blech.

Jordan bounded over. "Everyone's going to Afton's house to play Wii bowling. Can I go?"

What to do? Bag the movie idea and let her go? Maddy shot a glance at Alan. He was frowning. That decided it. "Not tonight, sweetie."

Jordan's cheery smile was replaced with a Grinchy scowl. "Why not?"

"We're having some family time," Alan said. "Remember?"

"All we were doing was going out to dinner, and we're done," Jordan pointed out.

"We had some other plans," Maddy said.

"What?" Obviously, nothing her parents could come up with would be as cool as hanging out with Afton and her mom and Mr. Scrawny.

"We're going to the movies," Maddy said.

There went the eye roll. "Okay, can Afton come over tomorrow?"

"We're going to Seattle to see Grandma and Grandpa," Maddy reminded her.

"Afton could come with us," Jordan suggested.

"Honey, let's catch up with Afton during winter break, okay?"

"Fine," Jordan said, her tone of voice saying it was anything but, and flounced off.

"I don't think we scored any points just now," Alan said.

"Maybe not, but we need to spend more time as a family before she moves on and it's too late."

Alan watched where Jordan stood with her friends, prolonging the contact. "I don't know. It might already be too late."

Maddy hoped he was wrong. All teenagers wanted to get away from their parents, but Jordan was barely a teen. Surely they had another year at least.

The gang left, and their daughter returned to the table, her pretty face marred by a very ugly expression. "Thanks, Mom," she said bitterly, and plopped into her seat.

As if it was Maddy's fault? The immature part of her wanted to say, "Blame your father. This was his idea." She silenced it, saying instead, "You'll have time to catch up later in the week. Now, let's see what's playing at the Falls Cinema."

"Whatever it is, we'll probably miss half of it," Jordan muttered.

Sigh. There was no forgiveness for past mistakes when you were the mother of a thirteen-year-old.

They did manage to find a movie, but even supplied with popcorn, Milk Duds and a gigantic Coke, Jordan was still pouting. *So much for a family evening,* Maddy thought as the opening credits began to roll.

Ivy stood outside in her red coat and her Santa hat passing out candy canes until she was sure her poor, frozen nose would pop off. She checked the time on her cell phone: 7:40. She decided her good deed was done. It had been fun at first, waving at people and giving out candy. After that she remembered why she so rarely volunteered for Mrs. Santa Claus patrol. Anyway, the snow was really starting to come down now and the wind was picking up. She hadn't seen a car in ten minutes. Nobody would be out driving in this.

She went inside and put on her favorite ratty black sweater and her fleece pajama bottoms, then fixed herself a nutritious dinner—popcorn and diet Pepsi. No pizza! She was just about to watch the holiday movie she'd recorded when her doorbell rang.

It couldn't be Deirdre. She'd had plans to go hang out at Zelda's with Courtney from Sleeping Lady Salon. They'd invited Ivy, but after the humiliating show she'd put on at the Man Cave the night before, she didn't trust herself not to offer some kind of repeat performance, and she'd opted out.

So who was here, catching her all glam in her fleecy

bottoms with penguins on them? She opened the door and found Tilda Morrison standing there with a bowl of cookie dough, looking as awkward as Ivy suddenly felt.

"My new stove isn't working. I made this cookie dough and…" She stopped, obviously uncomfortable with finding herself in need of neighborly assistance. Or maybe it was uncomfortable having to ask for help from the woman you'd sent home the night before, after she'd created a public disturbance.

Ivy stepped aside and pulled the door wide. "Come on in."

"Thanks. Were you busy? I mean, this isn't a big deal."

Ivy pointed to her outfit. "Do I look like it?"

Tilda smiled. Her whole face changed when she smiled. "I dress like that when I've got company."

"And never say cookies aren't a big deal," Ivy said with a smile. She peered into the bowl. "M&M's cookies. My fave."

"Mine, too," Tilda said. "I was going to bake them today, but that damn stove crapped out on me. It was just delivered this week, too."

"Don't tell me, let me guess. You bought it from Arvid."

Tilda scowled. "Yeah."

"I think he was a crook in another life," Ivy said, leading the way to the kitchen.

"I think he's a crook in this life," said Tilda.

Ivy started the oven preheating and got out a cookie sheet and two spoons. "Thanks for not arresting me last night."

"Cops aren't always out to get you. Sometimes they actually want to help. You know, serve and protect."

"Well, I obviously needed protection last night. From

myself." She pointed at the bowl with her spoon. "Mind if I sample?"

"Be my guest." Tilda picked up the other spoon and took a sample herself.

"Mmm, good."

"It's about the only thing I can make."

Ivy pointed her spoon at Tilda. "You can make hot buttered rum mix now, too."

"Yeah, there is that."

They each dipped out another spoonful of dough. "I haven't seen you around much," Ivy said.

Tilda shrugged. "I've been busy. I started working second shift."

"What does that mean?"

"Nights."

"Not great for your social life," Ivy observed.

"Most of my social life is with other cops and fire-fighters, and a lot of us are on similar schedules."

"But you've got a Saturday night off."

"It's rare. That's just how it worked in the schedule rotation this time. I'm on for tomorrow."

"Saturday night, and you're over here letting me eat your cookie dough. What's wrong with this picture?"

Tilda ate another spoonful. "Right now all I want to do is eat cookie dough." She looked at the shrinking ball of dough in the bowl. "Well, and maybe bake a few."

In unspoken agreement, they began dropping dough onto the cookie sheet.

"So you're home on a Saturday night, too," Tilda said.

"After last night, I'm never going out again."

Tilda smiled. "Hey, we all make fools of ourselves over men once in a while."

"Not you. I can't picture you making a fool of yourself

over anyone," Ivy said, dropping dough on the cookie sheet.

Tilda gave a snort and ate some more dough. 'Like I said, we all do it."

Ivy slid the sheet in the oven. "I thought I saw Devon Black over at your place the other day. What's with that?"

"Nothing's with that. He's not my type. I want someone more…responsible."

"Good luck," Ivy said bitterly.

"Yeah, men are a crapshoot. But at least we've got cookies," Tilda added with a grin.

"And popcorn. I made some. Wanna stay and help me eat it?"

"Sure. Why not?"

Why not indeed? "I've got pizza I can heat up, too."

Tilda's eyes lit up as if she'd been offered a bribe. "Yeah? Bring it on. I love pizza."

"Me, too," Ivy said. "But this one I'd just as soon see gone."

Tilda looked at her questioningly.

"My ex sent it."

"Your ex sends you pizza?"

"He wants to get back together." And she was sharing this with someone she barely knew because?

"Interesting. You taking him back?"

"He left me," Ivy said as she pulled the pizza out of the fridge. "Do you think he deserves to be taken back?"

"That's not for me to say."

Ivy kept her gaze on the pizza she was wrapping in foil. "What would you do if you were me?"

"Probably tell him to take a hike." Ivy was feeling justified until Tilda said, "But I'm not you. And I don't have kids to think about. Do you still love him?"

"When I'm not hating him, you mean?"

Tilda smiled. "Want me to run him in for heartbreak in the first degree?"

"Too bad you can't do that."

"The jails are too crowded already. Seriously, I know it's hard working stuff out, but if he really feels bad about his screwup and, deep down, you still love him, you may need to give him another chance. You've heard of the three-strike law, right? Not saying you should give him three chances," she added hastily. "But people do screw up sometimes."

Ivy did look at her now. "And everyone deserves a second chance?"

"I don't know. I can see how you wouldn't want to risk it."

The timer went off and Ivy took out the cookies.

"The only thing better than cookie dough is hot cookies," Tilda said once Ivy had transferred them to cooling racks. She helped herself to one, juggling the hot cookie in her hands.

"Cookies and milk," said Ivy, turning to the fridge.

"Cookies and milk, pizza, popcorn—girl, you sure know how to party," Tilda said approvingly.

"Thanks. Right back atcha." When she wasn't being a cop Tilda Morrison was pretty cool. Actually, Ivy thought, remembering the night before, she could be pretty cool even when she *was* being a cop.

Chapter Eighteen

*Remember, this is the season to be jolly. Your posi-
tive attitude can go a long way to fostering happi-
ness in your home.*
— Muriel Sterling, *Making the Holidays Bright:
How to Have a Perfect Christmas*

In spite of the pout she'd pasted on her face, Jordan enjoyed the movie and laughed at all the funny scenes.

"Thanks, Daddy," she said as they left the theater.
"That was fun."

"You should thank your mom, too," Alan said.

"Thanks," Jordan said, the sweetness vanishing from
her voice. Proof that you could make a child say the right
thing, but you couldn't make her have the right heart.

It was a cold walk to the car with an icy wind blow-
ing snow in their faces, but that was nothing compared
to the chill coming off Jordan.

"Let's hope they don't close the pass tomorrow," Alan
said.

As if on cue, the snow began to fall faster and the
wind whipped up, batting the giant fir trees hovering
over the theater.

"I hope we don't lose power," Maddy said. Trapped in

the house with her cranky daughter and no power. Oh, that would be fun.

There were only a few cars on the road, probably making their way home. As they turned onto Candy Cane Lane, Maddy heard a distant boom. Then all the lights on every house on the street went dark as if a giant plug had been pulled.

"Looks like a transformer blew," Alan remarked.

Lovely.

Once inside the garage, Alan found a flashlight and lit them into the house. Maddy got candles and Alan gave Jordan the flashlight to take to bed, then fetched one they kept charging in the laundry room. Power outages had become a rare thing, but when they did happen, Jordan loved it because it meant a fire in the fireplace, roasting marshmallows and her dad telling ghost stories. It was too late for that tonight, on so many levels. Jordan went straight to bed, a hug and kiss good-night for her dad and an icy peck on the cheek for her mean mom.

Maddy lay in bed that night listening to the wind howl and praying that the storm would end quickly and they'd be able to get over the pass the next day to see her parents. Her daughter obviously didn't want any mother-daughter time with her, but Maddy sure needed some time with *her* mother.

There was no power the following morning and the house was cold. So was her daughter. Jordan was still Little Miss Frosty, determined to make Maddy feel guilty for ruining her thirteen-year-old life.

All the houses were dark and so was most of downtown, except the end where the hospital was. It looked so…sad and deserted. "We can stop in Gold Bar and get breakfast," Alan said.

Jordan had set herself to Ignore mode and started texting at the table until Alan told her to put her phone away. That cut off all communication, especially with her parents.

Once at her grandparents' she was polite, but polite was as far as she could bring herself to go. It wouldn't do to ruin the abused-child facade.

"What's bothering our little girl?" Maddy's mom asked after Jordan had finished clearing the table and went to sit in a corner and text.

"I wouldn't let her hang out with her friends last night."

"Was she in trouble?"

"No. We were having some family time."

Mom nodded slowly. Sagely. "Do you remember how much *you* wanted to hang out with us when you were that age?"

Maddy sighed. "I know. I just…oh, Mom, she's growing up so fast. I feel like I'm losing her." She shook her head. "Sometimes I feel like I'm losing me. Between work and keeping everything going in the neighborhood… It sometimes feels like I'm hauling around a backpack with a baby elephant in it. And now I've got Corrine descending on us."

"This is a hectic time of year, honey. You have to prioritize."

"I know, but there's nothing I can cut out."

Her mom stopped washing a pot and looked at her. "Are you sure?"

"What are you trying to say?"

"Well, there was some talk about Candy Cane Lane at dinner."

More like complaining. Alan had joked that he saw more of Santa's wife than he did of his own these days, and Jordan had muttered her usual epithet regarding the neighborhood decorations. "Dumb."

"Your street is charming," Mom said, "but maybe you need to spend a little less time out on it and a little more inside with Alan and Maddy."

"People have been sick this year," Maddy explained.

"That doesn't mean you need to single-handedly pick up the slack," said Mom. "If you were around more, you could probably let go more."

"What's that supposed to mean?"

"I mean, make Jordan a higher priority during the week and you won't have so much trouble letting her go off with her friends on the weekends."

Maddy frowned as she poured soap in the dishwasher and shut the door. "I have to work during the week."

"Not at night. Look, this is just a suggestion, but I think maybe you should hang up your Mrs. Santa Claus suit for the year. Life will still go on if someone doesn't get a piece of candy. You've got the lights and all the pretty decorations, and that's what people really come for."

Mom was right, Maddy thought as they drove home, the trunk filled with presents to put under the tree. There weren't that many days left until Christmas. She'd take her mother's advice and stay inside. She and Jordan could wrap gifts, maybe even make some fancy Christmas cards for Jordan to give to her girlfriends. Jordan always liked making cards. And they'd start all this fun by putting up the tree and having a nice family evening decorating it.

The lights were on again downtown. Hopefully, they'd also be on at home. "So, who's for decorating the tree?" Maddy asked cheerfully as they entered town. It was only seven-thirty, plenty of time to get the tree done before Jordan had to go to bed.

The old Jordan surfaced. "Me."

"Me, too," said Alan, smiling.

They could see the lights from their street even before they got to it, a nimbus of Christmas glory in the night sky. "It does look pretty," Maddy said as they turned onto Candy Cane Lane.

"Yeah, it's nice," agreed Alan.

Jordan said nothing.

They were just walking in the door, loaded with presents, when the phone rang. "I'll get it," Maddy said, setting down her pile.

"Let it ring," Alan said.

"I won't be long," she promised.

"I'll have the tree inside and up in ten minutes," he said.

"She's gonna talk on the phone all night," Jordan predicted, grumpy again.

"Only for a minute." Maddy snagged the cordless from the hall table.

It was Carla. "Maddy, I got it!"

"Got what?" Maddy asked, slipping out of her coat.

"The license plate for that SUV. They came through again. Took the last of my candy canes and fishtailed on out of here. Almost hit another car in the process."

Maddy walked to the kitchen to boil some hot water for cocoa. "Oh, good job. Did you call the police?"

"Uh, no. I figured I'd give it to you since you've got an in with them. You know, being friends with Tilda and all."

"We're not exactly friends," Maddy said as she flipped

on the electric teapot. In fact, she got the distinct impression that Tilda Morrison didn't want to be friends.

"Well, anyway, you want the number?"

"Sure." It would only take a minute to call the police. "Let me grab a pencil."

Carla rattled it off. "I'd like to see 'em try and mess with us now," she said.

"Yeah, this should fix the problem," Maddy agreed, and wrote *Candy Cane Lane Vandals* next to the vital information. "Thanks."

Jordan walked into the kitchen. "Daddy's got the tree up."

"Great. You two bring the decorations from the garage and I'll be right with you."

"Okay. Daddy! We have to get the decorations," she hollered, and disappeared through the laundry room and out the door into the garage.

Alan came into the kitchen. "You ready?"

"Almost," Maddy said. "I've got water heating for cocoa."

"Great idea."

Maddy was just looking up the number for the police station when Shirley Shank called. "Did you hear? Carla found the vandals."

Jordan and Alan were coming back through the kitchen, each carrying a large plastic bin. "We're ready, hon," Alan called over his shoulder.

"Be right there," she said. Then to Shirley. "Yes, I just talked to her."

"Are you going to call the cops?" Shirley asked.

Why did everyone assume she'd be the one to call the police?

Because she was the one who did all the organizing

around here, from getting the neighborhood on board with the holiday lights to keeping everyone supplied in candy canes. Heck, she was the one who came up with everything—the best Halloween house contest, the summer block party. Christmas.

But somebody had to do it. And those were the things that brought people together.

"Mom!" Jordan yelled from the living room, her voice packed with irritation.

"I've got to go," she said to Shirley. "We're decorating the tree."

She made cocoa and delivered it to the living room. "Okay, here's hot chocolate."

"Is this how you want the lights?" Alan asked.

"We've got a gap in the middle," she said just as the phone rang again.

"Don't answer it," Alan said.

"It'll just take a minute." This time it was Mr. Werner. "Carla Welky told me you got those hoodlums."

"Well, we think we do," Maddy said. "We've got a license-plate number."

"Good. Make 'em pay. That's what I say. Kids these days have no respect for property."

"You're so right, Mr. Werner."

"Have you called the police?"

"Not yet."

"Well, what are you waiting for?"

A spare minute. "Don't worry, I'm going to." Now, what should she do? There was no point calling the station. That would be closed. Nine-one-one? This didn't exactly qualify as an emergency. She'd give it to Tilda. Looking through the directory, though, she discovered that Tilda Morrison had an unlisted number. Well, she'd run down the street to Tilda's house.

She pulled the piece of paper with the vital information off the tablet and went to grab her coat.

"Where are you going?" Alan asked as she took her coat out of the closet.

"I have to run this license number to Tilda Morrison."

"Now? Hon, we're ready to hang the ornaments."

"I'll be right back."

"No, she won't," Jordan muttered.

"This is important," Maddy informed them. "We got the license number of those vandals."

"Then call it in on Monday."

"They might be able to pick them up tonight. I'll be right back, guys," she said again, and slipped out the door.

The night was clear, and the air was fresh and crisp. Every house glittered like a giant jewel box and the lawns were covered with snow. Candy Cane Lane looked picture-perfect. In fact, someone should take a picture of it and make it into a poster. Or a Christmas card. Maybe she'd do that. But not tonight. Tonight she had to get back and help trim the tree.

She hurried down the street, her boots crunching in the snow. Tilda's Christmas lights were on and that silly dinosaur sat smack-dab in the middle of the yard. So tacky. The house certainly wouldn't win the prize for best-dressed holiday home at Maddy's neighborhood New Year's Day party, but at least she had some lights and her candy canes were up.

Maddy went to the door and rang the bell. No answer. Where was she on a Sunday night, anyway? Maddy followed with a gentle knock on the door. Still no answer.

With a sigh, she folded the piece of paper and slipped it under the doormat, which read *Do You Live Here?* (*Pick one.*) Beneath it were two option boxes. One said *Yes.* The printing next to it said *Welcome Home.* The other box was for *No* and said *What the hell do you want?* Was that supposed to be funny? Sheesh.

She turned and trudged back. Wherever Tilda Morrison was, Maddy hoped she got home in time to do something with that information.

Meanwhile, Maddy had things to do. The tree was two-thirds done when she walked in the door. "That looks lovely, you two," she said as she hung up her coat.

"Daddy and I had to do this all by ourselves," Jordan chastised her.

"We didn't need help, anyway," Alan said in an effort to lighten her mood. "We do good work, don't we?"

Maddy came over and dug a tissue-paper-wrapped ornament from one of the bins. She unwrapped it. "Look. Your Elsa ornament." Every year she bought Jordan a Christmas ornament. Last year's had been the Disney snow queen from the movie *Frozen.* Jordan had loved it.

Tonight she just shrugged and pulled out another ornament.

In the mommy doghouse again, thought Maddy as she hung Elsa on the tree. She had the distinct impression her daughter would like to hang *her* on a tree somewhere, and not as an ornament.

Quite the weekend of family bonding.

It was after bedtime when Rob finally returned the kids. "Sorry I'm late," he said. "We were at my folks'."

The annual extended family Christmas bash. It was the first one Ivy had missed since she was eighteen.

Her former mother-in-law had remained cordial, sending her birthday presents and Valentine's cards in an effort to atone for her son's bad behavior, but of course she couldn't include Ivy in this particular gathering. Being excluded still rankled, and it was one more loss to lay at Rob's new apartment door.

"Can Daddy stay with us tonight?" Hannah asked.

It was the same thing she'd been asking ever since Daddy and Mommy started having joint custody. Ivy gave her the same answer she always did. "Not tonight."

Hannah's lower lip jutted out. "I want Daddy to stay."

"Daddy can stay to hear your bedtime prayers," Ivy said, going up the stairs with Robbie in her arms. "Let's get your bath and get you into bed. It's way past your bedtime."

"I'll help you," Rob offered, coming up after with Hannah, who began singing. "Jingle bells, jingle bells, jingle all the way." Rob joined in, singing in his off-key voice.

Ivy had her own version. *Jingle bells, this sure smells. Wish he'd go away.* But did she? Really? Deep down? Yes! Three-strike laws worked fine for men who stole cars. Men who stole hearts and then broke them should be locked up for life. With no pizza.

With bath time over and Robbie in his crib (for about two seconds), it was time to hear Hannah's prayers. That, too, was a repeat. "God bless Mommy and Daddy and Oma and Opa, and Grandma and Grandpa B., and Robbie and Gizmo and Aunt Deirdre, and my bear and…" The list went on. Her Sunday school teacher, Mrs. Walters, all the children in the world, all the teddy bears in the world, all the dogs in the world.

"I think that covers it, honey," Ivy finally said.

"And please bring Daddy home to stay," Hannah finished. "Amen."

"Amen," said Rob, kissing her.

Ivy didn't add an amen. "Okay, you, in bed," she said, pulling back the covers.

Hannah bounced onto the bed, her newly cleaned curls bouncing, too. "Daddy, you'll be here when I wake up, won't you?"

Ivy could feel Rob's eyes on her. "No. You know Daddy lives someplace else."

Hannah's little brow furrowed. "But I asked God."

"Sometimes God says no, honey," Ivy said, trying to be as gentle with the hard news as possible.

Hannah started crying and Ivy felt like a rat. Why she had to feel like a rat when Rob was the one who'd caused this problem in the first place was a mystery. "But Daddy's not far away."

"I want Daddy to live with us again," Hannah sobbed.

"Come on, now, princess. Don't cry," Rob said. "You know we're going to spend Christmas Day together."

Christmas Day without her children, and the whole rest of the week, too. She'd never spent Christmas without her kids. The very thought of it made her want to cry. Instead, she kissed Hannah, then scrammed and left Rob to settle her down while she went downstairs to camp out on the couch and fume.

"What did you tell her?" Ivy demanded when he came downstairs.

"What do you mean?"

"You must have said something to set her off."

"I didn't say anything, Ive, honest. I'll be right back," he added, and slipped out the door.

"Don't bother." She got up and locked the door after him and enjoyed the satisfaction of listening while he turned the knob and realized he couldn't get in.

"Come on, unlock the door."

"Go home."

"I brought you something."

"Take it with you."

"Ive, please. Come on."

He'd stay out there banging all night, she rationalized, and opened the door.

He stepped in, bearing a bottle of chocolate wine. Her favorite. First pizza, now wine. This was definitely bribery. "You really think you can get me to take you back just because you ordered a pizza and bought some wine?" How easy did he think she was, anyway?

"I told you, I'm just trying to prove that I've changed. I'm up for doing whatever you want."

"Yeah? Well, take out an ad in the paper, tell all of Icicle Falls what a jerk you were." *Make a public spectacle of yourself like your idiot wife did.*

He nodded and set the wine down on the hall table. "Guess I'd better go."

"Yeah, I guess you'd better." He left and once again she locked the door behind him. Then she double-checked the lock she'd put on her heart, just to make sure it was still in place. So far, so good.

Except it wasn't. Nothing was good anymore, including Christmas. She got a piece of scratch paper from the kitchen junk drawer and wrote *Enjoy*, then signed the note and taped it on the bottle of wine. She marched it next door to Tilda's, where she put it on the front porch. Back home again, she snatched Muriel Sterling's stupid book from her nightstand, took it downstairs and dumped it in the garbage.

Then she ran a bubble bath and sat in it and had a nice, long cry. *'Tis the season to be soggy. Fa-la-la-la-la la-la-la-la.*

Chapter Nineteen

Plan a night of fun with your children. This will
make the season memorable for everyone.
—Muriel Sterling, *Making the Holidays Bright:*
How to Have a Perfect Christmas

Although Tilda knew her mom was going to be okay,
seeing her in a hospital bed had been a shock. It had
brought home clearly the fact that she wouldn't have her
crazy best friend around forever, and that thought was
terrifying. She'd returned to the hospital later in the afternoon but found Mom sound asleep, so she'd tiptoed
out and gone home, feeling at loose ends. Hanging out
with Ivy (who knew she'd ever want to hang out with
Ivy Bohn?) had been a nice distraction, but it couldn't
completely take her mind off where Mom was.

First thing Sunday morning found her back at the
hospital, smuggling in a couple of M&M's cookies.
She'd wanted to call in sick but Mom had shooed her
out. "You're watching me like a buzzard. Get out of here
and go do some real good for someone."

So now here she was, riding around town looking for
criminals and having to settle for trying to stump Jamal

with movie trivia questions. "Okay, how come Edward Scissorhands never got real hands?"

"And how old were we when that came out?"

"Five. Looks like you can't answer. Point for me."

"Uh-uh, not so fast. What's the answer?"

"Because the inventor who made him died before he could make his hands."

Jamal snorted in disgust and Tilda chortled. She was ahead.

"Okay," he said, "here's one you're not gonna get. What's the first movie that actually has the word *zombie* in the dialogue."

"Easy. *Shaun of the Dead.*"

"How'd you know that?"

"I like that movie."

"You're killin' me. I need a Coke. Let's swing by Safeway."

By ten at night the grocery store's parking lot was almost empty. The whole town was pretty much in slumber mode.

They got their sodas and went back to movie trivia until around midnight Tilda said, "Let's swing by my street and see if it's all quiet."

"Not again," he groaned. "You're not gonna catch whoever messed with the candy canes. It's too late and it's too cold."

"You're probably right, but at least I can tell Maddy Donaldson I tried."

"What's with this sudden need to keep Maddy Donaldson happy?"

"Hey, if you lived in the same neighborhood, wouldn't you want to keep her happy?" Tilda retorted.

"She's the queen bee over there, isn't she?"

"Oh, yeah. I think if anybody gave her a chance she'd rule the world."

They turned onto the street and all was, indeed, quiet. Everyone's lights were off, both outside and in, as the residents of Candy Cane Lane logged in their eight hours before the Monday-morning alarm went off. But it was almost a full moon and that, plus the patrol car's headlights, made it easy to spot the vandals.

"Bingo," Tilda said, pointing to Maddy Donaldson's house where two figures were busy knocking down candy canes, one of them taller than the other. A girl and a boy. Why was she not surprised? Half the time when girls got in trouble with the law there was a guy involved. Jamal floored it and, seeing them approaching, the kids took off, the boy galloping across the nearest front lawn, the girl running around the corner of the Donaldson house.

Jamal jumped out and took after him, while Tilda went after his accomplice. "Stop! Police!" That was always such a waste of breath. They never stopped.

This one didn't, either. The perp slipped through the fence into the backyard like a pro but Tilda closed the gap. Knowing she couldn't escape, the girl turned around and cried, "Don't hurt me!"

Good grief. The kid looked all of twelve. In fact, the kid looked…oh, shit.

Something startled Maddy out of a sound sleep. What was that noise? Someone hollering. The vandals! She shot out of bed and grabbed her bathrobe from the hook on the bathroom door.

"Maddy, what's wrong?" Alan asked, sitting up.

"Someone's outside!" she said, and ran out of the bedroom.

"Wha..."

She didn't wait to explain, but hurried down the stairs and flipped on the front porch light. A glance out the living room window confirmed it. Yes, there was the patrol car parked at a crazy angle at the curb, its lights flashing. And there was that big police officer stuffing a kid inside. Maddy squinted, trying to bring him into better focus. He looked a lot like the boy Jordan had a crush on. Tall, scraggly hair. Attitude.

Good. But why their house? Was he trying to impress Jordan? If so, this was the wrong way to do it.

And now here came the second officer, walking around from the side of the house. It was her new neighbor, and she had a hand on the other criminal's arm. So, there'd been two of them. But this one seemed so young and... Wait a minute. Maddy recognized that white parka. And the girl wearing it.

Oh, this couldn't be happening. This was the Nightmare Before Christmas.

If she was dreaming, that doorbell was pretty realistic. She went to the door on wobbly legs and opened it to see Tilda Morrison standing on her front porch with Jordan, whose face was as white as her parka.

Jordan rushed to Maddy, throwing herself into her arms and crying.

Alan was coming down the stairs now. "What's going on?"

"We caught your daughter destroying your candy canes," Tilda said.

"Come in." Maddy stepped aside to let Tilda pass. Jordan was glued to her and they moved like an amoeba.

Tilda came in. She sure was intimidating in that uniform. Maddy wanted to cry herself. "Jordan, was it you who's been wrecking everything?" It couldn't be.

"I'm sorry, Mommy," Jordan sobbed, her newly acquired teen-girl attitude completely gone.

"But why? Why would you do such a thing?" Maddy asked, trying to understand her daughter's bizarre behavior.

"Because I hate those candy canes! And I hate Candy Cane Lane! You care more about that than you do about me."

"Oh, good Lord," Alan muttered.

"Jordan, you don't really believe that, do you?"

"It's true. You never have time for me!"

Maddy hugged her daughter tightly. "Oh, sweetie. This isn't the way to get what you want. And why would you wreck other people's things?"

"We did it so you wouldn't sus...sus...suspect," Jordan wailed, trying to get the words out in between sobs.

"We, as in?" Alan prompted.

"There were two of them out there tonight," Tilda explained. "Who else helped you?" she asked Jordan.

"N-no one," Jordan stammered.

"There were *three* sets of prints in the snow last time," Tilda said. The way Tilda was looking at Jordan made Maddy want to cry out, "I confess."

"Jordan, did any of your friends help you do this?" Alan asked.

Jordan bit her lip. Tears were running down her cheeks. She shook her head vehemently.

"You're not doing your friend any favors by covering for her," Tilda said sternly.

Jordan buried her face in Maddy's bathrobe. "Afton," she sobbed.

"Afton?" Afton with the perfect mother? Maddy had to be hearing wrong.

"What's her last name?" Tilda asked.

"White."

White. Snow White, white as snow. Model child Afton. It was hard to believe.

"What happens now?" Alan asked Tilda.

"We can release her to you."

Thank God.

Maddy was just breathing a sigh of relief when Tilda added, "Yours wasn't the only property she's vandalized."

The Welkys wouldn't press charges, or whatever it was you did to misbehaving minors. Oh, but the Werners. Maddy felt sick.

"I'm afraid this will have to get referred to juvenile court."

"But it's Christmas," Maddy protested.

"We understand," Alan said.

Not Maddy. She didn't understand any of it. How could her daughter do such a thing? And more than once? She remembered Jordan's words after the first candy cane assault. *Wow, what happened?* What indeed? She was raising a criminal mastermind.

How was she supposed to handle this? There was nothing in the parenting handbook that dealt with holiday vandalism. Oh, yeah, there was no parenting handbook.

Her job done, Tilda left Maddy and Alan to deal with their domestic mess.

"Am I in trouble?" Jordan asked in a small voice.

"Yes, you certainly are," Maddy replied. "What you did was wrong."

Jordan hung her head. "I know." Then she hugged Maddy fiercely and started crying all over again.

"I think we've had enough excitement for tonight," Alan said. "Back to bed, girls."

Jordan was still crying. She cried as Maddy helped her out of her coat. She cried all the way upstairs to her bedroom. She cried as she got out of her clothes and into her pajamas. She was going to have the headache to end all headaches.

Maddy fetched a glass of water and an aspirin. "Take this."

Jordan stopped crying long enough to get the aspirin down and ask, "What's going to happen to me?"

Maddy wished she knew. Court. What did that mean? Would Jordan be sent to juvie? How Maddy wished she'd never started this whole Candy Cane Lane thing. She didn't want to see another candy cane as long as she lived.

And she wished she had a better answer for her daughter than "I don't know." Jordan sent up a howl and Maddy sat down on the bed next to her, rocking her back and forth. "But whatever happens, we'll get through it. And, hopefully, you'll learn that it's not okay to act out like this when you're mad."

"You wouldn't listen to me," Jordan whimpered.

Maddy kissed the top of her head. "I'm sorry, sweetie. I'm sorry you felt so neglected. I do love you. You know that, right?"

Except she hadn't shown it much lately. She'd been so absorbed in making sure her neighborhood was picture-perfect she'd neglected the most important people in the holiday picture—her family.

Jordan hugged her tightly, laying her head on Maddy's shoulder. "I love you, Mommy."

Her daughter's words were the best Christmas present ever.

Tilda didn't enjoy writing up the report of her night's adventure. And she hadn't enjoyed presenting Maddy Donaldson with her own daughter as one of the neighborhood candy cane killers. Probably the best thing that could happen to the kid, though. She'd been scared out of her gourd, and at that age, that was a good thing.

Tilda still remembered the time she got caught shoplifting at the drugstore at about the same age. Hildy Johnson had grabbed her by the arm and shaken her until her teeth rattled. Then she'd called Mom, who'd blistered her butt. Both Mom and Hildy had lectured her on how wrong and unfair it was to take things that didn't belong to her, and to give her a taste of how that felt, her baseball mitt had gone to the local thrift store and she'd had to go buy it back. The rest of her penance had been just as bad. Every week for the whole summer she'd had to walk to Hildy's house and mow her lawn. And Hildy had a push mower. All of which had convinced Tilda that crime didn't pay, especially in Icicle Falls.

Part of her hated to do it, but with other people involved, she had to refer this case to juvenile court. Whatever punishment got meted out to little Jordan Donaldson, Tilda suspected it would be made to fit the crime. That might mean a crappy Christmas for the Donaldsons, but in the long run, she hoped it would give them a happy ending with their kid.

Idiot kid. What a stupid stunt to pull. But then, that was what you did at that age—pull dumb stunts. It was enough to make Tilda rethink the idea of having a couple of kids to go with her new house. Kids were a pain in the butt. Maybe she'd get a dog and call it quits.

And what about adding a man to the equation? Ivy Bohn and her troubles with her ex sprang to mind. Then so did the vision of Devon Black waiting for her at the hospital. Every time she thought she had him figured out, he did something to break open the box she'd put him in.

He was a poor love risk, she was sure of it. But then, what did she know? She'd thought Garrett Armstrong, Mr. Responsible, was exactly what she'd needed, and look how that had turned out. Love was such a crapshoot.

But when it came down to it, all of life was a crapshoot. *Take a chance*, urged her hormones.

I will when I find the right guy, she assured them.

We're dyin' here!

Don't be rushing me. I'll give you some chocolate when we get home.

Chocolate. Pah! We want sex.

Well, all you're getting is chocolate, so shut up.

Her house was still lit up, the last one in the neighborhood. The lights illuminated a bottle sitting on her porch. Who was bringing her wine? There came the vision of Devon again.

She pulled the car into the garage, then went through the house and retrieved the bottle. Chocolate wine. The note on it said, *Enjoy*, and it was signed *Ivy*.

All right! Thanks, Ivy. But why was Ivy parting with perfectly good chocolate wine? It didn't take a crack detective to work that out. The wine was probably from the same man who'd brought the pizza. Looked like he wasn't making much progress.

Well, what did he expect? The worst crimes were

crimes against the heart, and this particular criminal was probably going to be spending the rest of his life trying to bribe his way back into his home. Served him right.

Still, Tilda would've kept the wine if she were Ivy. Making a guy pay was one thing, but why deprive yourself?

The next day she was back at the hospital, assuring herself that Mom was still breathing. "I'm doing fine," Mom said. "But I could sure use a cigarette."

"Not happening," Tilda informed her. "You're done."

"Just because you're a cop doesn't mean you get to boss me around," Dot muttered.

"No, I get to do that 'cause I'm your daughter. And I don't want you checking out anytime soon. You scared the shit out of me, Mom."

"I'm going to be around for a million years," Dot said.

"Yeah, if you quit smoking. This is the perfect time to stop. You've already gone forty-eight hours without a smoke."

"And it's killing me."

"So is smoking.You can do this."

"Do you know how many times I've tried to quit over the years?"

"None."

"That's not true. I've tried three different times."

"Well, fourth time's the charm," Tilda retorted. "Come on, Mom. Do this for me, will you? It'll be the best Christmas present I've ever gotten."

Dot sighed. "I'll give it a try. But no guarantees," she said, hedging her bets.

Tilda handed over the incentive spirometer. "You haven't used this yet."

Mom scowled at her. "You make quite the dictator, you know that?"

"I learned from the best. Do your breathing exercises and I'll buy you some Oreos."

An hour later the doctor came by and pronounced Mom ready to be discharged. "About time," she said. "Your food here stinks."

"Yep, you're feeling better," Tilda said.

"Good enough to make the yams for Christmas Eve," Mom said.

"You're not making anything. You get to just come and relax."

"I want to help you," Mom insisted.

"No need. It's all taken care of." Or it would be once Tilda got that turkey ordered. Which she needed to do before she went to work.

"How's the new stove working?"

The stove. With all the stuff going on with Mom, getting it fixed had completely fallen off her radar. "Crap. I still have to call Arvid to order a heating element for it."

"Heating element?"

"The oven doesn't work."

"You planning on having that by Christmas?" Mom asked skeptically.

"I'm counting on it."

"What about the turkey?"

"All under control," Tilda promised her. Or it would be soon.

As soon as she had Mom settled back at home, she drove to the store to order her cooked turkey. On her way she saw the sign outside Mort's Meat Market. *Order your precooked turkeys now.* The price was cheaper than what Safeway was charging. All right. She pulled in to Mort's and ordered a nice twenty-pound bird. That should be enough to feed everyone. And she'd saved some money. Oh, yeah.

"So, pick up on the twenty-fourth, 5:00 p.m.," Mort confirmed.

"Yep," Tilda said. That took care of the bird. She still needed to have her oven up and running for heating rolls and baking her green bean casserole, so she went to Arvid's to have a little talk about the faulty heating element.

"Not a problem," he said. "We'll replace that free of charge."

"Very nice of you, considering the stove is brand-new."

"Well, these things happen," he said philosophically. Old Arvid sure rolled with someone else's punches. "We'll order it in for you right away."

"What do you mean, order it in? Don't you have one around here somewhere?"

He shook his head mournfully. "I'm afraid not."

Why was she not surprised? "How long will that take?"

"We'll have it day after tomorrow."

"Wait a minute. Day after tomorrow is the twenty-fourth. My family's coming over for dinner that night."

"It'll be in by morning," he promised her. "Don't worry."

Don't worry? She'd seen how Arvid operated. She was screwed. She pulled out her cell phone as she left the appliance store and called Georgie. "Can you bring the green bean casserole?"

"I thought you were making that," Georgie said.

"Yeah, so did I. But that was when I thought I had a working oven."

"You have a brand-new stove!"

"With a dead heating element. Arvid's ordering a new one. It's supposed to come in on the twenty-fourth."

"I'll bring the casserole," Georgie said.

Okay, she had Aunt Joyce bringing candied yams and cookies. Georgie was bringing cookies, too. She'd get Caitlin to take charge of the rolls and cranberry sauce. Stuffing and spuds Tilda could do on the stove top. That, at least, was working. The turkey had been ordered. She'd pick up the wine and beer and some of her aunt's favorite holiday tea, and she'd be good to go. Christmas was now officially under control. And that was just the way Tilda liked things. Under control.

She picked up Mom's Oreos and delivered them, then swung by Christmas Haus where she picked up Christmas ornaments to give out on Christmas Eve.

"Finishing your Christmas shopping?" Ivy guessed as she wrapped them.

"Yep, this does it. Speaking of gifts, thanks for the wine."

"You're welcome. I hope you enjoyed it."

"There's still half a bottle left. You sure you don't want it back?"

Ivy frowned. "No, thanks. I'd choke on it." Tilda handed over her charge card and Ivy rang up the sale. "Do you think people can change?"

"I don't know." She wished she did. It would be so much easier to figure out love if you could look into the future.

Ivy gave Tilda back her charge card and her purchases. She shook her head. "Last year I wanted everything to be perfect, and it wasn't. This year I decided I was going to do whatever it took to make the holidays perfect and so far…"

"Things don't always work out according to plan." Especially when it came to love. "I guess you have to do the best you can and call it good."

Ivy nodded.

"You've got kids. That's got to put some merry in Christmas." Unless you were Maddy Donaldson. Tilda suspected her holidays were going to be pretty unmerry.

Ivy smiled at that. "You're right. Kids make all the difference." Her smile suddenly fell away. "Except Rob has the kids Christmas Day."

Tilda had no idea what to say to that. If she was going to be home, she would've invited Ivy to visit with her, but she had to work Christmas Day.

Not until the afternoon, though. "Hey, you can come over to my place in the morning if you want. Maybe I'll have a stove by then and you can teach me how to make pancakes or something."

Ivy looked at her, incredulous. "You don't know how to make pancakes?"

Tilda shrugged. "What can I say? Whenever I wanted pancakes I just went to the restaurant."

"Wow, we have some work to do," Ivy joked. She smiled. "Thanks for the offer. I might take you up on it."

Another customer had arrived, so that ended the conversation.

"See you," Tilda said, and started for the door.

"Merry Christmas," Ivy called after her.

Tilda gave her a backward wave. With her mom out of the woods, this *would* be a merry Christmas.

Chapter Twenty

Grandparents are one of life's greatest blessings,
especially at this time of year.
    —Muriel Sterling, *Making the Holidays Bright:*
               How to Have a Perfect Christmas

The twenty-third of December found Maddy and her
family on the way to court. What happened to the courts
being slow? Why did they have to deal with this right
before Christmas?

Because her daughter had misbehaved right before
Christmas, that was why. Obviously, there wasn't much
on the docket in Icicle Falls Juvenile Court these days.

Or maybe Tilda Morrison had greased some wheels so
things would move along fast. It was better to get through
this mess quickly than have it drag into the New Year.
Maddy just wished they hadn't gotten into the mess in
the first place.

If only Jordan had talked to her, told her how she felt.

She did, said that small voice in the back of Maddy's
mind, the one she'd been trying to ignore. *Your mom
tried to tell you, too.*

She looked out the window at the snowy yards along
Candy Cane Lane filled with nativity sets and reindeer

and inflatable snowmen, the myriad lights outlining rooftops and windows waiting to shine after dark. Such a magical place she and her neighbors had made. And yet she'd spent so much time focusing on the outside that inside, where true Christmas happened, she'd let the magic die. *But we made fudge*, she wanted to protest. *We decorated the tree. We made cookies, for heaven's sake!*

That had all been wedged in around higher priorities. Holiday lights and stupid candy canes. No wonder Jordan had acted out. And now look what was happening to her, all because her mother had given plastic decorations and lights and stupid striped candy higher priority than her.

Priorities had certainly fallen into place since then. They'd spent the past two nights together on the couch, sharing a blanket and watching movies. Or just talking. Most of the talking was done by Maddy, assuring her crying daughter that she wouldn't have to go to jail and wear an orange jumpsuit. (It was hard to tell which scared Jordan more, being incarcerated or having to wear orange.)

They'd met with the prosecutor. That had been an afternoon of tears, headaches and an early bedtime for Jordan, and tears, a headache and a sleepless night for Maddy. No one called and asked her to don her Mrs. Santa Claus suit and pass out candy canes. Just as well. Maddy didn't care if she ever saw another candy cane as long as she lived.

Of course, all the neighbors knew by now. Most had been sympathetic, at least to her face. She was sure they were laughing at her behind her back. Or they were heaving sighs of relief that their kids hadn't pulled a similar stunt. The few who grumbled every year about the fuss, the extra work and the increased traffic on the street must be taking devilish delight in her family's misery.

Maddy hadn't been able to down anything but half a cup of coffee before they left for court. That had been a mistake because it burned in her stomach like battery acid. Alan hadn't eaten anything, either. Neither had Jordan. Now she sat quiet and subdued in the backseat as they left the neighborhood behind and made their way to the courthouse. No texting. These days she wasn't speaking to Afton. Or the boy she'd found so fascinating. At least there was something to be thankful for.

The only time Maddy had ever been to court was to fight a speeding ticket, and she'd lost. *It's going to be okay*, she told herself. They'd met with the prosecutor and survived. Now they just had to go stand before the judge.

Maddy was going to be sick.

How was poor Jordan doing? Maddy checked her daughter in the rearview mirror. "It's going to be okay," she said.

Jordan bit her lip and nodded. A tear slipped down her cheek and another piece of Maddy's heart broke off. Her poor daughter. The courthouse was scary, and Maddy held her baby's hand as they walked down the hall to the room where Jordan's fate would be decided. There weren't many people in it; there was another case being heard before Jordan's and that was Logan's. Ah, yes, one of her partners in crime.

The judge gave him a stern lecture and ordered him to do a month of community service. "Don't let me see you back in here again," she warned.

He and his mother left. Her lips were pressed in a tight line, while he had a scowl on his face. She, too, scowled when they walked past where Maddy, Jordan and Alan sat, looking at Jordan as if it was all her fault. Her daughter the femme fatale.

Jordan had confessed all now, and yes, that little spree of destruction had been her daughter's idea, but he'd been all over it, encouraging her every step of the way. He and Afton had both thought it would be great fun to sneak out and help Jordan make a holiday statement. On the second occasion, the three of them had been together, the girls in the house, with him visiting a couple of blocks over—the perfect Christmas storm. His friend had better sense than to get involved in the prank, but Logan had a great time demolishing candy canes. Afton, the not-so-perfect houseguest, had been the one who'd suggested sneaking out that night. The third time he'd stolen his mom's car and taken a joyride to Candy Cane Lane. It was a wonder he hadn't run off the road or hit someone. Thank God Jordan was done with them both.

And now look who'd entered the courtroom, along with their lawyer—Afton and her mother. Only a couple of weeks ago Maddy would have been embarrassed to be seen in this humiliating situation by the other woman. Now, not so much. Afton's mother wasn't perfect, either, and Maddy found that realization oddly comforting. There was no such thing as a perfect mother. There were only mothers who tried. Granted, some tried harder than others, but in the end kids made their own decisions. When they were right, parents could be proud and hope they'd had something to do with it. When they screwed up? Well, it took a village to raise a child, as the proverb said, and here they were in the village courthouse where someone else was going to step in and take a hand.

Now it was their turn in front of the judge. Jordan was

as white-faced as the Welkys' inflatable snowman and Maddy suddenly felt faint. The proceedings were short. The prosecutor said his piece—"The defendant understands the seriousness of what she did"—and then the judge said hers.

"I'm sentencing you to community service," she told Jordan, who was wiping tears from her eyes. "You will help all your neighbors—every one of them—take down their Christmas decorations."

Did the judge have any idea how many decorations that involved? Next to her Maddy could hear a gulp.

"You will also write a letter of apology to everyone whose property you damaged. And that includes your parents."

Jordan nodded and wiped away more tears.

"Mom and Dad, you will check off all the names on the list and submit that to the court as well as a copy of the letters written. I'll expect them on my desk by January 13."

"Yes, Your Honor," Alan said.

"I trust I won't see you back here," the judge said to Jordan when she was done passing sentence.

Jordan was too terrified to speak but she managed to shake her head.

Alan hugged her as they left the courthouse and she burst into tears. Maddy, too, was tearful. But she was also relieved to have the torture over with and hopeful that both she and her daughter had learned some valuable lessons.

"I'm sorry, Daddy," Jordan sobbed.

"I know, and we forgive you. You did something wrong, and now you'll make it right."

Alan's cell phone rang, but he ignored it. Then Maddy's

rang. And rang. And rang. She let it go to voice mail. There was nothing anyone had to say that was more important than spending time with their daughter.

But whoever was trying to reach them was persistent. A moment later Alan's cell phone rang again. He frowned and pulled it out of his pocket, then swore. Phone to his ear, he said, "Hello, Mom."

Oh, no. His parents were flying in today. And expecting to be picked up at the airport.

"Oh, I'm sorry," he was saying. "It went completely out of my mind." He shot a self-conscious look in Jordan's direction. "Something came up. No, we're still in Icicle Falls."

That. Woman. "Alan, let me talk to her," Maddy said in her sweetest voice.

She was the family diplomat, and he was happy to hand over his angry mom for her to placate. She took the phone and, still smiling, said, "Corrine. So sorry we forgot to come and get you."

"Honestly, I don't know what you were thinking," Corrine sputtered. "I emailed you the flight and arrival time last week."

"Well, we've been kind of busy since then. And today we were tied up in court—"

"Why on earth…"

Maddy continued, talking right over her. "So I'm afraid you're going to have to rent a car and drive up here."

"Drive!" Corrine echoed.

"Yes, you know how to do that."

"Tom doesn't like to drive in the snow," Corrine protested.

"The roads are clear. You'll be fine. See you when you get here," Maddy said, and hung up.

"What did she say?" Alan asked.

"I have no idea. I ended the call a little prematurely."

"You hung up on Grandma?" Jordan asked, shocked.

His cell phone immediately started ringing again. Maddy dropped it in her purse. "I'm hungry. What do you say we go to Herman's?"

Alan grinned. "I'm in favor of that. We could all use some stress relief." Her trauma survived, Jordan skipped ahead to the car and he said to Maddy, "You realize we're going to have major stress once my folks arrive. Mom's going to be madder than a hornet."

"Compared to what we just went through? As far as I'm concerned, her stinger's been pulled out."

But once her in-laws finally arrived, Maddy realized Corrine's stinger was still in fine working order. "What on earth is going on?" she demanded as they walked in the door, her husband, Tom, struggling with a king-size suitcase and a carry-on. Corrine, on the other hand, held only her Gucci bag. As always, her makeup and hair were flawless. She wore a classic black wool coat over leggings and stylish boots, proving to the world that she refused to be outdone by the younger generation.

Her husband didn't worry about fashion. He was clad in a parka with jeans and the blue sweater Maddy and Alan had given him for Christmas ten years ago. Whereas his wife had frown lines around her mouth and between her brows, laugh lines had settled in around his eyes.

"I'm sorry you wound up having to drive, Tom," Maddy said. "We had a bit of a crisis."

"It was okay," Tom said.

"A *bit* of a crisis?" His wife frowned and cocked an eyebrow. "You left us stranded at the airport. I hope it was more than a bit."

"We've had some problems with Jordan," Alan said in a low voice.

"Jordan!" Corrine scanned the hallway for a sign of her granddaughter. "Is she all right?"

Jordan, on hearing the doorbell, had made herself scarce. Normally she would've been on hand to greet her grandparents. Today Maddy didn't blame her for scatting. She'd like to scat herself.

"She's fine," Alan told her. "Let's get you two settled and then we'll talk. Here, Dad, I'll take that," he said, and made his escape to the upstairs bedrooms with the suitcases, leaving Maddy to take the coats, along with the brunt of her mother-in-law's wrath.

"I don't understand what's going on," Corrine snapped as Maddy hung up her coat.

"She's about to tell us, dear," Tom said calmly. Tom was a saint.

"Come into the living room and sit down. Would you like some coffee?" Maddy offered.

"This late in the afternoon? I'll be up all night. Just tell us what's going on," Corrine demanded as they walked into the living room.

"Jordan was involved in some trouble," Maddy explained.

"Jordan! I don't believe it," Corrine said.

"What kind of trouble?" asked Tom.

"She and a couple of other kids vandalized some of our neighborhood Christmas decorations." Mostly hers, but she wasn't sure she wanted to get into that. Of course, how not to? Oh, this was awkward. And humiliating.

"Why on earth would she do such a thing?" Corrine demanded.

How to answer that?

"Why do kids do anything like that?" Tom shook his head. "Remember that time Alan took our car and went joyriding?"

Corrine's cheeks got a little pink. "We're not talking about Alan."

Okay, might as well come out with it. Corrine would find the dirt, anyway. "Actually, she was feeling ignored," Maddy confessed. "And she was mad at me. So she trashed our candy canes and a couple of other neighbors' decorations, as well."

Corrine fell back against the couch cushions and stared at her.

And now was the moment of truth, when she had to admit to both herself and her in-laws that she'd focused on all the wrong things. She took a deep breath. "I'm afraid I got so caught up in making the holidays special for our neighborhood, I fell short here at home."

Corrine shook her head in disgust, but Tom said, "I'm not buying that. You've always been a good mother—and a good wife to our son."

Corrine didn't add an amen to that. Instead, she said, "I need something to drink, after all."

"Of course," Maddy murmured. "Some tea? I have a special holiday blend."

Corrine looked at her watch. "It's almost five. After the way this day has gone, I'll take a glass of white wine. Please tell me you've got some."

Come to think of it, Maddy could use a glass herself. She fetched wine for all of them, including Alan, and returned to find him on the sofa, describing Jordan's community service sentence to them.

Tom nodded. "Suit the punishment to the crime. I like that."

Alan smiled as he took a glass from the tray. "I'm not sure Jordan does."

"Really, Madeline, with you hardly ever home, it's not surprising she got into trouble," said Corrine.

"Mom, she got into trouble in the middle of the night when we were both home," Alan said, defending Maddy like the loyal husband he was. "It's not Maddy's fault. Our daughter made some wrong choices, pure and simple."

"Still…"

"So," Alan said in an effort to turn the conversation. "How was your flight?"

He would've had better luck turning the *Queen Mary* with a rowboat. "The flight was fine. We only had problems after we arrived," said his mother. "I can't understand why you didn't tell us. We'd have been more than happy to come up early and help."

Maddy could just imagine what kind of "help" Corrine would have offered. I-told-you-sos and why-didn't-yous right and left.

"It's all under control now," Alan assured her.

"Is it? Does she understand that what she did was wrong?"

"I think so," Maddy said.

But at dinner that night Corrine made sure, grilling Jordan, telling her how wrong it was to damage other people's belongings. Would *she* like it if her mother came into her room and started breaking her things?

Before she was done, Jordan was in tears all over

again and running up the stairs to her bedroom, the last of her chicken and mashed potatoes abandoned. Maddy had gone to the store and picked up deli chicken earlier, knowing it was her daughter's favorite and hoping to end the evening on a positive note. So much for that.

"Excuse me," Maddy said, and hurried after her.

"You should let her go," Corrine said. "Don't indulge the child when she's been bad."

"Corrine, I think she knows what's best for her own daughter," Tom said. *Thank you, Tom.*

"I'm just saying."

"I think you've said enough."

Alan's words were the last Maddy heard as she left the dining room. *Thank you, Alan.* She might not need an antacid, after all.

She found Jordan on her bed, crying. "Everyone hates me!" she greeted her mother.

Maddy perched on the side of the bed and rubbed her daughter's arm. "Nobody hates you. We all love you."

"Then why is Grandma being so mean?"

Because that's what she does best. "Because she's disappointed." Hmm. Was that why Corrine was so sour? Maybe she was disappointed with how her life had turned out. Maybe she was disappointed that her son had gone away to school in Washington and never come home, that he'd married a girl who'd stolen him away.

Still, that was no excuse to berate Jordan. She'd already been judged in court. She didn't need her grandmother adding to the sentence.

"I wish they hadn't come," Jordan sobbed.

Boy, that made two of them. "You know what, sweetie, it'll get better. Grandma's said what she needed to say and now we won't speak of it again."

Jordan's sobs began to subside.

"We'll have a nice day tomorrow delivering Christmas cookies to the neighbors and…"

"Do I have to see the Welkys?" Jordan asked in a small voice.

"I can take a plate to the Welkys. If you write your apology note to them, I'll deliver it for you. Still, you'll need to see them eventually. You're going to have to help them take down their Christmas decorations."

Jordan nodded, keeping her attention fixed on plucking at a loose thread on her bedspread.

"I know this is hard, but we'll get through it, okay?"

Jordan nodded and whispered, "Okay."

"Now, how about you come back down and have dessert?"

Jordan shook her head vigorously.

There was no point in forcing her. Maddy didn't blame her. She didn't want to go back downstairs, either. "All right. You can join us later if you feel like it."

Jordan just bit her lip.

Maddy gave her a kiss and left. What her daughter had done was wrong, but that didn't stop Maddy from feeling sorry for her. Jordan's actions were paying a hefty dividend of humiliation. Hopefully, the experience would scar her for life in such a way that she'd never again be tempted to walk on the wild side.

Actually, if this was as wild as Jordan ever got, Maddy would be happy.

"Is she coming down?" Corrine asked when Maddy returned.

"She's going to spend some time in her room, thinking about what she's done."

Corrine nodded. "Well, good."

"I told her we're done talking about it." The look she gave her mother-in-law said, "Don't cross me."

Corrine bristled, insulted. "Really, Madeline, I don't know why you're looking at *me*."

"We do," Tom said. "Give it a rest, hon."

"Of course I'm not going to rub the child's face in it," Corrine said stiffly, and took a sip of wine.

"Who's for dessert?" Alan asked, rubbing his hands together.

With dessert came new topics of conversation—Tom's latest business investment, how things were going at the hardware store, what the plans were for tomorrow.

"Would you like to help Jordan and me put together our plates of cookies for the neighbors?" Maddy asked Corrine. "We always take around cookies on Christmas Eve as a…as something nice to do," she corrected herself. The cookies were a thank-you to the women who'd volunteered for Mrs. Santa Claus duty, but under the circumstances, Maddy decided it was best not to bring up the subject of Candy Cane Lane. That would only remind everyone of the trouble it had inspired.

"I'd be happy to," Corrine said, inclining her head like a queen conferring a favor.

Memories of Corrine's contributions a few Christmases past surfaced. She'd been very helpful, wondering why Maddy didn't use curling ribbon ("It makes a much nicer bow") to observing that Maddy hadn't baked her raspberry thumbprint cookies (which were Alan's favorite).

Maddy made a mental note to get Corrine to help her with the thumbprint cookies in the morning. "I thought we'd have an early meal since we have the Christmas Eve service at seven."

Corrine approved of that. "We don't want to eat late."

"We have a Christmas stollen from Gingerbread Haus for Christmas Day breakfast and then we can open presents," Maddy continued. "I thought I'd plan dinner for around two."

And after that they'd only have to endure her mother-in-law for a few more hours and the old bat would be gone. And Alan wouldn't have to drive them to the airport. Now, *there* was a lovely Christmas bonus.

"Well, son, how about a game of cribbage?" Tom suggested, obviously tired of going over the itinerary.

"Sure," said Alan, and escaped, leaving Maddy to entertain her mother-in-law. *Oh, great.*

"Corrine, is there anything you'd like to do?" *Maybe go to bed early. Now would be good.*

"Oh, whatever you'd like," Corrine said, sounding deceptively genial.

Other than bridge, which Maddy had never mastered, Corrine wasn't much for playing games. She wasn't big on movies, either. Conversation was a potential minefield as Corrine usually found it a wonderful platform for even more helpful "suggestions" on how Maddy could do better as a wife or mother. Inspiration hit. "You know, I recorded the latest episodes of *Downton Abbey.* Would you like to watch it?" She wasn't sure if Corrine watched the series, but since it was so popular she figured the odds were good.

"That's fine," Corrine said, and almost smiled.

They were halfway through when Jordan slipped into the family room and dropped a note on Maddy's lap, then fled. The note was written on lined paper. It only covered a small part of the page, but the tear splotches showed that it was heartfelt.

Dear Mommy,
I'm really sorry about what I did. I wish I could do it over cuz I wouldn't do it. I'm sorry I made you unhappy. Please forgive me and ask Grandma not to hate me. I love you.
XOXO Jordan

"Well, what does it say?" Corrine demanded.

Maddy handed it over and Corrine read it, her brow furrowed. "Why on earth would she think I hate her?"

"I guess she somehow read that between the lines."

"That's ridiculous. I love the child," Corrine said, her voice softening.

"She'd probably appreciate a hug at some point."

"I'm going to go talk to her right now," said Corrine.

"I think she just wants to be alone."

"Nonsense. We need to settle this," Corrine said, and left the room.

Maddy followed her out. "She's had a pretty emotional day."

"Well, then, a hug is just what she needs."

"That's all you're going to do? I won't have you scolding her." She never talked to her mother-in-law like that, but desperate times called for desperate measures.

"Honestly, Madeline, what kind of heartless shrew do you think I am?"

Maddy hoped that was a rhetorical question. She followed Corrine up the stairs, determined to run interference if necessary.

Corrine tapped on Jordan's door. "Darling, it's Grandma. I'm coming in," she announced, and entered the room like an invading general, startling Jordan, who was hard at work on another letter of apology.

But there was no further scolding. Instead, Corrine said, "I don't believe I ever got a hug. I could use one. Could you?"

Jordan looked warily at her, but complied.

Corrine kissed the top of her head. "We all make mistakes, darling. The important thing is to learn from them. I bet you've learned a lot, haven't you?"

Jordan's only answer to that was noisy sobs.

"There, now. You know we all love you. Everything's going to be fine, so no more hiding in your room. Come down and have some ice cream and watch TV with your mommy and me."

"I have to finish my letters, Grandma," Jordan said, still crying.

"Of course you do. It's important to make things right when you've done something wrong. You can come down when you're done. Agreed?"

Jordan sniffled and nodded.

"All right, then. And we'll say no more about this."

More sniffling and nodding.

"Good," Corrine said, and left the room. "There, now. It's all handled."

Corrine to the rescue. And to think they still had tomorrow to look forward to.

Chapter Twenty-One

Even the most carefully laid Christmas plans can experience a little hiccup.
—Muriel Sterling, *Making the Holidays Bright: How to Have a Perfect Christmas*

"**Y**ou might want to read this," Mutti said, handing the morning paper to Ivy when she came to drop off the kids. It was folded to a page in the Living section, dedicated to kids' letters to Santa.

"We didn't send a letter to Santa," Ivy said, taking it.

"No, but someone you know did."

"I want to write a letter to Santa," Hannah piped up. "Can we ask him to bring my daddy back?"

"We'll see," said Mutti. "Take your brother and go see what Opa's making in the kitchen."

Meanwhile, Ivy was reading.

Dear Santa, I want a kitty for Christmas. I'm nine now and I'll take good care of it. Carolyn.

She looked up at her mom. "That's cute, but…"

"No, no, farther down."

Dear Santa, Plees bring me a sooper soker so I kan hav water fits this sumer. Ned.

Somehow, she didn't think Mom wanted her to read about Ned and his Super Soaker. She read on. The paper was full of requests and love and adoration.

Dear Santa, can you bring me a little sister for Christmas? I love you. Mandy.

"The one signed Rob," Mutti said impatiently, poking the paper.

Rob? Ivy moved her gaze farther down the page.

Dear Santa,

Can you help out a big kid who was really bad and deserves nothing but lumps of coal for the rest of his life? What if that big kid is really sorry? Could you put in a good word for him with his wife?

I'm that big kid. I had a great wife and a great family and I threw it all away because I thought I wanted my freedom. I felt tied down. Now I realize I wasn't tied down. I was anchored in a snug harbor. Yeah, sometimes I felt like all we did was work. So I left. Went out on my own to enjoy the good life. But without my wife it wasn't good. It was lonely and useless.

Santa, I was a fool. Please help me. Ask my ex to give me a second chance. Tell her I'll do whatever it takes to earn back her trust. Tell her I don't want to drift anymore. I need my anchor. I need the woman I've always loved. Rob.

After reading it, part of her wanted to laugh with joy and run to the Sweet Dreams warehouse and find him, throw her arms around him and tell him to come home. Another part of her wanted to slap him for having the nerve to think he could do something like this and all would be instantly forgiven.

She glanced up at her mother. "I don't know what to say."

"Maybe you need to say you'll give him another chance."

"He left us, Mutti. Just walked out. He broke my heart."

"Yes, he did," her mother agreed. "And it was wrong of him, wrong of him not to stick around and try to fix things. But now it looks like he wants to try."

Ivy crumpled the paper and tossed it on the hall table. "Well, good luck with that. I've got to get to the shop."

Her mother caught her arm. "I know you love the shop. We all do. But there's nothing in it that can keep you warm on a cold winter night."

Ivy frowned. "I can't believe you'd side with him after the way he hurt me."

"I'm not siding with him, darling. I simply want you to be happy. Unforgivingness is a very destructive emotion."

"I can forgive him," Ivy lied. "But that doesn't mean I have to take him back." She kissed her mother and left for the shop. But on her way she stopped at the grocery store and picked up a copy of the paper.

Happily, nobody at work mentioned it. That didn't keep Ivy from thinking about it. She'd be closing the shop at three so everyone, including her and Deirdre, could go to their various family functions. Christmas Eve dinner at her parents' with extended family and a few old friends would start at four, followed by opening presents. Then at seven, everyone would go to the Christmas Eve service at church where they'd celebrate peace on earth, goodwill toward men. And the whole time she'd be thinking about one man in particular. How much goodwill was she willing to extend? *Could* they start over? Did she want to take that risk?

Christmas Eve was finally here. Which was more than Tilda could say for the heating element in her stove. Good thing she'd delegated all the casserole dishes. And the turkey was taken care of. Ha! So clever of her. Well, okay, clever of Devon Black.

She hadn't seen him since their last encounter. Just as well, she'd told herself. It would be too easy to get embroiled with him. What was he doing for Christmas Eve, hanging out with his brother? Not that she was interested. Just a passing thought.

One that kept passing through her mind on and off all day as she cleaned her house and set the table with the fancy Christmas paper plates and napkins she'd bought earlier. He'd fit in well with her wisecracking family.

Stop that, she scolded herself. *What is your problem?*

You know what your problem is, said her hormones. *It's us! We want attention.*

You'll get it in the New Year, she told them. *We'll go find ourselves a sheriff from Wenatchee. Or a firefighter from Yakima. Or...something.* But not a construction worker who tended bar in his spare time.

And came over with cupcake liners and saved kids from being squashed by cars.

They had nothing in common.

He likes to cook, whispered Team Estrogen.

Lots of men like to cook.

He probably likes to play video games.

We don't know that.

We could find out.

We could also concentrate on getting ready for company. And that's what we're going to do.

The hormones went away to pout and Tilda, resplendent in her black leggings, high black boots and the blue chambray blouse her cousins had talked her into getting at Gilded Lily's, went to Mort's to pick up her turkey. The turkey was ready as promised, all golden and gorgeous in its foil roasting pan. A work of art. Her family would be dazzled. Not to mention surprised.

Well, this would prove once and for all to them (and her) that she could be a domestic goddess when the occasion called for it. Tough cookies could have a soft center when they wanted. Maybe she'd host again next year. Maybe next year she'd even buy some china Christmas dishes. And that fancy platter.

She'd barely set the turkey on the counter when her mom arrived, toting a shopping bag filled with presents. "Hey, kidlet, smells good in here," Mom said as Tilda took her coat.

The last time Mom had seen the place, it hadn't exactly smelled like a rose garden. In fact, it still had a faint hint of wonky, which Tilda was covering up with a scented candle Georgie had given her last year when they'd had their gift exchange.

Mom looked around, taking in the furniture, Georgie's quilted wall hanging and Tilda's holiday decorations. Her fake tree sat in the corner, decorated with various collectible ornaments her mom had bought her over the years. The scented candle was on the kitchen counter, working hard to make the house smell like peppermint. The mistletoe was hanging over the entryway, still unused but pretty. Her table was crowded with its matching four chairs, along with some folding chairs she'd borrowed from the chief. She'd covered it with Mom's Christmas tablecloth, a vintage white cotton cloth decorated with green boughs and candy canes. In the center sat a glass bowl she'd found at Timeless Treasures and filled with red and silver foil-wrapped chocolates.

"Looks good." Mom set her shopping bag next to the tree, then pushed up the sleeves of her red sweatshirt that proclaimed I Put Out for Santa. "So, what do you want me to do?"

Was she serious? "I want you to sit on the couch," Tilda said firmly.

"I'm all well now," Mom insisted.

"And we'd like you to stay that way. Anyhow, there's not much left to do. I've got the spuds cooking on the stove and it'll only take a few minutes to do the stuffing."

"Stove Top?"

"Yep."

Mom nodded and smiled, then fell onto the couch with a deep sigh. "Put some Christmas music on that fancy equipment of yours."

Tilda obliged and in a minute Darius Rucker and Sheryl Crow were crooning, "Baby, It's Cold Outside."

A knock on the door signaled fresh arrivals, and Tilda went to let in Georgie and her husband, Jay, loaded down with food and presents. "Hey, it looks great in here." She gazed around approvingly. "Aww, and you hung up my quilt."

"Of course I did," Tilda said, taking the food. "I love it."

"I can teach you how to quilt," she offered.

"That's okay." One quilter in the family was enough. "I'll go put this in the kitchen. You know where the coat closet is."

"Presents under the tree?" asked Jay.

"Yep."

"I'll come with you." Georgie started to follow Tilda into the kitchen.

"No need. Everything's under control."

"You're going to need help when it's time to serve," Mom called from the couch.

"Not from you," Tilda called back. "You're not moving."

She'd just set a bowl of chips and some salsa on the coffee table when Caitlin arrived with Aunt Joyce and Uncle Horace. Both women also wanted to help, but Tilda assured them, too, that everything was under control. She took their food offerings to the kitchen and lined everything up on the counter. There it all was, everything they needed for an impressive dinner—green-bean casserole, rolls, candied yams and cranberry sauce, cookies and red velvet cake (not made by her, sadly, but there was always next year). Oh, yeah. Lookin' good. The potatoes would be done in a minute, then she'd pour off the water, add some milk and butter and beat the heck out of them with her new electric mixer. ("Don't forget to pour off the water," Mom had cautioned. *Gee, thanks, Mom, I wouldn't have thought of that.*) And there, on the stove top sat the crowning piece of the meal…the turkey.

It was calling her. *Come try me.*

Well, she did need to carve it and get it on the platter (borrowed from Mom). And while she was cutting, she'd just take a little taste. She loved turkey. Think of the leftovers. Turkey sandwiches, turkey stew…hmm. How did you make turkey stew? Well, she'd figure it out.

She got a carving knife from the knife block she'd found at a garage sale a couple of years back and started to saw into the bird. What was with this thing? She sawed harder. The knife was hardly moving. Were they making turkeys out of cement these days? What the... She bent over and examined the bird.

Wait a minute. How could this be? Oh, for crying out loud. Underneath its golden-brown crust the damn thing wasn't cooked.

Mort. She was going to kill him. She pulled her cell phone out of her jeans back pocket and dialed the meat market.

"We're closed for Christmas," said a pleasant voice. "We'll be open again December 26. Happy holidays."

Happy holidays? Were they kidding? They'd given her an uncooked bird. What was happy about that? The vision of her perfect first Christmas dinner in her new home flew away, leaving her to grind her teeth.

Okay, work the problem. What could she do? The microwave, of course. She'd stick the bird in the microwave, right on that rotating glass and...

It didn't fit.

Okay, don't panic. She set it back on the stove. What to do now? Try again and see if she could cut off enough pieces to put in the microwave and cook. She didn't go to the gym for nothing. She had muscles. She could do this.

She tried once more to saw into the bird. She got off one skinny little piece. *Shit. Shit, shit, shit!*

Meanwhile, music and laughter drifted in from the living room. Everyone was having fun. Eating chips. Pretty soon the chips would be gone and they'd want dinner. And turkey.

She started sawing for all she was worth. *Come on.*

Please! She threw herself into the task. Her final vigorous effort sent the bird scooting right off the stove top. It hopped out of its aluminum pan and landed on the floor with a thud.

She stared at it. Her Christmas turkey. Her perfect Christmas turkey. With a growl, she kicked the stupid thing, sending it across the floor and crashing into the cabinet. It bounced off and skidded into the middle of the kitchen. So, of course, she did what had to be done. She kicked it again. Then, when it came back for more, she jumped on it, determined to stomp it to death.

Mr. Greasy Turkey Dude slid out from under her foot, and her foot slid out from under her. "Ack!" Down she went, landing on her backside. The turkey sat there on the opposite end of the kitchen floor. Laughing at her.

"You...frozen giblet piece of shit." Teeth bared, she crawled toward it.

"What on earth...?"

She looked up over her shoulder to see Georgie standing in the kitchen doorway, gaping.

Okay, this was not cool. She'd just been caught talking to her turkey.

"Have you gone insane?" Georgie demanded.

Tilda scrambled to her feet and hauled her into the kitchen. "Don't say anything to anybody."

Georgie pried Tilda's greasy hand off her sleeve. "You're having a psychotic break in the kitchen, stalking our turkey and you don't want me to *say* anything?"

"It's not cooked," Tilda said through gritted teeth.

"What?"

"It's not cooked on the inside. Mort gave me an uncooked turkey."

"Oh, no! Well, we'll get it in the stove."

"The stove doesn't work. Remember?" Tilda turned her around. "Go back out there and stall."

"What are you going to do?"

"I'm going to go get...something."

Except her car keys were hanging by the front door and her coat was in the hall. "Bring me my keys, and don't let anyone see you."

"Why don't we just tell them what happened?"

"No! I can handle this. Just get my keys."

"Okay," Georgie said dubiously.

While she fetched Tilda's keys, Tilda paced the kitchen. She gave the turkey another kick, just to make herself feel better.

Georgie was back. "Here they are." She looked at the bruised bird. "What are we going to do with that?"

"Leave it." Tilda was going to save it until the twenty-sixth. Then she'd go in to Mort's and throw it at him.

She took her keys and snuck out the back and around the house, coatless, getting into her car. It was cold outside, but she was so steamed she barely felt it. Off she barreled down the street.

Two of her neighbors were loading presents into their car trunk. "Slow down," cried the woman, probably the same one she'd almost run over the other day in her mad dash to the hospital.

"Police emergency," Tilda muttered, and roared on past, sending newly fallen snow flying in all directions.

She got to the store in record time and ran to the deli.

"I need a turkey," she said to Mindy, the deli manager.

"Did you order one? I don't remember taking an order."

Okay, this was embarrassing. Tilda got a lot of stuff at the deli—sandwiches, Asian rice bowls, potato salads, you name it. She should have ordered her turkey there. They would've given her one that was cooked. But, oh, no. She'd had to be clever and save a buck.

"No," she admitted.

Mindy shook her head sadly. "I'm afraid I can't help you."

"You're out?"

"Sorry. We did up some extras but I sold the last one an hour ago."

"Do you have anything?" Tilda begged.

"Problems?" said a male voice at her elbow.

Of all the grocery stores in all the world... Tilda could feel her cheeks heating. "Shouldn't you be someplace?"

"Yeah, as a matter of fact. I was on my way over to my bro's when you passed me like a bat out of blazes. What's the emergency?"

"My turkey isn't cooked."

"Put it back in the ove...oh. I bet your heating element didn't come yet."

"You win," Tilda said miserably. To Mindy she said, "Got any chicken?" Surely they had some Southern-fried kicking around.

Mindy shook her head. "Someone just bought all of it. Said their turkey didn't get done."

"Probably ordered it from Mort," Tilda muttered.

"You might try the frozen food aisle," Mindy suggested. "Get some microwave chicken."

Oh, great idea. Tilda hurried there, Devon keeping her company.

"Where's the bird now?" he asked.

"On the floor." Okay, that was a little embarrassing.

"The floor," he repeated.

"It's dead. Ruined. Hopeless." Tilda paced back and

forth in front of the frozen entrées. Where was the chicken? "I've got a living room full of people waiting to eat, and green-bean casserole sitting on the counter getting cold. And…" And there was not a speck of chicken to be had. She pushed her hands to her forehead and tried to rub out the headache that was now in full bloom. "What am I going to do?"

"You're gonna go home and wash off your turkey."

"It's frozen. I can't cut it!"

"We can fix that."

We, such a comforting word. But… "How?"

"I can bring over what you need to deep-fry that baby. We'll get it cooked. Trust me."

Maybe it was because, even though he wasn't a cop or a firefighter, there was a nice guy underneath that cocky exterior, or maybe it was because she was desperate, that she said, "Okay."

"Go back home and give everybody some chips. I'll be there in ten."

So, back home she sped. She found her mother and Aunt Joyce in the kitchen, washing the turkey in the sink. A bucket and mop stood in the corner. They'd obviously cleaned the floor, too. *Crap.*

"I came out to get a drink of water," Mom said in her own defense. "We're going to get this washed off, then we'll take it over to my house."

"No need. Everything's under control," Tilda insisted. How many times had she said *that*?

The two women looked at each other the way people did when they were around someone who was, well, having a psychotic break.

"Really," Tilda assured them. "Everything's going to be fine." She pulled another bag of chips out of the cupboard. "The food's getting cold," protested Aunt Joyce. There was an understatement, considering the condition of the turkey.

As it turned out, everything wasn't getting cold. Tilda was just ushering them out of the kitchen when Aunt Joyce pointed to the stove. "The potatoes!"

Tilda dashed over and yanked them off. Fun. She was having fun. Lots of fun. What circle of hell was this, anyway?

"Throw in the towel, Tillie," Mom advised.

No way. There would be no towel-throwing here. No surrender. "I've got this covered."

Ten minutes later Devon was knocking at the back door. "Where's the dirty bird?" he joked.

She led him over to the sink.

"Looks like a good one."

"Yeah, well, looks can be deceiving."

"So can first impressions." he said, picking up the turkey. "But you should never judge a bird by its outside."

"We'll probably all get food poisoning." She could see the headlines now. Local Cop Poisons Entire Family with Bad Bird.

"Not on my turkey watch," Devon said, and carried it outside, where he'd set up a propane gas tank, a burner and a huge pot, which he'd already filled with oil.

She noted the thermometer clinging to the inside of the pot. The whole thing resembled some giant science project. "This is yours?"

"Nope. It belongs to Todd and Bailey. They're letting me borrow it."

"I bet you were supposed to be there for dinner." And here he was, rescuing her.

"They'll all survive without me for a while."

There was a telling word. He probably had parents in town for the holidays and here he was, bailing her out. "What'd you tell them?"

"That I got a better offer," he said with a grin.

The oil was boiling now and he stuck a hook in the turkey and lowered it in.

"Die, evil bird," Tilda said, which made him laugh. And that made her laugh. And suddenly her Christmas didn't feel quite so ruined.

Dinner wasn't served on time, but it did get served. The bird got cooked, Tilda mashed her potatoes, reheated the casserole in the microwave, turning the fried onions to mush, and managed to make stuffing from a box without ruining it. And they had one more person at the table.

"This is my friend, Devon Black," she told everyone. And yes, he was her friend. He'd proved himself more than friend worthy…which was more than she could say about herself. "He got our turkey cooked."

"A true hero," said Uncle Horace. "You saved us all from starvation, son."

Tilda could see Mom looking speculatively at him. "Well, Devon, I wouldn't mind if Santa put you in my daughter's stocking." Everyone laughed and Devon, the biggest flirt in Icicle Falls, actually blushed.

He stayed to help with cleanup afterward. Then he hung around to play "Wii Sports Resort" games, and her family took delight in seeing Tilda the champion fencer get knocked from her platform into the water by the newcomer.

But when it was time to open presents, he said he needed to get going. "I'll help you load your stuff," Tilda said, grabbing her coat and going outside with him.

Once his turkey torture equipment was loaded and

they were standing in front of the cab of his truck, Tilda suddenly found herself at a loss for words. Other than, "Thanks. You saved the day."

"Once in a while us ordinary guys put on our Superman capes," he joked.

"You don't look anything like Clark Kent."

He gave a snort. "I guess I don't look anything like Superman, either. For that you need a police badge and a bulletproof vest."

"Maybe," Tilda said. "Maybe not." Maybe she'd been wrong about a few things.

About time, said her hormones. He looked at her, a speculative smile playing on his lips. He had some five-o'clock shadow stealing across his jaw, and it was just plain sexy. Like the rest of him. Oh, he was trouble.

She was a cop. She knew how to deal with trouble. She took a step closer. "How am I going to thank you for saving my butt today?"

He smiled down at her and Team Estrogen said, *Go for it!*

"I bet you could come up with something if you thought hard enough. Or better yet, if you didn't think."

Let's stop thinking and get with the program, urged the hormones.

So she did. She took that lovely, five-o'clock-shadow-covered face between her hands, pulled it to hers and kissed him. And he slipped his hands under her coat and pulled her against him and kissed her right back. And her black lace thong went up in flames.

"Was that mistletoe I saw in your living room?" he murmured against her cheek after they came up for air.

"Yeah."

He smiled, a bad-boy glint in his eye. "We should do

something about that." He snuggled her up against him. "Got it hanging anywhere else in your house?" *Like the bedroom?*

"Just because you cooked my turkey..." *And set my panties on fire.*

"Yeah? What?"

It took her a minute to answer, since he was kissing her again, and the second helping was even better than the first. "Don't be getting it into your head that I'm sleeping with you."

"I don't put out on the first date," he said.

"This isn't a date."

"Then you aren't getting past first base," he said with a grin.

"Yeah?" All of a sudden she kind of wanted to get past first base.

"Maybe I'll stop by later and see if you can change my mind," he said with a grin.

Maybe that was a pretty good idea.

Chapter Twenty-Two

Forgiveness is the key to experiencing true joy.
—Muriel Sterling, *Making the Holidays Bright:*
How to Have a Perfect Christmas

The day had gone as well as could be expected. The Christmas cookies got delivered and Corrine helped assemble the plates with hardly a critical comment. "I don't know where you found time to bake all these," she said.

Maddy hoped that was a compliment. "I started early and froze them. And Jordan was a big help," she added, smiling at her daughter.

Jordan, who seemed to have reconnected with her sweeter side, had blushed and smiled. Not for the first time Maddy wondered if there was a connection between that and the dearth of texts now that she and Afton and Logan were no longer buddies. One thing she was grateful for—each kid was doing community service in a different area of town. She wouldn't have to see the other miscreants and neither would Jordan, at least not until school started again. And they would cross that snowy bridge when they came to it.

Now, with dinner over, it was time to head out to

church. Maddy was helping with refreshments, so that meant leaving a little early.

"Honestly," Corrine grumbled. "Do they really need cookies at a Christmas Eve service? And why on earth do you have to bring them?" Translation: *Why do I have to be inconvenienced?* Corrine had been up here for Christmas before. She knew the drill. She simply didn't like it.

"Everyone enjoys staying and chatting afterward." She shouldn't have to explain this to her mother-in-law. "And whenever people gather, there's usually food involved."

"Which is why so many Americans are overweight," said Corrine, the food police.

"If you'd rather stay home..." *Oh, please say you would.*

"No, no." Corrine waved away Maddy's suggestion. "We don't want to miss any of the fun."

No, because then how could "we" be on hand to throw a wet blanket over it?

"Let's go," said Alan, and everyone bundled into coats and went out to the car.

Even though they were early, several cars were already in the parking lot. Jordan saw a buddy and ran across the parking lot to greet her, slip-sliding as she went.

"Be careful," Alan cautioned as he helped his mother out of the car. "The temperatures have dropped and the ground is icy."

"Can't be falling at our age," added Tom.

Corrine still managed, though. Alan had just opened the church door and Maddy had gone through and was greeting one of her friends when a screech followed them into the foyer. Maddy turned just in time to see her mother-in-law landing on the ground. Not content to fall on her own, she'd dragged poor Tom down, as well. His reflexes not what they used to be, he was unable to avoid landing on top of her, which produced another screech.

Alan rushed to help them up. Maddy handed off her cookies and ran after him. Tom was struggling to get to his feet and assist his wife at the same time. Alan got his dad up and then pulled his mother to her feet, which brought a cry of pain.

Maddy hovered. "Are you all right?"

"No, I'm not all right," Corrine snapped. "Oh, Tom, my ankle."

Tom didn't look so good himself. His face was rapidly turning as white as the snow and he was cradling his left hand, which was bleeding.

"Here, come inside," Alan said, taking her arm.

She started to limp toward the door and let out another cry. "I can't put weight on it."

Alan scooped her up and staggered into the foyer, managing to get her to a chair before collapsing with her. Corrine wasn't overweight by any means, but Alan wasn't exactly in shape. Maddy hoped he wouldn't give himself a hernia in the process of being a noble son. Meanwhile, she took Tom's arm and escorted him inside.

"I'll get some ice for that ankle," offered Maddy's friend.

"Thank you," Corrine whimpered.

"Come on, Dad, let's get you cleaned up and take a look at that hand."

Tom nodded and limped off toward the men's room

with Alan, leaving Maddy to provide comfort as best she could.

"I'm so sorry," she said.

"It's not your fault," Corrine replied. She was being nice. What was wrong with her? "They should salt that entrance," she muttered with a frown. Ah, there was the Corrine they all knew and didn't love. But then she added, "Someone else might get hurt. We don't want to see someone's Christmas Eve ruined."

Okay, the woman was human, after all.

Maddy's friend was just applying ice to the ankle when Dr. Sharp, their GP, came in, bringing his mom and sisters. "What happened?" he asked, leaving the women to deliver their cookies to the church basement.

"I'm afraid my mother-in-law had a fall," Maddy explained. "Could you look at her ankle?"

"Of course." He knelt in front of Corrine and began to examine her ankle, which now resembled a baseball. The extra attention raised the whimpering decibel.

"Is it broken?" Maddy asked.

"It's hard to tell. I think you should go to the emergency room and have this checked out. You could've fractured it."

"Fractured," Corrine repeated weakly.

"Don't worry. We'll get you fixed up," the doctor said calmly, taking out his cell phone.

Tom was back now, and it was decided that he, too, should get checked out. Well, so much for the Christmas Eve service. Looked like Maddy would be spending it at the hospital, praying desperately that her mother-in-law hadn't broken anything. It would've been nice if her motives were altruistic, but alas, they were purely selfish. If

Corrine had broken her ankle, she'd probably extend her stay. Just what Maddy wanted for Christmas.

Ivy and her family arrived at church to find an ambulance in the parking lot. Its flashing lights bathed the man sprinkling salt around the snowy lot in red light. And there were Maddy and her family, leaving the church.

Ivy rushed over to her. "Is everything okay?"

"My mother-in-law fell," Maddy said. "We're on our way to the emergency room." She lowered her voice. "If she's broken her ankle, they'll have to stay longer. Please pray for us."

Ivy got the underlying message. "Will do. Hang in there."

Poor Maddy. She tried so hard to make the holidays ideal. So far, though, this Christmas had been anything but ideal for her.

So far this Christmas hadn't been ideal for Ivy, either. But today had been the capper. Rob had posted his very public apology and now everyone expected her to take him back.

"A hard thing for a man to publicly admit he's been an asshole," said her father. "Maybe he's learned his lesson."

And when her uncle Will had come in after dinner, dressed up as Santa for all the kids at the Christiansen family gathering and Hannah had reminded him that she just wanted her daddy to come home, all eyes had turned to Ivy. Somehow, it was all on her now. If she couldn't forgive Rob, if she didn't take him back, she would be the new villain of the Bohn family. How unfair!

The idea of letting him back in was tempting. What would it be like to have Rob home again, to snuggle up to him in bed at night, to feel his arms around her? To have another adult in the house? To feel loved? But it was Rob's fault that she'd felt unloved for the past year!

And now, as she and the kids seated themselves next to her parents, here he was walking into the sanctuary, looking tentatively around. He was wearing his favorite dark jeans and the red sweater she'd given him for Christmas two years ago, along with his North Face jacket. He was like red velvet cake—oh, so tempting and oh, so bad for a girl. He hadn't been in church in a year. But now that it was Christmas, here he was. *Do you see what I see?*

A creep, a creep, her inner song continued, *slinking through the night. I'd like to tell him to go fly a kite.*

And yet, under the anger, was a longing that had resurfaced like Scrooge's Ghost of Christmas Past, reminding her of what they once had. Could they find it again?

Hannah had seen him now. "Daddy!" she called, and waved to him.

He smiled at her and waved back. Then he made his way to where Ivy sat, looking like a man about to wade into shark-infested waters. He nodded at Ivy's parents and ventured a smile.

Her father acknowledged him with a nod, and Mutti said, "Rob, we haven't seen you in church in a while."

He ducked his head. "Yeah. I know."

"Sit with us, Daddy," Hannah invited him.

Rob turned to Ivy, his eyes asking for more than permission to join them in singing Christmas carols. "Do you mind?"

No more shuttling the kids back and forth. No more fighting over who got them when and for how long. No more lonely nights. No more feeling unloved and rejected. *If you sit down, you don't ever get to leave again.* Could she say that? And if she did, would it be that easy? He took her silence as consent and sat down next to her. Hannah immediately climbed over her and settled in his lap. "Are you coming home with us, Daddy?"

"I don't know," he said, looking at Ivy again. "Am I?"

She was saved from answering. The musicians had started playing and now everyone was singing "Joy to the World" with gusto. Ivy seemed to be the only one in the whole church who was waging an inner battle this Christmas Eve.

The congregation sang some more carols and Pastor Jim preached a minisermon. His concluding remarks seemed to be meant just for her. "This is the time of year we celebrate the great gift God gave us. He gave us all a second chance when He sent His Son to earth. Let's see if we can honor that gift by reaching out in love to those around us, by giving those who've wronged us a second chance. By giving ourselves a second chance. Tonight, let's every one of us go home and think about how we can do our part to bring about peace on earth and goodwill toward all."

It was a candlelight service, and every participant had been presented with a candle. Now the lights were dimmed and ushers walked down the aisles, lighting candles for the people sitting at the end of each row. That person then lit the candle of the person sitting next to him or her, so little dots of light began to spread in the darkness. A musician softly played his guitar and the congregation sang "Silent Night."

As Rob touched his candle to Ivy's, she couldn't help thinking back to their wedding ceremony when they'd lit that unity candle. Two becoming one. Could it happen again? Could they light that fire a second time and keep it lit? *All is calm, all is bright*.

Pastor said a prayer and the solemn moment ended. The lights came back up and the candles were extinguished and collected as the mood turned festive and everyone sang, "We Wish You a Merry Christmas."

"Merry Christmas, and God bless us, everyone," said Pastor Jim. "And now, let's go sample some of those wonderful Christmas cookies I saw earlier."

People chatted with one another and children dashed off to get into the cookies. A couple of people told Rob it was nice to see him again.

"I'm glad you two are back together," said Mrs. Walters, patting Ivy's arm.

"Thanks, Mrs. W." Ivy decided it was easier to play along than explain that their relationship was in the "it's complicated" stage.

"Let's get cookies, Daddy," Hannah said, tugging on Rob's arm.

"Just a couple," Ivy told her. "Then we need to go home and get you in bed so Santa can come."

"Santa, yay!" Hannah cried, jumping up and down.

Robbie was still clueless about Santa, but his sister's reaction was enough to make him bounce excitedly in Ivy's arms.

"Okay, one cookie and then Mommy will take you home," said Rob.

"You're coming, too, Daddy," Hannah insisted.

Rob looked at Ivy. *Am I?*

"Daddy will come over to help tuck you in," Ivy said. It was Christmas, after all, and she wanted her daughter to go to sleep happy.

And what about her? Did she want to go to sleep

happy? All she had to do was say the word and she could. Her tummy felt as though an entire flock of sugarplum fairies was dancing around in there.

Three cookies and a cup of punch later, Hannah was on a sugar high. "It's going to be fun getting her to settle down," Ivy predicted.

"She'll crash once you've got her in bed," Mutti said. She hugged Ivy. "Come on by tomorrow if you want." She sneaked a glance in Rob's direction. "Unless, of course, you get a better offer."

She had a feeling she was going to. The big question was, should she take it?

Rob helped her pile the kids in the car, then followed them home. No baths tonight. She popped both children into their jammies and settled them in bed, Gizmo trotting behind, supervising. Hannah wrapped her arms around Rob's neck after they'd tucked her in, reluctant to let him go. "I asked Santa for you to come back home, Daddy."

"You know, you don't need to ask Santa for stuff like that," Rob said. "I'll always be around for you, princess, whether I'm here in the house or down the street."

"But I want you *here*," she said, her voice tearful. "And I asked Santa. And God."

"Bringing in all the big guns," Rob quipped. He kissed her head and gently disengaged himself. "You need to go to sleep, so Santa can come."

"Okay," she said, and dutifully closed her eyes.

Ivy bent and kissed her cheek. "Good night, baby."

"Night, Mommy." Hannah sighed and snuggled into her pillow.

They quietly left the bedroom and went downstairs,

not talking. Then they were in the hallway and Ivy suddenly had no idea what to say.

Rob filled the silence. "Ive, can I stay for a while? Please?"

There went the sugarplum fairies again, dashing back and forth. "You want some hot buttered rum?"

"Sure," he said, and followed her into the kitchen, Gizmo beside him.

She gave the dog a treat and said, "Lie down." Happy with his reward, Gizmo went into the family room and curled up on his dog bed.

"He still minds you better than he does me," Rob said, and sat on a bar stool at the counter.

"He still likes you better." So did their daughter. But then little girls all liked their daddies best. Even when the daddies left.

He watched as she turned on the electric teakettle and pulled mugs from the cupboard. "Did you see today's paper?"

She concentrated on spooning the rum mixture into their mugs. "I did." *Say something more.* But she couldn't. Her lips seemed to be frozen shut.

"I know I was a shit."

All the hurt and anger she'd been carrying around for months sizzled to the surface and melted the freeze. "Yeah, you were. Rob, do have any idea what this year has been like for me? Having to hear about you taking up with that Ashley Armstrong in the New Year? And then that other woman this summer? To see you just moving on and partying, throwing aside what we'd had? Do have any idea of what Hannah's gone through? What it's been like around here having to hear her ask God every night to bring you home?" She poured the water into his mug, walked over to the counter and slammed it down in front of him. "I'm sick of you, sick of all the hurt you've caused, sick of trying to figure out what I did that was so bad you couldn't stay and fix it," she finished, her voice breaking. The thaw released a torrent of tears and she turned her back to him.

He was at her side in an instant. "Ivy, Ivy," he said, drawing her into his arms. "I was a jerk."

She laid her head on his chest—it felt so good—and let herself sob.

"Oh, baby. You didn't do anything. It was all me."

She looked up at him, tears stinging her cheeks. "How can I take you back? How can I trust you not to break my heart again?"

"I don't know. I really don't. I don't deserve a second chance."

"No, you don't," she said. But suddenly what anyone did or didn't deserve was a moot point. It was Christmas Eve and she was tired of holding on to the hurt. She wanted her husband back. She wanted him, period. She pulled his face to hers and kissed him.

His arms tightened around her and he drew the kiss out, their lips salty with tears. "Do you know how long I've wanted to do that?" he asked at last.

That had been the wrong thing to say. She freed herself and stepped back. "It couldn't have been *that* long since you were with those two other women. And they're only the two I know about," she added. She snatched her mug and went to the living room.

He trailed her in. "Ivy."

She was mad all over again. "I guess you weren't exactly moping around, dreaming of kissing me."

He settled on the couch next to her. "Yeah, I admit it. I thought life would be better with no strings."

Yeah, well, maybe she wouldn't have minded escaping those strings, too, getting a break from long hours at the shop, housework, babies up all night with ear infections. She scowled at her drink and set it aside.

"You know, I took Melody to my folks' for Thanksgiving."

"I don't want to hear this."

He held up a hand. "No, let me finish. Everyone was nice to her, but it was weird. We went to Seattle afterward but the magic wasn't there for us. It was like when you're putting together a puzzle and you keep trying to fit in a piece that's almost the right shape, but not really. You keep trying and trying to force it in. It never works, though, because it's not the right piece. That was when I knew I'd been fooling myself all along. I should never have left."

"But you did," she said sadly.

"I know. I was tired of the grind, tired of feeling like…" He shrugged. "I don't know, just another thing on your to-do list. We'd lost what we'd had, and I figured there was no point in trying to get it back."

"We could have gone for counseling."

He shook his head. "I didn't think it would work."

Why? And why hadn't he said all this to her back then, instead of just giving her vague excuses? "Rob, I would have done anything."

He turned and faced her. "Would you, Ive? Would you really? What about the times I suggested taking a weekend off? What about Thanksgiving weekend last year?"

"It's one of our busiest weekends!" she protested.

"Yep. I remember you saying that. More than once. That was the tipping point, though."

They'd gone to a fund-raiser dinner in October for Camp Summit, a camp just outside of town that focused on helping underprivileged kids, and Rob had bid on a weekend at a Seattle B and B in the silent auction. He'd wanted them to leave the kids with her parents and go away for a second honeymoon. "We could go Thanksgiving weekend," he'd said.

"We can't do that weekend. I've got the store."

"You've got employees. Your parents could help out."

"*And* watch the kids?"

"Okay, if not then, when?"

"We can't go in December."

"It's only good till the end of the year," he'd pointed out.

"I guess we can't use it, then," she'd said.

"I guess not," he'd agreed irritably, and stopped bidding.

The drive home that night hadn't been as happy as the drive to the fund-raiser. Rob had been ticked.

"We've got a business," she'd reminded him.

"No. *You've* got a business. I'm not part of it. And frankly, ever since you took over for your folks, that place has owned you."

Now, looking back, she realized it had. "So, it's my fault you left."

"No. It's mine. I was tired of being in second place and I walked out like a spoiled kid who can't get his way."

Second place. "Was that what you thought, that you came in second?"

"More like third or fourth, after the kids, after your

family, after the shop. And yeah, I know that makes me a supershit. I really don't deserve another chance, Ivy, but I'm hoping you'll give me one, anyway."

"What would things be like if you did come back?" Did he want her to quit working at the shop?

"Better than they were when I left, I hope."

"We'll still have kids. I'll still… Will I have a shop?"

"I know you love that shop. It's been in your family since dust. Hell, my mom remembers when it first opened as Kringle Mart. It was dumb of me to think I could separate you from it, especially since you'd been working there since we were in high school. So, yeah. Do what you gotta do. Just put me back in the picture."

"Or the puzzle," she said, managing a smile.

"Have we got a deal? Can I come back home?"

She bit her lip. Could they work things out?

He was looking at her so earnestly. He'd taken a risk in coming over, in writing that letter to the paper. She could get even right now and send him packing.

But she didn't want to. "Yes. Please come home," she said.

With a very unmanly sob, he pulled her to him and kissed her like a man who'd been marooned for a very long time and just been rescued. Maybe they'd both been rescued.

Their lovemaking was fast and heated, their clothes torn off with the same eagerness they'd been shed on their honeymoon. Afterward, when they lay together on the couch, he kissed her temple and murmured, "I love you, Ivy. I always have. I'm so damn sorry I hurt you."

So was she. But her joy in having him back eclipsed that sorrow. "You're here now and that's what counts."

"Daddy?"

The sudden sound of their daughter's voice made Ivy just about jump out of her skin.

"Shit," Rob muttered, grabbing for his pants.

"Hannah, go to bed!" Ivy commanded.

Hannah remained perched halfway down the stairs, rubbing her eyes. "Did Santa come?"

"Not yet," Rob said, trying to discreetly get himself back in his pants. Not an easy feat considering the fact that the couch and the two naked people on it were in full view.

"Mommy, where's your nightgown?" Hannah asked.

"Daddy's going to get it for her," said Rob, zipping up his jeans. He walked to the stairs, leaving Ivy to fumble for the throw on the end of the couch. "Come on, back to bed."

"When's Santa coming?"

"As soon as you've gone to sleep," he said, picking her up.

"But I went to sleep."

"You have to sleep some more."

They disappeared upstairs, and Ivy threw her clothes back on and got busy putting out presents for the kids— a pink bumblebee Pillow Pet and LeapFrog LeapPad for Hannah, and some Fisher-Price goodies for Robbie.

She found herself singing "I Saw Mommy Kissing Santa Claus." More like *I saw Mommy boinking Santa Claus.*

"Do you think we scarred her for life?" she asked when he came back down.

He grinned. "In a good way. She's sure that Santa's already been and gone—and left me here to stay."

"I guess he did," Ivy said with a smile. "Come on, let's go to bed."

"Great idea," he said. And once back in the bed they'd shared for so many years, the bed that had been half-empty for so many months, he proceeded to give her a very merry Christmas.

They were awakened that morning by Hannah bouncing on the bed. "Santa came, Santa came!" she cried, falling on her father and hugging him.

From his room Robbie was howling to be let out. As Ivy left to go and get him she heard her daughter say, "I knew you'd come home." This was followed by, "Thank you, Santa, thank you, God."

Her daughter's prayers had worked and she'd gotten just what she wanted for Christmas.

They all had.

Chapter Twenty-Three

So what really makes the holidays perfect? Two things—appreciating the message of joy that comes with Christmas and loving one another. After that everything else falls into place.
—Muriel Sterling, *Making the Holidays Bright: How to Have a Perfect Christmas*

Christmas Eve had not gone according to plan. Maddy's father-in-law had sprained his wrist. Corrine's diagnosis was less conclusive. X-rays had been taken and the doctor couldn't rule out a subtle fracture. The patient had been put in an ankle brace, instructed to use crutches, to remain non-weight-bearing and repeat the X-ray procedure in a week. Which meant—oh, joy—staying in town for another week.

They'd transferred the folks from the upstairs bedroom to the sleeper sofa, which allowed Corrine to complain about her back all through their Christmas-morning stollen. Tom, who'd had to cancel his appointment back home, simply said, "Oh, well," and got to work rebooking their flight. Now the Queen of the World was enthroned on the living room couch, her foot propped up on a pillow, while they opened their presents.

Jordan was delighted with the iTunes gift card her parents had given her (since Grandma wasn't going to come through) as well as the gemstone necklace and the decorative bed pillow that said Plant Face Here. Now she was opening a present from her grandparents. "An iTunes gift card. Thank you, Grandma! Thank you, Grandpa," cried Jordan, hugging first Tom and then Corrine.

"You're welcome," Corrine said. "That's what your mother said you wanted."

Jordan nodded eagerly. "Thanks. I did."

"I didn't know your parents were going to give you one," Corrine added, and looked accusingly at Maddy.

What to say to that? Nothing, of course.

Alan got a tin of his favorite hard candies, along with a shirt (the same thing he got every year) and a Rascal Flatts CD. He also received a MasterCard gift card.

"We figured you could use it to do something as a family," Corrine said. "It sounds as though you're not getting to spend much time together lately."

She might as well have added, "And, obviously, with the problems you've had with your daughter, you need it."

"Thanks, guys," Alan said. "That's nice of you. Isn't it, hon?"

"Yes, it is," Maddy agreed, forcing herself to smile.

Corrine shifted on the couch and let out a whimper.

"Do you need another pain pill?" Maddy asked her.

"That would be good," Corrine replied. "I'll have some more coffee, too," she said, holding up her mug.

"Of course." Maddy took the empty mug and went to fetch coffee and more painkiller. A whole week of this lay ahead. Santa sure had it in for her this year.

She returned with a pill and the coffee, and Alan

said with a sly smile, "Here's a present for Maddy." He handed her a small gold foil-wrapped box. The tag on the bow said *To the world's best wife. Love, Alan.*

Aww. She pulled off the paper and found a black velvet box from Mountain Jewels inside. "Oh, my. What's in here?"

"Something that's going to earn my son a lot of points," predicted Tom.

Tom had tried to earn points with Corrine by getting her a gold bracelet—and failed. Corrine had been eyeing a different one. What a surprise. "But it was very sweet of you to try," she'd said. "I'll exchange it when we get home." Charming. For the millionth time since they'd got married, Maddy found herself wondering how her husband had turned out to be such a great guy. Oh, yeah. He took after his father.

"Open it," Alan urged, nodding at the box in Maddy's hand.

She did, and there sat a pair of pink diamond earrings. "Oh, Alan, they're gorgeous!" she cried, and kissed him.

"Now, how come I don't get rewarded like that?" Tom joked.

"Trade this in for the bracelet I wanted, and you will," Corrine promised.

"Here's another present for you," Jordan said, handing Maddy a square box wrapped in expensive red foil with a gold ribbon. It was the same wrapping as Alan's and Jordan's presents, one of the gifts Tom had put under the tree.

"It's so pretty, I almost hate to open it," Maddy said. She'd probably like the wrapping better than what was inside.

Corrine smiled, the picture of self-satisfaction.

Maddy slipped off the ribbon and braced herself. Over the years her mother-in-law's presents had ranged from books on how to have a better marriage to workout DVDs (that one she'd given Maddy the Christmas after Jordan was born and she was trying to shed ten pounds). This year...

"Oh. Oven mitts." Sage green decorated with a French *boulangerie* print. Maddy's kitchen was done in Delft blue. Corrine had gone all out this year. "They're very pretty," she said politely. "I can always use oven mitts."

"That's what I thought," Corrine said, nodding. "One of them has something inside."

Maddy felt around in one. Nothing. She tried the other and her hand found a gift card. She pulled it out and saw it was for a chain department store.

"We looked online and saw they had one in Wenatchee," Tom explained. Tom had probably been the one to suggest adding something more to Maddy's present.

"Well, it was very thoughtful," Maddy said, smiling at him.

And that was the end of the presents. Now it was time to get dinner on. "Don't forget your oven mitts," Corrine called after Maddy as she started for the kitchen.

"Oh, yes. Can't forget those."

Maddy spent the next couple of hours putting together their holiday feast—ham, mashed potatoes, rolls, fruit salad and roasted vegetables. She enlisted Jordan's help in setting the table, then frosted the red velvet cake and waited on Corrine, fetching more painkillers, ice for her ankle and, of course, more coffee.

By the time dinner was over, Maddy was ready for bed. But the in-laws were still with them and had to be entertained. "Let's play a game," Jordan suggested.

"Okay," Alan said. "You pick."

Jordan picked the classic board game Clue, which they hadn't played together in a year.

"Oh, good choice," Tom said. "You know, I remember playing this with you and your sister when you were kids," he told Alan.

They had to set up the game on the coffee table because Corrine couldn't move all the way to the kitchen table. For a second Maddy imagined her mother-in-law laid out on the kitchen floor. Maddy Donaldson did it in the kitchen...with the oven mitts.

Surprisingly, the coffee table worked out just fine and Corrine enjoyed the game. She also enjoyed watching *White Christmas* later that day.

That evening Maddy served grilled ham and Gruyère sandwiches made with French bread. "These are great," Tom said. "You should make these, hon."

Corrine's smile was cold enough to turn him into a snowman. But then she said to Maddy, "They're very good. You'll have to give me the recipe." A compliment from Corrine? Whoa, what was in those pain pills?

Later that night Corrine said something else that nearly made Maddy's jaw drop.

"It's sweet of you to let us stay longer."

Yes, it was. Too bad Protestants didn't canonize people. She would surely have qualified for sainthood. Maddy Donaldson, patron saint of long-suffering daughters-in-law.

"You're a kindhearted woman," Corrine added, then picked up her crutches and swung off to her makeshift bed.

This time Maddy's jaw did drop. Wow. Would wonders never cease?

"It's been a strange Christmas," Alan commented later as they got ready for bed.

"It sure has," she agreed. But Corrine actually saying something kind to her—this just might have been the best Christmas she'd had in a long time.

The evening of Christmas Day was usually pretty quiet. Not tonight, though. Tilda and Jamal dealt with a B and E, which turned out to be a couple home from their holiday vacation a day earlier than expected. Their neighbors had been positive they were burglars. That was followed by two domestic disturbances, proving that there was, indeed, no place like home for the holidays, and a call from Mrs. Walters who was sure she'd heard something.

Tilda was equally sure Mrs. W. had imagined it, but she and Jamal walked all around the house, shining flashlights everywhere.

"I didn't think we'd find anybody," Jamal said.

"We can't tell her that. She'll worry that he'll come back."

"There's nobody to come back," Jamal pointed out.

"I know that and you know that, but Mrs. W. doesn't," Tilda said as they climbed the porch steps. Tilda knocked on the door.

"Who is it?" the old lady called.

"It's me, Tilda. You can open up."

Mrs. Walters opened the door, her bathrobe clutched tightly to her chest, and looked up at them with a mixture of fear and… Oh, now Tilda got it. Other than her excursions to Pancake Haus with her sis, this was the most excitement in Mrs. W.'s life.

"Did you get him?" she asked.

"We did," Tilda lied. "He's in the patrol car."

Mrs. Walters craned her neck, trying to see into the dark vehicle. Jamal moved slightly to block her vision. "Oh, thank God. Now I can sleep. You know, I didn't sleep very well last night. We were all at my niece's over in Wenatchee and I had some coffee. She told me it was decaf, but I don't think it was."

"You can sleep well now," Tilda assured her.

"Thank you, my dear. I don't know what we'd do without you. I'm so glad you moved into the neighborhood."

Actually, so was Tilda.

"You shoulda been a shrink," Jamal said as they left.

Back in the patrol car, they picked up the thread of an earlier conversation. "So, your mom finally got over being mad 'cause you were late for Christmas Eve dinner?" Tilda asked.

"Yeah, but next year she's threatening to make me come over the day before and spend the night."

"Now she's found that cute woman from her church, maybe you'll have to do that," Tilda said with a grin.

"I don't want to marry a chick from the 'hood. I don't know why I can't get that through my mom's head."

"She's afraid you'll take up with some trashy white girl."

"Yeah? You wish," he teased.

And, at one point, he'd wished it. But really, even though Jamal was big and beautiful and even meaner than her—everything a tough cookie could want—she'd had her heart set on Garrett Armstrong.

And now. She smiled. Now she was falling for Clark Kent in a tool belt.

"So, you never told me. How'd your dinner go?" Jamal asked.

"It went okay." More than okay. True to his word, Devon had come by her house late that night, and she and he and her hormones had enjoyed a very merry Christmas. And tomorrow she had a breakfast date with him. Oh, yeah.

She didn't see the point of mentioning that to Jamal, though. As far as he was concerned, Devon Black didn't make the cut. But, like her, he hadn't seen past the cocky facade. She'd gotten a good look this Christmas, and the more she saw, the more she liked. Construction workers weren't cops or firemen, but they were pretty handy when you owned a fixer-upper. They were probably good with dogs, too. And kids.

Pancake Haus wasn't the most private setting for a date, and she couldn't help wondering why Devon had suggested it, especially when her mom kept popping over to pour coffee neither of them needed. "Are you sure your dad's not single?" Mom joked on her third visit.

Devon smiled at her. What a smile. No wonder Mom was asking. Not that she really wanted anyone. According to Mom, men were more trouble than they were worth. "He's married, third time. He likes the ladies," Devon added.

"Like father, like son," Tilda murmured, and took another bite of her waffle.

"Nah. He can't cook."

"Well, I don't have time for a man, anyway," Mom said with a chuckle, and moved off to greet new customers, for once not leaving behind the smell of cigarette smoke. It looked like Mom had finally kicked the habit.

"Speaking of cooking," Tilda said, "I think my heating element's supposed to come in today."

Devon cocked an eyebrow. "Yeah? Maybe we should install it, see what we can heat up in your kitchen."

Like another black lace thong...

"I like your mom, by the way," he said, calmly returning to his pancakes after creating estrogen mayhem.

"I guess. Is that why you suggested meeting here?"

He shrugged. "I figure if I suck up to her, she'll put in a good word for me."

"You need my mom to plead your case?"

"No—because I think that closed mind of yours is finally open."

"Sure is," she said with a smile.

"Good, since my mom's still in town."

Tilda laid down her fork and stared at him. "What's this meet-the-mom stuff?"

"A guy always wants his mom to meet the woman he's going to marry."

"You're full of shit," she scoffed. Yes, she'd given him a warm (no, make that hot) welcome when he returned to her place Christmas Eve, but it didn't mean anything. Well, actually, it did, but she wasn't going to be stupid enough to say that.

"Why? Because I already know how this story's gonna end? I knew it practically the minute I laid eyes on you." He forked a mouthful of pancake into his mouth. "We're gonna spend the rest of our lives together. Which is just as well, since it'll take a lifetime to turn that dump of yours into a real house."

"That house is a great house!"

He nodded. "It will be."

"I'm going to get a dog."

"There's a surprise. A Rottweiler?"

"No. A poodle."

He almost choked on his coffee.

"They're smart. And I want a couple of kids, too." Now he'd run in the opposite direction.

"Works for me. We can all go to the batting range on Sundays."

She had never had this kind of conversation with Garrett. She'd never had this kind of conversation with any man. She pointed a warning finger at Devon. "You'd better not be messing with me."

He grinned. "That comes later, after we get to your place."

Happy New Year! hooted her hormones.

Yeah, it looked that way.

Happy New Year

The afternoon of New Year's Day saw lots of people coming and going at the Donaldson residence. Maddy had made enough appetizers to feed not only everyone on Candy Cane Lane but half of Icicle Falls.

"Honestly, Madeline, aren't you going a little overboard?" Corrine had asked.

"There's nothing worse than throwing a party and not having enough food," Maddy had replied.

"Except, perhaps, having to host your in-laws for an extra week?" Corrine teased.

"My in-laws are welcome anytime," Maddy said graciously. Actually, the extended visit hadn't been as bad as she'd feared. Corrine had been as negative, opinionated and demanding as usual, but there'd been a shift in their relationship, as if they'd called some sort of truce. Maddy would always be the woman who took Corrine's son away but, as she'd said one night, "My son could have done a lot worse." High praise indeed.

"You need to give me this recipe," Geraldine Chan said, helping herself to more of Maddy's Brie cheese in puff pastry.

"Nothing to it," Maddy told her.

"You say that about everything you make. Honestly,

Maddy, I don't know how you do it. You're a regular Martha Stewart."

She'd done much of "it" at her family's expense. Next year was going to be different. Maddy would still pitch in to make Candy Cane Lane the wonderful place it was— after all, her daughter needed to see the importance of volunteering—but she was resigning from being in charge of everything. She had her hands full just managing her family.

The Werners showed up and, seeing them come through the door, Jordan ducked out of sight. Encountering Mr. Werner was like having a run-in with Ebenezer Scrooge. Jordan had lucked out when she delivered her letter of apology, because his wife had answered the door. She'd probably hide until the Werners were gone, and Maddy didn't blame her. If it wasn't for the fact that she felt the need to make amends, she would've conveniently forgotten to invite them over.

"Where's that daughter of yours?" Mr. Werner demanded as his wife handed over a plate of *lebkuchen*. "I want her to come take down my decorations today."

"Mr. Werner, it's New Year's Day," Maddy protested.

"I tried to explain to him that you're having a party," put in Mrs. Werner.

"I can see she's having a party," her husband said. "But it's all grown-ups. Kids get bored with that kind of thing. The girl will be happy to escape."

Maddy doubted that spending time with grumpy Mr. Werner qualified as *escape*.

"Anyway, I'm more than ready to get that nonsense gone. Now, where is she? Ah, there she is," he said, and pursued Jordan into the kitchen.

Maddy followed, prepared to shield her daughter from a Werner onslaught, Mrs. Werner tagging along.

"There you are," he said, making Jordan jump. "I want my decorations taken down today."

Jordan kept her gaze on her feet and nodded. "Okay, Mr. Werner."

"What time would you like her there?" Maddy asked.

"The sooner, the better, while we still have some sunshine."

"I can come now," Jordan offered.

"Oh, honey, I'm sure Mr. Werner doesn't mind if you stay here for a little while."

"Now is okay," Jordan said.

Mr. Werner nodded. "Good girl. You know what you did was wrong." Maddy was about to inform him that her daughter had already gotten a lecture both from the judge and her grandmother when he added, "But I can't say as I blame you. I hate those blasted candy canes." That made Jordan smile. Until he pointed a finger at her and said, "But don't go around damaging my property again."

Jordan gulped and shook her head. "No, Mr. Werner."

"Okay, come on back to the house and let's get that crap taken down. We've also got some eggnog that needs to be finished off." And then, to Maddy's surprise, he put a hand on her daughter's shoulder and ushered her out of the kitchen. "You know, when I was just a couple of years older than you, my friends and I wedged our buddy's VW Bug between two trees."

"Oh, dear," said his wife with a sigh. "I don't think he's going to be a very good influence on her."

"I'm just happy he's forgiven her," Maddy said.

"Let he who is without sin cast the first snowball," his wife muttered, frowning at her husband's departing back.

Tilda Morrison arrived shortly after Jordan left, escorting Mrs. Walters. Tilda also had a handsome man with her whom she introduced as Devon Black. She didn't look like the same woman when she was out of uniform. In jeans and a red sweater and a printed scarf, she looked almost, well, feminine. Maddy had made a special point of inviting her so she'd know there were no hard feelings. She came about the same time as Ivy and...Rob?

"We're back together," Ivy said.

"I'm so glad," Maddy told her, hugging them both. And she was. As for Tilda...

Ivy smiled at Devon. "You guys...?"

"Are together," he said, and slung an arm around Tilda's shoulders.

Tilda shrugged. "What can I say? He can cook."

"Such a lovely party," Mrs. Walters gushed. "But then, Madeline, you always do everything to perfection."

Not everything. Certainly not parenting. She glanced over at Muriel Sterling, who sat in a corner, chatting with Carla Welky and her husband. *Well, Muriel, all we can do is try.*

She said as much to Ivy later, as they set out more cookies.

"Don't tell Muriel, but I threw her book away," Ivy confessed. "Too much to live up to. All those suggestions for a perfect holiday. They just weren't working for me."

"It's been far from perfect for us this year," Maddy said, looking to where her mother-in-law sat, reigning on the couch, well stocked with both appetizers and neighborly sympathizers. Somehow they'd all survived. In fact, it seemed that they were in better shape now than when they entered the Christmas season. "Funny how even the most imperfect Christmas can turn out perfectly," she mused.

Ivy smiled across the room at her husband, who was holding Robbie and talking with Devon, and he smiled back. "I'll second that," she said.

Tilda joined them now. "How's your daughter doing?" she asked Maddy.

"She's doing well. We all are. Even though what happened was horrible."

Tilda nodded. "Don't blame yourself too much. Kids do dumb stuff. And like my mom always says, it takes a lot of manure to make a garden grow."

"Then we should have a bumper crop of good things this year," Maddy said, pouring them all a cup of punch. "Anyway, there's always next Christmas."

And who knew what that would bring? For the moment, they had right now, and right now was just fine. She saluted her two neighbors with her cup. "Here's to imperfect Christmases and happy New Years in spite of them."

"Let's drink to that," said Ivy, and they did.

* * * * *